Praise for the novels of Catherine Spangler

"Her creative and innovative world building makes for an unrivaled, adventurous read. Highly recommended!"

—*Romantic Times*

"Ms. Spangler has humor, a great plot, sensuous romance, [and] riveting characters that give her romances lots of sparkle. Put these on your 'must-read' list now."

—*Reader to Reader Reviews*

"A definite must buy for your futuristic keeper shelf."

—*Romance at Heart*

"Some of the best romantic science fiction on the market today . . . Catherine Spangler spangles once again with this superb stellar story."

—*The Best Reviews*

"In this twist on *Beauty and the Beast*, Spangler imagines a well-drawn futuristic world."

—*Booklist*

"Ms. Spangler shines, her talent wonderfully evident as she takes us on a journey across galaxies, cultures, and brings us to a perfect understanding of her characters, their motivation, and their very personalities. I am looking forward to future novels by one of romance's brightest stars."

—*Sensual Romance Reviews*

TOUCHED BY DARKNESS

Catherine Spangler

BERKLEY SENSATION, NEW YORK

THE BERKLEY PUBLISHING GROUP
Published by the Penguin Group
Penguin Group (USA) Inc.
375 Hudson Street, New York, New York 10014, USA
Penguin Group (Canada), 90 Eglinton Avenue East, Suite 700, Toronto, Ontario M4P 2Y3, Canada
(a division of Pearson Penguin Canada Inc.)
Penguin Books Ltd., 80 Strand, London WC2R 0RL, England
Penguin Group Ireland, 25 St. Stephen's Green, Dublin 2, Ireland (a division of Penguin Books Ltd.)
Penguin Group (Australia), 250 Camberwell Road, Camberwell, Victoria 3124, Australia
(a division of Pearson Australia Group Pty. Ltd.)
Penguin Books India Pvt. Ltd., 11 Community Centre, Panchsheel Park, New Delhi—110 017, India
Penguin Group (NZ), Cnr. Airborne and Rosedale Roads, Albany, Auckland 1310, New Zealand
(a division of Pearson New Zealand Ltd.)
Penguin Books (South Africa) (Pty.) Ltd., 24 Sturdee Avenue, Rosebank, Johannesburg 2196, South Africa

Penguin Books Ltd., Registered Offices: 80 Strand, London WC2R 0RL, England

TOUCHED BY DARKNESS

A Berkley Sensation Book / published by arrangement with the author

PRINTING HISTORY
Berkley Sensation mass-market edition / January 2007

Cover art by Dan Oleary.
Cover design by George Long.
Interior text design by Kristin del Rosario.

For information, address: The Berkley Publishing Group,
a division of Penguin Group (USA) Inc.,
375 Hudson Street, New York, New York 10014.

ISBN: 978-0-425-21400-8

BERKLEY SENSATION®
Berkley Sensation Books are published by The Berkley Publishing Group,
a division of Penguin Group (USA) Inc.,
375 Hudson Street, New York, New York 10014.
BERKLEY SENSATION is a registered trademark of Penguin Group (USA) Inc.
The "B" design is a trademark belonging to Penguin Group (USA) Inc.

PRINTED IN THE UNITED STATES OF AMERICA

10 9 8 7 6 5 4 3 2 1

To Roberta Brown, a wonderful and amazing person. You've been there with me since the beginning. I can't thank you enough for your support and encouragement, and for your friendship, not to mention the Godiva chocolate. Oh—and also, for being a fabulous literary agent. You're the best!

Acknowledgments

This book required an incredible amount of brainstorming and general information. I couldn't have done it without the assistance of some very special people. My gratitude goes out to the following:

Angelica Blocker, Robyn Delozier, Beth Gonzales, and Carole Turner, my wonderful coworkers, who were actually cocreators with me on this story. They read pages, brainstormed, read more pages, and offered great ideas and endless support.

Chief Alexander of the Mustang Ridge Police Department, for information on the operating procedures of small-town police.

Beth Allen, for her impromptu survey on the most popular pickup truck in Texas.

Angelica Blocker (again), for her assistance with the Spanish.

Edward Heasley, for sharing his expertise on guns (as well as being one of my favorite uncles).

Sergeant Frank McElligott, for all sorts of information on Texas autopsy and gun laws, NCIC, and numerous other questions I threw at him.

Stacy Mefford, for sharing her knowledge of the Blanco River and surrounding towns.

Officials at Blanco State Park, for their geography lesson on the area.

Janet Underwood, nurse practitioner and lifetime friend, for her medical expertise.

My husband, James, for driving me through Texas Hill Country to explore settings for this story (and not stopping at too many antique stores).

Of course, any errors in the story are their fault—oh wait—those would be *my* errors. I'm sure the input was flawless.

More thanks goes to Cindy Hwang for being an amazing and gracious editor. And to the Musketeers: Jennifer, Linda, and Vickie, who've been in on this adventure long before the beginning.

Thank you all!

Glossary of Terms

Atlantis—A mystical, magical culture that some believe actually existed in the North Atlantic Ocean, bordering parts of what is now the eastern U.S. coast. It is also believed that Atlantis had an extremely advanced culture, and destroyed itself through civil war and the misuse of its great Tuaoi stone.

Belial—The cunning, evil leader of a rebel Atlantian faction, Belial advocated human slavery, human sacrifices, and the dark side of magic. His group gained control of the Tuaoi stone and orchestrated the destruction of Atlantis.

Belian—Followers of Belial (also known as the Sons of Belial). Adhering to their leader's original dark practices, Belians are now reincarnating in human form on Earth, and wreaking violence and havoc on its inhabitants. They thrive on chaos and terror and blood offerings to Belial. Although they occupy mortal bodies, they have superhuman abilities. They operate from the four lower spiritual chakras, and can shield their presence from Sentinels.

Belian Crime Scene (BCS)—The scene of a Belian crime. A Sentinel investigates the scene, absorbing the psychic energies left behind by the Belian, in order to track it down.

Belian Expulsion (BE)—A forced exile of a Belian soul to Saturn for spiritual rehabilitation. It requires the joint efforts of a Sentinel and the High Sanctioned.

Chakras—The seven spiritual centers of the human body, starting in the lower abdomen and moving upward. Each corresponds to a physical part of the body, and also to a specific color. The first four are the lower chakras and grounded to the Earth. The last three are the higher chakras and are linked to the Creator and the spiritual realm.

Conduction—The process in which a Sentinel and a conductor link spiritually through the seven chakras; most specifically, the sixth chakra and third eye. This amplifies the psychic energy the Sentinel has absorbed from a Belian crime scene and helps to identify the Belian. The process also raises powerful sexual energies and has a physical component—sexual intercourse, which further enhances the psychic energies. Often several conductions are required before the Belian's shields are breached.

Conductor—A regular human who is psychically wired to link with some Sentinels, and to magnify and enhance the Sentinel's psychic tracking abilities. Conductors are relatively rare, and a good conductor/Sentinel match is even rarer. A matched conductor is always the opposite sex of the Sentinel, and there's a powerful sexual attraction between them.

Crystal Pendant—A pink quartz crystal edged in silver, it's worn by many Sentinels. Attuned to the great Tuaoi stone, and to the Sentinel's personal energy, it helps focus and magnify psychic energies, and with shielding.

High Sanctioned—Those entities (souls) that were the high priests of the temple of The One on Atlantis. Generally, they don't occupy physical bodies, but act more as spirit guides for Sentinels. They assist with Belian expulsions.

Initiate—A fledgling, a young Sentinel who is still learning how to shield energies and use the Sentinel powers.

Law of One—The spiritual law and belief followed by most Atlantians, it acknowledged a higher Supreme Being and placed the focus on the Light, and positive energies.

Psychic Signature—The energy patterns left behind by a Belian, more pronounced if a violent crime has occurred. A Sentinel collects and absorbs these energies, and pieces together clues and mental pictures to help identify the Belian.

Sanctioned—Spiritually advanced Atlantian entities who served the high priests in the temple of The One. They occupy human bodies and are the overseers and the decision makers in the day-to-day Sentinel operations on Earth.

Saturn (Burning/Experience)—Saturn, the "grim reaper," rules the moral and karmic lessons souls must experience and overcome. Also called the "karmic initiator," Saturn is where Belian souls are sent until they learn their spiritual lessons. It is not a pleasant experience—more like purgatory.

Sentinel—An Atlantian soul reincarnating into a human body to track down Belians and dispense karmic justice. Like Belians, Sentinels are mortal, but possess superhuman powers. They operate out of the three higher chakras, making it difficult for Belians to sense their presence. They often use conductors to help them identify Belians.

Sexual Surge—The raw, powerful surge of sexual energy that occurs at the beginning of a conduction, when the lower chakras open and pull in Earth-based energies—which most resemble the vibratory levels of Belians. This surge helps the Sentinel get a better fix on the Belian.

Shielding—Using psychic energies to create a spiritual

shield that blocks the presence of either a Sentinel or a Belian.

The One—The Atlantian term for God/Supreme Being.

Third Eye—A spiritual center that is linked to the sixth chakra and the pineal gland, and represented by the color indigo, the third eye enhances "seeing" and "hearing" on an ethereal level. A Sentinel, often with the aid of a conductor, works through the third eye to track Belians.

Tuaoi Stone (The Great Crystal)—A huge spear of solid, multifaceted quartz crystal, the Tuaoi stone was housed in a special temple on Atlantis. It provided all power, as well as a means of communicating with The One, and was ultimately used to destroy Atlantis. It now lies at the bottom of the Atlantic Ocean, its power undiminished.

White Brotherhood—(Does not refer to race or gender.) This was the Atlantian priesthood established for the perpetuation of the Law of One. They had the ability to transport themselves in thought or body wherever desired. Many of them have incarnated as Sentinels, the Sanctioned, and the High Sanctioned.

PRELUDE

For in the life of the entity enters many of those conditions that may be made into miracles or crimes.

(Edgar Cayce Reading 2497-3)

The Beginning—Atlantis

THOUSANDS of years ago, luminous soul beings arrived on the planet Earth; bright and inquisitive spirits exploring an endless Universe. On Earth, they discovered physical sensations—and oh, what sensations! Only in this physical realm could they experience taste, touch, smell, hearing, and feeling.

So they stayed, creating new material forms to house their beings. Some became mermaids, unicorns, half-beasts. Most materialized into human forms. Thus Atlantis came into existence.

At first very peaceful and spiritual beings, they followed the Law of One: *There is only The One. All come from The One, all must return to The One. The One is the Light. You are the children of Light*.

They lived in great illumination; their technology and accomplishments were legendary. They had physical and mental abilities and powers far beyond those of humans today. What they could conceive, they could create.

They mastered particle physics, solar power, atomic power, gravity. They constructed spacecraft that moved faster than light through outer space and time. The great crystal, the Tuaoi stone, provided all their energy.

But then disharmony crept in. An evil faction, led by the cunning Belial, who advocated slavery and excesses of the flesh, began gaining power. His followers were known as the Sons of Belial, or Belians. They worshiped the darkness and renewed their life force through the blood of human sacrifices. They disdained the Light.

Through treachery and violence, they gained control of the Tuaoi stone and began terrorizing the citizens of Atlantis and surrounding nations. They used the Tuaoi as a death ray, tuning it to such high frequencies that it caused great upheavals of the land—and ultimately, the final destruction of Atlantis.

Then the Earth knew peace again. The Atlantian souls who had inhabited the planet abandoned it for thousands of years. But the twentieth century saw the rise of amazing scientific and technological advancements. Once again, Atlantians were drawn back to the Earth, to the familiar technologies.

The Belians first chose to return to a physical existence, where their superior powers would enable them to dominate the weaker humans, where they could thrive on terror and darkness and blood.

They are now entering the Earth through birth as humans or by possessing bodies. They have renewed their reign of evil, ruthless power brokers that some call dictators, serial killers, mafia, gang leaders, drug lords, and more.

Other Atlantians have been called into service to stop them. They are also reincarnating into human bodies to hunt down the Belians and dispense justice.

They are the Sentinels.

They answer only to The One and those who serve the Light. They walk among you, unrecognized, except to a few—human conductors who are able to enhance the Sentinels psychic abilities and help them track the unseen evil that threatens you.

Your Earth is once again touched by darkness.
But those who worship Belial will not win.
There is no escape from destiny.
The Sentinels will prevail.

ONE

For being afraid is the first consciousness of sin's entering in. . . .

(Edgar Cayce, Reading 243-10)

IT didn't start out as a day of horrendous memories—or of soul-numbing pain. It started as a beautiful, sunny Saturday, with the air so clear and crisp, one couldn't help but inhale deep breaths of the cleansing freshness, and feel as if a multitude of God's benevolent blessings must be shining down upon the entire world. Terrorism, disease, poverty and hunger, grief and despair were distant threads of reality, too dim to possibly exist.

Life was good, Kara thought, as she headed to town in her '98 Chevy truck. Like the few daffodils insistently pushing their way through the thick grass and weeds lining the two-lane road—despite the fact it was only early March—the heart could recover from overwhelming anguish, could return from a harsh, debilitating winter. Life could resume, with a reassuring ebb and flow of normalcy.

She glanced over at Alex, his head bent over his Game Boy Micro as he concentrated on FIFA Soccer. From an early age, he had displayed a superior intelligence, and could play games far above the level of most six-year-olds. Even so, she wouldn't let him play any of the fantasy games that most young boys indulged in. No magic or monsters. Those things too closely alluded to dark, shadowy realms; to otherworld entities, which were very real and far more dangerous than any mythical monsters, more terrifying than the average person could even begin to conceive.

A chill shuddered down Kara's spine, but she quickly shook it away. She had no more involvement with the supernatural darkness, was determined that their life from this point forward would be normal. Except that Alex . . . She also shook that thought away before it could fully congeal.

Our life is normal, she told herself fiercely. He—*they*—were safe from such a possibility. She had made sure of it, moving halfway across the country to take up residence in Texas. She was fortunate that she could use her medical skills anywhere.

And she liked the small town of Zorro, liked the close-knit community, and the simple way of life. She turned onto the main street of the town, rumbling past the antique and secondhand shops, home-style restaurants, hardware and feed stores, a dress shop with dowdy, "mature woman" fashions in the dusty display window. Traffic was sparse and leisurely, matching the laid-back pace here.

Kara pulled into a parallel space in front of Sal's Grocery and cut the engine. She reached over to tousle Alex's thick brown hair. "Hey bud, we're here."

He didn't look up from his game. "Just a minute, Mom," he wheedled. "I'm about to score."

"Pause it," she advised. "I want to get our errands done." She pulled the key from the ignition and dropped it into her sweater pocket, then swung open her door. "Come on."

She felt it the minute she climbed down from the pickup. It assailed her, surrounding her like the treacherous tentacles of a sea monster. Threatening, suffocating.

The power.

She grabbed the top of the door, suddenly struggling for

breath. *No!* She was just imagining it, still haunted by the terror of seven years ago. Still raw from Richard, even now. No one in this small west Texas town could wield such power. Alex was too young, and—God willing—would never learn to manifest it. She shouldn't have even let herself think about it on the drive here. That was the only possible reason she could be imagining the sensation.

But the feeling persisted, furtive, horribly familiar. *The sensation of the power.* Adrenaline surged, sending an awful tension through her body. She slammed the door shut, leaned against the truck, battling the beginnings of all-out panic. No, no . . . *no*!

Her frantic denial didn't diminish the effect of her pounding heart—or the insistent barrage of an outside force. It was coming from across the street, near Don Mason's feed store. Kara turned that direction, determined to tame her runaway imagination.

A man stood on the sidewalk in front of Mason's Feed, tall, dark, unmoving. A long black duster flapped around his jean-clad legs. The same breeze blew his midnight hair around a sharp face with chiseled features. His steady gaze fixed on Kara, an all-too-familiar glow flaring into his eyes. No . . .

"Mom? What are you doing?"

She felt sweat trickling down between her breasts, even though the day was chilly enough that she'd worn a sweater over her shirt. The power was like that, like an insidious fever that heated the blood, destroyed balance and rational existence.

Reminiscent of hell.

"Mom!"

Still staring at the stranger, she saw his gaze shift downward and to her left. *Oh, God. Alex.*

She looked at her son. He clutched her sweater, concern on his thin face. Dark brown eyes, sandy brown hair, and an expression so much like Richard's, she wanted to cry—something she had refused to do since about two weeks after his death.

Richard. Her gaze snapped back up. The stranger was striding toward them, staring intently at Alex. *The power.* Here, in Zorro. Panic coalesced into terror.

"Get in the truck!" she gasped, pulling Alex away from the vehicle and jerking open the door. She jammed her hand in her pocket, grabbing the keys. "Get in! Now!"

He stared at her, obviously confused by her irrational behavior. "But Mom—"

"Now!" she screamed, picking him up and heaving him across the bench seat. She didn't give him time to slide over, before she leaped in behind him. It seemed like an eternity before she could right herself from the sideways angle in which she landed, while Alex wiggled out from beneath her.

She leaned out to grab the door. The stranger was almost upon them, moving in steady strides. From painful experience, she knew his seemingly moderate speed was deceptive. Her heart battered her rib cage. She fumbled the key into the ignition as she swung the door shut.

The engine roared to life, the truck lurching forward as she floored the gas before the gears had fully engaged. The jolt snapped her head backward painfully. For one horrible moment, she thought the vehicle would stall. Frantically, she stomped the gas pedal again. Tires shrieking, the truck shot down the road, fishtailing and nearly crashing into the right curb, before Kara spun the wheel and got it under control.

She sped away, exhaust spewing out behind them. She had to look. Was compelled to look. In her rearview mirror, she saw the stranger, standing in the road, watching them. Watching her. Watching Alex. She began shaking uncontrollably.

And knew her bid for a normal life had just gone up in smoke.

The terror pressed down on her, the memories swirling through her frantic mind. Only she feared memories weren't the only monsters she now faced.

But real flesh and blood demons.

TWO

DAMIEN Morgan stared after the speeding truck, noting the license plate, in case he met with any resistance from the locals. Not that he expected to, but he preferred to keep mind probes or subconscious inducement to a minimum.

The surge of power he'd sensed when the blue pickup had driven past him had taken him totally by surprise. He watched the slender, auburn-haired woman climb from the truck, thinking it came from her. The power hadn't been very strong for a fully evolved Sentinel, nor had it been shielded.

It took him a moment to realize the energy emanated from the boy, which had been even more of a shock. The woman was obviously not one of them, but the boy was. Yet there were no other known Sentinels remotely close. They rarely overlapped territories. Even so, Damien had sent out a query before he left for Zorro, getting no response. He had believed he was the only Sentinel within miles.

Strange. A child with the power, left unattended, without guidance. Unheard of. Unless . . . none of the Sanctioned knew of his existence. And the woman . . . she wasn't one of them, but she had recognized Damien immediately. Only an initiate or a conductor could have sensed shielded power.

Turning possibilities over in his mind, Damien started toward Sal's Grocery. Since it was the only grocery store in the vicinity, most of the town's residents would shop there. The employees would surely know the identities of the auburn-haired woman and the boy.

Glancing around to be certain no one would see him, he turned his palms upward, visualizing what he wanted to manifest. A silk scarf whispered across his skin, in a gold color that he knew would complement the woman's coloring. He went up the cracked cement steps to the store.

A chime tinkled when he opened the door. Inside it was overly warm, but wonderful aromas permeated the air: coffee, cookies, cinnamon, and other spices. A checkout area with an ancient cash register stood in the right corner. Old-fashioned glass cases lined the first fourth of the store, displaying meat and cheese on one side; baked goods on the other. Farther down was a small produce section, then a dairy case.

The limited floor space was crammed with shelves piled with all sorts of goods. Toward the rear, tools and work clothing hung on the walls, indicating this was more of a general store than a grocery. Damien walked down the right aisle, his booted feet resounding on the wooden floor.

Halfway down, a man was stacking burlap bags of flour against the wall. He glanced at Damien, then took a closer look, apparently pegging him as an outsider. The man straightened and stepped forward. He was tall and gangly, with a gaunt face weathered by years of hard work, and a shock of white hair. He wore a blue and white plaid flannel shirt, tucked carefully into faded work jeans. Damien picked the man's identity from his mind. He was Sal.

"Can I help ye find anything?" Sal asked in a gruff voice with a strong country twang.

"You can help me find the owner of this scarf." Damien held up the gold silk rectangle. "She dropped it when she was getting into her truck. Drove off before I could catch her. She was driving a blue Chevy pickup. She had auburn hair and a young boy was with her."

Sal's brow furrowed as he took the scarf in his rough hands. "Well, now. Sure sounds like Dr. Cantrell ye just described. But I can't see her wearing nothing like this."

"Dr. Cantrell? Does she have a son?"

"Sure does. His name's Alex, and he's real bright." Sal considered a moment. "I guess I'll keep this and ask the doctor if it's hers the next time she comes in. She shoulda been by, if she was in town this morning. She usually does her shopping on Saturdays."

"Does she?" Damien smoothly retrieved the scarf before Sal could get a firm grip on it. "I'd rather return it myself. Thank you, though."

A dull red suffused Sal's face. Damien detected high blood pressure. "I woulda seen she got it."

"Oh, I'm sure you would have." Damien hastened to assure the old man. He sent a small burst of calming energy. "But since I'm now a resident of Zorro, I'd rather give Dr. Cantrell the scarf myself. It's a good way to meet a pretty woman, if you know what I mean." He winked conspiratorially at Sal. "Oh, unless she's married."

Sal didn't take the bait, instead giving Damien a thorough once-over. "New resident, eh? What line of business are you in, Mr—?"

"Morgan. Damien Morgan." Damien extended his hand, and Sal slowly accepted it with his own callused hand. "I'm a crime writer for *Society Magazine*."

"A crime writer? Not much crime around here. Hey, you investigating those murders over in Fredericksburg? Naw, you'd be staying over there if ye was."

There was more criminal activity in Zorro than the old man could possibly know. "I don't really investigate murders," Damien lied. "I leave that to the authorities. I do write about them, though, and I needed a quiet place to live, where I could find a slower pace and focus on writing."

Sal considered this. "Zorro ought to be slow enough for ye. Not much going on. Where you staying?"

"The Magnolia Bed-and-Breakfast, for the time being."

Sal nodded. "Belle Williams will take good of ye there."

"So where can I find Dr. Cantrell?" Damien persisted. "I'd like to meet her and return the scarf."

"Well, I don't give out other folks' addresses, not without their say-so. But you can catch Dr. Cantrell at her clinic on Monday. She's usually in from nine to four, and sometimes later, if she's needed. It's a small town, and she don't always work full days."

Damien had no intention of waiting that long. With the boy broadcasting power, it was only a matter of time until he attracted discarnate entities, or worse, the Belian that Damien was tracking. But he didn't want to arouse Sal's suspicions. "Where is her clinic?"

"One street over on Johnson." Sal hooked his thumb toward the west. "Take a right on Maple, then go right again on Johnson. It's about halfway down on the left. The doc is in if her pickup's out front."

"Thank you for the information." Damien started to leave, then turned back. "Occurs to me you might want to pay Dr. Cantrell a visit yourself. You look a little under the weather."

Sal grunted. "Ain't nothin' wrong with me, excepting a lot of years of living."

Knowing there was nothing more he could do, Damien headed for the door. "See you around."

He walked down the cracked steps and into the sunshine. The air seemed cooler after the overheated stuffiness of Sal's store, and he tugged the front of his duster closed as he headed toward his car. It was nothing flashy or obtrusive, just an older model gray sedan. Even so, he knew he stood out like a sore thumb, as evidenced by the curious stares of the good citizens of Zorro.

Although many small towns like Zorro, with their antique stores and bed-and-breakfast facilities, drew a fair number of visitors, Damien had never been able to blend well. His height and the chiseled harshness of his features drew attention. He often wore dark glasses to hide the intensity of his eyes and tried to dress casually, but it always took awhile for people to become used to his presence.

Ignoring the stares, he strode to his car and got in, starting it and pulling onto the main thoroughfare. He drove to Johnson Avenue and turned right per Sal's instructions. Apparently one of the older parts of Zorro, this street had once been a residential section. Now the old homes lining it were businesses of one sort or another. He saw antiques, art supplies, florists, law offices, and then the neatly painted sign identifying the medical office of Kara Cantrell, M.D.

Like the sign, the small house was well kept, painted a pale yellow with white trim and large pots of pansies flanking the front steps. A concrete driveway took Damien to a small parking lot behind the house. He was grateful for the rear entrance, which would allow him to enter the building without being seen or questioned.

The locked door was no challenge, and he readily located Dr. Cantrell's office. Moments later, he had what he needed—her address, and the knowledge that she wasn't married or dating anyone seriously. The latter came from a recent birthday card in which her brother had jokingly asked when she was going to get a boyfriend. Good. That would make things easier. Relocking the door behind him, Damien got in his car, consulted his map, and headed for the private residence of Kara Cantrell.

KARA paced the family room, rubbing her hands along her chilled arms. She had turned on the gas logs she'd had installed in the fireplace shortly after she and Alex moved into the old house. While charming, with its wood floors, rugged ceiling beams, and large country kitchen, the house was drafty, and she had neither the time nor the energy to deal with wood-burning fires. But right now, the efficient gas fire didn't begin to warm the bone-deep chill racking her body.

No, the cold went far deeper than that, into the depths of her very soul. And Kara knew why. The stranger in Zorro.

She tried to tell herself that she could have been mistaken about him, about sensing the power. That it was her overactive imagination, fueled by the memories of what had happened with Richard. But gut-deep intuition told her otherwise.

There was no doubt in her mind that the stranger was one of *them*. The power had been too strong, his reaction further confirmation, leaving no doubt he'd picked up on Alex. She didn't know what the stranger would do, but she felt certain they hadn't seen the last of him.

He could find out who she was easily enough. There was no anonymity in a small town. The knowledge of the stranger's true nature, that he could find her and Alex, sent a surge of hysteria through her. What should she do? Pack up? Run, like she had before? And then what? Richard had told her *they* were everywhere.

As long as Alex was broadcasting, he would always be at risk, wherever they went. Kara had tried to deny his power, had tried to tell herself that it was under control. But deep down, she knew better, and today had driven home that point. She'd denied it far too long, had denied it from the beginning, when Alex showed signs his was one of the special souls. It was right before he turned three. She could still remember the first time, as clearly as if it were yesterday.

"Mama, me been here before."

"What?"

"Me here before . . . before now. Me a woman in a scary place."

"Silly boy. What are you talking about?"

Alex had thrown his chubby arms over his head and burrowed against her. "Fire. Big rocks falling on me! Hurts."

She'd held him close, feeling his pounding heart, her own terror clawing at her throat. "It's just a story, sweetie. Just a bad dream, that's all."

"No," he'd insisted. "Real."

It had taken some doing to soothe her terrified son, but she had persevered. And as he got older, Alex seemed to forget the so-called memories, to forget his claim that he'd lived in another place and time.

It had also taken quite an effort to teach him to restrain his pointing and the ensuing results if he were upset or excited. Dishes spinning off the table, plants tipping over, scorched places on the floor or furniture.

Kara had hoped and prayed that the power would become dormant if not acknowledged and encouraged, that it could be repressed with conditioning. Alex was a good child, responsive to her parental requests. Now he never pointed at anything, and his normal placid nature dominated his moods. There had been no further incidents, and she'd begun to believe her prayers had been answered.

Until the past month, when strange things started happening around the house and Alex's school class. Things that seemingly were not a direct result of anything he did.

The faint ding of a timer broke into Kara's reverie. She drew a deep breath, trying to still her shaking. She'd almost begun to believe she and Alex were safe, that the past was behind them; she had almost convinced herself.

A foolish and fragile hope. But that same knowledge told her it was useless to run again. Until she could find some way to shield Alex, they'd be at risk of discovery wherever they went. For now, she was determined to keep his life as level and normal as possible.

"Alex," she called out. "I know you heard that timer. Turn off the television." She stepped closer to the fire, still cold. She limited the time Alex could spend on the computer or watching TV, determined he not become totally dependent on them for his entertainment. Already, he displayed loner tendencies like his father had, preferring solitude to the company of others.

A moment later, Alex came tromping down the hall, Mac, their mixed-breed dog, trailing behind him. "Ah, Mom," Alex protested, "There's a *Star Trek* marathon today. Ten episodes in a row."

"Then it will still be on in an hour," Kara told him. "You

need a break and some fresh air. You can work in the garden with me for a while. Get your jacket. And tie your shoes."

Alex rolled his eyes, but he dutifully knelt down and dealt with the dragging shoelaces, then went to the wall rack by the front door and took his denim jacket off its hook. Reluctantly leaving the fire, Kara decided to get a sweatshirt to garden in, instead of her bulky jacket.

Alex opened the front door as she started to her bedroom. The sound of a vehicle turning onto the graveled drive halted her. Mac's shrill bark filled the air. Another omen, as Mac rarely barked at anyone, unless he felt threatened.

"Hey Mom! Who do we know who drives a silver car?"

Apprehension sent adrenaline pounding through her body. She didn't need to see the car, didn't need to run through a mental inventory, to know who it was. She already knew.

"Alex, get inside," she said sharply, reaching the door in a few frantic strides.

He stepped farther out, his attention on the driveway. "It looks like that man we saw in town this morning."

"Now!" she ordered, her voice rising. She grabbed her son's arm and dragged him back. "Get in here!"

"Ow!" He stumbled and almost fell. "Mom!" He stared up at her with startled eyes. The intensity of Mac's barking increased. The dog sensed the danger.

She struggled to keep her voice calm. "Listen to me. I want you to go to your room. Turn on your television and stay there. Do not come out until I tell you to. Is that clear?"

"But—"

"Don't argue with me, son. Do it. Now."

"Okay." He shuffled off, throwing her one last look over his shoulder.

Kara turned back to the door. The adrenaline rushing through her had her shaking, made coherent thought difficult. She battled to draw a breath into her constricted chest, to stay clear headed.

Every instinct screamed at her to slam the door shut and

throw the bolt, to snatch Alex and run out the back of the house and through the fields, away from the stranger and the terror he represented. But bitter experience reminded her of the futility of such an act. There was no where to run from *them*.

She felt exposed, vulnerable, with no weapon or any means to defend herself and her son. Because of Alex, she refused to keep a gun in the house. Besides, Zorro was a quiet, safe community. She'd never before felt the need for weapons. She thought of Alex's baseball bat, stored in the utility room with the other athletic equipment, but she knew it would be no protection against a Sentinel.

The slam of a car door, along with Mac's frenzied barking, told her she'd just run out of time. Sending a prayer to a God whose existence she'd long doubted, she forced herself to step out onto the porch. The driveway was to her right, and the stranger was out and strolling around his car.

Still on the porch, Mac snarled and snapped, his hackles raised. The stranger stopped on the near side of his vehicle, raised his palm toward the dog, making a sharp motion. Mac immediately quieted, lowering his tail between his legs with a small whine.

The stranger turned toward Kara. She couldn't see his eyes through the dark glasses he wore, but the rest of him was intimidating. He was a big man. The black duster emphasized his tall length, made him appear even more ominous. His long midnight hair was sleeked behind his neck and tied, leaving bare the slashing lines of his lower face.

He didn't move for a moment, then slowly, deliberately, he raised his hand and removed the sunglasses. Steel blue eyes, glowing with a preternatural energy, seared through her. He made no effort to shield his power; rather he seemed to direct it outward, its insidious force penetrating her mental barriers, a psychic barrage.

Kara felt physically broadsided, emotionally violated. Any doubt about her earlier assumptions concerning this man's identity was evaporated by the blast of pure, unchallenged power.

She grabbed the doorjamb, digging in her nails, willing herself to remain upright and steady. Managed to find her voice. "What do you want?"

He slid the glasses in his duster pocket, then leaned against the car, seemingly relaxed. "To talk about Alex."

The shock of hearing him say Alex's name sent her reeling again. He knew her son's name! Anger followed on the heels of that knowledge. How dare this man pry into their lives; how dare he drag Alex into this?

She forced back the fury, reaching for calm rationality. There was nothing this man could do to Alex and her. True, he was one of *them. A Sentinel.* He was powerful beyond human imaginings, and very dangerous, but he was also bound by a strict code of ethics. He could never hurt innocent beings. She refused to let him intimidate her.

"I have nothing to say to you. Get off my property."

He straightened, all indolence gone, replaced by intense purpose. "I think we have plenty to discuss."

He strode to the steps and mounted them steadily, his gaze never leaving her. Kara stepped back involuntarily, grabbing the edge of the door. It wasn't far enough. The stranger's close proximity launched an invasion into her personal space.

She felt the electricity leap between them, a lightning bolt of raw chemistry. She'd only ever experienced such a reaction with Richard, had assumed it was specific to him and her. The horrifying realization that she could encounter the same thing with this man sent her staggering backward into the house. She groped for the door handle, gripped it tightly.

He tilted his head, his gaze assessing. "You're a conductor."

Oh, God. He felt the shocking chemistry, too. And he was far too close to another area that she had walled off seven years ago. Utter panic surged through her, evaporating all traces of indignation and anger. All thoughts of trying to deal with this man fled. All she could think about was survival. Getting away from him, and the threats he presented.

"Get off my property now, or I'm calling the police."

She slammed the door before he could move, shoving the bolt home.

Shaking violently, she ran to the phone by the couch and snatched it up. She punched 9-1-1, but nothing happened. She disconnected and tried again. It took another fumbling moment before the fact there was no dial tone registered. She heard the bolt on the door jiggle and looked up. Horrified, she watched as first the bolt, then the door handle, turned smoothly.

She threw down the phone and ran to grab her purse off the dining room table. The door swung open, and the stranger loomed in the doorway.

"Go away!" Kara screamed, fear pushing her beyond reason. She dumped her purse on the table, snagged her cell phone.

"It's no good," he informed her. "It won't work."

"It will, it will," she chanted like a mantra, trying to activate the phone. Nothing. It was dead, like the other one.

She stared at the phone, a sense of inevitability dulling the mindless panic. Along with it, she felt something else—a soothing swirl of reassurance, almost like a physical, calming touch. It took a moment to realize the source. She dropped the phone onto the table and turned toward the doorway.

"Don't," she said sharply, glaring at the stranger. "Don't use your so-called magic on me."

He stepped inside and closed the door behind him. "Then I suggest you calm down. Unless you want to upset your son further." He nodded toward the other side of the couch, where Alex huddled against the wall, sheet white, his terrified eyes huge as he clutched Mac against him. He had come back into the living room and probably watched everything out the window.

What a muddled mess her near-hysteria had caused, especially considering it had accomplished absolutely nothing. She went to her son, sinking down on her knees and wrapping her arms around both him and Mac.

"Oh, sweetie, I'm sorry I upset you." She kissed his

head, inhaling the musty scent of a little boy who needed a bath. "It's okay now."

"But Mom," he said, his voice wavering, "what about *him*?"

Kara lifted her head and glanced at the stranger, still standing beside the front door, watching them intently. "It's okay," she said carefully. "He'll only be here a little while. I'm sorry I yelled at you earlier and pulled on your arm. I guess"—she paused, not certain there was any way she could explain her erratic behavior—"I guess I lost my temper."

"But you never lose your temper," Alex said, then thought about it a moment. "Until today."

Remorse tore at Kara. Twice in one day, she'd not only yelled at her son, but physically manhandled him. She'd probably blasted him emotionally as well, since he was highly sensitive to the feelings of others.

"I'm sorry, sweetie," she said hoarsely, her throat tight. "I'm having a bad day. It's not your fault. We'll discuss it later. Right now, I need to talk to this man."

Alex looked uncertainly from her to the stranger. "He feels funny," he said. "I don't like him."

So he could sense the power. Kara had never had any way of knowing how Alex might react if he were around others of his kind—until now. She strove to reassure her son. "Silly boy. He's on the other side of the couch. How can you tell anything about him from here?"

But Alex remained serious, his distrustful gaze on the stranger. "Listen," Kara said, shifting back. "Why don't you go to your room and watch *Star Trek*? Take Mac with you."

Alex nodded, but he seemed reluctant as he stood and headed toward the hallway. With a low growl toward the stranger, Mac followed, his tail still tucked between his legs.

Dreading the coming encounter, Kara rose and walked to the fire, seeking its warmth. She turned her back to the flames, keeping a wary watch on the stranger. He shrugged out of his duster and tossed it over the arm of the sofa, then started toward her.

"I didn't invite you to stay," she protested.

"I don't stand on formalities." His voice had an odd rasp to it, not unpleasant. He closed the distance between them, moving to her side.

She realized it had been a mistake to position herself in front of the fire. Now the stranger had her virtually hemmed in, with the flames behind her. This close, he was even more intimidating, towering almost a foot over her own five feet, six inches.

He wore a red pullover sweater and faded jeans over his impressive physique. His face appeared even harsher, defined by high cheekbones beneath slashing steel eyes. His full, sensual mouth had a ruthless set to it. Energy sizzled between them, permeating her skin and moving through her body like molten lava. How could a virtual stranger have such an effect on her?

"So you're a conductor," he said, certainty in his voice.

What he thought he knew and what she would admit were two different things. It was far too frightening to go down the same path she'd traveled nine years ago. She forced herself to meet his penetrating gaze. "I don't know what you're talking about."

"Yes you do. In town this morning, you recognized my power immediately. Since you're not a Sentinel or a Belian, that leaves only one possibility." He stepped closer, and she tensed. "And there's no denying the energy between us."

His words, enhanced by the electricity arcing between them, conjured up shockingly erotic memories. Memories of Richard, and of him and Kara naked and entwined, their bodies locked together in a frenzy of passion. With them, it had been like a fever in the blood, a hunger that couldn't be sated.

Richard had told her it was a chain reaction of chakra energy, automatically ignited when certain conductors and Sentinels were in close proximity. Yet there had been more than just sex between Richard and her. She chose to believe that the reaction itself was simple lust, fueled by chemistry, no more, no less. It could be controlled—mind over matter.

"I don't feel anything," she lied. "You've barged into my house uninvited, talking foolishness. I want you to leave."

"You're a conductor, and your reactions to me, earlier and now, prove it. Besides, you just told me not to use magic. Why would you say such a thing, if you didn't know what I am?"

He had her there. She knew he wouldn't leave now. His extraordinary powers had ensured he'd be able to ferret out her secrets, despite her resistance. Not that she'd been very cool or levelheaded. She stepped away from the fireplace, putting some distance between herself and him.

She tried to still her trembling, to speak normally, but her voice came out as a hoarse whisper. "What do you want from me?"

He advanced, and she retreated, her legs shaky. He gestured toward the couch. "Sit, before you fall down."

Hating that he could see her fear, but knowing his suggestion was valid, she moved to the couch, sinking down on the sturdy blue corduroy. She was grateful he took the large armchair opposite her and that he now appeared to be shielding the energy. It wasn't the bombardment it had been.

"Tell me, Dr. Kara Cantrell, about your psychic abilities."

Another shock jarred through her. "I have none," she said adamantly.

Impatience flashed in his eyes. "Stop lying to me. Many conductors have some sort of ability—precognitive, empathic, telepathic. And you were able to sense me from a distance. You can't deny your abilities."

Kara shook her head, wishing she could block out the truth of his words. Her thoughts drifted back through the years, to events she would rather forget. The earliest memory was from age four, when she awoke from a particularly vivid dream and informed her parents, "*Grandpa went to visit the angels.*" Two hours later, they received a phone call with the news that her beloved Papi had suffered a sudden heart attack and died.

Then there was the terrible time, when at age eight, she again awoke from a dream—this time screaming—and told her mother that she'd "seen" her father crushed in his car. They soon learned a drunk driver had smashed into her father's vehicle, killing him instantly.

During her senior year of high school, while in her calculus class, she'd had a sudden vivid image of her brother Dan being shot in the left leg, his knee shattered. Dan, who was serving in Desert Storm, lost his left leg from the knee down that very day.

There were more, many more, incidents over the years. She'd felt like a freak, been unsettled by these unexplained occurrences, and rationalized them away as coincidence. She had taken refuge in science, which was logical and definable. And she'd worked hard at suppressing the events, training herself to awaken at the first hint of an unsettling dream. Of course, meeting Richard had opened her eyes to a world that couldn't be explained by logic. But she refused to acknowledge or enter that world again.

"I'm a doctor, with scientific training," she said. "I don't believe in unexplained phenomenon. Obviously, you have me confused with someone else."

"Do I? Your son is a Sentinel. Which means at least one of his parents is a Sentinel. In this case, it would have to be his father."

"Leave my son out of this." She had no intention of discussing Alex with this man. Alex was just a normal six-year-old boy. He attended first grade, played soccer, watched *Star Trek*. He—she clenched her eyes shut, not wanting to face what she'd known since Alex was three, what she desperately wanted to will away.

The sudden presence next to her, the startling feel of a hand over hers jolted through her like a burning brand. The stranger sat next to her on the sofa, having moved with astonishing stealth and speed—something she well remembered. She gasped and tried to pull back, but he tightened his grip on her hand. Currents of energy tingled up her arm.

"No more games," he said. "I will get to the truth of the matter, with or without your cooperation. I can help you. Alex needs protection until he can learn to shield himself."

What protection had Richard had? If her son was in danger from the same dark forces . . . God, why had she thought all that was behind them?

She pressed her free hand against her mouth, mortified by the sudden rush of hot tears in her eyes. "We don't need your help. Just go away."

His face impassive, he manifested a clean handkerchief in his palm and handed it to her. "Let's start from the beginning."

THE fool. He thinks he can hide from me, can keep his presence in Zorro a secret. But I'm too smart for him—and too powerful. It's only a matter of time before I uncover his identity.

Now that I have physical substance, I can't be defeated. A weakened body has given me everything I need. It might be diseased, but soon I will find a stronger body, and then the possibilities will be endless. The terminations . . . ah, how glorious! The rush, the adrenaline, the power.

Praise Belial for my descension into this plane. No Sentinel can discover or defeat me. There will be more terminations, more power.

I will have it all.

THREE

"YOUR son was fathered by a Sentinel," the man repeated, a ruthless determination underlying his deep voice. "Who?"

Kara knew he'd eventually uncover everything—already had, for the most part, but a deeply ingrained instinct for survival insisted that she continue to deny the facts. "What makes you so sure of that?" she challenged, wiping at her eyes.

"There's no denying Alex is a Sentinel, no matter how much you might wish otherwise. And there are only two ways a human can have Sentinel power. The first is to be born to parents where one or both have the power. The second is through possession of a body. I'll bet your son has no indications of being possessed—and believe me, you would know if he was. You are not one of us. Therefore, the transfer of the power came from his father."

She lifted her chin, glaring at him defiantly, although fear still pounded through her, barely restrained only through tremendous effort on her part. "And there are no exceptions to that rule, no anomalies?"

"None. The mother becomes pregnant only if a Sentinel soul chooses to enter the physical plane at that time and through those specific parents."

The soul chose? Both the time and the parents? This new knowledge skittered through Kara, adding to the emotional and mental overload.

"You didn't know this." Her surprise must have been evident, because he said it more as a statement of fact rather than a question.

Richard had told her there was no need for birth control, and she'd believed him. She'd been so head over heels in love with him, that she didn't care if they did have a child. But she hadn't known any details of how Sentinels came into the physical plane.

There was probably a lot more she didn't know, information that might be necessary to keep Alex safe. Resignation seeped through her, and she felt weary and drained. Any denials were futile in the face of the stranger's perceptiveness. She shook her head. "I didn't know how Sentinels came into being. I didn't even know I was pregnant until after Richard"—she paused, closing her eyes against the pain—"until after he was murdered."

The stranger leaned closer. "Tell me about Richard."

Surrendering to the inevitable, Kara steeled herself against the grief. "I met him in Birmingham, Alabama. I had just finished my residency in family practice. He was a medical examiner for the county coroner's office."

That fateful moment flashed through her mind: Bored to tears at a stuffy American Medical Association honorarium dinner, she'd glanced across the room to see a tall, handsome man staring at her. Normally she would have ignored him, but the attraction had been mutual and instantaneous. She'd watched as he threaded his way through the crowd with a purposeful tread, his gaze never leaving her, and a shiver had swept through her body . . .

"Birmingham." The stranger's voice jolted her out of the memory. "You must be talking about Richard Wayman. His physical entity perished after a mortal encounter with a Belian, which had incarnated as a state trooper. Seven years back, I believe."

A mortal encounter? No, that was too neat and clinical. It had been a massacre . . . *The trooper, his inhuman eyes shielded behind mirrored sunglasses, coldly gunning down innocent people as they screamed in terror and tried to run. Smiling as he stepped over bodies sprawled around him like broken, bloody toys. Daring Richard to stop him—a challenge no Sentinel could ignore.*

With a gasp, Kara tried to shut out the horrific images that she had witnessed seven years ago. She channeled her emotional upheaval toward the man now sitting beside her. She wouldn't allow his unemotional reduction of Richard to nothing but a statistic.

"Richard Wayman was more than a *physical entity*," she snapped. "He was a flesh and blood man, and he cared about people, really cared what happened to them."

So much so that he had answered the Belian's challenge. Had stepped forward so no more innocents would die. She clenched the handkerchief, dug her nails into the fabric.

The stranger appeared unaffected by her outburst. "And you conducted for him?"

Other memories swirled forward, heated and erotic: *Richard rising above her, stroking inside her deep and hard.*

"That's it, baby. That's it. Just let yourself go, and don't worry about the energy. I'll handle it."

Light flashed around them, electricity arced between them, and her body began convulsing, in the throes of the most powerful orgasm she'd ever experienced. "Oh, God, Richard . . . oh my God!"

Then the light and feelings became so intense, she couldn't see, couldn't think, could only be swept away by sensation.

"Kara?"

Her heart was pounding again, and her breasts felt painfully swollen. She drew a deep breath, looked into the stranger's glittering eyes. "Yes. I conducted for him."

"Did you work together long?"

Worked together, lived together, loved together. "Almost two years," she murmured.

"Yet you had no idea what to expect, or that your child would have the power."

She blew out her breath. "No, but we've handled it without any problems."

"You can't continue to do it on your own. Alex needs to be initiated into the Law of One. He needs to be instructed in the proper use of his power and the fulfillment of his purpose on this plane."

"We've been fine until now," she insisted stubbornly. "I want my son to live a normal life."

"You can't keep denying the reality, Kara. An unshielded initiate can draw discarnate entities, or worse. The Belian I'm hunting could eventually pick up Alex's power and prey upon him."

"What are you talking about? There can't be any Belians in this area. There haven't been any murders. No crime at all, in fact."

"You're wrong about that. There has already been at least one murder in Zorro. But the authorities labeled the death as accidental."

Another chill swept through her, and she clenched the handkerchief until her hand ached. "I don't believe it. David Thornton was the only recent death, and he drowned six weeks ago. He never could swim, but he always insisted on going out in the water to fish, even in January."

"He didn't drown. I believe an autopsy would show that he died from other causes."

"What other causes?"

"A blow to the head."

She knew when a Sentinel visited the scene of a crime or a death, and was able to pick up a psychic trail, the Sentinel could often "see" what had happened. But she couldn't bring herself to accept what the stranger was telling her.

"He was battered badly because the current carried him

over several dams, and it was two days before they discovered his body," she said.

"That was the official report. But Thornton was dead before he entered the water."

It didn't surprise her that this man had been able to access the police reports, just as she understood why, even if he had "seen" David's death, he didn't know who had committed the alleged murder. A highly advanced Belian could obscure its presence, so it would only appear as a blur in a psychic vision.

But she still wouldn't accept that David had been murdered. Couldn't accept it, because it would herald the end of the normal existence she'd carved out for Alex and herself.

"No," she persisted. "The medical examiner would have discovered the blow to the head, and the death wouldn't have been ruled accidental. There are no Belians in Zorro. The population has hardly changed since I've been here. Besides Alex and me, nobody new has moved to Zorro in a number of years."

His expression hardened; impatience again flashed in his eyes. "You're not that naive, Kara. We just talked about it. Not all Belians come to Earth through physical birth."

Horrific possibilities flashed through her mind. "Possession," she murmured, feeling even sicker.

"Exactly. You probably also know such a thing is easier if the possessed person's body or mind is weak." He leaned forward, his frigid gaze fixed on her. "There are two things you will do for me. You will give me a list of your patients with serious physical or mental conditions. And you'll help me track down this entity."

"I won't do either of those things. I'm not going to allow you to terrorize innocent people."

"I can get the medical records, with or without your help," he informed her grimly. "And you *will* conduct for me."

She knew she couldn't keep him from accessing her patient records, unless she destroyed them, and she would give that serious consideration after she got rid of him.

As for the conducting, although he possessed the power to force her compliance, the code of honor that all Sentinels followed did not allow him to use his power that way. A conductor had to be willing to be called into service.

"I won't conduct for you, or anyone else." She rose from the sofa, finding strength from her resolve. "We've talked. Now you can leave."

He rose, too, and she instinctively took a step back from his intimidating frame. "You must conduct for me. This Belian is eluding me. I need you to provide the focus and magnify the energy. Like you did with Richard."

Another emotional blow added to the staggering overload of the day. "Richard and I—it was different. We loved each other."

"Love has nothing to do with conducting. It is the physical bodies that are the conduit, and the balancing of female and male energies." He closed the gap between them, grasping her shoulders. Energy arced from him to her, sparking through her body like fireworks.

He leaned down, his breath a harsh caress against her face. "It is not love, but the power of the *sexual* surge, which facilitates the seeking."

She jerked away from his grip, stumbled back. "Go to hell, Sentinel."

He straightened, his hands dropping to his sides. "We're already there, Kara. Hell is here, on Earth. And it's here in Zorro. I can guarantee you it's going to get a lot worse."

"Get out."

He didn't move. "What about Alex? You can't leave him unprotected."

Alex was her weak link, and this bastard knew it. She drew a deep breath, looked at the pictures on the mantel, her son's beloved face reflected in each of them. She couldn't discount the possible danger to Alex. "I'll think about what you said."

"You do that. And you—*we*—need to take action soon, Kara. Very soon." He picked up his duster and strode to the door, which swung open as he approached. "One more thing." He paused in the doorway, glanced back at her. "Check the autopsy report on Thornton."

She had the sinking feeling she wouldn't like what she found. "I intend to do that."

He reached into his rear jeans' pocket and pulled out a card case. "I'm staying at the Magnolia Bed-and-Breakfast, but you can reach me on my cell phone." He held out a card, and she took it, feeling as though she'd just grasped an activated hand grenade. "Even if I don't hear from you," he informed her, "I'll be back in touch."

He left then, the chill afternoon air drifting through the open doorway, not refreshing and soothing, but insidious, like a harbinger of evil. She stood there long moments after the sound of his car faded into the distance, too mentally battered to marshal her thoughts into any cohesive pattern.

Then she walked slowly to the door, closed it, and bolted it, before she finally looked at the card in her shaking hand. *Society Magazine*, Damien Morgan, Staff Writer. His cell number was listed at the bottom.

She wanted to scream. To knock things over and kick furniture. To grab Alex and Mac, and load their most important stuff into the truck and drive far from here. Far from this resurrecting nightmare of Belians, of madness and murder. Most of all, she wanted to be far from Damien Morgan and the unsettling memories he'd managed to raise, after she had so carefully packed them away.

But now she feared there was truly nowhere to hide. She couldn't outrun the fact Alex was a Sentinel, or the possibility that his burgeoning power might be a signal to other Sentinels and Belians alike.

Another memory came out of nowhere, sucking her back to the vivid horror of Birmingham . . .

The state trooper held a terrified pregnant woman against him, his police-issue pistol pressed to her head. "Better show yourself real quick like, Wayman. Or I might get bored and send some more souls to your cursed One. Ah, there you are."

He smiled broadly as Richard stepped from the shadows. "Throw down your weapons—all of them—Sentinel, or she dies." He waited until Richard complied, tossing down both his gun and knife. Then, still smiling, he raised his own gun, aimed toward Richard, shot him . . .

No! Shoving the mental pictures away, Kara stared blindly around her living room, willing herself to focus on the here and now. She wouldn't—couldn't—allow Alex to develop his powers or attempt to use them. It was too dangerous. She had to find a way to hide his abilities, to help him shield himself.

Even with her determined resolutions, she still didn't know what to do now, or how to extricate Alex and herself from any involvement with Damien Morgan.

Morgan was right about one thing. Hell truly was here on Earth.

"I'M sorry, Dr. Cantrell, but we don't have any records on a David Thornton," the assistant medical examiner told Kara.

"There has to be a mistake. Mr. Thornton drowned six weeks ago. You must have some record on him."

"I'm sorry, doctor, but there are no files here on anyone by that name. As far as I can tell, this office hasn't done an autopsy on a Zorro resident in the past six months."

Kara disconnected from the Travis County Medical Examiner's Office and took a deep breath. There had to be an error somewhere. She picked up the phone receiver again and dialed the police station, requesting Tom Greer. "This is Kara Cantrell," she said when he came on the line, then pushed forward without further preliminaries. "Did you order an autopsy on David Thornton?"

There was a pause before the police chief said, "Why are you asking about that, Dr. Cantrell?"

"Because I need the information for David's medical

records," she lied. "Did you, or didn't you, request an autopsy on him?"

"No, I did not."

She didn't want to believe what she'd just heard, but as the unrest churning inside her intensified, Damien Morgan's scenario began to fall into place. "Why not?"

"I didn't see the need." Chief Greer's gruff voice came back over the phone. "It was obvious David had drowned. The dang fool was always too darned stubborn to wear a life jacket and he never could swim worth a damn. The medical examiner's office in Austin has a huge backlog right now, on account of those murders in Fredericksburg, and with the flu epidemic, and so many affected folks dying at home. There wasn't any need to tie up David's body and prolong his family's grieving."

"So you just released the body?" Kara clenched her pen, dread circling through her like a vulture over a cow carcass.

"I did. And there's no reason to make a big deal over it," Tom said evenly. "It was a judgment call, and I made it."

"Who signed the death certificate?"

"Bill Sampson, the JP over in Johnson City. He's worked with us many years, so it seemed easiest to let him do the paperwork."

And it had also left Kara, who liked to do things by the book, out of the mix. She was the outsider, and a woman besides. She hung up the phone and stared blindly at the neat stack of lab reports on her desk.

She couldn't believe the police chief hadn't reported an unattended and potentially suspicious death, and that Bill Sampson had gone along with it. For one thing, the law demanded that Tom do so, and for another, as far as she knew, he had always followed correct protocol. Why had he deviated in this instance?

Unless he had been psychically influenced by a Belian . . . or . . . *unless he had been possessed by the Belian.*

Panic pressed down, threatening to suffocate her. She shoved back from the desk, almost tipping over her chair. Forcing her trembling legs to move, she paced back and forth, making herself take deep, steady breaths. It couldn't be true. She still had no real evidence that Damien Morgan was right, only the ghosts of her past resurrecting all the old fears.

She was a physician, scientific and logical. Chief Greer's reasoning made perfect sense. Why would anyone want to murder David Thornton? He'd been a genial, good ole boy, who'd lived in Zorro all his life and was liked by everyone. It was too preposterous.

Yet Kara found herself in the small alcove off her office, where her patient files were stored, spurred by Saturday's confrontation with Morgan: particularly with one specific, horrifying aspect of the discussion.

"You're not that naive, Kara. . . . Not all Belians enter the earth through physical birth."

"Possession."

"Exactly. You probably also know such a thing is easier if the possessed person's body or mind is weak."

Those words reverberated through her, and Damien Morgan's dark, chiseled face flashed into her mind. Forcing his vivid image away, Kara pulled David's file, along with those of Tom Greer and some patients who had chronic health problems. She felt compelled to review them closely, while at the same time, she found herself praying that the suspicions beginning to take root were totally unfounded.

She didn't know what she'd do if they weren't.

DR. Kara Cantrell's blue truck was parked on Johnson Avenue in front of her office. It was 2:00 P.M., and hopefully she had afternoon appointments. Damien had plans that would go more smoothly without interference from Dr. Cantrell.

Not that he minded dealing with her. On the contrary, he found her fascinating. Few humans, conductors or otherwise, offered much resistance, but Kara Cantrell had been an intriguing blend of strength and defiance. Her inner light had glowed with a fierce vitally.

Physically, she wasn't hard to look at, either. He saw her clearly in his mind, her hair a rich auburn color, cut in a classic style that fell, straight and smooth, to curve below her stubborn jawline, framing a face that was strong, yet feminine. Her eyes, a shade that was not quite gray, but not quite blue, had that odd translucence that seemed common to true psychics and conductors (often one and the same). Her complexion was the pale, creamy hue common to many true redheads, her nose was ordinary, and her mouth a little on the thin side, as if she kept it firmly compressed, finding little in life to smile about.

Hers wasn't a striking beauty, but rather an understated attractiveness, with an appeal that was enhanced by her obvious intelligence and integrity.

Not that female conductors had to be beautiful to be effective. Why some women made good conductors and others didn't was one of the universe's mysteries.

One theory was that conductors were reincarnated souls of the wretched creatures who had been created in Atlantian experiments and enslaved by the Sons of Belial, and whom the enlightened Atlantians had tried to help. Perhaps that had created a karmic link between the rescued creatures and the Children of One, now facilitating conductors helping Sentinels track down the Sons of Belial, but not even the Sanctioned knew for sure.

Psychic ability was often present in conductors, but not always. There was no doubt in Damien's mind that Kara was both psychic and a conductor. The connection with her had been undeniable. The minute he had stepped onto her porch on Saturday, Damien had felt the familiar flare of chemistry and sexual energy surging from the base chakras of his body.

It was fortunate he'd found her, because conductors weren't all that common. It was even more fortunate that they matched so well, because putting a Sentinel and a conductor together didn't automatically guarantee a powerful enough chemistry for conduction. It was like sex—some partners created potent heat together, some partners left each other cold.

Damien had connected with a few of the conductors he'd met—enough to get his job done. But he'd been pleasantly surprised to so readily find a conductor receptive to his particular energy, especially in rural Texas. And his and Kara's connection was very powerful. He'd thought he'd gotten used to the one-two punch of lust and the ensuing hormonal rush over the years, had honed his control over his body to minimize the effects.

Yet he had experienced an immediate, primal response to Kara's energy, his body reacting as if he were a green initiate rather than a seasoned Sentinel. He'd been grateful his duster hid his obvious physical arousal. Such a thing hadn't happened to him in years, and while it was unacceptable, it was also proof positive that Kara was indeed a matched conductor, and a very powerful one at that, no matter how much she might deny it.

Even now, thinking about her sent a sexually charged rush through him. Startled, he mentally clamped down, focusing his thoughts with ruthless precision on the matter at hand. Kara Cantrell might have a surprising effect on him, but he had years of experience and discipline to fall back on. He would not—could not—ever allow himself to be affected by the conductors with whom he worked. Painful experience had taught him that, and it was his ironclad, unbreakable rule.

He would handle Kara's resistance to helping him, and his unprecedented response to her—although he needed to rethink his approach. He wasn't known for subtlety, and he realized his aggressive approach on Saturday had shaken her up and hadn't been conducive to gaining her cooperation. But he'd deal with that later.

His immediate goal was to talk with the boy, to determine the extent of the boy's powers, so he could report back to the Sanctioned, and a decision could be made regarding the boy's future.

Damien didn't know whether or not Kara normally picked up the boy from school, but he assumed that if she did, she would have alternate arrangements for the days she was tied up with patients. He'd called the elementary school earlier, and knew classes let out at two thirty, so he drove to the small red-brick building and parked half a block from the main entrance.

A battered school bus was already in front of the building, and several cars were parked behind it, although they appeared unoccupied. Most likely the small groups of women standing nearby, chatting among themselves, were the owners of those cars, and were visiting together while they waited for their children.

Damien settled back to observe and wait, his senses automatically flaring out to check for unusual psychic traces, but he found nothing out of the ordinary. The tinny sound of the school bell signaled the release of classes, and students began emerging from the building, dispersing to the bus and the cars, with a few trudging off on foot. There weren't a large number of students; the Zorro population was around three thousand, and had only one elementary school. Damien readily spotted Alex.

Not only did he recognize the boy, with his mop of sandy hair and serious brown eyes, but Damien picked up the thread of power the child was subconsciously broadcasting. Although it was unlikely anyone or anything else could pick up on the faint broadcast, it still was not a good thing, and something that must be remedied quickly.

The boy got on the bus, and Damien waited until the bus pulled away from the school before following at a discreet distance, wondering if Alex would go to his mother's office or a daycare of some sort. After quite a few drop-offs, the bus eventually turned on the road leading to Kara's house, then stopped in front of her home.

The blue truck was not outside, and Damien was surprised

that Kara would allow the boy to go to an empty house. But a young, Hispanic-looking woman came to the door. Alex greeted her with familiarity, and she smiled and ruffled his hair as they went inside.

Damien was undeterred by the presence of a strange woman, as he could usually manipulate human minds, unless the subject was especially strong willed. He waited a few moments for the bus to lumber out of sight, then pulled up in front of the house. He walked up to the door, knocked.

The boy opened the door, his eyes going very round when he saw Damien. Behind him, the dog went into a frenzy of barking. Damien quieted the animal with a mental command, turned his attention to the boy. "Hello, Alex. I'm sure you remember me."

Still silent, the boy began backing away. He radiated a blend of fear and power, his Sentinel force even stronger because of that fear. Damien glanced into the house, didn't see the Hispanic woman. He squatted down, grabbed Alex's arm, felt his alarm spike wildly. "I'm not going to hurt you," he said quickly, sending a burst of calming energy to the child. "I just want to talk to you. We can do that right here. Okay?"

Alex stared at him with wide, distrustful eyes. "My mother doesn't like you. She wouldn't want me to talk to you. I don't like you, either."

"You don't have to like me, Alex. But it's important that you talk to me, about your power. Do you know what I mean?"

The boy stood frozen, like a terrified rabbit trapped in a snare. "You know what I'm talking about, don't you?" Damien persisted. "Can you make things happen with your thoughts, Alex? Or by pointing at something?"

The boy stared at him mutely.

"Answer me, Alex. Can you?"

"M-my mother doesn't like me to make things happen. I don't do anything!"

"But you can, Alex, if you want to."

The boy continued to stare at Damien, his dark eyes

looking far older than his physical age. "You can do stuff, too," Alex said finally. "That's why you felt funny when you were here before."

Damien grasped Alex's other arm and leaned closer, his gaze boring into the child's eyes. "Yes, I can. I'm a Sentinel. So are you."

"What's going on here?" came a shrill voice.

Damien looked up to find the Hispanic woman he'd seen earlier bearing down on them. He rose as she grabbed Alex and pulled him to her.

"Who are you?" she demanded, glaring at Damien. "What are you doing here?"

KARA studied the file on Belle Williams, who was battling breast cancer. She tried to imagine the middle-aged Belle, who harbored a generous heart beneath her no-nonsense, businesslike exterior, murdering David Thornton. The chemotherapy treatments that Belle was undergoing in Austin had definitely weakened her, leaving her open to the possibility of possession by a Belian.

But quite a few of Zorro's residents had life-threatening conditions, and any one of them could be susceptible. Kara added Belle's name to the list of possibilities and rubbed her aching temples. Closing Belle's file, she reached for Sal's chart just as the door tone chimed, indicating she had a visitor. Since she was the only one in the office, she put the chart back on the stack and went out to the reception area.

She felt a momentary flash of pleasure when she saw her visitor was Doris Burgess, and her smile was genuine. "Hello, Doris. What brings you here?"

Doris, a spry lady of seventy-five years of age, was Kara's closest neighbor, as well as one of her favorite patients. She insisted on being addressed by her first name, refusing to surrender to encroaching age, or to the diabetes that had been diagnosed when she was sixty. She dressed very stylishly, drove a sporty car, and was computer savvy, with a lot of e-mail contacts. She was also a wonderful baker, and Alex loved to help her in her kitchen.

Doris glanced around the empty waiting area. "Where is everyone? Are you closed?"

"It was a light day, and I didn't have any appointments this afternoon, so I let Bonnie and Susan go home."

"I hope I'm not intruding. I know I don't have an appointment, but I saw your truck outside and thought it might be all right to come by without one. I need medical advice."

In the six years that Kara had been practicing medicine in Zorro, Doris had never dropped in without first making an appointment. A frisson of suspicion ran through Kara, knotting her body. Surely it wasn't Doris who might be possessed. She and Kara crossed paths almost every day. Surely Kara would have sensed something. But even as she tried to rationalize her fear away, Kara knew better. A Belian could often shield itself from a Sentinel, who had far more powerful psychic abilities than any human.

"Dr. Kara, are you all right? Should I come back another time?"

Kara pushed her suspicions away—for now. She still had no real proof of Damien Morgan's supposition. She needed to act as if everything were normal, for both herself and Alex.

"I'm fine. You know you don't need an appointment to see me." She put her arm around Doris, giving her an affectionate squeeze, yet at the same time she found herself reaching out mentally for any sign of a dark energy. She hated this. "You know I'm always available for you, Doris, day or night."

"Well, thank you. Even though I'm watching my diet, I've had some trouble regulating my blood sugar, and I thought I'd better check with you about adjusting my insulin dosage."

"Absolutely. You need to be careful when you're dealing

with insulin." Kara gestured toward her office. "Come on in here. I don't think we need an examining room for this."

Doris pulled a small notebook from her purse as she walked into the office. "I've got all my glucose readings and my medication log with me." She always kept exacting records that made Kara's job of controlling her diabetes much easier.

"I wish all my patients were like you." Kara settled Doris in a chair facing her desk then went to get her glucose meter and Doris's chart.

"Now then," she said when she returned. "When did you last eat?" She held the pen over the open chart, and found herself searching Doris's lively green eyes for any glimmer of evil. Again, she had to shake away her suspicions. "I'm sorry. What time did you say?"

She notated the time, pricked Doris's finger, put the strip in the meter, and studied the readout. "One hundred sixty-five, and it's been three hours since you ate lunch. That *is* too high. You're right, as usual. We need to adjust your insulin."

Doris nodded. "I thought so, and the information I found on the Internet backed up my theory."

"You and that computer. Have you signed up for an online dating service yet?" Kara teased, trying to convince herself that Doris was normal, that *everything* was normal.

Doris laughed, her eyes dancing with her usual zest for life. "Certainly not. I don't want some old man desperate for someone to pick up after him." She leaned across the desk. "Now you, young lady, should be surrounding yourself with handsome young bucks, although I think they call them 'hunks' nowadays. You're too young and pretty to be devoting all your time to your son and your patients."

Kara sighed mentally. She was perfectly happy in her roles as mother and doctor, despite the attempts of well-meaning family and friends to steer her back to the dating world. "Doris, you know the only man for me right now is

Alex," she said lightly, despite the tension still stringing her nerves. "I'm very content with my life just the way it is."

"You always say that," Doris replied. Her unwavering gaze made Kara uncomfortable.

The older woman always managed to see more deeply into Kara than others did. And if she was now possessed by a Belian—*Stop!* Kara ordered herself fiercely. *You are not going to let Morgan's unverified claims turn you against your patients and your friends.*

"Being content may be all right for a while, but you can't stay in a safe little bubble forever, my dear," Doris continued. "You need to get out and live. The years go by way too fast."

"I know what you mean," Kara said. "I can remember when Alex was just a baby, and he'll be seven on his next birthday. I can't believe it."

"How is that young man doing?"

A new concern nagged at Kara, but she firmly told herself she and Alex would deal with the issue of his powers, and successfully put the matter to rest. Damn Morgan for coming into her life and putting all these fears into her mind. She would not live like this.

"Alex is wonderful," she said evenly.

"Is he still coming on Thursday to help me make cakes for the town hall bake sale?"

Did she dare let Alex go over to Doris's house? He was so excited about helping Doris bake. But now . . . Kara felt the strong urge to pull Alex from school and keep him home until the matter of the Belian was laid to rest.

That was her emotional side. Her logical side knew that she and Alex couldn't live that way. She had to accept the fact that evil resided wherever there was opportunity; there was no place she and Alex could run to that would ever be completely safe. She had to allow him to follow his usual routine as much as possible.

"I'd like to help with the baking, too," she said. She'd keep life on its regular course, but she would take extra precautions. "Can we both come over Thursday afternoon?"

"That would be wonderful. It will be much easier to make all those cakes with two extra pairs of hands." Doris picked up her pen. "Now, if you can tell me what my new insulin dose should be, I'll get out of your hair, and let you get home to young Alex."

Kara read Doris's notes to see what doses she'd been taking, made a copy of the notes to put in the chart, and calculated the amount of a slightly higher dosage. Doris wrote down the information, then read it back.

"The American Diabetes Association website says you can't be too careful with insulin," she said, tucking her notebook into her purse. "And I always worry about getting too much and going into insulin shock."

"That's always a concern," Kara told her. "But you're very conscientious, plus you're on premixed medication that has both regular and long-acting insulin, so you don't have to juggle two bottles for your injections. If you'll be sure to eat within thirty to forty-five minutes after your injections, you'll be just fine."

"I always do. I set my stove timer as soon as I have the shot, and start fixing my meal." Doris rose and leaned over to give Kara a maternal hug. "Thank you, Dr. Kara. I'll be looking for you and Alex on Thursday afternoon." She left, leaving behind the airy fragrance of the Liz Claiborne perfume she always wore.

Seeing Doris should have been a pleasant ending to a stressful day, but Kara couldn't seem to shake the dark cloud of suspicion hounding her. She closed Doris's file and was rising to put all the charts away when the phone rang. She saw on the caller ID it was from home, and figured Alex was wondering why she wasn't home yet. Feeling her mood lighten, she smiled and picked up the receiver. "Hello there."

"We have a problem here."

Kara's smile faded at the concern in her combination housekeeper and nanny's voice. "What's wrong, Luz?"

"There is a man here at the house. I've never seen him before. He came to the door while I was in the kitchen, and

Alex let him in. He was talking to Alex, and Alex is very upset."

"Oh, no," Kara murmured, certain of the intruder's identity. "Has this man threatened you in any way? Did you tell him to get out?"

"No threats yet," Luz said, her voice shaky and her accent thicker than usual. "I told him I would call *la policía* if he did not leave immediately. He said to call you first, that you knew him."

"Did he tell you his name?" Kara asked, although she knew.

"Damien Morgan. He is very arrogant. He said I could call the police if I wanted, but he's staying here until you arrive. I sense that he is *muy peligroso*. What should I do?"

Kara felt as if a huge hand had closed around her heart and was squeezing unmercifully. "Don't call the police," she said sharply. "Mr. Morgan won't hurt you. I'll be there in a few minutes. Just keep him away from Alex until I get there."

She slammed down the phone, grabbed her jacket and purse, and raced out of the building as if a Belian were pursuing her.

A distinct and horrifying possibility.

He thinks he can track me, but I'm far smarter than he is. I was able to pick up on his power, even with it shielded. I don't know who he is yet, but I will find out. I know he was somewhere near the school today. I wonder what he was looking for. Or maybe who *he was looking for. I did pick up a second, faint echo of energy. There must be someone else in Zorro with the power.*

I will have to investigate that possibility further. Since the Sentinel was lurking near the school, perhaps it's one of the children. Now, that would be an interesting development—and one I would enjoy remedying. I'll have to check out the school-aged brats. Discreetly, of course. I'm far too clever to ever fall under suspicion.

Before I'm through with this pitiful excuse for a town, my power will be legendary, and I'll be unstoppable. The Sentinel, whoever he is, will be just a fading memory in the chronicles of the Sanctioned.

And these bumbling idiots will never even know what hit them.

FOUR

KARA slammed into the house, her heart racing. She wasn't sure what she had expected to find, but she stopped short when she saw Damien sitting on the sofa, idly flipping through her latest *JAMA* magazine. Luz stood in the archway between the living room and dining area, Alex's baseball bat gripped tightly in both hands and resting against her shoulder as if she were preparing to swing at a ball.

Alex stood just inside the hallway leading to the bedrooms, his dark eyes wide and fixed on Damien. His clenched fists were the only visible sign of his agitation. Mac lay on the floor in front of Alex, his gaze on Damien, his ears and his hackles up.

The scene, and this man's invasion into her home, spiked Kara's fury to a new level. Damien calmly turned a magazine page, looked up when she stormed toward him. "What the hell do you think you're doing here?" she demanded, surprised at how hard she was shaking.

He tossed the magazine onto the coffee table, sat back. "I wanted to talk with Alex about his"—he glanced at

Luz—"situation." His steel blue gaze shifted to Kara, piercing her with its intensity. "And I wanted to continue our discussion."

She forced herself to take a breath and speak calmly. "I told you Saturday that I don't want you anywhere near Alex. You're not welcome here."

"Then maybe you should have let your maid call the police." He rose, towering over her, and stepped closer.

Resisting the automatic reflex to back up, she stood her ground. "She's not a *maid*. Get out. *Now.*"

He didn't move. "Did you check on David Thornton today?"

The doubts flooded her again. She glanced at Alex and Luz. The young woman reached over to the dining room table and picked up the portable phone. "I can call the police."

"No, Luz, that won't be necessary. Mr. Morgan is leaving. I'm going to see him out. Alex, get started on your homework." Kara looked back at Damien, jerked her head toward the open front door. "Outside." She whirled and strode through the doorway, certain he would follow.

The pulsing waves of energy behind her were the only indication that he was behind her. Absurdly, she wondered how so large a man could move with such utter stealth.

The cool afternoon air flowed over her, and she shivered, thinking she might never be warm again. Over her shoulder, she watched Damien close the front door behind them. Mentally bracing herself, she turned to face him. The relentless electrical static that surged between them only agitated her more. "Can't you shut that off?"

"Shut what off?"

"That damned energy. It's . . . disconcerting."

His brows arched. "Is it now? Well, I suggest you go with the flow here, and acclimate yourself to it. You should know I can't do anything about the conductor/Sentinel reaction."

"I know you can stay the hell away," she snapped, wanting to advance on him like a boxer on an opponent, to crowd his personal space and throw his own tactics back at him. But she knew that would be a bad move, so she opted to stay where she was.

He stood motionless on the porch, his duster draped over his arm. He was dressed in a black turtleneck and black jeans and boots. His midnight hair was tied back, denying any relief to his stark features. In the fading sunlight, he looked dark and menacing, like a secret agent for Satan.

He appeared oblivious to the chill in the air, radiating a body heat she could feel even across the three or four feet separating them. Richard had been like that, too, with a superhuman metabolism and higher body temperature.

"You checked on David Thornton," he said.

There was no sense lying to him when he could readily obtain the information. Telling him she knew the truth, but still had no intention of helping him, might be a stronger offensive tactic than playing dumb. "I tried to locate an autopsy," she said. "One was never ordered."

He didn't appear surprised. "Who made that decision?"

She didn't want to have this conversation, didn't want to consider the ramifications. But what she wanted didn't change the facts. "The police chief, Tom Greer, decided it was an accidental drowning, and that an autopsy was unnecessary." That would put Tom at the top of Damien's list of suspects.

"So now you know I'm right about Thornton."

"All I know is that an autopsy was never done. There's still no evidence David was murdered." But her words were sheer bravado, because she knew on an intuitive level that Damien's suspicions were correct.

"My psychic visions are never wrong," he said. "A Belian killed David Thornton. I need your help to track it."

She rubbed her chilled arms, kept them folded protectively across her chest. "I won't do it."

He watched her a moment. "You're stronger than you realize, Kara."

"Yeah, I'm familiar with the Sanctioned company line."

She turned away from the eerie blue glow of his eyes. "Tell me, is there some sort of pain meter you Sentinels use as a gauge? Do you compare notes to see which conductors can endure the most pain, the most stress, the most horror? Who's strong, and who's weak? Who can take on the most powerful and terrifying demons from hell? I've got a news flash for you, Morgan. I'm no longer on the list of candidates."

Not that she owed him an explanation. She'd already paid her dues. She had faced unspeakable monsters and a shadowy void so immense, she could only pray God was strong enough to win, that the light could prevail, and the world wouldn't be plunged into the abyss of darkness . . .

The state trooper laughed as Richard struggled to get to his feet, slipping on the blood from his gun-wounded leg. "What's the matter, Wayman? You letting a little thing like a bullet keep you from saving this human here? Maybe this will help."

He pressed the gun barrel to the terrified woman's swollen abdomen, oblivious to her pleas to spare her baby. Before he could pull the trigger, Richard flicked his hand toward them. The gun jerked away from the woman and fell, skidding between lifeless bodies.

With a roar, the trooper threw his victim aside and went after the gun. Richard channeled more energy to send the gun flying farther away, and the Belian charged him. They both hit the ground, rolling. Sparks flew in the air as each battled to manipulate and direct energy. Kara could only watch, knowing they were locked in mortal combat . . .

Her breath hissing out, she forced away the memory—and those that followed.

"Turn around, Kara. I don't want to have this discussion with your back."

The way Damien said her name in that husky voice of his was reminiscent of intimate, whispered conversations in the heat of the night. She refused to fall under its spell. "There's nothing more to discuss."

With a sound of exasperation, he grasped her shoulder, pulled her around. His touch sent tendrils of sensation spiraling through her. She damned the innate chemistry that existed between certain Sentinels and conductors, damned the fate that had visited such a curse on her.

She jerked away. "Don't touch me."

"Then don't ignore me. And look at me, damn it."

She lifted her chin, glaring at him. "I've heard what you have to say, Sentinel. I've already made my contribution. I conducted for two years. The Sanctioned have gotten more than the designated pound of flesh from me."

"You haven't heard everything. There's a lot more at stake here than you realize."

"And you haven't been listening. *It doesn't have anything to do with me.* Even if you're right, even if there's a Belian in Zorro, I won't help you." *She wouldn't watch anyone else she loved die, lying in a pool of blood.*

"What about Alex?"

Everything inside her froze. That was the million-dollar question, wasn't it? "I don't know. I have to think about that situation some more."

"He was broadcasting today, as he came out of school and got on the bus."

Adrenaline churned through her. "He couldn't have been. We had a long talk about it last night, and he promised to be more careful—"

"I told him I'm a Sentinel, and that he's one, too."

His words had the impact of a physical blow. Staggered, she reached out to brace herself against the house. He definitely knew how to pull the trigger of an emotionally shattering weapon. Fury rose swiftly.

"Damn you!" She swung at him.

He grabbed her arm before she could land a punch and dragged her to the wooden bench glider at the end of the porch. She tried to dig in her heels, but his superior strength won out.

"Sit," he ordered, backing his words with a small push. Making contact with the hard seat, she glared up at him, debating the wisdom of leaping back up and kicking him. It might be crazy, but she had no doubt it would be very satisfying.

"Don't do it," he warned. "Stay there and calm down."

She clenched her fists. Was the man a mind reader as well? He took his duster off his arm, shook it out, and tossed it over her. She didn't realize she'd been shivering until the first wave of warmth hit her.

The consideration of his action diffused some of her anger, but didn't diminish the intensity of the situation. She huddled into the garment, breathing in the tantalizing scents of sandalwood and male, and tried to collect her racing thoughts. *What should she do about Alex?*

The glider jolted and swung backward as he settled next to her, his large body sending another source of heat her way. The wood creaked as he sat back. She glanced sideways at him.

He stared straight ahead, his jaw tensed. He probably hated dealing with overly emotional females as much as she hated acting like one. Normally, she was calm, the logical voice of reason. But after the seismic shocks of the past few days, she'd been batting zero.

"Are you always this emotional?" he asked.

"No, I'm usually very rational," she shot back. "But arrogant, domineering men tend to bring out the worst in me. Are you always such a bastard?"

"Yes, actually, I am."

"I already figured that out," she muttered.

A movement at the corner of her eye caught her attention. She saw that the blinds in the large picture window were raised; Luz stood there, still holding the phone and baseball bat. She looked at Kara questioningly, held up the phone. Kara shook her head in the negative, mouthed *"It's okay."*

Damien turned his head, stared at Luz, who gave him an evil-eye look. He shrugged dismissively, and the glider shimmied as he shifted back to face Kara. "Calmer now?"

Her anger flared at his condescending remark. "How would you feel in my place?"

"You need to put aside your personal feelings about Sentinels and let me help you and Alex."

"I don't want your help."

"How are you going to protect Alex? Keep him in an insulated, underground chamber?"

Doubts plagued her. "How strongly was he broadcasting today?" she asked. A terrifying thought occurred to her, and she leaped to her feet, the duster sliding to the porch. "What if a Belian has already picked up on him? I can't let him go to school anymore!"

"Whoa! You're getting ahead of yourself. Alex is definitely broadcasting, but it's not very strong yet, and it's still on the higher chakra frequencies. I'm probably the only one who can pick it up right now. But if he gets excited or feels threatened, the signal will project more. As he gets older, his projections will become stronger and more erratic—unless he learns how to control them. Eventually, it will only be a matter of time until a Belian can sense him. Then he'll become an easy target."

A target . . . Oh, God . . .

The Belian/trooper and Richard rolled around on the bloody street. The Belian was larger, and Richard was weakened from blood loss. Kara saw the sudden flash of a knife in the Belian's hand, saw him plunge it into Richard's chest. Saw her beloved jerk from the shock. Saw the knife go in again and again . . .

Pain slashed like a physical blow. She felt her knees go weak, reached out blindly to keep from falling.

"Kara! Are you all right?" A strong hand grasping her elbow steadied her and jolted her back to the present.

But the images lingered on the edges of her consciousness, like a nightmare in the darkest hours of the night. Only it hadn't been a dream. It was real—the reality she'd faced seven years ago, and a powerful reminder she couldn't allow Alex to be discovered. He would *never* become a statistic as Richard had, not while she had a breath in her body.

Playing ostrich hadn't worked, and she could no longer

selfishly avoid her personal pain. A new wave of emotion barreled through her—steel determination that she would do whatever it took to protect Alex. *Anything*—including accepting the help of a Sentinel, as much as she hated to.

"I want my son safe," she demanded fiercely, staring up at Damien. "And I want your word on that, Sentinel."

"You know there are no guarantees—"

"No!" she practically screamed. She dug her fingers into his sweater, pushed against him. *"My son will be safe!* Do you hear me?"

He clamped his hands over her wrists, pulled her hands to the side. "I will do everything in my power to protect Alex. That's all I can promise."

She hated his calmness in the midst of her mental chaos, hated the cool logic and total lack of emotions he displayed. But he was a Sentinel, trained to hunt and destroy evil, a killing machine. He wasn't human, despite the mortal body he inhabited. Yet Richard had been different.

Richard was gone. And this man was Alex's best chance for survival—at least for the time being.

She pulled her wrists free. "What are you proposing?"

"That you allow me to act as his mentor, providing basic instruction, until the Sanctioned can appoint a permanent one."

"Leave the Sanctioned out of this," she said sharply, a new concern wedging in with all the others. "I don't want them involved. They might try to take Alex away from me."

The resultant silence sent off warning bells and she looked at Damien in alarm. "Don't tell me you've already told them."

"I contacted them on Saturday, after I left your house. It was my duty to do so."

Her body went rigid. She knew how the Sanctioned operated, knew they were merciless in their quest to defeat Belians, with no compunctions about sacrificing their own for what they considered the "higher cause." And that would include Alex, if it suited them. "Why did you do that?"

"It was my sworn duty," he repeated. "It had to be done."

Of course it did, in his mind. Sentinels fulfilled their purpose of tracking Belians, and kept complete secrecy and order by adhering to a strict code of duty and honor. There was no gray in the Sentinel world—only black and white. Kara felt a sense of inevitability, like the moon's pull on the tides.

The fight left her body. She turned and stared at the dissipating sunset. "You know, when Richard first told me he was a Sentinel, I thought he was joking. Up until then, he'd been so serious and down-to-earth."

Except in bed. The sex had been amazing, electrifying, incredible bursts carrying them to the stars. Multiple orgasms that should have left her utterly exhausted, rather than burning to have Richard inside her again. It had been exhilarating—until he blew away her concept of reality.

They were in bed after a marathon lovemaking session, him on his back, with her curled against his side, when he dropped proverbial bomb. "Kara, there's something I have to tell you. I'm . . . different. I'm not really human."

"Hmmm, you can say that again. You're definitely superhuman *in some areas."*

"No, I'm serious. I'm a Sentinel. My soul originated in Atlantis. I came into this life to track Belians, other Atlantian souls, but very evil."

Still seeing the moment as clearly as if it were yesterday, Kara pulled herself back from the memory. "Then, when I realized he was totally serious, I thought he was crazy."

Damien shifted behind her. She was hyperaware of the heat and strength of his big body. Oddly enough, his presence was comforting. "I'm sure it's a shock to realize the world is not as you envisioned it," he said.

That was an understatement. She let out a ragged breath. "Yeah, it was a shock, all right." She turned to face him. "There's so much Richard didn't tell me, like the fact that Sentinels are born to other Sentinels, although that's a logical assumption. He also didn't tell me that sometimes the good guys lose." She pushed away the sharp rise of pain. "I guess he wanted to protect me from your world."

"Just like you want to protect your son." Understanding softened Damien's harsh voice. "The best way to do that is to educate him."

She hated it that he was so damn right. "That doesn't mean the Sanctioned need to come anywhere near Alex. You're the only one I want working with him."

His face remained impassive. "I will suggest they let me handle this without interference, at least for the time being. That's the best I can do."

Kara didn't like it, but it was better than nothing. A Sentinel's word was pure gold. She turned and walked to the opposite side of the porch, letting the cool air wash over her like a blast of chilling reality. "I want you to show Alex only how to control his powers. I think we should hold off on giving him information about the Sentinels."

"He already knows he's a Sentinel."

Damien's voice was right behind her. Startled, she whirled and found herself facing his chest. She kept forgetting how quickly and quietly they moved. But it was impossible to forget the ever-present chemistry that sizzled between Sentinel and conductor.

She took a step back, angled her chin to meet his gaze. "He's not ready for this. And neither am I. I'm asking you to hold off for a while. And I want to be present whenever you're with him."

He stared at her a long moment, his features hard. Finally he nodded. "All right. We'll work on Alex controlling his powers and shielding himself. For now."

Kara blew out a sigh of relief. She'd won this battle, but knew she faced an entire war. A war against beings who had been a part of Earth, off and on, for thousands of years.

But go to war she would, if it would keep Alex from the abyss.

* * *

"WHO is that man?" Luz demanded the minute Kara came inside and closed the door, bolting it for good measure—although as Damien had already demonstrated, locks were no defense against a Sentinel—or a Belian. "I have never seen him around before. *¿Quién es él?*"

Kara held up a hand to stop Luz's tirade as she waited to be sure Damien was gone. When she heard the sound of a car starting and driving away, she slumped against the door, feeling as if she'd just run a marathon.

"Who is that man?" Luz asked again. "And why was he talking to Alex?"

Kara mentally scrambled for an explanation that would sound plausible. "Damien Morgan is a writer for a magazine. He—he was an associate of Alex's father."

Luz sniffed. "He's *muy* arrogant. I didn't like the way he just barged in here, and then refused to leave."

"I don't want him here, or anywhere near Alex, unless I'm around," Kara said firmly. "If he shows up again when I'm not home, don't let him in, and call me immediately."

Luz nodded her agreement. "There's something about him," she mused. "Not quite evil, but dangerous . . . and powerful. *Muy machista.*"

"He's interested in Alex, partly because of his association with Richard," Kara said, hoping to distract Luz from her musings. As a *curandera*, a folk healer, Luz moved in a culture that often dealt in superstitions and believed in evil spirits. She was highly intuitive, and Kara didn't want her sensing anything unusual about Damien. "He might be spending some time with us," she added.

"He could be a threat to you personally," Luz said, "You need to stay away from him."

"I'm not worried about that," Kara said, although that was only a half-truth. She turned toward the kitchen and the enticing smells of food cooking, but she didn't think she could eat anything. "Where's Alex?"

"I sent him to his room to watch TV." Luz leaned the baseball bat in the corner beside the front door. "I did not want him to hear you arguing with that man. He is very sensitive."

"I'm glad you thought to do that." For the hundredth time, Kara wondered how much Luz had discerned about Alex.

It was probably unwise to have an intuitive *curandera* taking care of him after school, but Luz loved children, and she was great with Alex. Kara preferred that arrangement over daycare, because Alex was so sensitive to the emotions of the other children. And it was heavenly to come home to a clean house and a cooked meal on weekdays.

She sighed, questioning the wisdom of many of her decisions over the years. But there would two things she could *never* regret: the love she and Richard had shared, and having Alex.

"Your dinner is ready," Luz announced, getting her red leather coat and matching purse off the wall rack. "My sister has my truck, but I called her five minutes ago, so she should be here." She looked at her watch. "I have a . . . an appointment."

Kara suddenly realized that her working late and then the altercation with Damien had kept Luz past her usual departure time. "I'm sorry I delayed you. Would your appointment happen to be a hot date with a certain rancher by the name of Matt Brown?"

Luz smiled her *Mona Lisa* smile. "Perhaps."

Luz and Matt had been dating off and on for number of years. They'd met when she was seventeen and had gone to work as a housekeeper at his family's luxurious home. Kara suspected that Luz had stronger feelings for Matt than he had for her.

There was a soft knocking on the door, and Luz opened it. Her sister Serafina stood there. Although younger than Luz, she was taller and larger boned, with less refined features that made her look older. But she had the same vivid coloring and beautiful skin. She was a waitress at a Hispanic bar on the outskirts of town, and had a reputation for going out with a lot of men.

Kara didn't know her very well, but had always liked her. She was quiet and polite, and talked to Alex whenever she saw him. She and Luz came from a large family, and they both seemed to adore children.

"Hello, Serafina," Kara said. "How are you?"

"*Hola.* I am well."

"She is working too many hours." Luz slipped on her coat, pulling her long, shimmering hair free. The coat's red hue enhanced her stunning dark hair and eyes. *"Hasta mañana."* She turned toward the hallway, raised her voice. "Alex, I am leaving. *Adiós, hijo.*"

"Bye Luz," came a faint, little-boy voice.

"You watch out for that man," Luz told Kara, then with a swirl of her coat, she was gone, trailing a scent of cinnamon and something rich and provocative. Serafina nodded good-bye and followed.

Luz must have a *really* hot date with Matt, Kara thought, closing the door behind her. For a moment, she rested her head against the wood, feeling drained and exhausted. But an entire evening stretched ahead of her, filled with the mundane and comforting rituals that made up the fabric of their lives—dinner, homework, talking about their day. And she had to tell Alex that Damien would be coming tomorrow night. With a sigh, she straightened and turned, calling out, "Alex, it's time for dinner. Wash your hands and come on."

His bedroom door opened a crack. "Ah, Mom, *Home Improvement* is on."

He loved television, perhaps too much, but then he didn't have many friends outside those on his soccer team. In addition to science fiction, he really liked shows about families—those with a father, a mother, and kids (especially the ones where there were siblings). Kara felt the familiar regret that Alex had never had a normal family life.

Her mother and stepfather lived in northern Alabama, a

fifteen-hour drive from Zorro, and he only saw them two or three times a year. Her only sibling, her brother Dan, lived in Oregon with his family; they were lucky to see him once a year. Kara had never met any of Richard's family, didn't even know how to contact them. So she and Alex were pretty much on their own.

"It's already late, and I need to talk to you," she answered. "So cut it off and get out here."

"All right," he said, managing to sound grievously put upon.

He shuffled into the kitchen a few moments later as she was putting their food on the table and pouring his milk.

"Mom, why was that man here again?"

She turned to answer, but could only stare at her son. Had he ever been a child? He was always so intent, so serious, seemed so far beyond his years. Standing there, watching her solemnly, he looked just like Richard. *God, so much like Richard.*

She went to him, dropped to her knees, and hugged him against her tightly.

"Mom!" he protested, his voice muffled against her chest.

She loved him so much. He was her heart, her soul, her world, and all she had left of Richard.

"Mom! You're hugging me too hard!"

"Sorry." She loosened her hold a little. "Have I told you today that I love you?"

Most six-year-old boys would have been embarrassed, but Alex seemed to sense her angst. "I love you, too, Mom."

"You'd better." Reluctantly, she released him. "Let's eat."

"Yeah!" he said enthusiastically. "Luz made an apple pie for dessert."

Kara forced herself to smile. "Yum. I guess we'll have to have some ice cream with that."

"All right!" Alex crowed and headed for the table.

For the moment, Kara thought, they were back in an

ordinary, comforting routine. But the sense of normalcy and safety was now a facade. While she was determined to hang onto the life she and Alex had as long as possible, and to keep him safe, she knew they were teetering precariously . . .

Near the touch of darkness.

FIVE

AT six o'clock the next evening, Damien pulled into the gravel driveway, behind Kara's truck. He sat there a few moments, staring at the white frame house, elevated on the frame-clad pier-and-beam foundation so common in this part of Texas. Wide cement steps leading up the wrap-around porch were painted country blue, as were the shutters. Neatly trimmed shrubs lined the front. Like Kara's office, the house was well kept and homey. He climbed out of the car and shut the door.

The dog appeared at the chain-link gate at the end of the driveway and went into his frenzied barking routine. Damien didn't bother with silencing him. He would see that the animal remained outside during the session with Alex.

He went up the walkway. Purple and yellow pansies lined both sides of the last third and skirted gaily around the steps to the porch. The plant beds were weed-free and covered with shredded bark. Sudden memories of his childhood home surged into his mind. His father had been an avid handyman, puttering around their duplex in central New York, keeping both home and yard immaculate.

As a young boy, Damien had loved hanging out with his dad, watching him work on some weekend project. Dad often let him help, showing him how to dig flower beds and fertilize plants, how to hammer nails, and even letting him paint things. Although reserved with everyone else, Damien had talked to his father about everything. His father had known and accepted what he was, and he didn't have to hide his abilities when he was with his dad. It had been an uncomplicated, blissful time in his life, free of the worries of the world.

But those idyllic times had ended abruptly with the destructive violence inherent to Sentinel existence.

Taken aback at this emotional slippage, Damien shook off his thoughts, forcing them behind a self-imposed barrier. He couldn't think about the past, couldn't afford to indulge in memories or emotional sentiments. He would not entertain thoughts that might distract him in any way from his life's mission. Nor would he ever allow emotional attachments. They led to mistakes, errors in judgment—and ultimately, tragedy and pain.

As Damien reached the top of the steps, the attractive Hispanic housekeeper came out the front door. She was wearing a red leather coat and carrying a purse, so he assumed she was leaving.

Her gaze narrowed when she saw him, and she leaned back inside. "Kara, *that man* is here. Do you want me to call the *policía*?"

She obviously didn't like Kara's answer; she frowned and whirled from the door, leaving it open. Glaring at Damien, she stalked past him. "Good evening to you, too," he murmured, but got only a spate of rapid Spanish that didn't sound friendly.

He pondered her strange reaction as he entered the house. Most women didn't have that response to him. Usually he was the one who had to maintain his distance. Not only that, but he sensed a different sort of energy from the young woman, one that was unfamiliar and intriguing. He didn't think it was shielded Belian energy, but decided it might be good to keep a close eye on her.

Kara met him in the living room. She was wearing a soft sweater in a shade of blue that brought out the color of her eyes, and a pair of worn jeans that hugged her gently curving hips. Damien might have self-imposed mental barriers and preternatural abilities, but he was still a flesh and blood man, and not immune to the allure of an attractive woman.

Especially not to the allure of a woman who was also a precisely matched conductor, as evidenced by the strong sexual rush he felt when Kara reached him. But he had years of experience in controlling his reactions and ruthlessly forced his responding body into submission.

Kara obviously felt the spark, too, but didn't have the practice he'd had in controlling his body, as evidenced by the puckering of her nipples through the sweater. Damn, the woman wasn't wearing a bra. Not that it mattered, he told himself firmly. The energy snapping between them was a *good* thing, one that would help him track the Belian in Zorro.

"You're right on time." Her arms crossed defensively over her chest, and she turned away. "Alex is in the kitchen."

She glanced over her shoulder as she led the way. "We just finished dinner. Are you hungry?"

The aroma of food drifted from the kitchen, and Damien's heightened sense of smell told him they'd had beef, potatoes, carrots, and bread for their dinner. He couldn't remember when he'd last had a home-cooked meal; probably not since his youth.

He experienced another rare nostalgic punch. Both his parents had enjoyed cooking—hearty soups and stews on cold New York winter nights, and French toast or waffles on the weekends, replete with bacon, fresh fruit, and real maple syrup. But the family meals had ended thirty years ago—

Damn it! What was the matter with him? He was methodical and logical, able to maintain an intense focus on whatever task was at hand. He didn't indulge in going off on mental tangents in general, much less forays into his past, especially into his childhood. That life was over and long gone.

"I've eaten," he said brusquely, stepping into the kitchen behind Kara.

It was an inviting and cheerful room, with pale green walls, rustic, white-painted cabinets, and a warm terracotta tile floor. A white wooden table and four matching chairs were grouped in a breakfast nook on the left side of the room. Alex sat in one of the chairs, playing with the remaining food on his plate.

He shot a quick sideways glance at Damien, looked back down. Damien could feel the boy's heightened tension. He knew he'd be more effective if he could present himself more as a friend and put the boy at ease.

"It smells great in here," he said to Kara. "Do you do the cooking?"

A small snicker came from the table. "No." She shook her head. "I'm not much of a cook, I'm afraid."

"No?" Damien looked toward Alex. "So, young man, does that mean you're the cook?"

A quick shake of the head, brown hair bouncing; Damien thought he saw the flash of a smile. "Then it must be your maid"—he stopped, corrected—"or housekeeper, or whatever she is."

"Luz takes care of Alex after school and cleans the house and keeps us from starving to death, at least during the weekdays," Kara said. "Have a seat, and we'll get these dishes out of the way."

He pulled out a chair and sat before prodding to find out more about the housekeeper. "Luz is very protective of you and Alex."

Kara picked up the leftover meat loaf and potatoes and carried them to the counter. "Yes, she is protective, and she's very good at swinging a baseball bat."

"She's not a conductor," he mused, ignoring her inference, "yet I sense unusual mental strength in her."

"She's a *curandera.* Not only can she swing a bat, but she can put a curse on you."

Another snicker came from the table, followed by, "Oh, Mom!"

"Ah, a healer." Damien considered a moment. "What is her specialty?"

Kara shot him a surprised look. "Well. I'm impressed, that you even know what a *curandera* is, and that they practice different kinds of healing. Luz is a midwife and herbalist."

"She looks too young to be very skilled," he commented. "And I would think what she does would be in conflict with your scientific approach to medicine."

"Not really." She pulled some aluminum foil from a drawer and began wrapping the meat loaf. "Most of her patients would never go to a conventional physician. Luz is very knowledgeable. She learned from her mother, who was a skilled *curandera* for many years. At least she'll contact me if one of her patients has childbirth complications. That's better than nothing."

"True enough," Damien agreed.

"Alex, please clear your dishes off the table." Kara bent down to look in a lower cabinet, giving Damien a tantalizing view of jeans stretching across a very fine rear. She retrieved a storage container and stood to put the potatoes in it.

Alex picked up his plate and glass and carried them toward the sink, but detoured to open the back door. Before Damien could protest, Mac rushed inside, already barking. Damien started to send a mental command to the animal, but then he saw the flicker of Alex's hand toward Mac, felt the quicksilver flare of power.

With a final growl, Mac subsided. Kara, getting the bread and carrots from the table, didn't see the action, nor did she see the quick glance Alex shot at her, then at Damien—or the flash of triumph on his face and the little smile.

Damien contemplated the boy's too-innocent demeanor.

So, Alex must have observed him silencing Mac on Saturday and again on Monday, and figured out what he'd done and then replicated it, which showed intelligence and ability. Not only that, but Alex was obviously experimenting with his powers.

That wasn't unusual for a curious boy who could sense things most humans couldn't, but it could prove dangerous with a Belian nearby. Without working closely with Alex on his powers, there was no way for Damien to know how long he'd been using them, or how gifted he really was. But he'd told Kara he'd hold off as much as possible, and he intended to honor that.

Considering, Damien sat back in his chair. Alex turned to the sink, Mac settling expectantly on his haunches, his full attention on the plate the boy was holding. Alex paused at the sink with his back to them; Damien saw a piece of meat loaf falling into a dog dish on the floor.

Kara sank into the chair to his right. "Every night, I tell him not to give Mac scraps, because I don't want Mac begging at meals," she said, her voice pitched low. "And every night, he sneaks scraps to Mac anyway, and I pretend not to see." Her voice hitched, and she paused until Alex stepped onto a small stool by the sink and turned on the water to rinse his dishes.

"I love the *normalcy* of our little games and routines." She clenched her hand into a fist on the table, her gaze hardening. "Fate has no right—*no right*—to take this away from us! I don't want to give up the life we've built here."

At least her tirade hadn't included Damien as a villain, which he considered a sign of progress. But unfortunately, Sentinels and conductors were not fated for "normal" lives. "I can understand you wanting that," he said quietly. "But as I've already told you, there are no guarantees."

Alex shuffled back to the table, with Mac right behind him, nudging his hand, probably hoping for more scraps. She turned toward Alex, her expression changing, and her face taking on a glow. As she looked at her son, she radiated love. Damien found the transformation fascinating. He vaguely remembered his parents looking at him like that—once upon a time, in a carefree world he hadn't known for years.

"Sit down, sweetie," Kara told her son. "You know Mr. Morgan is here to talk to you."

Alex slid into the chair across from Damien, his expression wary. Damien leaned forward, maintaining direct eye contact with the boy. "Do you know what I'm here to talk about?"

"Kinda."

Without dropping his shields, Damien deliberately projected energy. "Can you feel anything?"

A pause, then a small nod. "You feel funny. Like you did on Saturday, and yesterday."

So Alex could sense the power, even when it was shielded. Sentinel energy vibrated on a very high frequency. Conductors and Sentinels could usually pick up that energy from other Sentinels because they operated through the three higher chakras. Belians operated only on the four lower, earth-based chakras, with two consequences. The first was that they couldn't readily sense Sentinels or conductors, which was fortuitous. But it also made it difficult for Sentinels to sense them.

"What you're feeling is a special energy that I have," Damien explained.

"So you're different." Alex looked down, played with a napkin left on the table. "Like me. I've always been different from the other kids."

"You're a very normal boy, Alex," Kara interjected. "You're smart and good, and I'm very proud of you. Your thoughts are just unusually strong sometimes, that's all."

Damien placed his hand over hers, gave a small shake of his head to let her know he didn't want interference. "Do you agree with your mother, Alex?"

"No." He scuffed his feet against the floor, looked at Kara. "It's more than that, Mom. I can tell if someone is sad or happy, or angry. I can always tell when you're upset. And if I think hard enough, I can move things with my mind. Although I know I'm not supposed to," he added hastily. "I know we've talked about it a lot. I don't think the other kids at school can do any of that stuff. I'm not like them."

"Does being different bother you?" Damien asked, keeping a warning hand over Kara's.

"Sometimes, 'specially since I can't tell anyone about it. Mr. Morgan . . ."

"Yes?"

"What's a Sentinel?"

Damien felt Kara tense, sensed she was about to jump in. He squeezed her hand. "I'm not going to discuss that with you tonight. I will say most people don't know anything about Sentinels, which is why you should never mention them to anyone."

Alex thought about that for a moment. He appeared to be very deliberate in his words and actions, reminding Damien of himself as a boy. "You told me I'm a Sentinel, like you. That we both have power." Alex tilted his chin up. "My special powers—the ones the other kids don't have—are those Sentinel powers?"

"Alex—" Kara began, jerking her hand free, but Damien cut her off.

"Yes, they are."

"Did my dad have those powers?"

"Yes, your father had them."

Alex's eyes flared, darkened. "My dad was a Sentinel," he said, making the obvious connection.

Kara leaned forward, placing both her hands on Alex's arms. "Sweetie, those Sentinel powers are part of the reason your father died. This is why it is very, *very* important that you must never use them. You must never talk about them, and you must be very careful to shield your thoughts."

His brow furrowed. "Shield my thoughts?"

"Kara, let me handle this," Damien said firmly. "I gave you my word we'd only discuss shielding tonight, and I will hold to that. But you can't ignore the boy's questions. That will only confuse and upset him further."

"I'm not upset," Alex protested, then chewed his lower lip. "Not 'zactly."

"I'll let you handle it, as long as you stick to our agreement," Kara told Damien. She returned her attention to Alex. "Mr. Morgan is going to work with you on shielding your powers. He can help you control them. Will you work with him on that? For me?"

Damien watched as the boy considered. A gleam sparked into his eyes, and Damien suspected he found the idea intriguing. Kara had been stifling any urges or inclinations he'd displayed toward using his power all of his life, and he had to be a little bit curious. "I guess so," he finally said.

"Good." Damien leaned back in his chair. "There was a game my mother taught me when I was about your age. I would imagine sucking all my energy and thoughts deep inside me. Then I would pretend I was locking them into a box, so they couldn't get out. Do you think you can do that?"

He waited until Alex gave a slow nod, then continued, "That's basically shielding your thoughts. But the first step is to learn how to center yourself. Let's try something. Sit back and close your eyes." He waited until the boy complied, then continued, "Now, take a deep breath, and imagine all your energy is right in the middle of your body, and it's forming a straight line going from the top of your head down through your abdomen."

The boy's brow furrowed. "What?"

Damien tried to think of a comparison he would understand. "Do you know what a lightsaber is?"

"Like in *Star Wars*. Yeah!"

"Just like in *Star Wars*. Imagine that your energy is inside a lightsaber, and when you turn it on, the energy comes out in a perfect, straight line of light. Now keep that light beam in the exact middle of your body. Can you imagine that?"

His eyes squeezed tightly shut, Alex nodded. His excitement caused his energies to fluctuate wildly. "Keep the light steady and straight, and at the same time, take deep, even breaths," Damien said. "That's called centering, and you should do it whenever you want to shield yourself."

Alex would also use the same technique when he wanted to use his powers to track, but that would be a later lesson, if Kara ever allowed the boy to be trained as a Sentinel.

"Do I always have to close my eyes?"

"No. It helps to visualize things at first, but soon you'll learn to center yourself automatically, without closing your eyes. Right now, imagine you're turning the lightsaber off, and all your energy is sucked inside the metal handle. Can you see that?"

"Yeah! Cool, just like Luke turning off his saber."

"Now imagine a box made out of something very strong, like steel."

Alex's brow furrowed again. "Or the stuff they use for streets and parking places?"

"Do you mean cement? That's good. Any box that's very thick and strong will work. Once you see the box in your mind, put the lightsaber—which contains your energy, right?—into the box, close it, and lock it. Now your power and energy are inside that box, and no one can see or feel or know they're there."

"But . . . if all my energy is gone, will I still be alive?"

The boy was very astute. "Of course you will," Damien told him. "Your energy will still be there inside you. It will just be protected."

"Like from Darth Vader?"

"Absolutely, and from anyone else who's evil. Do you think you can do that?"

"Maybe."

"Let's practice. Visualize the lightsaber projecting the energy in the center of your body, then turn it off and lock it in the box. Try it."

They worked at the process several times, and Alex quickly became very adept at "hiding" his power, even from Damien.

"That's good," Damien said, after Alex had shielded himself the fourth time. "You must practice this every day, especially when you're not at home. When you're at school, or with your friends, or out anywhere, you need to center yourself by visualizing the lightsaber. Then suck your energies into it and lock everything inside the box. *It's very important.* It will help keep you safe."

"Keep me safe from what? Strangers?"

Damien guessed that was a valid question, as Kara had probably been warning Alex about strangers all his life. "It's to keep you safe from anyone who doesn't like Sentinels."

"Why don't people like Sentinels?"

Damien knew tonight wasn't the time to bring up Belians, so he replied, "Because some people don't like anyone who is different from them."

"That's cause they don't know better," Alex said, accepting this with the innate wisdom of a child, along with the intelligent comprehension of his Sentinel birthright.

Damien felt a pang of regret that this precocious, serious child would probably never have anything approaching a normal life. He reminded himself that Alex's soul had freely chosen this path.

"Yeah, they don't know any better," he answered. "So for now, I don't want you to mention Sentinels to *anyone*, not even your best friends. Again, you need to lock your energies and thoughts in that imaginary box *every single day*, especially when you're not at home. All right?"

"Okay," Alex said, but it was apparent he still had a lot of questions.

"We'll talk about more ways to shield your energy and powers after you've worked with locking them in the box. Try it for a few days, then I'll come back for another visit," Damien said. "Call me if you have any problems. Your mom has my telephone number."

"Sure, Mr. Morgan," Alex said, his dark eyes reflecting a maturity far beyond his six years, and a knowing that told Damien it was going to be next to impossible to keep the boy's Sentinel heritage at bay—no matter how much Kara might fight against it.

SIX

THE next day, Kara managed to keep herself convinced she'd made the right decision in letting Damien Morgan work with Alex on shielding his energies—until her cell phone rang while she was driving home late that afternoon. She reached over and snagged the phone, saw it was from home. "Hello!" she said, expecting one of the normal after school calls she often got from Alex.

"Get home immediately," Luz said, her voice tense.

Alarm roared through Kara. "What's wrong?" Sudden childish shrieking sounded in the background, and her alarm coalesced into panic. "Was that Alex? *What's wrong?*" She was practically screaming herself.

"Espíritu malo. ¡Hay un espíritu malo en la casa!" Luz lapsed into rapid Spanish, something she did only if she was truly rattled.

"What? For God's sake, speak English!" Realizing she had edged into the other lane and into the path of an oncoming car, Kara swerved back, barely missing the vehicle. "Is Alex all right?" Her heart was pounding so hard, she had to strain to hear Luz.

"Evil spirit," Luz gasped. Another shriek came through the phone. "There's a . . . a *fantasma*—a ghost, in the house."

"What do you mean, a ghost?"

"Something not human is in this house," Luz shrilled. "We cannot see it, but it is throwing things around, and Alex says it is 'talking' to him. The boy is terrified, and I don't know what to do. You must come. *¡Pronto!*"

"I'm on my way." Kara's mind was reeling, her body shaking from adrenaline overload. *A ghost?* A cold vise gripped her heart. Her experiences with Richard had taught her that discarnate entities—what some considered "ghosts"—did indeed exist, and they were often very evil and dangerous. Sometimes they were even displaced Belians.

All-out terror ripped through her at hurricane force, impeding cohesive thoughts. She had to stay calm. Her son was in danger. *Think, Kara!* Damien—they needed to get Damien over there.

"Luz, get Alex out of the house now!" she ordered. "Go to Doris. If that—that *thing* follows you, call the police. I'm going to find Damien Morgan."

"Him? He is probably the cause of this. *El trajo la fantasma en esta casa.*" Luz went into another spate of rapid Spanish.

"Luz!" Kara shouted, wrenching the truck over to the side of the road. "Just get Alex over to Doris's house. I'll be there as soon as I can."

She shoved the gear stick into park, dumped her purse's contents on the passenger seat, her hands shaking. "It's got to be here. I know it's here," she muttered, shoveling through the items, looking for Damien's card.

There! She snatched it up, trying to slow her pounding heart as she punched in the numbers. Then she put the truck in gear and roared it back onto the road, pressing the phone to her left ear as she floored the accelerator.

It seemed like an eternity before the line rang, once, twice. "Pick up!" Kara tried to keep her attention on the road, but all she could think of was Alex. Three rings, four . . . "Answer, damn it!"

The connection clicked. "Morgan."

"I need your help. Luz says there's a discarnate entity at my house. It's after Alex."

There was a pause. "Kara?"

"Yes! I need you at my house. You're the only one who can help."

"A discarnate entity?" he asked, sounding incredulous. "What happened to draw one?"

"I don't know. Please come. I can't handle this." She was starting to feel as hysterical as she sounded.

"All right. Calm down. I'll be there as soon I can. Where are you?"

"I'm—God, I can't think. I'm about a mile from home. I told Luz to take Alex to the neighbor on the north side."

"Good," he said. "Go straight to your neighbor's, and I'll meet you there. Do not go into your house, or let anyone else go in. Understand?"

"Yes."

He disconnected without another word. Kara drew a deep breath, felt a little more in control. She might not like having to call on a Sentinel, but if a Belian was involved, she needed Damien's help. He was far more powerful than a human male, and more capable of handling anything supernatural.

She made that last mile in record time, heaving a sigh of sheer relief when she saw Luz and Alex in the doorway of Doris's house, standing behind her glass storm door. The fist around her heart finally loosened, and she slammed the truck door and ran up the driveway and the steps. "Alex!"

"Mom!" He flew out the door and into her arms. She held him tightly, thankful he was all right. Trembling, he clung to her. "Mom, it was freaky."

"It's okay. You're safe now." She looked over his shoulder at Luz's pale face. She'd never seen Luz look so shaken.

"Here now," Doris said briskly, coming from behind

Luz and holding the storm door open. "You come on inside and get out of that cold air." She hustled them into her immaculate living room with its contemporary, simple furniture in soothing neutrals, and burgundy Oriental rug over a gleaming hardwood floor. Lush green plants thrived in the large bay window, and the scent of baking cookies wafted through the house. "Have a seat, and I'll make some hot chocolate."

She paused, looked from Luz to Kara. "You sure I don't need to call anyone?"

Kara didn't know what Luz had told Doris, but was grateful the older woman wasn't asking a lot of questions. She shook her head. "I already did. He's going to check the house."

Doris nodded and went to the kitchen. Kara sank onto the couch with Alex, who still clung tightly to her. "What happened, sweetie?"

"I was in my room, just"—He paused, looked at Luz, and a strange expression crossed his face—"doin' stuff."

Kara was instantly suspicious, but simply said, "Then what?"

"Then it felt"—he glanced at Luz again—"It felt weird. Then one of my books fell off the shelf. Then a poster fell down." He looked up at Kara, his eyes troubled. "It was my Captain Picard poster."

The priorities of a little boy. She hugged him again. "Oh sweetie, that's okay. We'll put it back up or get another one. What happened then?"

"I started calling for Luz and she came. She saw stuff happen, too."

Kara looked at Luz, who nodded her confirmation. A chill went down Kara's spine. "At least both of you are all right," she said. "And Mr. Morgan is coming over to try to figure out what's going on."

"I do not know why you would call that man," Luz muttered. "He's probably the cause of it."

"Luz, don't say such things!" Kara said sharply. "I don't believe that."

"Do you think he'll be able to fix it, Mom?" Alex looked at her solemnly. "Because, he's . . . *you know*."

"I think he can help," she said neutrally.

Doris returned with a tray bearing four cups of hot chocolate and a plateful of cookies. "Here we go." She set the tray on the elaborately carved cherry wood coffee table. "Something hot to chase away the chills—in more ways than one."

She handed them each a mug of steaming hot chocolate and napkins and cookies before settling down in a big wing chair with her own mug. "Mine's sugar-free," she informed Kara with a smile and took a sip. "Got to watch the carbohydrate intake."

"How's the new insulin dosage working?" Kara asked.

"Just fine. I feel great."

"Mrs. Burgess, do you believe in ghosts?" Alex asked.

Doris considered thoughtfully. "Well, I don't know for sure. But I do think there are a lot of unexplained and unusual things in the world, don't you?"

He nodded. "Socks disappear in our dryer all the time, and Mom says there must be a black hole behind it."

Doris laughed. "Out of the mouths of babes."

"I'm not a baby," Alex protested.

"Of course not. You're a fine young man." Doris held out the plate of cookies. "Have another cookie. They always make things better, don't you think?"

Alex happily took another. "Yes, ma'am."

Kara finally felt some warmth seeping back into her body. She sank back with a tired sigh. "We've definitely had some strange experiences lately." She reached out and mussed Alex's hair, needing to touch him again. "But we're going to get back to normal real soon. Right, champ?"

"Right, Mom," he dutifully replied, but she heard the doubt in his voice.

She steered the conversation away from ghostly topics, and Luz and Doris took her cue, instead talking about the annual bake sale at the town hall, which raised funds for senior citizen programs.

"Are you still coming over tomorrow to help me make cakes?" Doris asked.

Alex looked at Kara, who nodded. "I'm coming, too," she said, once again reminded of her concerns about a Belian taking possession of a body, and cursing fate—and Damien—for bringing doubt and distrust into her life.

"Cool," Alex said. He loved helping Doris in her kitchen, partly because he got to sample the goods.

A brisk rapping on the front door alerted them to Damien's arrival. Doris's eyes widened when she opened the door and saw him. He filled the doorway, an imposing figure in his duster with his hair banded back, and his dark glasses giving him a menacing appearance. He didn't remove the glasses and was brief but courteous with Doris, refusing her offer to come in.

"I need for Kara and Alex to come with me," he said. He looked at Luz. "And you, as well."

Stepping back he held the storm door open. Luz took Alex's hand. "Come, *hijo*, we will see if our *fantasma* is gone."

Alex drew back. "I don't want to go home," he whispered.

"I'm sure it is all right now. Yes?" Luz stared at Damien, who gave a curt nod. "There, you see? The arrogant man has assured us all is well." She swept past Damien, pulling Alex with her.

Squaring her shoulders, Kara walked to the door. She gave Doris a quick hug. "Thank you for letting us barge in on you like this. I'm sure"—she hesitated, hating to lie, but feeling it prudent to play this down—"I'm sure that whatever happened at our house was nothing."

"And I'm sure you're in *very* good hands." Doris gave Damien another look, leaned close, and whispered, "What a specimen! Now that's the type of hunk I was talking about the other day."

"Oh, uh, no." Kara drew back. "He—I—It's not what you think. He's just an . . . associate."

Doris looked at her over the rim of her glasses. "Whatever you say."

"Thank you again," Kara said, well aware that Damien possessed superhuman hearing and had probably heard every whispered word. "You're always here when we need you, and it means a lot."

"Any time." Doris stepped back. "I know you usually work until four. Is five o'clock tomorrow afternoon a good time for you and Alex?"

"Sounds great."

"See you then." Doris smiled at Damien. "Good-bye, Mr. Morgan."

He nodded and closed the storm door behind Kara. "Is it safe to go home?" she asked in a low voice.

"I wouldn't allow you to return if it wasn't." He turned and strode after Luz and Alex.

She got her truck and drove it back to the house, while the other three walked over. When she pulled into the driveway, she saw Max was in the fenced backyard. He stood at the gate, barking to let them know he didn't appreciate being left behind. She told him to hush and joined the others on the front porch.

They entered the house, Damien going first, then Kara. Alex and Luz entered warily behind them, looking toward the hallway leading to the bedrooms. Alex moved a few steps closer to Damien. While Kara hated being dependent on Damien in any way, she had to admit she was glad he was here. She knew he wouldn't let anyone—or anything—harm them while he was around.

Damien took off his sunglasses and slid them into a pocket, then removed the duster and tossed it on the sofa. "Take the boy into the kitchen until I call you," he instructed Luz. He looked down at Alex and the harsh granite of his face seemed to soften a fraction. "It's all right to be here now," he told her son. "Your ghost is gone."

Face pale, eyes wide, Alex stared up at him. "Will it come back?" he asked, his young voice quavering.

"We'll work on that later. You go to the kitchen with Luz and wait there." Damien turned to Kara. "You come with me."

She put her purse on the end table, apprehension tingling through her. She didn't like being frightened in her own home, or knowing that Alex might not be safe there. So she focused on Damien's attitude instead.

"Boy, you sure know how to influence people and win friends," she muttered, unbuttoning her jacket as she followed him down the hall.

Beside Alex's bedroom door, he turned to face her. "Meaning what?"

"Meaning you're rude and abrupt. You snap out orders like a general. Has it ever occurred to you that you can catch more flies with honey than with vinegar?"

The corners of his sensual mouth twitched ever so slightly. "Now why would I want to catch flies? Pesky things."

Kara was taken aback. Had she just detected a trace of humor? Surely not. Most Sentinels were deadly serious at all times, and Damien appeared to be straight from the master mold. She pulled her attention back to the ghost. "Now what?"

"No we go in and let you 'see' Alex's visitor."

Her heart leaped in her chest and she took a quick step back. "Oh, no. I am *not* doing a conduction."

"I'm not asking you to," he said, exasperation evident in his tone. "This was not a Belian, but it was a discarnate entity. I didn't sense any malevolence, though, no evil. I'm not sure what it was doing here."

Relief flowed through Kara. She felt like she'd been on an emotional roller coaster the past four days; first on a peak of tension and fear, then plummeting to a valley of respite or at least the feeling another fire had been put out—if only temporarily—then starting back up the stressful, frightening slope again.

"Is the thing really gone?" she asked.

"For now." He opened Alex's door. "Come on."

She followed and observed the signs of chaos that went beyond a young boy's normal messiness: books knocked onto the floor, the Captain Picard poster lying on the bed, some of Alex's framed soccer award certificates hanging askew on the walls.

"Do you feel anything?" Damien asked. "See anything?"

Reluctantly, she sent out tentative mental feelers as she looked around the room. "No."

He held out his left hand. "Give me your hand."

"I don't know if I want—"

"Damn it, Kara, I know you're not a coward. Give me your hand."

She took a deep breath, placed her hand in his, and felt the static electrical shock of touching him. "Now what?"

"Close your eyes. Use your other sight."

She closed her eyes, but she didn't want to tap into that dark part of her that she had always despised, that ability to see actual events in her dreams. She'd worked at walling it up all her life.

In addition, the sexual energy from her physical contact with Damien was slapping at her. Her body tingled and her breasts felt heavy. She tried to pull away, but he tightened his grasp.

"Just go with it, Kara. Ignore the physical sensations, and focus on the nonphysical."

Resigned, she did her best to push away the sexual energy, to open her senses to the other energies in the room. In her mental vision, tendrils of gray fog swirled and snaked, luring her deeper into an unfamiliar dimension. The fog began to dissipate, and she "saw" Alex's room, only it was distorted, as if she were looking at it through a camera lens.

A flash to the right caught her attention, a trail of light in a zigzag pattern along the walls. It looked similar to the pattern Tinkerbell had made in *Peter Pan.*

Then she realized the light was still moving, in streaks that would end one place and then begin again in a different location. There were also flashes of light, these more like the pattern of light made by fireflies at dusk in the summer. A faint humming sound permeated her mind.

She tightened her grip on Damien's hand. "What's happening?"

"Our energy link is allowing you to see what I see."

She was so startled, her eyes flew open, and the images vanished. Instead, Damien filled her field of vision, big and solid, dressed in a royal blue sweater over black slacks. "You're conducting for *me*?" she asked.

"No. The conductor/Sentinel link enables our energies to merge, but this isn't a conduction. That, as you know, involves the third eye, which all humans have, but few can access. In a conduction, the third eyes of both the Sentinel and the conductor are activated, and the individual powers of each are merged and then magnified exponentially. You're not seeing through *your* third eye right now, you're seeing through *mine*. There's no expansion of energies through the chakras, and therefore no magnification."

She should have realized that, from the simple fact that the sexual surge was absent. She simply felt the pull of the sensual energies that always occurred when Sentinels and conductors were in close proximity. "So what did I just see?"

"You saw the energy trail left behind by the entity. Much the same way you see the remaining vapor trails of jets in the sky. Because it was in spirit form rather than physical, you won't see any clear images. Did you feel anything dark or threatening?"

"No," she said slowly, trying to recall what she'd actually felt. "It didn't feel good or bad, it was just . . . there."

"You'd have known if it was a Belian. The negative energy would have been very strong. That's why I believe this was a benign entity. Sometimes you can also smell things, usually unpleasant."

She hadn't noticed any odd odors, although now she picked up Damien's scent—that same soap and sandalwood blend that had permeated his duster. He smelled enticing, probably a side effect of the sexual energies swirling between them. There were definite disadvantages to heightened awareness and senses, she decided.

"No unpleasant smells," she said, shaking off her wayward thoughts.

"Another indication this being was benign. Did you hear anything?"

He was instructing her, she realized, broadening her knowledge of supernatural occurrences, something Richard had never done. "Yes. I heard a faint buzzing sound—not like a bug, but almost like the sizzle of electricity."

"A good description. That was the sound the entity's movements created."

"But you said it's gone. How could I hear it?"

"From the residual energy left by the sound. What you just saw and heard was facilitated by a psychic vision."

She had to think about that. "*Your* psychic vision?" she gasped, as comprehension dawned. "I was seeing what *you* see when you're following a psychic trail?"

Approval flashed in his eyes. "Right. Our energy link allowed you to see my vision."

"Amazing," she murmured. She'd never gone with Richard on one of his preliminary tracking sessions, where he gathered initial data from a BCS, the Sentinel term for a Belian crime scene. She'd only participated in the conductions that followed later, and could be done from any location, using the initial psychic signature of the Belian that Richard had extracted from the crime scene, and stored in his own psyche.

"I wanted you to see and hear what I did," Damien explained. "I think you can learn to do this on your own, and it will help you if the entity comes back."

"But I don't have Sentinel abilities."

"No, but I suspect your psychic abilities are very strong—or would be if you didn't repress them."

She didn't want to dwell on abilities she considered a curse; she was far more concerned about the ghost. "Do you think that thing will come back?"

He shrugged. "I have no idea. I don't know why it was here in the first place. I suspect it was drawn here."

Kara felt a sinking sensation. "By Alex?"

"Most likely. Why don't we find out?"

Shaken, she followed him to the kitchen. Luz, bless her, had Alex working on his homework at the table while she started dinner. Kara smelled chicken baking, saw the makings of a fresh salad in the large glass bowl on the counter.

Luz eyed Damien with animosity as they entered the kitchen. "Are you going to require me here much longer?" she asked Kara. "I need to leave."

"I know we've kept you late again. I'm so sorry, Luz." Kara looked at Damien. "Any reason she can't go?"

He leaned against the door frame, studying Luz. "Just a few questions. If you don't mind."

Sullenly, Luz picked up a tomato and a knife. "What do you want to know?"

"Do you work much with spirits?"

She shook her head, sliced the tomato with more force than necessary. "No. I deliver babies, compound herbs."

"But you believe in them," Damien persisted.

Alex, who had abandoned all pretense of doing his homework, darted his gaze between Luz and Damien. Kara went to sit next to him and put an arm around him. If the questioning got much scarier, she'd take him out of the kitchen.

"Of course I believe in them!" Luz snapped, with another *thwack* of the knife.

"Do you ever come across evil spirits?"

"A few. But the evil spirits I see are those that cause illness, bad luck, or a man's *pene* to shrivel up." Luz stared meaningfully at Damien's crotch. "Sometimes it is deserved."

"Mom," Alex said in a loud whisper, "do you think she's talking about his pe—"

Kara clamped her hand over his mouth. "Shhh. You're interrupting. I'll tell you later."

"But I have never seen *un espíritu* show up from nowhere to torment a little boy." Luz waved the knife in the air. "Not until you came." She tossed the mangled tomato into the salad.

"I've been accused of worse." Damien crossed his arms over his chest. "Did you sense anything truly evil in Alex's room today?"

Luz considered, finally looked at Damien. With a sigh, she shook her head. "No. I'm not certain it was evil. I did not sense *el Diablo.* But it was wild—throwing books across the room." She made the sign of the cross. "I'd never seen such a thing. My little man was so scared, *me asustó.*" She looked at Kara and Alex. "I'm sorry if I overreacted."

"I'd have done the same thing." Kara tightened her arm around Alex. "It must have been very scary."

"*Sí.*" Luz wiped her hands on her apron and untied it. "If you are finished with your questions, I really must go." She dropped a kiss on top of Alex's head and murmured to him in Spanish. Damien stepped aside as she swept past him.

"Good night, Luz. Thank you for everything," Kara called after her.

As they heard the sound of the front door closing behind Luz, Damien settled into the chair on the other side of Alex. He tapped the paper lying on the table. "What are you working on there?"

"Just some homework," Alex muttered.

"Looks like math. Aren't you too young to be doing that?"

Alex raised his chin. "I'm in first grade. We've been doing addition and subtraction since November."

"That soon, huh? I guess kids start on the hard subjects at a younger age these days."

"Math is easy," Alex informed him. "But health is boring." He shot a glance at Kara. "Sorry, Mom, but it is."

"I didn't like it, either," Damien sympathized. "Why don't you tell me what you did today to draw that discarnate?"

Kara felt Alex tense, saw his chin quiver, a sure sign he'd been up to something. "What's a dis-car-nate?" he asked. She knew he was stalling.

"It's another word for ghost." Damien leaned forward, his gaze intent. "What did you do to call it?"

Alex stared down at his homework. "Nothing."

"Alex," Kara said in a warning tone.

"Nothing much." He raised his head and looked at her. "I was just playing with . . . things."

What had her son done? She felt herself starting up the roller-coaster slope again, driven by returning panic. "What things?" she demanded.

"Just thoughts, just . . . moving some stuff around."

"With your mind?" Damien interjected.

Alex nodded mutely.

"But Mr. Morgan and I told you not to do that." Kara forced herself to speak calmly, although fear churned inside her. "He explained this to you last night. You promised you wouldn't use your powers."

Tears welled up in Alex's eyes. "I know, Mom, I know," he said, his voice wobbling. "And I kept my thoughts in the box all day at school, just like Mr. Morgan showed me." He sniffled. "I waited until I got home and I was alone in my room. I only wanted to 'speriment, to see what I could do." The tears overflowed and tracked down his cheeks. "I would never have done anything outside the house. Honest!"

Kara knew she was too upset to speak calmly and rationally right now. She shoved away from the table, and strode over to stare out the back-door window, willing herself to calm down. The sun had set, and it was gray outside, not yet fully dark. She vaguely heard Max barking in a far corner of the yard.

"Alex," came Damien's calm voice from behind her. "Tell me what you were doing, and what happened after that."

"Well . . ." Alex paused, and Kara could tell he was reluctant to tell Damien, probably afraid he was going to be punished.

"Tell Mr. Morgan what he wants to know," she said, turning from the door. "I won't get mad again."

"Okay. I was just playing around with moving stuff."

Damien leaned closer. "Tell me what you can do."

Alex's eyes lit up. "I can move lots of stuff. I look at something and imagine it in another spot. Like I 'drove' my model car across my desk without touchin' it. I made my book slide over to me. I moved my shoe and scared Max. It was really frigid!" He looked at Kara, seemed to belatedly remember their earlier conversations. He looked down at the table. "Sorry, Mom."

She didn't need the cool warning glance Damien shot her to remind her not to overreact. "Just tell us everything, son."

"Well." He fiddled with his pencil. "I was trying to shoot my thoughts to the tree outside my window to see if I could move the branches from inside the house."

"Did it work?" Damien asked.

Alex brightened. "Yeah! It was iced. So I kept doin' it for awhile."

Kara walked to the table and sat down. She felt utterly drained. Why had she thought a six-year-old boy would be able to resist the lure of such powers?

"What happened then?" Damien pressed.

"I don't know." Alex looked at him with big eyes. "I was just watching the tree limbs shaking back and forth, and all at once, a book went flying off my shelf. It was lots faster than I could have moved it. Then my poster fell down, and my soccer award things started turning on the walls. Max went crazy and barked a lot. It was freaky."

"Did you see or hear anything?"

"I didn't see a form or a white blob, or anything like that. But I kept hearing a noise, like whispering. Like something was trying to talk to me."

"What did it say?"

"I don't know," Alex's voice dropped to a whisper. "I was too scared to listen. But it felt—" He hesitated.

"What did it feel like?" Damien urged.

"It felt like it was real excited or stirred up—like Max is when he sees you."

"Kind of upset?" Kara suggested.

"Yeah. That's it." Alex nodded solemnly. "The ghost was upset, maybe frightened. Only ghosts don't get frightened, do they?"

"I think ghosts can have the same feelings they had when they were alive," Damien told him.

Alex considered that. "Will it come back?"

"Probably not if you don't use your mind to move objects. That's most likely what attracted its attention."

"Oh." Alex's lower lip trembled. "Mom told me it was bad to move things or try to do any stuff with my mind."

"It can be bad, if you don't know how to properly control your powers or shield yourself. But we're working on the shielding, aren't we?" Damien gave Alex's shoulder a reassuring squeeze. "I know you didn't mean to draw it here."

Damien was good at that, Kara thought, knowing when it was appropriate to touch, when to offer physical comfort. He was a strange, dual combination of arrogance and sensitivity. But then, the Sentinel nature was chameleon-like and crafty, a necessity in dealing with both humans and Belians.

"How do I control my powers?" Alex asked.

Damien looked at Kara, his steely gaze locking with hers. "That's something else we're going to work on. But right now, I need to talk to your mother."

Kara knew she wouldn't have any valid arguments, or be able to counter his demands to work with Alex on his powers this time.

I picked up another energy surge this afternoon, stronger than the previous ones. As before, it was not the pattern of a full-fledged Sentinel. It certainly wasn't the other unknown Sentinel, may Belial curse his soul. But the power was there, and it came from the general vicinity of Virginia Avenue. And there was that energy spike yesterday, at the school. Interesting . . .

It appears we do indeed have a fledgling Sentinel in this backwash town. While my power is growing, I am limited by this pitiful shell of a body that I must endure. A fledgling would provide me with more power, and then I could get a new body. Belial will make it so.

Until then, I must have more energy. It is time to claim my next victim and shake up that Light-spawn Sentinel. I will make my move tonight, and they'll never even know it was my handiwork.

I can hardly wait for the rush of the kill. As always, Belial provides for my needs. Glory to Belial, to the blood, and to the undefeatable power of the darkness.

SEVEN

KARA and Damien talked on the front porch because she didn't want Alex overhearing their conversation. However, he was anxious about being in the house alone, so they brought Max inside. Damien assured Alex that Max would know and react immediately if any ghosts entered the house. Kara raised the blinds on the picture window and turned on the porch light, so Alex could keep them in sight.

She donned a warm jacket, ensuring Damien wouldn't have to offer his duster again—and she wouldn't be subjected to its alluring warmth and male scent. She sank onto the wooden glider, waited for him to join her.

"Do you really think that thing won't come back?" she asked.

"I can't make any guarantees. If it's drawn to Alex and is trying to tell him something, it could return any time."

"Is there anything you can do to keep it away? Put some protective energy around the house?"

"I'm a Sentinel, not an exorcist. I don't go around chasing away ghosts."

"I'm wondering now if it was a good idea for you to work

with Alex. If you hadn't told him he was a Sentinel and had powers, maybe he wouldn't have experimented with them."

Damien's mouth thinned and his gaze bored into hers. "Wrong. He was bound to use his powers eventually, which could attract any number of entities. And there *is* a Belian in Zorro, whether or not you admit it. Sooner or later it will pick up on Alex. It's time to acknowledge the reality of the situation and deal with it."

The truth of his words deflated her protests, like the air leaving an inner tube. He was right.

"You don't have any choice in the matter, not with Alex's powers developing so rapidly," he added quietly.

"I don't understand how this happened. Alex promised me he wouldn't do anything with his mind."

"I'm sure he meant it. He appears to be a fine boy. But how can he control something if he doesn't even know what it is, or how it works?" Damien leaned closer, his gaze intent. "Knowledge is power. The more Alex knows about his abilities, the more he can control them. The better he can *protect* himself. That's why every young Sentinel is assigned a mentor if his or her parents are—if a Sentinel parent isn't raising the child."

She was certain he had started to say if the Sentinel parent or parents were dead, a strong possibility, as she well knew. Chilled, she pulled her knees up and huddled into her legs.

"I need to work with Alex on using his powers," Damien said. "So he can learn how to properly control them and protect himself from Belians and discarnate entities."

She could see his point all too clearly, and she hated it. But denying the reality could only put Alex in danger. "All right," she said tiredly. "But only for control and protection—no tracking energies. I still want to be present whenever you're with Alex."

"There's one more thing we need to do."

Anticipating him, she was already shaking her head. "No."

He grasped her shoulders and turned her toward him, his

gaze boring through her eyes and into her soul. "Yes, Kara. *Yes*. You've got to conduct for me. It's my best chance of catching this Belian and keeping it from sensing Alex."

Fear for Alex, and pain from the past, rushed over her. She was torn between a mother's fierce need to protect her child, and the preservation of her soul. She wanted Alex safe more than anything, but how could she take care of him, be there to protect him, if she was mentally and spiritually devastated? Conducting for Damien would take her back down the path that had almost destroyed her seven years ago.

She stared at him, paralyzed by the past. "I can't do it," she whispered. "I just can't. There has to be another way to protect Alex."

He shook his head with a frustrated growl, released her. "All right, then. We'll concentrate on Alex. For now. But the time will come, Kara, when you won't have any choice in the matter."

She knew he was right—her reprieve from the terror of Birmingham was just temporary. But as long as Alex wasn't in the direct path of the Belian, she simply didn't have the courage to face the past yet.

Not that her cowardice changed anything. With Alex's growing powers, he was moving closer to a Sentinel's existence. And she could only watch helplessly as their lives were irrevocably altered.

THE dreams returned that night.

The surreal feel of being suspended out of body permeated Kara, and she knew on some deep instinctive level—as she always did, even while asleep—that this was a precognitive vision in the form of a dream. *No!* her mind screamed. She thrashed and tried to break the bubble of the dream. Tried desperately to force herself to consciousness.

Her efforts were futile—as they had always been. Trapped within the vision, she could see everything happening in crystal clear real time, as if she were watching a movie, only she was drawn into the action.

A person was moving down a dark hallway that looked vaguely familiar. Kara followed behind, unable to see the person's face. The bulky overcoat and dark pants and outline of some sort of cap on the head gave the person a masculine look, so she assumed it was a man she followed.

He radiated malevolence; a black, terrifyingly familiar aura surrounded him. Kara had seen auras like that on several occasions, when she had been conducting for Richard. This man—this monster—was a Belian. She wanted to turn and run, to escape this essence of pure evil, but she was under the dictates of the dream. She could only follow; would be an observer no matter how much she resisted.

His feet, encased in boots, made no sound on the lush carpet. He reached an open doorway, paused, listened. She listened, too, heard the sound of steady breathing. Someone sleeping, so it must be a bedroom. He entered, and she followed. A night-light was plugged into the right wall, sending a low glow over the furniture and a figure in the bed.

She didn't recognize the room. The man moved to the figure in the bed. A woman with light-toned hair lay there, facing the opposite wall, her features hidden.

Familiarity stirred, yet Kara couldn't place the woman. The man turned slightly, and she saw he wore a baseball cap pulled down low over his face. She could see only his silhouette in the dim lighting, couldn't identify him.

"Who are you?" she asked, horror crawling through her. He might have a human body and a human name, might be someone she knew. But he was really the Devil incarnate. "What are you doing here?"

Ignoring her, he reached into the pocket of his coat with a hand encased in a flexible black leather glove, and drew out two objects. He deftly popped something off one object, then held up a small bottle, and placed the object against one end. Kara realized it was a syringe and some sort of drug he held. Dread pounded with every beat of her racing heart.

"What are you doing?" she demanded.

He leaned over the sleeping woman, pushed up the

sleeve of her gown. The material was a light-colored background, Kara noticed absurdly, covered with little cup and saucer motifs. The man placed the hypodermic against the woman's upper arm.

"Stop!" Kara ordered sharply, panicked. "You have no right to do this!" But she was frozen in place, unable to move or impede his actions in any way.

Giving no response, the man injected the woman's arm. Oh God, oh God, oh God, don't let this happen, *Kara implored as she watched, impotent in the throes of the vision. She knew, with every fiber of her being, that she was witnessing an atrocious act. And she could do nothing, nothing . . .*

Gasping for breath, Kara surged upright in bed. Her heart was pounding. She shook uncontrollably. Still unable to catch her breath, she looked around wildly. She was in her own bed, in her own room. Alex, too frightened to sleep alone, was sprawled next to her, his covers kicked off. Numbly, she covered her son, then curled around him, trying to console herself with his warmth and life energy. He didn't stir.

She prayed fervently to an ambiguous, distant God, asking for protection against the evil forces epitomized by the man in her vision. She prayed for the soul of the woman in the vision, knowing that soul was likely now winging its way from the Earth plane. She hadn't been able to see the woman's face, had no idea who had just been the latest victim of a Belian. Just as bad, she didn't have a clue on the identity of the Belian.

Basically, her vision was worthless—although she had no doubt of its accuracy. Despite her adherence to scientific data and logical explanations, her dream visions had always been eerily prophetic. This was just another horrific experience to add to those of the past few days.

She cursed the return of her psychic dreams, cursed Damien Morgan's appearance, which had probably been the impetus for shaking loose her carefully buried psychic abilities. And she mourned the loss of the life she had so carefully built for Alex and herself over the past six years.

More than ever, she felt she was barely balanced on the edge, and the slightest push would send her into the abyss.

IT had been years since she'd had a psychic experience, but she hadn't forgotten the physical aftermath, the nausea and nagging headache reminiscent of a hangover. But that wasn't the reason Kara moved through the next day with a sick feeling in the pit of her stomach.

She couldn't stop thinking about the woman in her dream, kept steeling herself to hear about another death. It crossed her mind to call Damien, but she shrugged the thought away. There was nothing he could do now, and she was determined to keep her contact with him to a minimum. They had agreed he would come over two nights a week to work with Alex, but that would be the extent of her cooperation.

"Dr. Kara?" said a soft voice, breaking into her thoughts. "Are you okay?"

Kara forced her focus back to the present and managed to smile at Sara Thornton. "I'm fine, Sara. Sorry, but I was just . . . thinking about Alex."

Sara, a short, thin woman with a heart-shaped face and straight, dark brown hair stared back at Kara. Her thick bangs emphasized her large brown eyes—and the circles beneath them. Kara had smelled alcohol on her when she came in with her two children, and her heart ached for the family. She knew they were struggling to survive after David's death.

"Well," she said briskly, lifting ten-year-old Julie down from the exam table. "I'm pretty sure both Julie and Michael have strep." She picked up the two cotton swabs lying on the stainless tray. "I'll run the test, but I expect it to be positive."

Seven-year-old Michael scrunched up his face. "Ah, bubble gum medicine *again*?"

"What, you don't like it?" Kara teased. "Would you rather have pills?"

He made another face. "Yuck."

"Let's run the test first. Why don't you two go ask Miss Bonnie to let you pick out some stickers while I do that?" Kara opened the exam room door and watched the children scamper toward the reception area. They were thin and dirty, although they showed no signs of malnourishment or abuse, and Sara seemed to genuinely love them. The woman just wasn't coping well.

"Sara, it's been over two years since you came in for a checkup," Kara told her. "You need to come in for a Pap smear, at the very least."

Sara brushed her dark hair out of her eyes. "I know, but money's been tight—and I've been busy."

"You still have the health insurance from David's job, and I'll waive the co-pay, just like I will today. But you have to take care of yourself, so you can be there for the children."

"I know," Sara whispered. "It's just so hard with David gone—" She sniffed, scrubbed her hands over her eyes. "I can't stop thinking about him. Can't sleep, most nights."

Kara would have offered medication to help her sleep, but she was reluctant to because of the drinking. "You might try warm milk or herbal tea, and going to bed by ten every night," she suggested. "A regular schedule will help. Have you considered counseling?"

Sara shook her head. "No, I don't have the money, and it wouldn't help. Nothin' will."

Kara gave her a quick hug. "You can call me anytime you want to talk, anytime at all. You have my home phone number."

"Thank you." Sara drew back and picked up her purse. "We're lucky to have you, Dr. Kara. You really care about folks."

Guilt swept through Kara. She didn't feel very caring. She hadn't done anything about her dream, hadn't reported it to anyone. But she knew such an action wouldn't help—if it followed the pattern of her past visions, it was already too late. She turned toward the door. "Let me run these tests."

Later, when she got home, she felt tired and defeated.

As much as she adored Doris, she didn't feel like baking cakes and having to be upbeat and pretend everything was all right. But she had promised, and Alex was eager to go. Luz had just left to deliver a baby, promising to call Kara if there were any complications. Kara wasn't wild about home deliveries, but knew many of Luz's patients were very superstitious and didn't trust Western medicine. At least Luz had been well trained by her mother.

So Kara put on a cheerful front for Alex. They got their coats and let Max out in the backyard. Then they raced each other, laughing, over to Doris's, with Max barking madly after them. It was a gorgeous, almost-spring afternoon, and the sun beamed down benignly. The crisp air and revelry revived her sagging spirits. Letting Alex beat her to Doris's house, she collapsed on the front steps, pretending to be totally winded.

"Beat you!" Alex crowed, his face flushed and his eyes bright with pleasure.

"Yes, you did." Smiling, feeling better than she had all day, she rose and dusted herself off. She admired the pretty pansies bursting out of two terra-cotta planters on the porch. Doris had an amazing touch with plants and flowers.

"But I bet I'll decorate more cakes than you," she teased.

"Uh-uh," Alex said. "I'm the fastest helper Mrs. Burgess has. She told me so."

"Well, then I challenge you to a cake decorating contest." Kara climbed the steps and opened the storm door to knock on the ornate wooden door.

She knocked again, then rang the bell. She didn't hear the sound of footsteps or other activity. "That's odd. I know Doris was expecting us."

"She's probably in the kitchen," Alex said. "She told me she doesn't hear too good sometimes."

"Doesn't hear too 'well,'" Kara corrected automatically, a dark twinge niggling her. She tried the door handle, found the door unlocked. She opened it and stepped inside. "Doris! It's Kara and Alex."

The silence that answered had the static sound of an empty house. Kara walked farther in. "Doris? Are you here?" She heard a plaintive meow, as Doris's cat, Tom, padded into the room. He meowed again, twined against Kara's legs, then moved on to Alex, who squatted down and gave him the attention he demanded.

A heaviness settled in Kara's body. Something felt wrong. "Stay here with Tom," she told Alex. "I'll look for Mrs. Burgess."

"Mom, wait." He stood and scooted to her side. "I don't want you to go. It feels bad in here."

The fact that he sensed something wrong only deepened her own uneasiness. "It's all right," she said, although she didn't believe it. "You'll be fine right here."

He shook his head. "It feels *really* bad. Kinda like that time I watched *The Sixth Sense*."

"Which you borrowed from Ben Martin without my permission," Kara reminded him. "Stay here by the front door, and leave it open. If you see or hear anything really scary, run next door and get Mr. Roberts. Okay?"

He nodded reluctantly and squatted by Tom again. She walked across the living room and through the dining room to the arched entryway to the kitchen. A quick glance told her the kitchen was empty. The table was completely clear and spotless, as were the counters. No baking items were out. Very strange.

Her apprehension growing, Kara went through the kitchen and breakfast nook to the neat den, which was also empty. She headed for a hallway she knew led to the bedrooms, although she'd never been in that part of the house. Entering the hall, she froze.

A sense of déjà vu rushed at her. The length of hallway became distorted, the walls wavering. Suddenly lightheaded, Kara braced herself against one wall with her right hand. She forced air into her lungs, blinked to clear her vision. And stared down the same hallway she'd seen in last night's dream. *Oh, God, no.*

While one part of her wanted to turn and run, she knew she had to go down that hall, *had to know . . .*

"Mom? Did you find her?" Alex's anxious voice came from behind her, and she whirled.

"Uh, no, sweetie, but she might be sick." She crouched down beside him, tried to keep her voice level. "Do me a favor, and go wait for me on the front porch. I'm going to see if she's okay."

His expression turned fearful. "It feels even badder here. What if that ghost came over here and—"

"No," Kara said firmly. "The ghost didn't come over here. Go sit on the porch. You can take Tom with you."

"Okay." He turned and tromped back outside, with a wheedling, "Come on, kitty, kitty, kitty." A meowing flash of white and gray fur followed him.

Kara turned back and stared down the hallway, which reverberated with an ominous energy. "Please be wrong," she whispered. *"Please be wrong."* She walked slowly down the hall, barely able to breathe, terror whipping through her, but she had to keep going. *Not Doris. No.*

Yes, some inner voice whispered. *You know it's true.* Her dream visions had never been wrong. Her feet grew heavier and heavier as she approached the last door on the left. Her pulse pounded in her temples; the light-headedness returned. The doorway was just like her dream . . . *but she had to find Doris.* She closed her eyes, opened them again, stepped through the doorway.

And stared at the body in the bed. Stared at the cream-colored pajamas decorated with colorful cups and saucers, horror welling inside her like a tidal wave.

She didn't need her medical training for a diagnosis. There was absolutely no life force in the room.

DAMIEN browsed through Sal's Grocery. It was almost six thirty in the evening, but Sal stayed open past his usual six o'clock closing if he had customers in the store, and apparently it had been a busy evening. Damien had spent the day in Fredericksburg, trying to determine if the murders there were linked to that of David Thornton, but hadn't found any psychic trails to confirm it. He was of the opinion that Thornton was the first victim of this particular Belian, which meant it had recently come into possession of a body.

Tomorrow, Damien planned to revisit the river and wooded area where Thornton had gone into the water. For tonight, he was looking for something to eat, while listening to the Zorro residents in the store and simply feeling the energies. He'd also use a police scanner to monitor violent crimes, but so far, there wasn't much criminal activity in Zorro.

He got a loaf of bread, a jar of peanut butter, a quart of milk, and a package of Oreos. It was a lot of carbohydrates, but he had a super-fast metabolism and could eat whatever he wanted, which suited him just fine, as he had a definite sweet tooth.

He caught himself wondering what Kara liked to eat. She was so slender, he suspected she was a light eater. She probably exercised regularly, as there was a hint of substance and muscle beneath the neat slacks and feminine sweaters she favored.

She'd been in his thoughts a lot, and more than once, he'd had to redirect his focus back to the boy and to the Belian he was tracking. It was her resistance, he told himself, the challenge of gaining her cooperation that held the fascination. His mantra of never getting involved with his conductors was so ingrained, it was virtually automatic.

He did everything in his power to ensure his noninvolvement, to the point that he didn't kiss his conductors, not even in the throes of hot, steamy, conduction-induced sex. And it was only sex; he would never allow it to be otherwise. He knew firsthand, and very painfully, what happened when things became personal between a Sentinel and a conductor.

He'd have to hold a little more firmly to his resolve

around Kara, because they had the strongest chemistry that he'd ever experienced with any conductor. The longer they were together, the stronger it pulsed and tantalized.

When—not if—she finally agreed to conduct for him, he had no doubt it would be an incredible conduction, which would require great care, because this Belian was very powerful, and might well be able to detect the sexual surge. But the being wouldn't escape him. Damien had never failed, and didn't intend to now.

He carried his items to the counter and set them down. "Hello, Sal."

"Evenin'." Sal started to ring up the food. He glanced sideways at Damien. "Hey, did ya ever find Dr. Cantrell to give her back that scarf?"

"As a matter of fact, I did." Damien reached for his wallet.

"I hear there was some bad news out her way earlier this evenin'."

Damien froze, his wallet halfway out of his rear pocket. "What happened?"

"Had a death out there. Your total is $9.71."

Damien's heart sped up as his senses went on full alert. "Who died?"

Sal peered over his glasses at Damien. "Dr. Cantrell's neighbor, an elderly lady. Don't have any details yet, exceptin' Doc Cantrell's the one who found her."

Damien tossed a twenty onto the counter and grabbed the bag of groceries. He strode from the store, ignoring Sal calling out, "Ya forgot yer change!"

As he left, an absolute, chilling calm came down over him like a blanket settling over a bed. His power began to throb, already tuning itself for the hunt.

Heading for Kara's house, he slipped into full Sentinel mode, ready to track and destroy the enemy.

EIGHT

FIVE vehicles lined the street in front of the house north of Kara—the same house where Luz had taken Alex after the discarnate entity made an appearance. One vehicle was an ambulance, sitting silent, with its rear doors closed and no sign of interior activity. Two vehicles were police cars, but their engines were off, and there were no flashing lights. The house, however, had lights blazing from almost every window.

Inevitably, a group of people had accumulated outside to watch the comings and goings, despite the descending night and the cooling temperatures. It was probably more excitement than a quiet town like Zorro experienced in a year. Grimly predicting that would change in the near future, Damien parked and strode around the knot of people and up the sidewalk.

The area hadn't been cordoned off, and no one was posted at the front door, an indication that this wasn't being treated as a crime scene. Inside, two uniformed police officers were standing in the immaculate, stylish living room, one of them making notes on a clipboard. They went on alert when they saw him, started forward to head him off.

"Chief Greer wants me here," he said, sending a slight mental push to back up his words. "I'm supposed to be here. It's all right for me to look around. You won't find any of my actions unusual or strange." As with most humans, it was easy for him to manipulate their minds, and they nodded and relaxed.

Damien took a deep breath to center himself and lightly touched the medallion resting beneath his sweater. Made of the purest pink quartz crystal, it was attuned to the energies of great Tuaoi crystal that lay amid the ruins of Atlantis, in the depths of the Atlantic Ocean. Hanging from a chain of silver, the stone was framed in intricately woven silver. Both the crystal and silver were conduits for the wisdom of The One.

Wearing the crystal was a calculated risk; any Belian who saw it would recognize it and know the bearer was a Sentinel. But the crystal facilitated a quicker rise of higher chakra energies and strengthened their focus, especially on a psychic scan of a Belian crime scene. Only a human conductor could offer a more powerful magnification.

Taking another deep breath, Damien allowed the crystal's power to flow through him and open his chakras, as he expanded his awareness, letting it flare out around him. He mentally slammed against a wall of darkness, felt the oppressive weight of evil and utter absence of divinity. A Belian had been here.

As he made the connection, images came to him, like a movie, only choppy and uneven, as if a strobe light were flashing in the scene. He saw a human form engulfed in an overcoat, with a cap pulled low over the face. He couldn't see any features; Belians were adept at blurring their psychic projections.

In jerky images, the figure jimmied the lock on the front door, slipped inside, and headed to a nearby hallway. The outside darkness in the vision told Damien it was nighttime, and Mrs. Burgess had been alive yesterday afternoon, so that narrowed the time frame of the murder. There was no doubt she'd been murdered. If a Belian was involved, there would be no other alternative.

He followed the dark trail to the hallway and down it as he watched the psychic replay of the Belian's actions. It was more difficult to pick up an actual signature. He had learned to create a mental sphere, surround it with the powerful, protective energy of the Light, and then suck the negative, oppressive energies into the sphere.

Later, he could work with the energies and manipulate them into the Belian's psychic signature. With the help of a conductor, he could amplify the signature even more, and begin to differentiate characteristics that would lead to the human identity of the Belian.

The stench of evil became more pronounced as Damien went down the hall, his vision leading him unerringly to the last doorway on the left. On an ethereal level, he watched the man/Belian enter the room, while on a physical level he heard voices as he approached the doorway. There were at least two men and Kara. He recognized her voice, pitched higher than usual, her agitation evident.

"Mr. Sampson, there's no way you can declare this a natural death," she was saying.

Damien paused outside the door, abstracted the energy that was even more decadent and evil here. "Dr. Cantrell, there's no evidence to the contrary," said a brisk male voice.

Damien stepped to the doorway, balancing the psychic replay of the previous night with real time. In the replay, a shadowy figure approached the sleeping woman in the bed, visible only in the faint glow of the night-light.

In the here and now, all lights in the room were on, people and equipment framing the centerpiece of attention—an elaborate, four-poster bed bearing the lifeless, stiff, and bent body of Mrs. Burgess. He felt a brief flare of pity for her soul and its ruined shell, but ruthlessly quashed it.

Kara faced two men, her hands clenched by her side, looking pale but determined. At the foot of the bed, two

EMTs, a man and a woman, waited beside a raised gurney. Their black leather equipment cases sat on the floor, closed up, useless in the face of death. Everyone looked Damien's way as he entered the room, letting go of the psychic trail for now. He'd come back later to study the crime and the energies.

He recognized Chief Tom Greer, a weathered, middle-aged man with thinning, graying black hair and brown eyes. He was dressed in jeans and a sweatshirt and sported cowboy boots, and had a cowboy hat clutched in his left hand. Apparently he'd been off duty when the call came in.

The police chief's eyes narrowed when he saw Damien. "What the hell are you doin' here?"

"I'm here to offer my assistance," Damien said, moving to stand by Kara. He felt her tension, and maybe a tingling of relief, as she shot him a quick glance before returning her attention to Greer.

"Well, you can just take yourself out of here," the chief said. "We don't need a reporter, and an outsider at that, snooping around at a time like this."

"I'm a writer, not a reporter. And I'm not here in an official capacity. I'm here because of my association with Dr. Cantrell." Damien left it at that, and let them draw whatever conclusions they would. They'd better get used to him and Kara being together, because he intended to spend a lot of time with her until the Belian was identified and Atlantian justice dispensed.

"I don't give a damn about your so-called association with the doctor," Greer snapped. "I want you out of here now."

Her eyes wide, Kara stepped in front of Damien. "Chief Greer—"

"Is this a crime scene?" Damien asked, taking her arm and moving her to the side.

"Not at this time," Greer said, placing his hand on his gun in an intimidating gesture. "Now get out."

"If there's been no crime, then you can't possibly object to my presence here." Damien met Greer's gaze squarely, although he was reluctant to use a mental push with the chief, because he didn't trust the man, didn't want to alert anyone or anything to his identity. "Unless, of course, you want me to air any suspicions I might have regarding Mrs. Burgess's death in my magazine."

His face turning red at the implied threat, Greer took a step forward. "Now see here—"

"Let it go, Tom," said the other man. He was dressed in a dark wool suit, and was older, with a shock of white hair and a gray mustache and vivid blue eyes. "It doesn't matter if this man is here, because this isn't a crime scene."

"I don't agree with you, Mr. Sampson," Kara protested again. "I'm not convinced Doris died of natural causes."

Damien glanced at her sharply. She knew something, or had sensed something. Or perhaps her previous experiences with Belians had led her to the logical conclusion that this was the work of one.

"But there's no reason to believe that Mrs. Burgess met with foul play," Sampson told her.

"He's right, Dr. Kara," Greer said. "There's no evidence of forced entry."

"The front door was unlocked when I got here." Kara turned her attention to him. "I know Doris keeps her doors locked."

"She probably just forgot to lock it, then," Greer replied. "As I said, there's no indication the lock was tampered with. And there's no sign of injury to the body—to Miz Burgess. She was an old woman—what? Seventy-eight, seventy-nine?"

"Seventy-five," Kara said. "And she was very healthy for her age. I just saw her on Monday."

"Seventy-five ain't all that young. It's not uncommon for an old person to die in their sleep," the chief pointed out. "And Miz Burgess had diabetes. That tends to take some years off a person's life." He turned to the two EMTs. "Either of you see anything suspicious when you examined the body?"

They shook their heads in the negative.

Kara's expression became more determined. "Think what you will. I still want an autopsy performed."

"It costs us almost two thousand dollars for every body we send to the medical examiner in Austin," Greer argued. "That's a lot of money, and our budget is limited, especially since we bought those new police cruisers."

"*By law*, unattended or suspicious deaths require an autopsy. Part of the same laws you've sworn to uphold. Just because you have the signature of a justice of the peace"—Kara paused and shot Sampson a hard look, alerting Damien to the man's identity—"on the death certificate, doesn't make it legal, or right."

"No, it doesn't," Damien interjected, throwing in with her. It was actually to his advantage that people knew Mrs. Burgess had been murdered. If they were on the alert, it might be harder for a Belian to operate in their midst.

"As a crime writer," he continued, "I know the state laws better than most. Texas law requires an autopsy for all unattended deaths, unless there are special circumstances. If there's any doubt in the matter, then I would suggest you err on the side of caution, and defer to the letter of the law."

"Damn it!" Greer slapped his hat against his thigh. "A sick old woman dies of natural causes in her sleep and you folks want to go and make a crime out of it—and spend the police department's money."

"I'm not signing the death certificate without an autopsy," Kara said. "Of course, Mr. Sampson has the authority to do it, but elections are coming up in, oh, eight months?" She stared pointedly at Sampson. "Aren't you up for reelection, Mr. Sampson?"

He made a sound of disgust. "Fine. Let's keep this clean. Tom, request the autopsy, and let me know the results." He turned toward the door. "I'm done here."

Greer gestured to the EMTs to load up the body and left behind Sampson. They prepared to move the gurney to the side of the bed.

"Wait," Kara said. "Just a minute, please." She walked to

the bed and stared at Mrs. Burgess a long moment, reaching out to stroke the stiff face. "Good-bye, my friend," she whispered. "I'm sorry I doubted you." She leaned down and pressed a kiss to the old woman's forehead. Slowly, she stepped back, her grief and sadness tangible. Tears rolled down her cheeks.

"Come on." Damien moved to her side and took her arm. "There's nothing more we can do here."

"I know." With a last glance at Mrs. Burgess, she swiped a palm over her face and allowed him to lead her from the room and out of the house. In the living room talking to his officers, Chief Greer looked up and glared at them as they went by, but had nothing to say to them.

The cold outside air hit them like a slap, but Damien found it refreshing, a welcome change from the oppressive stuffiness of the house and the smell of death, tainted with the stink of evil. Kara seemed uncertain in her direction, so he steered her toward her house, across the grass and away from the curious onlookers. Fortunately, Chief Greer had just come out on the porch, and the crowd's attention focused on him.

Damien maintained his hold on Kara's arm as they walked. He could feel her tension. "I'm sorry for your loss," he said, knowing words were never enough, yet all he could offer.

"Yeah." She stared straight ahead, the thick fall of her hair framing her face.

He couldn't see her features. Like most small-town roads, Virginia Avenue had no streetlights; the only illumination came from lighted windows, and the stars and nearly full moon above. She stumbled as they walked across the uneven yard, and he tightened his grip on her arm to steady her. "Where's Alex?"

"Oh no! How could I have forgotten him? He's with the Roberts family, on the other side of Doris. He took her cat over there." She tried to twist back the way they had come. "I have to get him."

He tugged her forward. "Not right now. You need a little time to pull yourself together, and to decide what to tell him."

"No, I—" She dug in, turned to face him, her face a pale oval in the moonlight. "This is my fault. I dreamed about Doris's murder last night. I should have done something."

Her words went though him like an electric shock. She had *dreamed* about the Belian crime? "Did you see the Belian's face?"

"No." She pulled free of his grasp. "I didn't even realize it was Doris in my dream, because I'd never been in the back of her house, and she was turned away in the bed. But I should have known. *I should have known!*"

"There was no way you could know," he said. "This is not your fault. Surely you realize that."

"When I had that dream vision last night, I knew what it was—that it would come true. And I didn't do anything. Not a damned thing! I should have called the police, should have told someone." She wrapped her arms around herself. "And all this time, Doris was just lying there, all alone."

She started toward her house. He followed, knowing she was suffering both grief and shock. He'd seen it enough times to recognize the signs. It didn't matter how many powers he had, he couldn't heal a wounded, grieving human spirit. He didn't speak until they were on the porch and she was opening the front door.

"Kara, listen to me." He waited until she angled her head and met his gaze, tear trails glistening on her face. "Even if you'd known for sure it was Doris in the vision, by the time you had the dream, it was already too late to help her. The best way you can help her now is to work with me to catch her killer. We've put this off longer than we should have. This thing is escalating, and we have to stop it. You *must* conduct for me."

She slowly turned toward him, anger flaring in her eyes. "You *would* use Doris's death to your advantage. You bastard!"

"Yeah, you're right, I would. I would use anything to catch this Belian."

"And that's all you care about, isn't it? It doesn't matter to you that an innocent woman is dead. That she probably had ten good years left, that she's leaving behind three children and five grandchildren, who all adore her."

In his mind, he saw the pitiful, bent body of Doris Burgess. Any death of an innocent was unacceptable. He felt a chasm in his tightly held control, felt the simmering rage slip through.

"Yes it matters," he said fiercely. "God damn it, it matters! How do you think I feel, knowing there's a monster within my reach, and if I don't stop it, more innocents will die?"

Fury ripped through him, and he whirled away, his fists clenched, needing to tear something apart. He settled for stomping down the steps and picking up a thick branch that had fallen off the nearby pecan tree. He snapped it like it was a twig, and hurled the pieces away. "I have to live with two murders already, knowing it's *my duty*, *my responsibility*, to stop this monster, and that I've failed so far. And every day that goes by is more time for it to destroy someone else."

He kicked at another branch, set it flying. His chest heaved, and he fought to bring himself under control. The red haze receded, but the frustration and knowledge that he was no closer to stopping this Belian continued to torment him. He raked his hands through his hair, vaguely aware of his leather binding falling off and the feel of hair flowing against his face.

Damnation. Somehow Kara managed to get beneath his skin, to shake up his control. He looked up to find her standing mute on the porch, her eyes huge and dark as she stared at him.

"And to know," he continued, "that for every person who dies, others are devastated by the loss. That a human life touches many other lives, that one single violent action has an exponential ripple effect, the potential of causing pain on many levels." *As well he knew, from personal experience.*

He exhaled deeply, tossed his hair from his face, and mounted the steps to the porch, willing himself to calm. He felt his Sentinel persona returning, slipping into place like a weapon into a holster.

"Yeah," he said, his gaze locked with Kara's. "I'm a bastard, all right. But, as The One is my witness, I will hunt down and destroy this Belian."

Her expression hardened. "Good." She turned and went inside.

He followed her to the kitchen, leaned against the counter while she telephoned Mary Roberts and told her she'd be over for Alex within the hour. Then she put two mugs of water in the microwave and dug out some tea bags. He'd have preferred coffee, and that laced with something with an alcoholic kick, but was willing to go with the flow, especially if it soothed Kara.

She remained silent while she fixed the tea, and he welcomed the time to ensure his own emotions were again deeply buried. She was still pale, her eyes haunted, and her hands shaking slightly as she handed him his tea and then seated herself at the table. He slid into the chair next to her and waited for her to work through the trauma of the evening. He would still push for—insist on—a conduction, but he'd give her time to settle down first.

She stared down at her mug. "Doris was my friend. And these past few days, I doubted her. I thought she might be the"—she shook her head, looked at him, tears glinting in her eyes—"I thought she might be possessed. How could I think such a thing?"

"Because anything is possible with a Belian, especially one this strong. It could have possessed any number of bodies. Old or sick people are easier targets. Your logic was sound."

She dropped her gaze back to her tea. "I know that, but still . . ."

Chaos, doubt, suspicion, hatred, despair. Belians had

that effect on everything around them. They were the spawn of Belial, may his soul burn in the Fires.

He leaned forward. "What can you tell me about your dream?"

She relayed what she'd dreamed, methodically and with an astonishing amount of detail, although her voice shook at times. He was amazed at how closely her vision resembled the psychic picture he'd "seen" at Doris's house.

"What do you think was in the syringe?" he asked.

"I don't know." She thought about it a moment. "It could have been insulin. An insulin overdose would be fairly quick acting and could produce symptoms of heart failure. A needle mark in her arm wouldn't be suspicious, because she is—was—Oh, God." Her voice broke again, and she took a deep breath before continuing. "Doris was diabetic and took insulin injections."

"So that would be a logical way to take her out, and if that proves to be the case, then the Belian wants the deaths to look accidental—for now," Damien mused. "It also means it knew Doris well enough to know she took insulin, and how to get around her house."

"Which reinforces the theory about the Belian possessing the body of someone who lives in Zorro," Kara said. "I didn't want to believe it."

"But it sure looks that way." Damien noted the time. "I'm going back to Doris's house later tonight. I didn't have a chance to gather all the information, but I suspect it's going to be very close to your vision."

"Oh, it will be." She gripped her mug, her knuckles white. "My cursed dreams are accurate right down to every bloody detail."

"Kara, you should have called me immediately when you found the bod—Doris. You knew, or suspected, the Belian had killed her. You also know it's very important that I scan a Belian crime scene as soon as possible."

"I didn't think." She stared sightlessly at the opposite wall. "I couldn't think of anything, except how she looked, lying there in that bed. Then . . . I grabbed my phone, and it was an automatic reflex to dial 9-1-1. It was all I could manage."

"I know it was hard. But it's crucial that I know right away if anything else happens. Is that your phone?" He pointed to the leather case clipped on her belt, and she nodded. "Let me have it a moment."

She unclipped it and handed it to him without comment, watched as he entered his mobile number into her directory, then handed the phone back to her. "My number is in there now, and if anything happens, I want you to call *me* first. Don't call anyone else until you talk to me. Understand?"

"Sure, whatever," she said dully.

They sat in silence a few moments, Damien mulling over how to convince her to cooperate on a conduction, without having to use coercion. Suddenly she turned toward him, determination firing her gaze. "I'm not going to let Doris's death go unchallenged. And I'm not going to let this—this *thing* hurt anyone else. I'll help you track this monster."

He came to full attention. "You'll conduct for me."

She held up a warning hand. "Only on one condition."

"And that is?"

"There will be no physical intimacy. No unnecessary touching, no kissing, and *no sex*."

He started to protest. Sexual intercourse created the most powerful conduction and would be more effective with this strong Belian. But he saw the resolve on Kara's face, knew her past experiences as a conductor had put her through hell. She wouldn't capitulate. He was lucky he wouldn't have to go against the Sentinel code of honor and force her. He'd take what he could get.

"All right," he said. "We'll do it tonight."

NINE

KARA stared down at her son. He was sprawled on her bed, one hand tangled in Mac's fur. Both were sound asleep, courtesy of a mental push from Damien. She hadn't been wild about that, but knew Alex was too wound up to sleep. She told him Doris had died in her sleep and hadn't suffered any pain—probably true, although it glossed over the fact Doris had been murdered.

Alex had still been upset and clingy, and worried that now Doris's ghost would join that of the other ghost and come to their house. Which Kara supposed was a disturbingly real possibility, given the way things had gone lately.

She felt a brush of heated energy behind her, knew Damien was there. Apprehension and physical awareness swept through her. She leaned down to smooth Alex's hair and kiss his cheek before she straightened and faced Damien. He had returned to Doris's house to finish examining the crime scene, while she calmed and fed Alex, and got him ready for bed. Damien returned in time to send boy and dog into a deep slumber, assuring her they wouldn't awaken during the conduction.

Now he stood there, waiting for her, the unspoken expectation hanging between them like a pending execution. He was dressed differently tonight. She had been surprised to see him in full business attire when he'd shed his duster earlier—an expensively cut black suit that made him look even bigger, his shoulders even wider. With it, he wore a white shirt and bloodred tie. He told her he had some official business earlier in Fredericksburg, and sometimes his work required a suit.

He'd removed the suit coat and the tie, and rolled up the shirt sleeves, exposing strong muscular forearms. With his dark skin and five o'clock shadow, and his midnight hair flowing freely about his shoulders, he looked like a modern-day pirate, threatening on many levels she didn't want to probe. It didn't help that he'd returned from Doris's house radiating excess psychic energy that jangled her already taut nerves.

"Ready?" he asked.

She was mentally and physically exhausted. There was a gaping hole in her heart, created by the loss of a friend she couldn't yet properly mourn. Instead, she had to hold it together for her son, subject herself to the trauma of a conduction, and at the same time, maintain her dignity in front of this Sentinel. "Hell no, I'm not ready," she muttered.

He held out his hand. "Come on."

Willing her hand to remain steady, she placed it in his, felt the tingle of electricity.

"Alex's room?" he asked.

"No," she said firmly, although a bed was the standard setting for a conduction—along with tangled sheets and nude, writhing bodies. But she refused to cross those boundaries. "The living room."

His brow arched at that, but he said nothing as they walked to the main room and over to the couch. "Sit here." He indicated one end of the couch and pulled the overstuffed chair around to face it. "I'll take the chair."

They seated themselves, adjusting furniture so they fully faced one another. He scooted the chair forward until his knees touched the couch, with her legs sandwiched between his thighs, far too close for comfort. Her heart was jumping like a panicked frog in a net, and memories of Richard crowded into her mind. She shoved them away, stared into Damien's mesmerizing silvery gaze.

"No intimacy," she said again. "No unnecessary touching."

"So we agreed." He reached toward her, pausing when she flinched involuntarily. "Kara, we have to touch *some*."

She felt like the naive, starry-eyed high school girl she'd once been, too shy and intimidated to say hello to the football quarterback on whom she'd had a huge crush. *This is ridiculous,* she told herself.

"I know." She wiped her palms on her sweatpants (the most coverage she could find) and held out both hands.

He took them, turning her left palm faceup and placing his right palm down against it. Then he turned his left hand faceup against her right hand, completing the familiar, standard position for opening energy pathways between Sentinel and conductor. Leaning forward, he shifted their pressed-together hands to rest on her thighs. He inhaled deeply, exhaled; she knew he was centering himself and creating protective shields.

Already, without any other initiation, she could feel the flow of psychic energy beginning to cycle through their hands. She couldn't believe that just a simple physical link could initiate the energy. Good thing she'd kept her bra on and donned a thick sweatshirt, because her nipples were already painful nubs. She felt another flare of panic, caught her breath.

"Easy now," he murmured. "Close your eyes and breathe through it."

Simple for him to say. She closed her eyes, managed a few deep breaths. The energy began pooling in her groin, quickly heating to an urgency that spread like fingers across her abdomen. On an intellectual level, she understood it was just the base chakra activating and expanding; this chakra controlled ovaries/gonads and reproduction and therefore sexual urges. But on a visceral level, it was an awakening of desire.

With astonishing speed, the energy cycled upward to just below her belly button, bursting through the second chakra, setting her abdomen aflame. With it came the sexual surge, creating a physical need so violent, she had to clamp her thighs together to keep from crying out. The energies were rising fast, much faster than she remembered with Richard. She struggled for air, unable to assimilate the overwhelming rush of energy.

"Breathe!" Damien commanded. "Just breathe and go with the flow."

The third chakra opened with an audible pop, energy pouring through her lower rib cage. "Too fast," she gasped. It had been too long since she'd done this. . . . "I can't do it."

"Let go, Kara. Let it carry you along."

"I can't—" She was vaguely aware that she had her fingers wrapped around his hands, that he had pressed his legs tightly against her thighs . . . it was too much.

"You don't have to do anything. Just hold on, go with the current." His voice was like steel, a command she was helpless to ignore. She felt tossed like a buoy in a stormy sea.

Another pop, and green filled her field of vision. Warmth flooded her fourth chakra, spread through her chest.

"We're through the lower chakras now," he said, sounding calm and impassive. "All you have to do is hang on." He meant that symbolically, but her fingers convulsed around his hands, desperately seeking an anchor. She felt his fingers curl around hers in return, felt the solidness of his grasp. "It's all right," his deep voice soothed. "Keep breathing."

The pressure eased somewhat, but her throat burned as the energy moved into the fifth chakra, the first of the higher three centers. They were in the Sentinel realm now, in the spiritual chakras that facilitated links with God and with the super-consciousness many referred to as the Universe.

The slight easing was short-lived. There was a blinding starburst of light, followed by a sharp spear of pain in the top of her head. The sixth chakra was now open, but she had no time to process it. The light spilled into the center of her forehead, into the seventh chakra. An electrical tingling began there.

With all the chakras open, the energy had a full range to flow and began racing through all seven centers in a figure eight pattern. It created a rocking sensation along her spine. She felt like she was being jerked off the couch, but knew that was just her perception. She also knew her "third eye," which was linked to the sixth chakra, was now engaged with Damien's. Colors flashed behind her eyelids—red, orange, yellow, green, blue, indigo, violet—alternating with light-speed images she couldn't decipher. Faster and faster and faster.

Clawing, sexual desire permeated it all. Kara's heart raced, her breasts ached, her vagina throbbed with basic, primal need. This was when most Sentinels and conductors came together physically. When the steady pounding of the male into the female set up a cadence that merged with the lower-based chakra energy signature of the Belian, slipping into that energy like a key into a lock.

This was when Richard would have entered her body, filling her, slaking her desperate need, as their energy merged to surround and pattern the Belian's energy, culminating in an explosive climax and leaving strong mental images that would lead Richard to the identity of the Belian.

But there would be no relief for her this time. No physical release or the bonding of minds and souls, or the glow of the spiritual aftermath. No lying in bed afterward and piecing together the parts of the Belian puzzle, then making love again, this time with leisurely tenderness. No Richard. Ever again.

Grief engulfed her, but not even that pain could dull the relentless sexual demands of her body. She wrenched her thoughts to Doris. For her, she could handle this—she *would* handle it. She'd come this far, and Doris's murderer was not going to get away with his crime. Kara reached deep, trying to ride the waves of energy and focus on the stunning starburst radiating in the center of her mind.

The images flashing through her mind in a super blur meant nothing to her, but that didn't matter. Damien would be able to interpret them. Her job as a conductor was to magnify and focus his psychic abilities, allowing him to chisel away at the Belian's psychic blocks. She was simply a conduit, albeit a very powerful one.

The energy began to slow, as did the rocking motion. The color and image flashes became weaker, began fading. She felt the surge receding, leaving behind a tingling sensation, like that of a limb falling asleep, then reawakening. But the sexual heat didn't recede. The four lower chakras were tied to the Earth, encrypted with the survival instinct of mating. Her entire body reverberated with a now highly charged libido.

Mind over matter, she told herself, clenching her teeth. Or maybe a bath in ice water. She felt Damien withdraw, mentally and physically, and it left her oddly bereft. Blowing out a shaky breath, she opened her eyes. He had pushed the chair away a few feet, and lounged back in it, watching her. He appeared composed and completely unaffected by what had just transpired, while she suspected she was rumpled and wild-eyed, with her hair going all directions.

Damn him. How could he be so impervious? He was in a human body, wasn't he? She squinted at his lap, trying to see if he had an erection. He should have a raging one, if he was experiencing even one tenth of the lust she felt right now. She couldn't tell, not with the dark suit and the dimness of the room.

Stop it! she told herself. She was just feeling the aftereffects of the conduction, not a true attraction. Fatigue and exhaustion seeped through her.

"You all right?" Damien asked.

"Just fine." She tried to get up, found her rubbery legs wouldn't support her.

"Careful there." He was out of the chair in a single movement, his hands on her arms the only thing that prevented her from toppling over. "You're shaking. Here, lie down for a few minutes until you get your balance."

"I'm okay, really." But she sank onto the couch and let him swing her legs up and settle her on her back as if she were a child. She didn't like it, but it was better than pitching forward onto her face.

"Sure you are." He pressed warm fingers against her neck, his gaze fixed on her face. "Your pulse is pretty fast."

No kidding. That was late-breaking news. Reaching a sexual flash point tended to have that affect on a woman. Kara shook her head to clear it, and to chase away the inane thoughts. She was definitely punchy, and she couldn't remember ever being this bad after a conduction.

He returned to the chair. "That was a very powerful conduction."

"It did seem pretty strong," she conceded, telling herself to focus on the images produced rather than the physical aftereffects. A cold shower was going to be the first order of business, as soon as her legs decided to work. "Did you get anything?"

"Not much, although some details might clarify when I do my evening meditation."

"You'll meditate *tonight*? After all that energy's been let loose?"

"It will be much more controlled. Regular mediation doesn't snap all the chakras open like that. It's gradual and regulated." He tapped his fingers on the arm of the chair. "I did get a sense of water during the conduction."

She remembered seeing flowing currents in some of the swift flashes of scenes. "I did, too. It could have been the Blanco River."

"Yes," he agreed. "It was clear water that looked green because of the rocks. I also got images of a road running beside the water."

"That would probably be River Road—an original name." Kara rubbed her forehead, now battling a sudden headache. "Do you think what you saw has to do with David's death?"

"No, they're not the same images I got at the place where I believe he went into the water. More likely, they're related to the Belian."

"Perhaps it goes there a lot?" she asked.

"Maybe. Either that, or it lives there. One way or another, it is a connection to the Belian."

"Oh, well, then." She made an effort to turn on her side and face him, wincing as the movement made her head throb worse. "If it lives there, that narrows the suspects down to about one or two hundred people who reside along River Road."

"It's still a clue, and it gives us a place to start looking. I also saw a live oak tree."

"Only a few thousand of those," Kara muttered.

"Smart-ass," he said, with a hint of a smile. "No, this tree is very odd looking. It's missing a big branch, but not a clean break, and most of the bark on that same side is splintered off. The tree was probably hit by lightning. It's unique, and I think I'll know it when I see it." He drummed his fingers on the chair arm again, seemingly lost in thought. "This is a very strong Belian. It's got some solid blocks in place. It's going to be a challenge to identify it."

"I have a feeling you're used to challenges." She tried to stifle a yawn. How could she suddenly be sleepy when she was still sexually wired and had a four-ibuprofen headache working?

"I don't object to a challenge, but any delay could result in more deaths. How are you feeling?"

"I feel great," she lied, swinging her legs to the ground and trying to get her body vertical. Her head protested violently, forcing an involuntary groan.

He was instantly up, moving like a great cat. "What's wrong?" He sat on the couch beside her.

She didn't want his concern, or his disconcerting touch. She was ready to be away from him, to be alone with her pain and grief. "Just a small headache. Some drugs and sleep and I'll be as good as new."

"Let me help you." His hands slid upward, one possessively grasping her neck, the other cupping her forehead.

"No, really, I don't need—"

"Just hush and be still."

A soothing warmth penetrated the tension in her neck and drifted inside her head. Immediately the pain eased. She relaxed and, for a moment, savored his trademark sandalwood scent and the stroking of his fingers along her neck. Until she felt the subtle mental push.

"Stop that!" She tried to squirm away.

"I said be still." He slid closer, pinning her against the side of the couch while he continued massaging her neck and sending the warmth into her head. "What is it you want me to stop?"

"I can feel your mental manipulation, and I don't like having my mind invaded."

"I'm merely calming and relaxing you, nothing more. And you object to this after the mental intimacy of a third-eye meld in a conduction?"

"Well . . . yes."

He dropped his hands. "Fine. Some aspirin or ibuprofen ought to be sufficient to keep the pain from coming back. If you'd allowed the conduction to be completed properly, the energy would have been fully dispersed, and you wouldn't have a headache."

"Spoken like a typical guy." She rubbed her neck, marveling that the pain was gone. "Most men think sex is the solution for everything."

"I wouldn't disagree with that." The silky seduction in his voice sent a shudder through her. She wasn't sure if it was the human or Sentinel side of him, but the man oozed raw, animal magnetism.

He rose from the couch and stared down at her. "And in this particular case, with such a powerful Belian, sex might be a necessity. It all depends on how badly you want to help me track it down."

He strode to the dining room to retrieve his duster from the back of a chair. He slid into it, picked up his suit coat. "I need to spend some time with Alex this weekend, especially after this latest occurrence."

Alex. A sudden memory shot through her. "He felt it."

"Who felt what?"

"Alex sensed the energies when we went inside Doris's house this afternoon." Kara stared blindly at the fireplace, reliving the horrendous events of the day. "He said it felt really bad in the house. He was frightened." She looked back at Damien. "I think it was the Belian he sensed."

"I have no doubt of it. This is another example of how quickly Alex's powers are developing, with or without direction. It drives home how important it is that Alex gain total control of his abilities, so he can manipulate them, rather than the other way around."

"I know." She sighed. "You've made that point quite clear. But I still expect you to keep his exposure to the Sentinel existence to a minimum."

"He chose this," Damien said quietly. "His soul exercised its free will, and came into this Earth plane, choosing the path of a Sentinel."

"He's just a boy! He's not old enough to choose anything. *I'm* his mother, and I have to make decisions for both of us. He's too young to fully understand being a Sentinel, and I intend to protect him as long as I can."

"You can't control the unfolding of his powers, Kara. Nor can you control what Alex senses, or his natural instincts. Better he learn to master them."

She could find no reply as he walked to the front door and opened it. He cocked his head toward her. "I'll call you tomorrow to arrange a time to come over. Think about what I said about tracking the Belian. I know it took a lot of guts for you to agree to a conduction, in light of your previous experiences. But what we did tonight may not be enough. The safety of Zorro's residents could well depend on your willingness to have sex with me."

AH, the power coursing through me! It is like the nectar of Belial, giving me new vitality. The old woman had more life force than I expected. Why did I wait so long to again feel the glorious rush of claiming a life to strengthen my own existence? There is no need to be so cautious—they'll never know. Not even the Sentinel can identify me; I'm far too powerful.

But he tried, oh yes, he did. I could feel the surge of power, and a sexual surge at that. So, there is a conductor involved, as well. Very intriguing, and much to consider. A Sentinel and a conductor working together will pose more of a challenge, but I have the supremacy of Belial behind me. I am more than a match for them. I will watch and listen carefully, so I can determine the identity of my enemies and destroy them.

To prepare for battle, I will need more power. To that end, I will experience the rush of the kill again soon.

Very soon.

KARA locked the door after Damien; she also checked the back door and all the windows, although nothing could keep out a Belian. She didn't get much rest that night, plagued by vivid images of Doris's stiff, cold body and the sense of evil that had permeated her house. Those images led to Kara's firsthand memories of the terrors a Belian could unleash on an unsuspecting human population.

Whenever she tried to vanquish those visions, Damien's last words took their place: *"The safety of Zorro's residents could well depend on your willingness to have sex with me." The hell with that,* she thought, tossing and turning, while Alex slept soundly beside her.

And yet, she was hard-pressed to come up with a single, logical reason for refusing to enter into conduction-induced sex, except for the fact she had never been one to indulge in sex with no emotional attachments. There was certainly no emotional bond between her and Damien Morgan. Just her personal ghosts and the fact he was a trained assassin.

Her thoughts went in circles most of the interminable night, and during that time, she decided to do something she had sworn she'd never do. With the decision made, she finally drifted into an uneasy sleep, where she was plagued by nightmares of Richard and Doris being murdered, and ghosts chasing Alex.

When they got up the next morning, Alex was clingy and still upset by Doris's death, so Kara let him go to her office instead of school. She felt better having him close by, anyway. She drew comfort from his presence, especially when her first order of business was a phone call she dreaded making.

Alex spent most of the morning in her office, working on school assignments and playing games on her computer. Once she caught him researching ghosts on the Internet. She put an immediate stop to that, threatening to take away all computer privileges if he didn't stay within permitted boundaries. She was amazed a six-year-old even knew how to surf the Internet, but then Alex had never been an ordinary child, and he had been reading since he was four.

Around noon, she was finishing up with Tina Meyers's six-month immunizations, her ears ringing from the baby's screams of pain and outrage, when her nurse, Susan, cracked open the examining room door. "Dr. Kara, you have a phone call from Damien Morgan. Do you want to take it?"

"Yes, I do. Please have Bonnie tell him I'll be with him in a moment." She turned back to Amanda Meyers. "Be sure and give Tina some baby Tylenol when you get home. She'll probably be fussy for the rest of today. Take care, and call me if you have any questions."

She stepped out of the room, thinking her ears might never recover, but she preferred to give the babies their shots rather than letting Susan do it. She loved doctoring children, and had almost chosen pediatrics over family medicine for her specialty.

Entering her office, she glanced over to see that Alex was playing an approved computer game. "Hey sweetie. I need to take a phone call in here."

"Sure Mom." His attention never deviated from the screen.

Resting her hip on the side of the desk, she picked up the phone and pushed the line button. "Hello."

"Are you okay?"

Somehow, Damien's deep, rough voice was oddly comforting, made her feel less alone. "I'm all right," she replied. "What about you?"

"No closer to knowing anything than last night. Can you estimate how long it might be before the autopsy on Mrs. Burgess comes back?"

Just the mention of the autopsy put Kara's stomach into knots. The subject had come up earlier today when she called Doris's daughter to offer her condolences. Sharon Wills had been distraught with grief, made worse by the fact that she couldn't plan her mother's funeral until the body was released to the funeral home.

It had been an upsetting conversation, made worse by Kara's guilt from the knowledge that she'd been the one to insist on the autopsy. She sighed, forced her thoughts back to the present. "Unless they have a big backlog, the medical examiner's office should do the autopsy within two or three days. The report might take longer, maybe to the end of next week."

"It won't affect our search for the Belian; we already know Mrs. Burgess was murdered," Damien said. "But it might affect how the police deal with the situation. By the way, were you aware that Alex called me an hour ago?"

She glanced sharply at her son, but he was engrossed in the game. Turning away, she lowered her voice. "No, I wasn't. I don't even know how he got your phone number."

"He told me it was on your 'flippy thing.' "

"Oh . . . he must mean my Rolodex. Yes, I put it in there after the gho—after Wednesday afternoon."

"I see. Well, he's obviously very resourceful."

"You've got that right. What did he want?"

"Questions about ghosts. About whether or not Doris was in heaven, or if her spirit was still here, that kind of thing."

Kara rolled her eyes. "Great. What did you tell him?"

"That we would discuss it more tomorrow. How about I pick both of you up around two?"

"Pick us up? Why not at the house like before?"

"When I work with Alex on controlling his abilities, he might accidentally broadcast. I don't want to take a chance of attracting anything."

Ghost or Belian, she thought, suddenly chilled. Her middle-of-the-night decision firmed into a solid resolution. "All right," she said. "We'll see you at two."

"Bring jackets." He disconnected.

"Good-bye to you, too," she muttered, putting the receiver back into the cradle.

"Who was that, Mom?"

"Mr. Morgan." She faced her son. "Don't you think you should have asked me if you could call him?"

He fidgeted with the mouse. "Sorry. He told me to call him if I had any questions, and I found his number in your flippy thing."

She wanted to tell Alex that being so fearful about the ghost wouldn't help anything, but how could she tell her son not to be afraid when there was so much to fear? *So very much.* She tensed, thinking about her newest decision. "It's called a Rolodex. I don't mind you calling Mr. Morgan when you have questions, but from now on, please tell me first, okay?"

He nodded solemnly. "Okay."

She rose from the desk. "I have to run an errand. If you'll stay here with Bonnie and Susan—and keep off the Internet—I'll bring us back some lunch."

"Why can't I go with you?"

"Because I have some business I need to take care of. But I'll bring you a hamburger from the Busy Bee. How does that sound?"

He considered a moment. "With cheese fries?"

"All right."

"And a strawberry milkshake?"

"You're pushing your luck, buddy."

He grinned, and the world suddenly seemed a little brighter. "We can share it."

"You're taking advantage of the situation," she accused, reaching over to give him a quick hug. "But I'll do it, just this once."

She got her purse, spoke briefly with Bonnie and Susan, and left. Getting the food from the Busy Bee was the easiest part of her trip. It was the other item of business that weighed on her.

THE gun she purchased at Turner Sporting and Hunting was a Beretta semiautomatic, which could be fired repeatedly without having to reset it—or so Jerry Turner assured her. He also said the flat design was easier to conceal, and the .40 caliber had good stopping power. Kara held the gun, testing its grip, and a wave of memories rushed at her, taking her back to Birmingham, over seven years ago. She had learned how to use a gun when she and Richard were together, but at the time, she'd had no way of knowing what was going to happen. . . . No, she wouldn't go back down that path.

At least she knew she could handle the kick of the .40, once she was back in practice. And she intended to practice as soon as possible—tomorrow morning, before Damian picked them up. With so many hunting enthusiasts in central Texas, there were gun clubs and practice ranges in the general area.

It only took a few minutes for Jerry to run Kara's information through NICS, the federal program denying or approving gun sales; then the gun, along with ammunition and a packet of forms to apply for a permit to carry a concealed weapon, was hers, and she was out over six hundred dollars. The cost had surprised her, as had the ease with which she'd been able to obtain the weapon. And that's what it was—a weapon, at least against the human body inhabited by the Belian in Zorro.

She hated bringing a gun into the house, hated subjecting Alex to both the danger and the reality that they might need protection. But her determination to keep her son safe far outweighed her concerns over having a potentially deadly weapon in the house.

There would be a grim discussion on gun safety and strict rules against Alex even looking at the gun (which would also be placed where he couldn't readily access it). Kara could handle that part; it was explaining *why* they needed a gun that worried her most. As far as she knew, Alex had assumed that Doris had died in her sleep; but then, he was able to sense many things, so that was only an assumption.

Still, she had no intention of telling her son that she'd bought the gun because there was a murderer—and a supernatural being at that—in Zorro.

TEN

"MOM bought a gun yesterday!" were the first words out of Alex's mouth when Damien entered their house Saturday afternoon.

"I know." Damien slanted a glance at Kara, who glared at her son in exasperation.

"*You know?* How—no, wait." She turned to Alex. "Get your jacket, young man. Then go give Mac some fresh water." When he started to protest, she pointed toward the wall rack by the front door. *"Now!"*

"Fine." He stomped to the rack, pulled down his coat, and dragged it behind him as he moved toward the kitchen.

"Watch the attitude," Kara told him, "and pick up the pace. Stay outside with Mac until I call you." She waited until they heard the back door open and close, then shook her head. "He's such a—"

"Boy?" Damien provided. "He's just a kid. You getting a gun probably made a big impression on him."

"You could say that. He's been full of questions since I told him about it. So how did you know?"

"I heard it at Sal's yesterday. I usually shop there in the

afternoon, and just listen in and see if I can pick up information."

Kara eyed his large frame. Today he was wearing stonewashed Levis, a dark gray turtleneck sweater, and black, tooled-leather western boots. He'd traded in the duster for a tailored black leather jacket that looked killer on him. The man could definitely wear leather, and the dark colors suited him.

As always, the electricity hummed between them, stirring up physical urges. The firsthand knowledge of just how powerful that chemistry was hovered uncomfortably in the back of her mind. What did you say to a man who'd been inside your body figuratively, had been inside your most intimate thoughts and feelings; who'd felt your raging lust; and who would have been all too willing to screw your brains out—even if it was theoretically for an altruistic purpose?

It had been all right talking to him on the phone, but facing him in person after Thursday night's conduction was unnerving. She took a few safe steps to the fireplace, busied herself straightening the pictures on the mantel. "You're pretty noticeable," she said. "Don't you think lurking around Sal's might raise suspicions?"

He shrugged. "I'm a stranger in town and that automatically makes me a suspicious character. It's possible the Belian will home in on me because I'm new here, but that's a risk I'll have to take. Tell me about the gun."

She leaned her back against the mantel. "It's a Beretta, semiautomatic, .40 caliber."

"Nice weapon. But it might not offer much protection against a Belian."

"The Belian is in a human body, isn't it? At least the body can be killed, be it Belian or Sentinel," Kara said fiercely. "I can tell you that for a fact, from personal experience."

"I know that."

"You carry weapons. Don't tell me you don't," she challenged. Richard had always carried a gun and a knife, at the very least. He'd said that sometimes the only choice was to kill a Belian outright, without performing the expulsion.

"Yes, I carry weapons," Damien said. "But I'm prepared to use them. Are you?"

"I am." Her chest tightened. "It's not like I *want* to kill anyone. I'm a doctor, for God's sake! I'm sworn to save lives, not take them." *But sometimes, there was no choice.* She curled her fingers into fists. "No one is going to hurt my child. I'm not just going to sit here and hope nothing happens. If push comes to shove, I'll do whatever it takes to protect Alex."

"I'm not telling you not to protect yourself. Just be sure you can pull the trigger, and don't underestimate the Belian. Don't let the gun give you a false sense of security. Do you know how to handle it?"

Oh, yes. She managed a nod. "Richard insisted I get training in using a gun. After he . . . died . . . and I learned I was pregnant, I disposed of my gun before moving here. I was determined I'd never need it again, and that my child would never be exposed to that sort of violence." She managed to draw a breath into her constricted lungs. "Obviously, I was wrong."

His silver gaze was steady, disconcerting. "Kara, despite free will, we can't always control the paths our lives take. Some of that is pre-patterned before we're born."

She resented the implacable logic that seemed to be an innate Sentinel trait. "Yeah, well, I intend to control what I can." She walked around him to get her coat. "Where are we going?"

THEY went to Blanco State Park, on the southern edge of the town of Blanco. It was situated right along the Blanco River. Damien suggested they go where they could be near the water, but didn't want to risk working with Alex too close to the part of the river that edged Zorro.

Kara had always liked the small park, with its grassy

expanse that ran along the green water, and the assortment of mature trees—gnarled live oaks, bald cypresses, cottonwoods, to name a few.

When Damien mentioned the park, she'd had the foresight to pack a blanket and two thermoses—one with coffee and one with hot chocolate—before they left. And somehow, a soccer ball got thrown into his car, although no one would claim responsibility.

They arrived at the park and found it had a fair number of visitors. Even in March, people came to fish, and sat along the bank in canvas chairs, casting their lines; some even perched on the dams stretching across the narrow river to fish. A small gaggle of geese honked noisily and waddled around, looking for food, in the form of handouts from visitors.

Kara spread the blanket on a grassy, sunny spot on the riverbank, a discreet distance from the people who were fishing. The geese immediately headed their way, but a quick flick of Damien's hand sent them the other direction.

"Cool," Alex said, his eyes glowing.

"Nothing you need to be trying," Kara told him.

"Your mom's right." Damien settled on the blanket next to Alex. "If you try to do stuff like that, you might not stay shielded."

Grateful for his input, which she knew would hold more weight with Alex than her motherly nagging, Kara settled on the other side of her son. He had carried the soccer ball from the car, and it rested on the ground beside him.

A slight breeze amplified the coolness of the day. She poured herself a cup of coffee and wrapped her hands around the mug, savoring the warmth. Damien rested his right forearm on his upraised knee, leaning down to talk to Alex, who mimicked his position. The sunlight reflected off the glossy black of Damien's tied-back hair, and not for the first time, she wondered if he had Indian or Hispanic ancestors. His coloring created a stark contrast to Alex's much lighter brown hair and warm skin tones.

"Water can enhance conduction of energies," Damian

was explaining. "Are you allowed to have the radio or blow-dryer near the bathtub?"

"No way! Mom would split a seam."

"Why?"

"If the blow-dryer fell in the water, I could get 'lectrocuted."

"Do you know why?"

Alex considered a moment. "Somethin' about electricity."

"Exactly right," Damien said. "The water acts as a natural conductor for the electricity, which travels through it very quickly, and at a greater intensity. It works the same way with your powers."

"Does it work that way for you, too?" Alex asked, wide-eyed.

"Yes. As Sentinels, we are of the water. It grounds us, carries the essence of our heritage."

Kara gripped her mug more tightly, reminded herself to not interfere unless Damien went too far over the line.

"Maybe that's why I like to stay in the shower so long," Alex said. "I get all wrinkled, and Mom makes me get out."

"I'm sure that's part of it. So a good place to work on making stronger shields or controlling your powers is in the shower, or near water, like the river, which is why we're here today. But," Damian added, with a glance at Kara, "you never head off to the river or a pool without telling your mom first, right?"

"Right." Alex nodded his head vigorously. "She'd ground me for a month if I went anywhere without telling her or Luz."

"All right. Have you been working on centering yourself?"

Alex nodded again.

"Then let's start by centering ourselves." Damian placed his hand over the middle of his chest, curled his fingers slightly and took a deep breath. Kara felt a flare of energy.

Alex must have felt it, too, because he reached up and grasped Damien's hand. "What did you do? It feels different. Why is your hand like that?"

"It's an automatic reflex. I wear a crystal that helps me to center more quickly," Damien explained, patting his chest. "And it helps me use my powers."

"I can feel it." Alex looked up at him. "Can I see it?"

"In a moment." Damien closed his eyes, took another deep breath.

Kara felt the energy again, only this time it seemed to be flowing around them. She guessed he was expanding his own shield around all of them. Richard had always shielded her if she were nearby when he was working.

"Now then." Damien reached beneath the edge of his shirt, pulled out an exquisite yet sturdy silver chain. Dangling from it was a piece of pink-tinged quartz, framed in silver wire.

A jolt went through her. Richard had worn a similar stone, which had been attuned to the great Atlantian crystal buried in the Atlantic Ocean. He had also imbued it with his own energy, and it had been a personal touchstone, acting as an amplifier for his powers.

The trooper/Belian reached down and ripped the chain off Richard's lifeless body. With a triumphant roar, he held up the stone, blood dripping off it. "I am victorious! Praise be to Belial!" he shouted, grinning triumphantly.

Then he turned his malevolent gaze on Kara. "And the woman becomes mine." He stalked toward her, the necklace dangling from his fist, reflecting the flashing lights and the blood . . .

"Wow," Alex said in an awed voice. "Can I touch it?"

"Sure." Damien leaned farther down, offering the stone. "Hold it in your hand, if you want."

"Wow," Alex said again. "I can feel the energy. It's shaking in my hand." He looked up at Kara. "I can really feel it, Mom!"

"That's great," she said, taking a shaky breath.

"Do all Sentinels have these?" Alex asked Damien. "Can I have one?"

"Many Sentinels have them, but you need to wait until you're older, and see how your powers develop."

"Aw," Alex groaned.

"Also, you must never tell anyone about this crystal," Damien said. "Because then someone might figure out I'm a Sentinel, and remember, we've already agreed that should always be a secret."

"I remember." Alex looked at him solemnly. "Some people don't like Sentinels."

"They don't understand, and they're afraid. It is important to keep it secret," Damien replied. "Now, let's see how well you're shielding yourself."

Alex showed him how he'd been pretending to lock his special abilities in a box, and Damien seemed pleased with his progress. "Very good," he said, and Alex practically beamed. "Now, we need to work on 'listening' or 'feeling' without lowering your shields."

"Listening? That's about my ears."

"I'm talking about listening with your senses. When you feel energy, like you felt with my crystal."

Alex nodded. "Or like the really bad feeling I got at Mrs. Burgess's house."

"Yeah, like that. What do you think that was?"

"I don't know." Alex's forehead furrowed. "Maybe it was Mrs. Burgess's ghost. Or maybe it was from the bad person who hurt her."

So he did realize Doris might have been murdered. Kara shouldn't have been surprised, given how sensitive he was.

"Was Mrs. Burgess a nice lady?" Damien asked.

"Yeah. She was really cool, for an old person."

"Since her ghost is basically her soul, do you think it would be mean?"

Alex considered, shook his head in the negative.

"That means two things," Damien said. "The first is that if Mrs. Burgess's ghost does come to see you, you don't need to be afraid. And you could try to listen to her ghost, because it might be able to tell you something important. The second thing is that if you sensed something else, and if it felt bad, then it came from a bad person. You need to learn how to sense when someone or something is bad so that you can protect yourself. And you need to be able to do it without lowering your shields. Are you ready to work on that?"

"I don't know. Feeling bad things is kinda scary."

"It is," Damien agreed. "But it's something that Sentinels do, so they can help people. And you can learn to do it without getting hurt."

After more consideration, Alex finally agreed to let Damien show him how to listen with all his senses. Kara held her silence, although it was hard. She wanted to protest, to insist enough was enough, and to take her son home. But the safe world they'd known a week ago no longer existed, and she knew Alex had to be able to sense danger in order to run from it.

She had to admit Damien was good with her son. "You keep your shields up," he explained, "only you crack them just a little. Do you have screens on your windows?"

"Yes."

"Do you know what they're for?"

"Yeah, so we can open our windows to let the air in, but keep the bugs out."

"Exactly," Damien said. "You want to open your shields slightly, but keep up a screen, only it's not for bugs. It's to keep your energies in, and to filter out the energies you let inside. You have to be careful what you pick up. Let me show you what I mean."

They practiced the technique for another thirty minutes or so, and Kara didn't need any special senses to see that Alex's abilities were already quite pronounced. It was very unsettling, and she had to grudgingly concede—again—that Damien was right that it was safer for her son to learn shielding and control.

Damien called a halt when it became obvious that Alex was mentally tiring. But it took a lot more to spend the physical energy of a healthy young boy. Alex immediately snatched up the soccer ball.

"Let's play some soccer!" He pointed to a sizable tree about twenty yards away. "That can be the goal, but you hafta actually hit it with the ball. We can play one-on-one."

He went down on one knee, pulling his calf up behind him. "C'mon Mr. Morgan. You gotta stretch first."

The incredulous expression on Damien's face was priceless. Kara knew from firsthand experience that Sentinels did not play at anything. They were ultraserious, ultrafocused on the evil beings they pursued day in and day out. She had often suspected Richard had been born a miniature adult and had never experienced being a child.

Even Alex, without the traditional Sentinel upbringing, was often more serious than not, had always seemed older than his years. He did love soccer, though.

Alex extended his leg out behind him, doing a lunge stretch. "C'mon! Gotta warm up your muscles."

She should probably come to Damien's aid, but couldn't resist the opportunity for a little payback for the upheaval he'd brought into their lives.

"Yeah, Morgan," she said, rising, and grasping her right ankle behind her for a standing quadriceps stretch. "Come on. You should be able to hold your own against a little boy and a mere woman. Unless, of course, you're not up to the *challenge*." She gave him a feral grin as she changed ankles.

His eyes narrowed to silver slits. He came to his feet in a smooth, lithe movement and stepped into her personal space. "Oh, I'm *up* to any challenge," he said softly. "And I do know how to play the game."

Heat and awareness flooded her body, and her throat tightened. She should know better than to bait a Sentinel, especially one who was so synchronized with her conductor energies. Determined to hold her own, she let go of her ankle and angled her chin at him. "Good. Try to keep up, will you? Alex, give me that ball."

She snatched the ball from Alex and whirled, tossing it toward the goal-designated tree. She was after it in a flash. She'd done her own stint at soccer in her preteen years, and she often scrimmaged with Alex.

"Hey!" Alex shouted. "You're supposed to wait until the whistle blows."

"Don't have a whistle." Laughing, she glanced back

over her shoulder to see Alex barreling after her, his small legs pumping furiously. She'd run track in high school, so she had good speed and was well ahead. She looked past him just as Damien tossed his jacket onto the blanket and casually pushed up his sweater sleeves, as if the competition hadn't started.

Kara stopped and stared, telling herself she was just getting her breath and letting Alex catch up with her. Then Damien took off like a rocket, racing toward her with superhuman speed, determination hardening his face. A frisson of panic shot through her, followed by an adrenaline rush. She spun, kicked the ball ahead, and raced after it.

Alex was almost up with her, and still shouting. She slowed slightly to let him catch up, saw Damien was upon them, the heat of battle in his eyes.

Alex took advantage of her distraction to kick the ball toward the goal tree. Both Kara and Damien raced after it. She was in the lead, but he had Sentinel speed and no compunction about using it. Even so, she was determined he wouldn't get past her. As he came abreast of her, she deliberately careened into him, giving him a hard push for good measure. Caught off guard, he lost his balance and tumbled to the ground.

"Hey!" he shouted after her as she commandeered the ball and maneuvered it toward the tree. "That's a foul."

"And cheating," Alex added, running behind her.

She lined up the ball, took aim, and kicked. By sheer luck, it grazed the tree. "I've got a point, I've got a point!" she chanted, doing a little victory dance.

Standing, Damien brushed the leaves off his jeans. "That was a foul *and* cheating."

She put her hands on her hips, stared both males down. "Oh, poor babies. And who are you going to tell? The referee? The point stands."

Damien's eyes flashed. "Is that so?" He edged around her, toward the ball. "I'm going to win, even with you cheating."

"Really? And just what do you call that Robocop speed thing you do?"

"Natural ability." He made a dash for the ball, scooped it up on the run. "Alex, go out for a pass."

Giggling, Alex dashed away at a perpendicular angle and Damien heaved the ball about forty feet toward the tree line. Alex expertly took control with his feet and moved it back toward the goal.

"Damn Sentinel powers," Kara muttered, chasing after the men. "Hey, this is soccer, not football!" she yelled.

"Deal with it," Damien called over his shoulder.

"Yeah! Deal with it," Alex repeated, looking back and grinning from ear to ear.

Her son was having a blast, Kara realized. And he appeared totally at ease with Damien, who was far more intimidating than any of the other men in Alex's life. Yet Alex didn't appear at all intimidated, and she could only guess he felt more comfortable with his own kind. A disconcerting thought—that her son was a member of another race.

Refusing to dwell on those thoughts, she raced after the guys. Jumping back into the skirmish, she managed to "accidentally" trip Damien and send him sprawling again. She quickly learned the error of her ways when an invisible shove sent her flat on her butt a moment later. Sitting on the ground, she glared at Damien, who was a good fifteen feet away.

"Do you really want to talk about cheating?" she demanded.

He offered a feral grin similar to her earlier one. "No, I want to talk about winning."

Rediscovering the competitive spirit of her youth, she pushed off the ground and took off after the ball. They went at it hard, laughing and shouting, until she finally collapsed on the blanket. "No more," she said, gasping and still laughing at the same time.

Alex collapsed next to her, and flopped onto his back. "Hey Mom, you have leaves in your hair. You look really funny."

"Well so do you, kiddo. You have dirt on your face and

your hair is sticking straight up. Mr. Macho Robocop over there doesn't look much better."

"Ah, but I won." Damien strolled to the blanket and stood over them like a giant vulture. Grass stains covered his sweater and jeans.

"Yeah, right, you used brute force to make those last two points."

"A win is a win," he said smugly.

"Hey!" Alex bounced up like a jack-in-the-box. "I'm starving! Can we go get something to eat?"

"I don't know." Kara glanced at her watch. The daylight was already fading. "It's getting late, and Mr. Morgan probably has other plans."

"Mr. Morgan, don't you want to eat with us? Say yes!" Alex pleaded.

Damien hesitated, as if considering his options. "If your mother doesn't mind," he said finally, meeting Kara's gaze. "I'm pretty hungry myself."

"Well, then," she said, surprised. "I guess that settles it. Dinner at the Busy Bee?"

"I have another idea," Damien said. "How about the Gristmill in Gruene? I've never been there, but I've heard it's a great place to eat." He glanced at his own watch. "We should be there by six, before it gets really crowded."

"It's always crowded." Kara started gathering up the thermoses and mugs. Alex was on his knees, rocking up and down and giving her his *Please Mom, please!* expression. "But okay," she conceded. "They do have good food."

"Yes!" Alex crowed, leaping to his feet to do a victory dance. "The Gristmill! *Yes!*"

More surprises, Kara thought as the evening progressed. It had taken about thirty minutes to wind their way down 281 and 46 to Gruene, and then another twenty minutes just to find a parking space and navigate the people and cars to get to the Gristmill, right around six o'clock, just as Damien had predicted.

The restaurant was already packed, despite it being off-season for tourists, so they put their name on the waiting list and hit the bar before finding seats on benches in the outdoor courtyard. Damien had a draft beer, while Kara had a glass of red wine and allowed Alex a soft drink.

A two-piece band played guitar and banjo and sang country ballads, while the names of those whose tables were now available were scrawled on the huge blackboard and then erased with amazing speed. It was chilly, but fun, despite the oddity of being there with Damien, or with any man for that matter. They didn't talk much over the music, just listened and sipped their drinks.

After a twenty-five-minute wait, they were shown to a table that was fortunately inside rather than on one of the outside tiers. It was impossible to see the Guadalupe River running alongside the restaurant at night anyway, and it had gotten even colder. Kara watched in amazement as Damien consumed two more beers and chicken poblano quesadillas for an appetizer, a huge Gristburger smothered in queso sauce, and every one of the round-cut fries on his plate.

"Fast metabolism," he said when he caught her staring.

"I know." She picked at her grilled chicken salad, remembering Richard's incredible metabolic rate. "Disgusting."

"No, actually, it's a boon when the food is good. Anyone want dessert?"

Kara declined, but Alex was all for it. He and Damien agreed to split a chocolate supreme, but Damien ended up eating most of the fudge pie and Blue Bell ice cream (after Alex took care of the whipped cream and cherries). The man obviously had a sweet tooth and she sourly hoped he had lots of cavities—it was only fair—but she knew better.

Sentinels also had an amazing immune system and recuperating powers, and rarely suffered malaises regular humans did. Richard had never had a cavity in his life, and Damien would probably be the same. Alex was almost never sick, had never even had strep throat.

They left Gruene around eight, Kara pleasantly full and definitely starting to wilt, energy wise. She must have fallen asleep during the drive back to Zorro, because she came awake abruptly when Damien said her name.

She looked around, disoriented, and squinted against the interior car light. Damien was outside the car, leaning into the back to unfasten Alex's seat belt. Her son was sound asleep. "Where are we?" she asked, still groggy.

"Your house. Both of you slept most of the way."

"I'm sorry." She unfastened her seat belt, pushed out of the car on stiff legs. "That was rude of me."

"You needed the rest." He stood with Alex in his arms. "I'm guessing you haven't been sleeping very well."

"I guess you're right. Mac, hush!" she admonished the barking dog as she started toward the house, pulling her keys from her purse. "If you don't mind carrying Alex inside, you can just put him in bed. He probably won't wake up."

"I think we wore him out."

"Yes." *Wore me out, too,* she thought wearily.

She pulled back Alex's covers and Damien lowered him to the bed. She tugged off her son's jacket and shoes, covered him, and kissed him.

"I'd better go and let you get some rest. Tomorrow—" He let the word trail off, and Kara thought of what lay ahead. Today had simply been a temporary diversion from a vicious reality.

She followed him to the front door. "Thank you for being so patient with Alex, for taking the time to instruct him. Do you think he's catching on to shielding himself?"

"Yes. He's very smart, very intuitive." Damien's gaze locked with hers. "Kara, his abilities are developing at a rapid rate. There is nothing you can do to stop their natural progression."

Her chest tightened. "I know." Just as she knew she could no longer ignore Alex's powers or make them go away.

"He's a fast learner." A slight smile teased Damien's mouth. "But I think he liked the soccer game best."

"I have no doubt of it. He really misses having a regular male figure in his life. *However*, cheating to win a game is *not* setting a good example for him." She strove to keep her tone and gaze stern, but failed miserably.

"Really." Now Damien did smile. "I think striving to win is a worthy goal."

"Is that a male, or a Sentinel, viewpoint?"

"Both," he said, exuding dangerously charismatic masculinity.

She grasped the door handle, decided to change the subject. "Thank you for dinner. You didn't have to pay for ours."

"It was my pleasure. Good night, Kara." He turned and strode into the darkness.

She locked the door behind him, sank onto the sofa, and sat there a long time. She couldn't remember how long it had been since she'd had such an enjoyable day. Damien had been attentive, fun, even charming. It was unsettling, though, because Sentinels simply weren't social beings.

Richard had been very much the loner, although once he understood that social events and niceties were important to Kara, he'd made an effort to attend the occasional party, to take her out to eat, to remember holidays and special occasions. But it wasn't an intrinsic part of his nature and had required a deliberate effort on his part.

Yet Damien had seemed relaxed, had appeared to truly enjoy himself. While that should have put Kara more at ease, should have been reassuring, instead it was disconcerting. Because, she realized, it made Damien seem human. That was a very dangerous assumption to make.

She didn't want to be attracted to him, not as a conductor to a Sentinel, and certainly not as a woman to a man. But her innate honesty forced her to admit to herself that she *was* attracted to him; and worse, being around him seemed to be awakening a gaping loneliness within her.

For years, she had suppressed her personal needs in order to take care of Alex, and to build them a safe life. But now, she felt a longing for male companionship. For all the things a relationship entailed—adult conversation, holding hands, kissing and being held, sizzling sex, the daily ins and outs of sharing lives.

She missed the feel of a man's hands on her, of his physical possession of her body, missed the intimacy of bed talk and cuddling in the dark hours of the night. While she had convinced herself over the past seven years that her life with Alex was enough, now she found herself envying those couples who had normal, loving relationships.

But there was nothing *normal* about Damien, or about the situation that had brought him to Zorro. She must remember that. Her loneliness was causing her attraction to him—a futile and dangerous attraction, at that.

Besides, this wasn't about her, or her needs. It was about a monster without conscience, and the threat to Zorro—and her son. If the Belian Damien was tracking stayed true to form, there would be more murders.

Then she would have to decide how far she was willing to go to help Damien hunt down this monster . . .

And how much of herself she would sacrifice.

ELEVEN

DAMIEN did his daily meditation on Sunday morning. Then he worked out, using the free weights he always carried with him, and doing lengthy sets of abdominal crunches and push-ups. He also worked through several of his martial arts kata routines, repeating them until his moves and kicks were flawless.

After that, he ran five miles, most of it along River Road. He kept his senses tuned as he ran, but he didn't pick up anything, nor did he see the lightning-damaged tree that he'd envisioned during the conduction.

Returning to the bed-and-breakfast, he showered and spent the rest of the day researching all the murders in central Texas over the past year, and compiling a progress report for the Sanctioned. When he got to the part about Alex, he sat back, considering that aspect of this current assignment. He'd never before been appointed a mentor to a developing Sentinel; perhaps because most children who needed a mentor had lost their Sentinel parent.

Damien had not only lost his Sentinel mother, but his human father as well, in one vicious Belian act. Even now, he had to work to keep the pain buried, and maybe that's why the Sanctioned had never marked him for mentor duty.

He'd had no siblings, so he had little experience with kids. But damned if Alex wasn't getting to him. The boy was incredibly bright, with a mischievous grin that could probably melt the strongest Atlantian alloy.

Alex's powers were strong and true, like a pure, bright beacon against a murky Belian soul, assuming the foul beings even had souls. The Law of One said they did—that every being had a soul, every being had the spark of The One inside them, awaiting awakening and guidance. With Belians, that spark had become enshrouded in a darkness that was fed by violence and fear and chaos.

Nothing new there, Damien thought. But his growing fondness for the boy, and the previous day's events, were a unique experience. He, Damien, had actually played soccer yesterday. He couldn't remember playing any game since he'd been about ten, and certainly not with such abandon.

And Kara—well, there was another aberration. It was hard to tell for sure, because of the ever-present chemistry that hummed between them, but he felt a growing bond with her. She was a good mother—firm but loving, devoted to her son. She had spunk and personality, and a surprising sense of humor.

He wasn't used to laughing, but he found himself often doing just that when he was around her. He also found himself looking forward to seeing her, found himself waiting to hear the next quick-witted remark she uttered. That type of bond wasn't a good thing to allow, for myriad reasons.

At this point, there was nothing to be done but to keep his emotional distance as much as possible. He had to work closely with her; their Sentinel/conductor link was the most precise and most charged one he had ever experienced. He might never again find such a good match.

The Belian he was tracking was quite possibly the most powerful one he'd ever encountered. He could request another conductor be sent to Zorro, but he didn't believe the conduction results would be as productive as they would with Kara. So he would resist the human attraction, repressing the part of him that was simply a man.

He finished the report and e-mailed it. It might seem incongruous that a group of beings whose roots could be traced back over thousands of years so enthusiastically embraced the Internet age—except that before Atlantis was destroyed, its technology had far exceeded current Earth technology. *Coming back full circle,* Damien mused.

That done, he powered down his laptop and headed out to find something to eat, since he only got breakfast at the bed-and-breakfast. His room there was nice enough, with a real fireplace, a tall four-poster bed, and a huge claw-footed bathtub that also had a shower. Belle Williams served a great breakfast, and had quickly learned he ate a lot and increased his portions.

He walked down a curving staircase carpeted in a burgundy floral pattern, to a foyer that smelled faintly of beeswax and potpourri. The stately old mansion had once belonged to Samuel Williams, the founder of Zorro, and the great-great-grandfather of Belle's husband. She was just coming in from outside, juggling two Wal-Mart bags. "Here, let me help you with those." Damien commandeered the bags, and Belle gave him a small smile.

She was an attractive woman, although she'd passed middle age and was heading toward senior status. She had honey blonde hair, fixed in a midlength, full style that was probably the product of the local hair salon. Her eyes were an alert blue behind bifocal glasses; she was of average height, with a thickening waistline and extremely generous breasts.

Her one outstanding asset was her legs, which were shapely and surprisingly youthful. Today she wore a soft floral skirt, and stylish red pumps that showed off her legs.

"Where do you want these?" he asked, hefting up the bags.

"The kitchen," she said briskly. "I believe you know the way."

"Sure do. It's my favorite room in the house." He started through the antique-appointed dining room to the swinging door into the kitchen.

"That's because you like what comes out of it," she said, her footsteps echoing behind him. "I figured I'd better stock up on more food to keep you fed. And I have three new bookings next week, which is unusual for this time of year. Probably want to see if the fish are biting in the Blanco River." As they entered the big, gleaming kitchen, she pointed to the long, spotless tile counter. "Put the bags there."

Damien did, inhaling the pleasant scents of coffee, cinnamon, and the ham steak and eggs he'd enjoyed at breakfast. "Got anymore to bring in?"

"Yes, and I'd thank you to get them from the truck. I'm feeling a little under the weather." She began unloading the groceries. "The dear Lord willing, I'll be better soon."

He'd noticed she'd looked a little pale and tired the past few days, but had been too distracted to give it much thought. Now, however, his instincts kicked into full alert. "What's wrong?"

"Oh"—she paused, seemingly flustered, and then waved a hand in the air—"just a medical problem needing regular treatment."

While he didn't like badgering or embarrassing older ladies, he needed to know about any serious medical conditions among the residents of Zorro. A weakened body was the easiest point of entry for an incorporeal Belian soul. Since Belians worked only out of the four lower chakras, they didn't have the ability to heal the bodies they possessed.

Sometimes the original soul inhabiting the body remained, so the person retained their basic personality, with only blips of erratic behavior that might or might not be noticed.

Even if the original soul fled the onslaught of the dark Belian soul, Belians were crafty and very clever, often impersonating the human they took over with amazing accuracy. They could maintain normal behavior and mannerisms for long periods of time, while secretly wreaking havoc on innocent lives.

"Mrs. Williams, what is it you need treatment for?" Damien persisted.

"Well, it's a little personal."

"Is it cancer?" he asked quietly.

She looked annoyed. "Well yes, if you must know"—she hesitated, sighed—"breast cancer. They found it five months ago."

"I'm sorry to hear that. Are you undergoing treatment?"

"Yes. My doctor recommended chemotherapy. We did it for three months, then took a few weeks off. We started another round last week, and it's making me feel a little puny."

"I hope you have a full recovery," he said, eyeing her hair and thinking it could very well be a wig. His gaze wandered to her ample breasts and he wondered if one might be a prosthesis. He'd be researching breast cancer in the near future.

"Well." She nodded briskly. "Thank you. My daughter Nancy takes me to Austin for the treatments, and my doctors say the prognosis is pretty good."

"I hope they're right. Let me get the rest of your bags." Damien spent the next fifteen minutes helping Belle put away her purchases, then accepted her offer of a cup of coffee.

She'd been fairly reserved when he arrived ten days ago, but had warmed up to him, becoming more talkative. Now she piled some of her homemade oatmeal cookies on an exquisite china plate, poured them both coffee, and sat at the table with him.

"Did you know Doris Burgess?" he asked.

"Yes, I did. I've known her all my life. We saw each other at church most every week." Belle shook her head and stared at her coffee. "Such sad news, her passing. She seemed to be in good health."

"Did you know she had diabetes?"

"Sure did. Probably what killed her."

"Why do you say that?" Damien asked.

"Well, havin' diabetes and havin' to take insulin wears out a body. And Doris had been taking insulin awhile. At least ten, maybe twelve years." Belle considered. "I can't remember for sure."

So Doris's condition had apparently been common knowledge.

"My aunt Susan also had diabetes," Belle continued.

"Did she? What happened to her?"

"She died in her sleep when she was sixty-two. The doctors said her heart just stopped beating. Said sometimes when a person has diabetes, the body just gives out." She offered him the plate of cookies. "Have another one."

"Thank you." He took a cookie, considered the fact that Belle had so much knowledge about diabetes.

"How much longer will you be staying in Zorro?" she asked.

"A little while," he replied evasively. "I'm not sure yet. I'm still working on several articles for my magazine, and I need a quiet place to write. Your bed-and-breakfast suits my purposes very well."

"Seems to me you'd be wanting to investigate those murders in Fredericksburg. Nothing to write about in Zorro."

"I don't know. I've learned that wherever there are people, there's usually crime. Can you tell me anything about past crimes in this area? Any murders? Suspicious deaths?"

She chuckled. "Not really. But we do have some colorful folks around here."

"Tell me about them," he invited, and they chatted as they drank a second cup of coffee, and he devoured the rest of the cookies.

Belle was a great source of information about the citizens of Zorro, and he made several mental notes on people he wanted to investigate more closely.

"Thanks for the coffee and the cookies, which were

great," he said thirty minutes later, taking his cup to the sink and rinsing it out. "Any ideas on where I should go for dinner?"

"You just ate an entire plateful of cookies!"

"That's just not enough for a growing boy like me." Damien patted his flat midriff. "I need some meat and potatoes."

"You and that appetite of yours. I don't know how you stay in shape." Belle stared at him thoughtfully, and he hoped his eating habits hadn't exposed him. "Well, if you want something besides the Busy Bee, which closes at eight on Sundays anyway, you can head up 165. The Country Kitchen has good food and stays open until nine, every day of the week."

"Thanks. I'll head out now. You have a good evening." Damien went back upstairs to get his duster and left the house.

He drove north on 165 and found the Country Kitchen. He had some great chicken-fried steak with mounds of mashed potatoes and gravy, and flaky biscuits dripping in butter, then some excellent homemade apple pie, which he ordered with Blue Bell ice cream. The ice cream reminded him of the night before, sharing the dessert with Alex.

Thinking back, he couldn't remember when he'd last shared a meal with anyone other than another Sentinel. Belle chatted with him a few minutes at breakfast every morning, but then left him alone with his food and a newspaper. Their visit in her kitchen today had been unusual, but fairly brief and impersonal.

Last night, however, he'd actually spent a social evening with someone, had laughed out loud and acted like a regular human being. Maybe that was part of the attraction he felt toward Kara and Alex; it appealed to the human side of him. But it was ill-advised, and he couldn't allow it to become a habit.

He got back to Zorro around ten and decided he'd have a beer at Jim's Tavern. It was another good place to hang out and possibly hear some useful information. Besides, he needed some time to digest all the food he'd eaten. The bar was relatively busy for a Sunday night, with about ten cars in the gravel parking lot behind the building.

Damien parked and got out of his car. He saw a man and a woman standing beside an oversize, king-cab pickup truck, but it looked like they were just talking, and he didn't give them much thought.

He was headed around to the front when he heard the woman's voice hitch up. The tone alerted him, and he turned back. With a Belian loose in Zorro, he had to be aware of any possibility. His superhuman hearing made it easy enough for him to eavesdrop.

"Matt, you're too drunk to drive," the woman said. The voice was familiar—he'd heard it before. She had her back to him, so he couldn't see her clearly.

"Let go of me," the man said, his words slurring. He shook the woman's hand off his arm. "I didn't ask for your company tonight."

"What's wrong with me joining you for a drink? I shouldn't have to wait for an invitation from you."

A faint accent, a slightly husky voice . . . Luz. It was the *curandera* who worked for Kara.

"And a man shouldn't be bothered when he just wants to have a drink with the guys." The man grabbed the door handle, tugged on it, but it didn't open. "Son of a bitch!"

"It's locked," she said. "Let me drive you home."

"Leave me alone!"

"Give me the keys, Matt." She reached for his pocket.

"Fuck you!" He shoved her, and she staggered back. Damien started toward them.

"How dare you talk to me like that?" she hissed. "*¡Cabrón!*"

She lunged at him, and he slapped her hard, the sharp sound of the physical contact carrying across the night air. The white haze descended around Damien, throwing him into Sentinel fight/protect mode. Power, and the instinctual need to protect this female human, roared through him.

Luz let out a screech and drew back her fisted hand. Damien was already there. He stepped between her and the man who'd hit her. He backhanded Matt, sent the man flying against the truck. Matt slid down to the ground in a crumpled heap. Reaching for control, Damien called upon the Light to sweep the haze away, to focus on his vows that he wouldn't harm innocents. Although he didn't know how innocent a man who would hit a woman could be.

"*Jesús.*" Luz knelt by Matt, ran her hands over him. "He's never acted this way before, even drunk. It's like he's possessed." She made the sign of the cross over her chest.

Matt groaned, looked toward Damien, his eyes unfocused.

"You have no business striking a woman," Damien growled. "You want to pick a fight, you do it with someone your own size. And next time, I won't be so gentle." He turned his attention to Luz. "Are you all right?"

"*Soy bien.*" She shoved her hand into Matt's coat pocket, pulled out a set of keys. Rising, she faced Damien, her attitude anything but grateful. "You didn't need to interfere. I can take care of myself."

She glanced down at Matt, her expression hardening, her eyes glittering fiercely in the moonlight. "He will be sorry he treated me this way, *el pendejo*." Pivoting, she threw the keys out into the field behind the parking lot. "I don't want him to kill himself or anyone else trying to get home tonight. I want him alive so I can make him pay."

She straightened her red coat, bent to retrieve her purse off the ground. Without another word, she stalked to a white Ford pickup truck, got in, and drove away.

Damien stared after her, sensing barely restrained fury and other emotions that had nothing to do with healing. He also felt a flare of power. He considered her words about Matt acting possessed. Interesting.

He pulled out a small notebook, wrote down the make, model, and license tag of Luz's truck, and then did the same for Matt's vehicle. He watched impassively while Matt struggled unsteadily to his feet. Satisfied that, for now, the man was no danger to anyone but perhaps himself, Damien headed for the bar entrance.

He'd have that beer, and maybe pick up some new tidbits of information, but he had already learned a lot today—and tonight.

ALEX didn't mind going to school, and he usually liked Mondays, because he had his two favorite subjects, math and art, on Monday. But he was having trouble focusing today. He kept thinking about stuff—the ghost on Wednesday, then going into Mrs. Burgess's house and that awful feeling inside it. Then there was all that neat stuff Mr. Morgan was showing him.

He'd been thinking so much about the ghost and Mr. Morgan, when he should have been doing math, that Mrs. Miller had given him a demerit, so now he had to sit out two recess periods. He was glad when the final bell rang.

As he gathered up his things, he did his shielding, pleased he didn't even have to close his eyes to "see" the box. It was getting easier, and made him feel a little bit safer. He walked over to Michael Thornton's desk. "Hey Michael! Wanna walk out with me?"

Michael was stuffing wadded papers into his backpack. He was a little older than Alex—he'd already turned seven—but he was small for his age, and even skinnier than Alex. He looked up and smiled shyly, his shaggy blond hair almost covering his eyes. "Sure. I just gotta get my books."

He was Alex's best friend, and they played soccer together and sometimes shared secrets—although Alex hadn't told anyone about his powers—not even about the ghost. He knew his mom and Mr. Morgan would split a seam if he did. Besides, Michael had lost his dad earlier that year, and Alex figured ghost stuff might upset him.

"Hurry up, Mikey," he said. "I don't want to miss the bus."

"I'm ready." Michael grabbed his jacket, dragged his backpack off his desk. The two boys lugged their things out into the hallway.

"I've been practicing soccer in my backyard. My mom got me one of those special nets," Alex said as he followed his friend through the main entrance to the covered area where the bus waited. "Hey, maybe you can come over one day after school this week, and we can practice together."

"Maybe," Michael replied, but he didn't look too hopeful. "It depends on my mom. She's been kinda sick since—" He stopped, looking stricken.

Alex felt a flare of sadness, and suddenly realized he was sensing his friend's emotions. Way cool. Maybe he could pick up more from Michael. Concentrating, he thought of a pretend screen, like Mr. Morgan had told him. He imagined a window lowering—just a little bit—and stuff coming inside, so he could "listen."

He felt it then, something bad. Something *really* bad. It was dark and scary and made him feel sick, like he'd felt at Mrs. Burgess's house. He froze, fear racing through him. What should he do? What would Mr. Morgan want him to do? He thought hard, remembering that Mr. Morgan said Sentinels had to listen.

Trembling, Alex knew he had to try, 'cause he was a Sentinel. Very carefully, he lowered his guards and tried to listen.

"Hey Alex! What are you staring at?" Michael's voice distracted him. "My mom's here. I gotta go."

"Okay. Bye." Alex looked around, trying to see if there were any strangers or people who looked bad hanging around. He didn't see any odd people, so he tried to listen again. It hit him—a feeling so scary, he dropped his backpack, and his books spilled out. Panicking, he stooped and frantically tried to cram his things back in.

He had the sudden sense of something dark coming closer. Looking for something, looking for . . . *him*. Scrambling to his feet, he glanced around, but everything seemed like a crazy blur.

The darkness moved toward him. He was terrified. He wanted his mom. He wanted Mr. Morgan.

It was coming after him. And he didn't know what to do.

TWELVE

KARA left examining room two and went to the sink in the lab area to wash her hands before going to the next patient. She felt a little more rested today. Damien hadn't called yesterday, and she and Alex had spent a quiet Sunday, going to church in the morning, working in the yard through the afternoon. They spent a nice evening watching *The Incredibles*, which he loved. Something about the superpowers the family members possessed really appealed to him, and perhaps now he even identified with them.

She wished Alex wasn't so enamored of being a Sentinel. Yet, she had to wonder if his fascination with his powers and with Damien was instinctual, like birds migrating hundreds of miles to an invisible lure. Two things Damien had said ran through her mind: *Some of that is prepatterned before we're born. . . . Alex chose this. His soul had free will, and came into this Earth plane, choosing the path of a Sentinel.*

"Dr. Kara, you have a phone call," Bonnie called out from the reception area. "It's Luz, and she says it's urgent."

Trepidation shot through Kara. She tried to repress her

alarm as she strode toward her office. But the word *urgent* filled her with foreboding. That and the fact she knew full well what a Belian was capable of. She closed her office door, picked up the receiver, and engaged the line. "What is it, Luz?"

"It's Alex." Panic laced Luz's husky voice. "He is missing. I can't find him anywhere."

"What?" Kara braced herself against the desk, a burst of fear jolting her heart. "What do you mean, you can't find him?"

"I decided to pick him up at school today, so we could run some errands. But when I got to the school, he was not there."

"The bus. He must have taken the bus."

"No, he didn't. I thought the same, so I followed the bus most of the route. He didn't get off at the house, and I flagged the bus at the next stop. Alex wasn't on it, and Mr. Meyers said he hadn't seen him. I thought maybe he'd gotten a ride and I went back to the house, but he is not here."

Suddenly unable to breathe, Kara pushed away from the desk. "Maybe he went home with—"

"No!" Luz's voice rose. "I called everyone I could think of—the Roberts, the Kirklands, the Libbys, the—"

"The Thorntons. Michael's his best friend." Kara's voice shook. "Did you call them?"

"*Sí.* Michael said Alex walked out with him, and headed toward the bus. Michael said he didn't see Alex after that, because he got in his mother's car and they drove off."

"There's got to be an explanation. Maybe he went home with someone else." Kara pressed a hand against her mouth.

"I don't know who." Luz let out a little sob. "All I know is my little man is missing, and I don't know what to do."

Blood was everywhere, almost iridescent in the flashing lights. Richard's body lay in a pool of it, broken and bent like a rag doll carelessly thrown aside. The Belian stalked toward Kara, its soulless eyes radiating a malevolent darkness. She stepped back, slipping in blood and almost falling. In a moment, he would reach her, and it would be over . . .

Alex! Thoughts of her son snapped her back. Surely the Belian hadn't found him. *Oh please, God, no!*

"Kara, are you there? What should I do?"

She battled back rising hysteria. Losing it now wouldn't help Alex. She had to think. *Damien.* She had to find Damien. "Call 9-1-1 and tell them Alex is missing," she told Luz. "I'll meet you at the house as soon as I can get there."

She clicked off and stared dumbly at the phone, the blood roaring in her ears. Her chest was so tight, she couldn't breathe. For a moment she thought she might black out. But her son needed her. She threw down the receiver and ran around the desk to retrieve her purse. Her hands shaking, she dug out her cell phone, punched the directory pad, and scrolled through the numbers. Where was it? There! *Damien M.* Thank God he had put in his number, because she wasn't sure she could find his card right now, much less dial the number.

She hit Send and listened to the rings, rocking back and forth, terror rolling through her in sickening waves. Alex, her baby, her child, her life. He was all right. *He had to be.*

"Morgan."

"Alex is missing. Damien, he's *gone*!"

"Tell me what happened." As always, he sounded calm, while her world had just tilted off its axis.

"He wasn't at school when Luz went to pick him up, and the bus driver said he never got on the bus."

"Have you checked with his friends? Maybe he's with one of them. Or maybe he found another way home."

"No, he didn't. He's not at the house, and Luz called his friends. No one has seen him."

"So he's missing from school."

"What does it matter? He's gone! My son is gone!" Her voice broke, and she forced a ragged breath.

"Kara, you have to stay calm, and help me figure this out. I need to know where Alex was when he disappeared."

Adrenaline and fear had her both jittery and sluggish, making it hard to think. "He was—he must have been at school. I dropped him off this morning."

"Call the school and confirm whether or not he was there all day. Then call me back."

"I think he was . . ." A memory nagged at the edge of her mind, and then she remembered what Luz had said. "Oh, wait, I know he was. Michael Thornton told Luz that Alex walked out with him after school and went toward the bus."

"That's what I needed to know. I'm headed to the school now."

"I'll meet you there."

"No. Your emotional state will affect my tracking. Contact the police and make sure they issue an Amber Alert."

Tracking? An Amber Alert? The reality of the situation lanced through her like a spear. Thoughts of child predators—and worse—ran through her head. Alex knew better than to go anywhere with a stranger but if it was someone he knew . . . "Do you think the Belian—"

"I don't know what to think yet. Let me do my job, Kara. Call the police, then go to the house."

"But—"

"Just do it. That's the best way to help Alex."

He disconnected with his usual abruptness. Anger flared through her, but she welcomed it, preferring it over the debilitating fear. She knew Damien was her best hope for finding her son. And his plan—as terrifying as the implications were—was sound. She fumbled in her desk for her Rolodex, picked up her phone, and called the police station.

DAMIEN parked in front of the school and turned off the car. He placed his hand over the quartz crystal resting beneath his shirt and centered himself, initiated the flow of power through his chakras. As he got out, he let his senses flare. Immediately, he hit a wall of darkness and depravity that signaled Belian energy. *Damn!*

For a moment, fear and concern for Alex gripped him. He was beginning to bond with the boy, to feel affection toward him. The thought of the child in the hands of the Belian sent rage and other, unfamiliar emotions through him.

Stop it, he told himself. He could not afford to form emotional attachments to the boy, or to let his feelings affect his judgment. Emotions could get him killed, and wouldn't save Alex. He must remain calm, objective.

He flared his senses again, saw the choppy, murky images created by a shielded Belian. He saw the psychic replay of the children coming out of the school, obviously leaving for the day, as they had jackets and backpacks and books, the bus and waiting cars edging the peripheral.

The vision jolted, moving across the kids, as if searching; the Belian must have been looking for someone. The focus appeared to be on the children rather than the adults who were present, raising the concern that the Belian had indeed picked up Alex broadcasting. But did it know Alex was the broadcaster?

The visual scan continued, and Alex walked out of the school, beside a pale, blond-haired boy. The scan swept past Alex, slowed, and started back in his direction. But before it came back to him, the vision blurred, faded to gray. Something must have caught the Belian's attention, broken its concentration.

Damien tried to pick up the ethereal trail again, but hit a psychic blockade—another indicator of the power and cleverness of this Belian. There was no way to tell if it had fixated on Alex or not, and what had happened after that. *God damn it!*

Senses fully alert, Damien walked along the sidewalk to where the children had been getting on the bus or in cars. Then he walked to the other end of the loading area. No other vibrations or twinges. Frustrated, he turned and started back. Outside of the initial psychic trace from the Belian, there was nothing. It was as if he were operating in a void.

A very slight wisp of energy brushed his mind; a faint stirring of something—or someone. He reached out mentally, carefully, broadcasting only through the higher chakras. *"Alex? Can you hear me? If you can, try to send me an answer, like a thought, but keep your shields up."*

He waited, got nothing. He tried again. *"Alex? Where are you?"*

The dead silence felt like a weight dragging him down. He had absolutely no idea where to look next, except to drive along River Road and hope he saw the misshapen oak tree he'd seen during the conduction—and what were the odds of that? His failure to keep the boy safe burned in his gut as he turned toward his car.

He felt it then, another faint whisper of energy. He froze, waited. There it was again—so soft and distant, he wasn't sure what it was. *"Alex? Is that you?"*

"Help . . . me . . ."

Damien turned full circle, scanning the entire area. *"Where are you?"*

Despite his intense concentration, he couldn't pick up the thought form again. Its weakness, and the fact the sender hadn't been able to sustain it, convinced him it must have been from Alex, who didn't yet have the power or the skill to project clearly. But where was he?

Damien closed his eyes, used his third eye to search for more energy trails. There! Fading swirls of brown, orange, and blue—the murky brown indicative of a lack of focusing skill, and the orange indicating agitation. The blue told him it wasn't Belian energy—he'd have seen black instead. The swirls appeared to be coming from the main doors of the school. He pivoted sharply and strode toward the entrance. There, the energy felt more pronounced. *"Are you inside the school?"*

He felt a small energy surge and took that as a yes. Now it became a question of where in the school. And was the Belian with Alex? Damien tried the glass door, found it locked. He focused his mental will, felt the bolt on the other side turning. Then he pulled open the door and went in. *"Alex, talk to me. Tell me where you are."*

"Dark . . . Afraid . . ."

Damien strode to the corridor on the right and turned down it. He followed the energy trail, feeling it grow stronger. Up ahead, a wizened man in a rumpled khaki uniform and scuffed work boots was mopping the tile floor. When he saw Damien, his head snapped up in surprise. Before he could react, Damien silenced him with a forceful mental push. Knowing the man's mind would be temporarily blanked, he moved past.

He slowed, however, as he approached a closed door. The energy seemed strongest there. Damien studied the door. It didn't have a window in it, and it didn't appear to be a classroom. Some sort of storage, maybe. And *something* was on the other side.

Damien grasped his crystal and called upon the forces of earth and water to give him strength and focus. Then he pulled his gun from the shoulder holster he'd strapped on after Kara called him.

Grasping the door handle, he turned it and pulled the door open.

KARA watched Luz's white pickup truck drive away and battled the all-out panic attack that lurked inside her. Officer Ben Rains had left ten minutes ago, after taking her statement and telling her he'd check into activating the Amber Alert. This was the first child disappearance for Zorro, and they had no firsthand experience with this.

Then Luz, who had been monitoring the progression of the labor of one of her patients via cell phone, told Kara she couldn't stay any longer. "I must go now, *mi camadre,* or Estella's *bebé* will birth itself. I am so sorry. I do not want to leave, especially with no word on my little man." Tears glistened in her eyes as she picked up her coat and purse. "But I am *una curandera,* and I must honor my obligations. Another *chiquito* needs me also. Promise you will call as soon as you hear anything."

Kara nodded. "Yes. Yes, I will"—her voice broke, and she turned away—"I-I'll let you know when I hear."

"I will pray that *los espíritus buenos,* good spirits, will watch over our little man, bring him back to us," Luz said softly, and then left.

There was nothing for Kara to do but pace back and forth, praying to God to bring her son safely home. An awful, incessant pit of fear spread through her until she could barely breathe. Horrific scenarios kept flashing through her mind, and she couldn't turn them off.

She felt the frantic need to do something, and several times started to reach for her car keys, determined to go to the school. But each time, she thought of Damien's words and stopped. She knew she couldn't control her emotions right now, and she also knew he had the best chance of tracking Alex. She couldn't do anything to endanger his chances.

She felt as though she was going insane as each interminable minute crawled by. She thought of calling Chief Greer, but had already spoken with him twice, and once with Officer Rains.

She desperately wanted to talk to her mother and stepfather, but didn't want to alarm them. Besides, they didn't know the truth about Richard, or the secret life Kara had led in Birmingham for two years. She didn't have any close friends, having left her old life behind when she fled to Zorro seven years ago. One person she might have told, Doris, was dead.

Feeling sick and dazed, Kara continued to pace and pray. Time blurred, so she wasn't sure how long she'd paced when her cell phone rang. Her heart leaped, and she snatched it up. "Yes?"

"I have Alex," came Damien's deep voice. "He's fine."

"Thank God." She sagged against the table, weak with relief, but then doubt dug in its talons. "Are you sure Alex is okay? You're not just saying that?"

"He's fine, Kara. I promise."

She let out the breath she'd been holding. "Where was he?"

"Let me get him home, and then we'll figure everything out. In the meantime, you'd better contact the police."

"Yes, yes I will." *Alex was all right!* She could leap tall buildings, could handle anything, even dealing with Chief Greer. "What should I tell them?"

"That Alex missed the bus and decided to walk home, and got sidetracked."

"Is that what really happened?" she asked incredulously. Alex had never missed the bus, and would have gone right back into the school office if he had.

"No. But you have to tell them something that sounds plausible, so it doesn't raise anyone's suspicions. Just so you know, Alex didn't do anything he shouldn't have. It's not his fault he missed the bus and didn't come home."

That couldn't be good, but she was too frazzled to consider the implications right now. "All right," she said. "I'll call Chief Greer."

"We'll be there in ten minutes."

She put down the phone and sank into a chair, her heart pounding from both the stress and sheer joy. But another part of her knew this wasn't a random event, that it was somehow tied to the Belian.

Bringing them one step closer to the edge . . . and the darkness.

KARA was watching anxiously out the window when she saw the flash of headlights turning into the driveway. She was instantly through the door and running toward Damien's car. She had the passenger door open before he even had the car in park, unsnapping Alex's seat belt and sweeping him into her arms.

"My baby!" she cried, holding him tightly. "Thank God you're safe! I was so worried."

"Mom!" He held on to her, wrapping his legs around her waist and pressing his head against her shoulder. "Someone was after me. It was awful."

"You're safe now." She stroked his hair with a trembling hand. "I'm not going to let anyone get close to you."

She carried her son inside, but couldn't bear to let him go, so she sank onto the couch and continued to hold him. She inhaled a deep breath of little boy and tears filled her eyes.

Damien's hand came down on her shoulder. "Easy now. Alex is very shaken up, and he's affected by your feelings."

She nodded, getting his clear message. She needed to be calm, for Alex's sake. Dabbing at her eyes with one hand, she looked up at Damien. "Thank you," she whispered. "Thank you for my son."

His expression unreadable, he stepped back. "He's all right, but he's cold and in shock. A hot bath and some food will help. I'm going back to the school."

"No!" Alex squirmed away from Kara and lunged for Damien, grabbing his duster. "Don't leave! Please!" He stared up at Damien, his face even whiter. "I don't want you to leave."

Damien's harsh expression softened, and he squatted down so that he was eye level with Alex. "I won't be gone for long. You won't be alone tonight."

"But what if that person comes looking for me again?"

"It's not a real person, Alex. It's a Belian that looks like a person. Your mother will be here with you until I return, and then we'll discuss what happened today. You'll tell us what you can remember, and we'll decide what to do. All right?"

Alex nodded, his eyes haunted.

"Don't talk about it yet," Damien repeated as he stood. "Give it time to settle, to let your mind be thinking about what happened. Take a bath and get warm, eat some dinner. When I get back, you can tell us everything. Kara, a word with you."

She rose from the couch, touching her son lovingly as she walked past him. Damien turned his back to Alex and spoke in a low voice. "Where's your gun?"

"In the nightstand by my bed, first drawer. The magazine is in the second drawer." She hated having them that reachable, but knew the gun offered no protection if she didn't have ready access to it. Fortunately, Alex didn't know how to load the magazine or chamber a cartridge. Plus she'd threatened him within an inch of his life if he even looked at the gun, and made her bedroom off-limits unless she was there.

Damien strode into her room, and returned a moment later with the gun and the loaded magazine. He slid the magazine into the pistol, racked the slide, and gave the firearm to her. "Keep this with you until I get back. And don't hesitate to use it if you feel threatened in any way."

The gun felt cold and lethal in her hand. She glanced toward Alex, saw his wide-eyed gaze fixed on the weapon. Swallowing hard, she nodded. Alex's safety took precedence over his childhood innocence being irrevocably shattered.

ALEX was in his Batman pajamas and eating dinner when Damien returned, with a wheeled suitcase and a briefcase in tow. "I'll be staying here for a while," he told Kara, and Alex perked up at that, his relief evident. Damien set his things in the dining room, then joined Alex at the kitchen table. "How's it going?"

"Fine, I guess." Alex played with the macaroni and cheese Kara had fixed for him. His other hand patted Mac, who sat hopefully by his chair, on the lookout for falling food. Normally Mac wasn't allowed in the kitchen during meals, but she had made an exception tonight.

Damien studied the boy. "Why don't you finish your dinner, then we'll talk."

Alex shoved his plate away. "I'm not really hungry."

Easing into a chair, Kara watched him, concerned. He

was still pale, with dark smudges beneath his eyes. He'd been quiet since he'd gotten home, going through his bath and dinner with a frightening lethargy.

"Then let's talk about today," Damien said. "Tell me what happened first."

"It was time to go home, and I walked outside with Mikey."

Damien's ebony eyebrows rose. "Mikey?"

"Yeah. His real name is Michael Thornton, but I call him Mikey. Only his best friends are allowed to call him that." Alex paused a moment, then offered, "His dad died last month."

"I'm sorry to hear that. So you walked outside with Mikey. What happened then?"

Alex picked at his napkin. "He saw his mom's car, so he went over there. I started to get on the bus." His fingers clenched the napkin. "But I felt somethin' funny."

"You felt something?"

"Well . . . Mikey and I were talking about his dad, and I felt his sadness." Alex twisted and untwisted the napkin. "I thought maybe I could feel some other stuff, so I 'listened,' like you showed me." He looked up at Damien, his small face pinched with remorse. "I kept my shields up, I promise! I just kinda imagined a screen, like on the window—just like you showed me—and lowered the shields just a little, so I could 'listen.' "

Damien placed his hand on Alex's arm. "It's all right, son. It's good you kept your shields up. What did you feel?"

Alex squared his shoulders. "It felt real bad, kinda like when we went in Mrs. Burgess's house."

A chill swept through Kara, and she clenched her hands in her lap.

"Okay." Damien's voice was pitched low and soothing. "Did you sense anything else?"

Alex nodded. "Yeah. It felt dark—like I could almost see black. It was really scary. I dropped my backpack and my books fell out. I tried to stuff 'em back in." His lips trembled and he looked at Kara. "I left my backpack, Mom. I guess it's lost. I'm sorry."

She forced air into her lungs, managed a weak smile for her son. "It's okay, sweetie. I'm not worried about the backpack. It's probably in the school's lost and found anyway."

"What else did you see or feel?" Damien asked.

Alex looked back at him, his eyes wide and dark. "Something was coming closer, and it was looking for someone. I looked around, trying to see it, but I only saw regular people."

Kara knew one of those "regular people" might have been the Belian, and terror shot through her like an insidious infection. She leaned forward, stroked her son's hair. "What grown-ups did you see there today?"

"Mr. Martin, Mrs. Roberts, Mikey's mom, Mrs. Williams . . . Principal Anderson . . . that's all I can remember."

"Mrs. Williams? Belle Williams?" Damien asked.

"Yes," Kara answered for Alex. "Belle has a granddaughter she often picks up after school. Sal Martin has two grandchildren, so he's frequently at the school as well." She thought a moment. "And Luz was probably there, because she told me she decided to pick up Alex today."

"I didn't see her," Alex said.

"All right, we know some of the people who where there," Damien said. "What happened next?"

"I could feel the bad thing getting closer, like it was coming after me. I got really scared." Alex's voice quivered. "I didn't know what to do. So I ran back into the school, and I hid in the closet by Mrs. Randolph's room."

"That was a very smart thing to do," Kara told him, grateful he'd had the presence of mind to hide.

"It was very smart," Damien agreed. "Did you feel anything else after that?"

"No . . . the bad darkness kinda faded away, but then I was in the closet darkness, 'cept it didn't feel as scary."

Alex looked from Damien to Kara. "But I didn't know what to do after that. I was afraid to come out, in case the badness came back."

"You did the right thing. Always stay where you're safe until you're absolutely certain it's all right to come back out," Damien reassured him.

Alex nodded, obviously still replaying the day. "I stayed in there a long time, and then I heard your voice in my head, Mr. Morgan." Awe replaced the fear in his eyes. "It was way cool! How did you do that?"

"You can 'talk' the same way you 'listen' with your senses. But that's another lesson. Besides, you answered me, at least enough that I could figure out where you were." Damien ruffled the boy's hair. "You did good. And you're safe now."

Still radiating tension, Alex didn't seem convinced. "But what about tomorrow?" he asked. "What if that person or bad thing comes back tomorrow?"

"We're going to come up with a plan to prevent that," Damien told him. "Your mom and I are going to figure out a way to keep you safe. We're not going to let anything happen to you."

Alex visibly relaxed. "Will I still get to play soccer?"

Kara's heart went out to him. He was just a boy, and it was patently unfair that his life had been disrupted, tainted by evil. He deserved a normal life, damn it!

"Of course you'll play soccer," she said, determined he would continue to have a regular childhood, even if she had to subject herself to a hundred conductions to make it so. But her first priority right now was his safety. "We just have to find the person who's doing all this bad stuff and send them away."

Alex considered that. "Like to jail?"

Kara looked at Damien, noted the hard set of his jaw and the steel determination in his eyes. "Something like that," she said. *Or something much worse, akin to a super-hell.* She certainly wouldn't want to be on the receiving end of a Sentinel's dispensation of Atlantian justice.

Damien pushed his chair back and stood. "I need to talk to your mother now," he told Alex.

The fearful expression returned to Alex's face. "Are you going to talk on the porch again?" It was obvious he didn't want to be left alone, even with the close proximity of the porch.

Damien glanced at Kara. "No, I think we can talk in the front room. You can stay right here in the kitchen with Mac, if you want."

"And you can rinse the dishes and put them in the dishwasher," Kara put in. Now *that* chore would definitely make it seem like life was returning to normal.

Alex scrunched up his face. "Ah, Mom!"

She rose from her chair. "It will just take you a minute. Get a book from your room, then you can sit at the kitchen table and read after the dishes are done."

She walked into the living room, with Damien behind her. She whirled to face him. "It was—" She stopped, seeing Alex walking through the dining room and into the hallway to his bedroom.

She lowered her voice. "It was the Belian, wasn't it?" She saw the acknowledgment in Damien's eyes before he answered.

"No doubt about it. I picked up the same psychic signature that was at Doris's house."

Fresh terror sent her heart racing. "And now he's directly in the path of this monster."

"But he's not without resources, Kara. If he hadn't been able to shield himself today, and to sense the Belian, then he most definitely would *not* have been safe."

Meaning Alex would not have *survived* today, had it not been for Damien's instruction.

"I know what you've taught Alex probably saved his life today," she said, feeling mentally and physically exhausted—and a whole lot afraid. "I-I really appreciate you showing Alex how to shield himself, and finding him at the school this afternoon—" Her voice broke and she turned her face away. She was *not* going to cry in front of this man.

She started when he reached out and took her cold hand. His warmth seemed to radiate up her arm, along with a jolt of sparking awareness. "I'm glad I found him, too. He's a great kid."

"Yeah." She sniffed. "He is." She faced Damien again. "He can't go back to school, now that that thing knows about him."

"I'm not convinced the Belian knows that Alex was the one broadcasting. I think it knows there's a fledgling Sentinel in Zorro, and is searching for him. But if it had known for sure, it would have tracked Alex down today. It would have been able to lock onto him and follow him into the school."

She couldn't even bear to think about what might have happened. But she had no intention of taking any chances. "You don't know that for sure," she argued.

"No, I don't. That's why I'm moving in with you for the time being. If the Belian has tagged Alex, then it's likely to come here after him. And you will be its next target—as will I, since we've spent time together."

Richard lay in his own blood, his eyes open, pupils fixed. She knelt beside him, numb with terror and grief, and took his blood-splattered hand. It was still warm . . .

No! She couldn't go through that again. "We can't take a chance, not if there's the slightest possibility it already knows Alex is the one," she said, her voice thick. "He can't be alone at any time. He'll have to come to my office every day until you track the Belian down."

"And you can keep Alex safe at your office?" Damien's silver gaze bored into her. "Are you willing to take your gun to the office? How will you explain Alex's absence from school, and his presence at your office?"

Suddenly overwhelmed by it all, she stumbled to the couch and sank down. "I don't know. I'll have to think of something."

The couch sagged as Damien sat beside her. "Is there anywhere you can send Alex until this is over with?"

Would it ever be over? she wondered wearily. She didn't

want Alex out of her sight, but Damien had some good points. "I could send him to my mother and stepfather in Alabama . . ." she said slowly. "They adore him, and he feels the same way about them. It's just that I would—I would miss him so badly."

"But he would be away from this Belian and safe."

"How do I know there wouldn't be a Belian in Huntsville, and that Alex might accidentally broadcast while he's there? Is there any place on this earth that's safe?"

"I won't allow Alex to go without protection," Damian said. "First off, I'll work with him more tonight, and be sure he has the control he needs. Secondly, I'll get someone to keep an eye on him."

"Another Sentinel?" Kara felt torn, wanting Alex to be protected, but not further exposed to the Sentinel world. "What if he starts giving Alex information on Sentinels?"

"I can't make any promises, but I'll forward instructions that Alex is to be guarded, but not mentored, unless it becomes absolutely necessary." Again, he pinned her with his intent gaze. "That's the best I can do."

She knew she'd have to settle for that. "Well, I guess it's the best offer I've had all day."

His lips twitched. "Some days are like that."

She looked away from his mouth, appalled that she could find it enticing at a time like this. "I'll have to call my mother, then figure out how to get Alex to Alabama. And then I'll have to tell him."

"We'll explain it to him together. He'll understand. As for getting him to Alabama, he's old enough to fly alone, if we can get a direct flight." Damien stood. "You call your mother, and I'll use my laptop to search the Internet for a plane ticket."

Kara felt a wrench at the thought of Alex leaving, much less flying by himself. She *knew* it was the best thing for her son, but he was her world, and she would be bereft without him.

Damien must have sensed her mood, for he said, "You're doing the right thing to keep Alex safe. You know that."

"Yes, I know."

But she felt as if her heart were breaking.

And the darkness was growing closer.

THIRTEEN

DAMIEN paused in his Internet search—being conducted with Alex's assistance—and listened to Kara talking to her mother.

"No, Mom, I'm fine, really. Nothing's wrong. I'd just like to send Alex to you for a week or two. . . . No, he's fine, too, but there's a serious measles epidemic in this area. . . . Don't you remember? He had a bad reaction to his first MMR shot, so he never received a booster, so he might not be immune. . . . Yes, that's the time he had a convulsion. . . . That's great! I really appreciate it. Let me check the airlines and I'll get back to you when we have flight information. . . . Oh, that's right. He might have to fly into Birmingham. Would that be a hardship for you and Frank? . . . Good. Thank you. You're the best. . . . All right. Love you, too."

Damien couldn't help but wonder if he'd have been having telephone conversations with his own parents if they were still alive. But they weren't, and he'd learned to function very well without a family safety net. He returned his attention to his search.

"Very clever to think of a measles epidemic," he said when Kara joined them at the dining room table.

"Mom, is there really a measles 'demic?" Alex asked.

"No, sweetie, I had to tell a fib. But I didn't think we should discuss Sentinel stuff with Grandma and Grandpa, or scare them. Don't you agree?"

Alex nodded. "Yeah. I guess." He wasn't at all sure he wanted to go off to Alabama, much less fly on a plane by himself, but he was being a real trooper.

Damien had spent an hour working with him more on shielding and safely sending and receiving thoughts. Alex was shaken up, and he was fearful and tired, yet he still exhibited an amazing ability to focus. He was rapidly becoming very proficient with the skills.

"Was your mom making up the bad reaction to the immunization, too?" he asked Alex.

"No, I wasn't," Kara interjected. "Alex had a convulsion after he got the first shot in the series. Fortunately, there wasn't any permanent damage." She paused, gave her son a teasing smile. "Oh, wait, maybe there was. It would explain a lot of things."

"Mom!"

Kara laughed and hugged him. "You know you're absolutely perfect. Just stay away from anyone with mumps or measles."

"You don't have to worry about Alex getting sick," Damien said. "Sentinels have very powerful immune systems."

"So I noticed. He's always been healthy as a horse. Have you two found any flights?"

"Yeah," Alex said. "Mr. Morgan's computer is really cool. Look." He showed her what he and Damien had lined up. There were no direct flights to Huntsville from either Austin or San Antonio, so Alex would have to fly into Birmingham.

"Maybe I should fly with him," Kara suggested. "Make sure he gets to my parents safely."

"You can," Damien replied. "But I don't think that's

necessary. There's no way the Belian can know our plans, and I'll make sure no one follows us from Zorro to the Austin airport. Even then, there would be no way to know what flight Alex is taking. And he can shield himself completely now. No other Belians will be able to pick up on him. He'll be fine, Kara, and we'll draw less suspicion if you remain here."

His logic was sound, so Kara conceded. She phoned her mother back and confirmed that the grandparents could pick up Alex in Birmingham tomorrow, and the ticket was booked.

One fire put out, Damien thought, as he powered down his laptop. But there was another matter that had to be handled tonight: a conduction. They couldn't put it off, not with the possibility that the Belian might have identified Alex. If that were the case, then all three of them were at risk. Damien had to push for any information that could give him the jump on the Belian.

He would wait until Alex was down for the night before he approached Kara. So he bided his time through the bedtime rituals—snack (he and Mac participated in that one), brushing teeth, and reading a book, along with a lengthy question-and-answer session, because Alex was anxious about going to Alabama, and the flight.

When Alex and Mac were ensconced in Kara's bed, her usual concession when Alex was upset, she sat on the edge of the bed and kissed her son. "Good night, you two," she said.

"I don't want to go to sleep." Alex pulled the covers under his chin.

"Why not, sweetie?"

"I might not know if the bad person comes back. And I might have bad dreams."

"I don't think the Belian will come back, but if it does, I'll make it go away," Damien said. *Permanently.* "And you won't have any nightmares. I want you to close your eyes and think of something fun—like winning a soccer game."

"Okay." Alex closed his eyes. A mischievous grin flashed on his face. "Hey! I just scored a goal."

"Great." Damien sent him a mental push toward sleep. His guard was down, and he went under readily, as did Mac. Damien deepened their sleep level, gave Alex a powerful, subconscious suggestion that he wouldn't remember any of his dreams.

Kara watched her son a long moment. "I hate that you have to do that."

"And you know I don't do it without good reason—in this case, two reasons. Alex was exhausted, and he needs a good night's sleep without disruption from fears or nightmares. You know the other reason."

She looked at him steadily. "Yes, I do." She stood, squared her shoulders. "Let's get this done."

He had to respect her determination and grit. She was practically swaying on her feet from exhaustion. She'd eaten very little dinner, and her skin was as pale as fine porcelain. Fatigue clouded her eyes and created dark circles beneath them. A conduction would wipe her out completely.

The feelings of concern and regret over pushing her to do this tonight caught him off guard. While he had certainly never mistreated a conductor, he'd never before hesitated to do what had to be done. He couldn't allow himself to feel regret, or to care. Any weakness could get him—get all of them—killed. There was no option of delaying the conduction, and Kara knew it as well as he did.

He followed her into the living room and pulled the chair up as she settled herself on the sofa. As he slid his legs on either side of hers, he caught a whiff of her Chanel perfume. It was faint, probably put on this morning, but his sense of smell was many times keener than a regular human's. The fragrance was subtle, earthy and rich, like Kara herself. Mingled with her natural scent, it was enough to send the first flare of sexual awareness through him. And he hadn't even initiated the chakra energies yet.

Focus, he told himself. He pulled the crystal from beneath his shirt, held it in his left hand, centering himself mentally and spiritually. He cast protective shields around

Kara and himself, around Alex, and the entire house. Dropping the crystal, he offered his hands to Kara, his left up and his right down.

She wiped her palms on her pants, like she'd done the first time. He felt her resistance, her hesitation, saw her chest heave, before she fitted her hands to his. Her skin was cool, yet the effect of the contact was instantaneous. Slashes of blue and red exploded on the edges of his peripheral vision; his nerve endings tingled—again, without any initiation. Her palms quickly warmed against his, and the air sizzled around them.

A deep breath, and then he commanded the rise of the energies. It was like opening a floodgate and releasing an avalanche of pure electricity. There was no buildup to the sexual surge. It burst upward like a geyser, rushing through the first three chakras so fast and furiously, they snapped open with pops that sounded like gunfire. Kara gasped and jerked backward.

He tightened his fingers around her hands. "Stay with me," he ordered in a guttural voice, although he was just as shaken.

He was rock hard, his erection straining uncomfortably against his jeans. It took all his will to marshal his control and maintain his focus on the energies. By the Light, this was no way to perform a conduction.

"Oh, God," Kara gasped. He could feel her tremors. "Damien, I can't—"

"Yes you can. Breathe! And let it happen. You can do this, Kara."

Yet it took everything he had to ride the turbulence as it roared through his chest and up his spine. The crystal resting against his chest pulsed with the energy of the great Tuaoi stone to which it was linked. Brilliant light and heat flowed through him, and for a moment, the mystical veil that separated lifetimes raised, and he could see the glistening green lands of Atlantis, the sapphire blue water surrounding it.

He could feel the purity and power that had resonated in

the magnetic disks in the sacred Temple, where The One had spoken directly to the Children. He was connected to his birthright, his past, his future. The light gathered and burst into his head with a blinding flash, brighter than a thousand suns, spilling over between his eyes. The veil dropped back down, the brief moment of divinity gone, but the spark had ignited the seeking.

Now all seven chakras were open, and the energies circulated through them so fast, his body felt jerked around like he was on a roller coaster. Colors whirled past like photo flashes.

He projected through his sixth chakra and its companion third eye, locking the link to Kara's third eye, and ensuring the psychic images projected only in the upper chakras. This would keep them in the Sentinel realm, and hopefully prevent the Belian from detecting them.

"We're there," he managed in a relatively level voice. "All you have to do is hold on, Kara. Hold the link."

She clutched his hands in a death grip, and a groan escaped her lips. Or maybe it was a moan. He doubted she was capable of more communication than that. He wasn't sure he could utter a coherent word himself. He needed to be inside her, needed her legs wrapped around him, to be claiming her, allowing the sexual surge to build to a crescendo, creating a vibratory rate that would attune to the Belian's energy pattern and break through its psychic barriers.

Belians were tied to the lower, earth-bound chakras, which resonated on the vibratory level of sexual energies. He needed to tap into those energies for the clearest images. And damn, his body needed release.

But Kara had said no sex, and coercion was not an option. No Sentinel would ever take a conductor by force. So he gritted his teeth, and dug deep and wrenched his focus back to the images he was able to discern through the third-eye link. He committed them to his photographic memory as they flashed by in one-second bursts.

Throughout the process, sexual need rode him like a razor-edged sword. He could feel the heat of Kara's body, could smell the musky scent of her need, could hear the hammering of her heart in conjunction with his. But discipline and training, along with his iron will, managed to override the physical deluge.

The psychic images began dissipating, and he initiated the process of bleeding off the energy into the ethereal and sealing off the chakras, this time from the top down. The rocking motion slowed, the various chakra colors faded in foglike wisps; the link between him and Kara evaporated like a sigh on the wind. Tiny aftershocks tingled through him, and he knew she felt them as well.

He released her hands and sat back in the chair, drawing deep breaths. The psychic, higher-chakra energies continued to calm, but not the adrenaline and sexually laced energies of the lower chakras. His body screamed for release, and he was still painfully hard, his jeans about three sizes too small. It was a lot more difficult to diffuse physical energy. He shoved the chair backward to a safer distance.

He'd never experienced such a powerful conduction. This one had been even stronger than their first one. It had required all his power to control the energies, so he could only assume it had upended Kara. He saw she had her own struggle to get air into her lungs. Her body shaking, she braced herself with a hand on the couch cushion.

"You okay?" he managed to ask.

With a barely perceptible nod, she sank against the cushion behind her. Her chest heaved as if she were struggling for air. "White," she said slowly. "I kept seeing a white expanse. And it was *moving*. That doesn't make any sense."

"It does, actually, because I think it was a white truck that was being driven."

"A truck . . ." Her eyes narrowed in concentration. "An *F*. I saw an *F* floating on the white."

Damien was surprised she could recall that much from the light-speed images. "You're correct, because it was a white F-150 Ford truck."

She considered that. "It could have been a white truck I saw. Do you think that's what the Belian is driving?"

He closed his eyes, turned inward to focus through his third eye. "I'm getting that impression."

"Great. That's about as helpful as River Road and the live oak. The Ford F-150 is the truck of choice around here, and white is the preferred color, because of the heat. There are probably three hundred of them in the area."

He let himself drift on the ethereal plane a little longer, sifting through the images again, then he mentally clicked off, settled back into his physical body. "Even so, it's a clue, and I've got precious few of them, against this Belian." He drummed his fingers on the chair arms. "That's basically all I got."

"It's so little to go on." She shifted upright and immediately groaned, her hand going to her head.

"Another headache," he said, but it was a statement, not a question. He could feel the pressure pounding through her head, could sense the pain radiating off of her. "Maybe you'd better lie down."

She just stared at him, her eyes large in her flushed face. Cursing silently, he lunged up, resisting the urgent need to adjust his jeans.

He grasped her shoulders, turning her and lowering her to the couch, just as he had the first time. He could feel the burning heat of her skin through the delicate, feminine sweater she wore. It was unbuttoned partway down, revealing the alluring slope of her breasts and the matching camisole beneath, as well as the outline of her taut nipples.

She obviously hadn't changed from her work clothes, probably hadn't even thought about it, not during the crisis with Alex. Now Damien wished she'd taken time to put on the sweats she'd worn the first conduction. Not that anything could dampen conduction-induced lust.

She swung her legs onto the couch before he could do it for her. He stepped back, intending to retreat to the relative safety of the chair. A shudder ripped through her. Her body vibrated with intense sexual need—as did his.

He could have resisted that, could have called on his higher self and his honor as a Sentinel to respect her request that there be no physical intimacy. He could have returned to his chair, and continued the discussion on the conduction images with relative calmness.

But she lifted a hand toward him. "Damien—" She stopped, dropped the hand. Her gaze locked with his, myriad emotions flooding from her to him. Fear, grief, and the need for comfort. She looked so vulnerable . . . so alone.

Her world was not only coming apart, it was colliding with a horrific past. But she wasn't giving in without a fight. She was courageous and fiercely determined to defend her child. She was allowing herself to be subjected to the emotional and physical drain of conductions to help fight a monster, despite her past experiences.

Yet at the end of the day, with her friends and neighbors dying—murdered—her child in danger, and the life she'd built threatened, she had no one to turn to.

He was not a man who knew how to be gentle, or give comfort. Nor was he a man to woo and soothe a woman; all things feminine and soft were totally alien to him. He was a trained tracker and executioner, the sole purpose of his existence to hunt Belians. His was a solitary path, free of human relationships and emotional entanglements.

Yes, there had been numerous female conductors in his life, along with steamy, uninhibited sex, but never a commitment beyond performing conductions to identify a Belian. However, most female conductors played the game willingly, either for the rush of the danger or the exceptional sex. The world's permissive societies gave rise to many conductors of both sexes, who didn't balk at working with several Sentinels, and didn't expect anything beyond the temporary, conduction-based liaisons.

Kara wasn't like that, and she had entered into a committed relationship with her Sentinel, suffering the inevitable consequences. With Damien, she'd been unwillingly drafted into service.

Now she was paying a heavy physical price for the bottled-up energies that were normally released during sexual conductions. He saw the lines of pain etched on her face as she pressed both hands against her head, could feel the throbbing in her temples. The headache was obviously escalating into a major migraine, and her libido hadn't calmed; he could still sense her need.

He might not be able to offer her emotional comfort or reassurances, but he could banish the headache and ease her body's relentless demands. *Not a good idea,* his analytical side argued. Even as every instinct he had told him to back away, he walked back to the couch.

He stared into her shimmering gray eyes, found himself kneeling beside her, unable to leave her like this. Her torment was too great. He reached out, cupped her face, marveled at the satiny texture of her skin.

She allowed his touch, turning into his hand. His own lust resurged like fast-flowing lava. "Let me ease you," he said hoarsely. "Let me take away your pain."

He slid his other hand behind her neck, rubbed away the tension. At the same time, he sent soothing, calming energies into her head and a subtle command to end her headache. The pain eased, but her body was still as charged as a live wire.

He moved his hands to her shoulders and down her arms and hands, massaging and kneading away tension. Her eyes closed, she offered no resistance, just gave a little sigh. He moved to her feet, massaged the pressure points, and this time she did moan. "Oh, that feels wonderful."

From there, he worked his way up her legs, along the sides of her hips. He felt the leap of tension go through her, the unabated sexual energies refiring. His body was pulsing, straining with its own demands, but he overrode it with fierce determination. This was for Kara, and there was only one way to rid her of the high-wire tensions that would otherwise leave her lying awake in bed most of the night.

He moved his hands upward, brushing lightly against her abdomen and midriff, settling them along the sides of her breasts.

Her eyes flew open. "Damien, what—"

"Hush," he murmured, watching her breasts swell at his touch. "Lie still."

"But—"

"Just lie back, and let me do this for you," he ordered hoarsely.

Before she could object, he feathered his thumbs over her nipples. She gasped, arching upward.

AS Damien's fingers stroked her nipples, shock chased a hot rush of sheer lust that torpedoed through Kara's body. She tried to protest, but a red, blurry haze filled her mind, and her dry mouth felt as though it was full of cotton. But the rest of her came alive—sharp, vibrant, pulsating with desire so intense, she felt engulfed in white-hot flames.

She moaned as his hands moved down and beneath her camisole, stroking back upward over her bare skin, his fingers trailing fiery electricity in their wake. Then they were slipping beneath the lacy edges of her bra, and her breath caught. She tried to protest again, but then he unhooked her bra and slid his hands over her breasts. The breath hissed from her lungs and she dug her fingers into the couch. *Yes . . .* How could she object when it felt so good, and when she craved it like an addict craved drugs?

She must still be in thrall to the conduction-induced energies, because as Damien stroked her breasts, colors and images flashed through her mind. She heard his voice in her head, speaking in a language she didn't know, his words flowing over her, holding her in place for his touch. It was like a dream where she knew what was happening, but was paralyzed. She didn't feel threatened by him, but her out-of-control body, desperately straining against his hands, was another matter.

He moved one hand down her body, undoing her slacks and sliding his hand beneath her panties, over her abdomen. An evocative, tantalizing touch, with a promise she desperately needed fulfilled. Of their own volition, her legs parted for that seeking hand. He stroked the wet flesh between her legs and a lightning bolt of electricity shot through her body.

"Damien!"

He seemed to understand, seemed totally attuned to her body. He slid a finger inside her, slow, deep, and her entire being shuddered. Yes, this was what she needed—and it had been so long. How could she have thought she could ignore such a raging demand?

Now that the flood was unleashed, what he was doing wasn't nearly enough. She could barely articulate anything, much less the all-consuming need. "More." Her voice was a guttural whisper, barely audible. But he knew. He was inside her mind, just as his finger was inside her body. He slid a second finger into her, and she shuddered again.

He stroked his fingers in and out, and with a little cry, she arched against his hand. It was too little, it was too much, it was everything she needed at this moment.

His thumb circled over the sensitive nub above those magic fingers buried deep inside her. "Let go, Kara." Then his voice was in her head, whispering in that strange language again, and she felt the mental push, hurtling her toward the edge.

She couldn't refuse, didn't want to refuse. She went into free fall, her body screaming as the climax pounded through her. The fall seemed to go on and on; in the throes of the explosion, she couldn't focus on anything but the sensations.

Even when the climax began to fade, leaving her a quivering, boneless mass, even when Damien pulled away from her, she couldn't seem to form a coherent thought, much less speak.

He stared at her a long moment, his expression inscrutable. "I know we agreed there would be no intimacy," he said, his voice raw. "But—ah, hell, Kara. This was necessary for your well-being."

She stared back at him, shocked. *My well-being?* He

made it sound like he'd given her a dose of medicine for an illness. Or worse, like he was maintaining a valuable asset: *Have to take care of the little conductor so she can continue to conduct for me.* It was certainly cold and impersonal. *Saw the problem, wham, bam, fixed the problem, now let's get back to business.*

Those thoughts sent a flare of anger through her. How dare he think of sexual need, of desire, as a *problem* to be *fixed*? And just what was she supposed to say now? *Thank you?*

She managed to find her voice, struggled to sound calm and unaffected. "Are we through for the night?"

Some unidentifiable emotion flashed in his eyes. "I guess we are."

"Good," she said coolly. "You should find everything you need in the cabinet in the bathroom. There are towels, and clean sheets for Alex's bed." She closed her eyes, willing him gone. She knew when he left, felt the crackling energy fade, felt the utter emptiness that settled around her like a heavy weight. She lay there, still stunned, and too shaky to stand.

She felt a rush of mortification, and her face heated. She had been totally out of control. If women ever started going into heat, she could be the poster girl. Yet Damien had remained cool and contained throughout, which made it even worse. She wouldn't—couldn't—think about that just now. Keeping Alex safe and stopping the Belian had to come before her personal embarrassment.

She pushed up from the couch, not surprised her legs were trembling. She zipped and buttoned her pants, yanked her camisole and sweater down without bothering to rehook her bra. As she managed to walk the distance to her bedroom door, she heard the shower running in the main bathroom. Maybe Damien hadn't been as unaffected as she thought. Then again, he might shower every night. She didn't know what to think—or feel—at this point.

The heat flared to her face again, and she entered her bedroom. Alex was on his stomach, his arm flung over

Mac, and both were snoring softly. She went into her bathroom, grateful that the previous owner had added it, along with a roomy closet, using one end of the large bedroom.

The house had been built in the forties, with only one bathroom and tiny closets. Kara's built-on bathroom was tiny, with a shower stall crowded in with a toilet and pedestal sink, but it afforded the privacy a woman sometimes needed.

She stared at herself in the mirror. Her eyes were too bright in her flushed face. Definitely postorgasm symptoms. Disconcerted and disgusted with herself, she stripped, stepped into the shower, and scrubbed thoroughly. She dried off and put on a pair of sweats and some fuzzy socks. It was way too late to dress protectively, but she still felt more secure.

She sat on the edge of the bed, brushing the tangles out of her damp hair. Despite her best efforts, she couldn't banish what had happened with Damien from her mind. Nor could she forget how he had looked tonight—first when he had worked patiently with Alex, both on his shielding and on the laptop. Then again later, when he'd sat across from her for the conduction, in his faded jeans and sweatshirt, his hair loose and glossy around his face.

The fact of the matter was that the man was sexy as hell. Realizing her mouth was dry, Kara got up to get a glass of water. *Damn.* What was the matter with her? *I will not be a slave to hormones—or Sentinel/conductor-induced lust,* she told herself fiercely.

Even if Damien had just given her one of the most earth-shattering orgasms of her life. It ought to hold her for the next seven years or so.

It would have to.

FOURTEEN

ALEX'S flight left on time, so it was only midmorning when Damien and Kara drove back from Austin-Bergstrom International Airport. She never showed her concern to her son while telling him good-bye, but in the silence of the car, Damien could feel her distress. He'd been pushing her, but something had to give in order to capture this Belian.

He shouldn't have initiated *any* form of sexual intimacy last night. Yet in his mind, he could still see the longing and sadness on her face, could smell her erotic scent. Could remember the feel of her skin, warming against his touch, the feel of his fingers inside her, her cries as her body arched up against him. Her need, her heat, her passion were imprinted on his senses.

He was used to being turned on when he was around a conductor, to the ongoing, sexual frustration every Sentinel endured as part of his or her job description. He knew better than to let his control slip, to let himself be affected by sexual energies. But last night, he'd stood beneath a cold shower and relieved his raging need in order to insure he'd be able to maintain that control—a very rare occurrence for him.

Kara was getting under his skin, and while he needed to put some distance between them, he'd already ruled out trying to find another conductor. They simply didn't have the time. This Belian was too powerful, and he knew it would strike again soon.

Kara dug her phone out of her purse. "I need to call Luz and tell her Alex is gone."

"Just stick to what we discussed. Tell her the same thing you told the school principal."

She did, telling Luz that Alex had gone to visit his grandparents because he had a special opportunity to take a trip with them. Since he might also be gone the following week, during school spring break, she told Luz to take two weeks off with pay.

"Well, that's that," she said, closing her cell phone. "Now I have to clean house for the next thirteen days, and either live at the Busy Bee or starve to death."

"You won't go hungry," Damien said. "I can cook."

Her auburn eyebrows lifted. "You can? Where did you learn?"

"My father taught me. He was the chef in our household."

She shifted toward him. "*Was?* Is he deceased?"

Damien suppressed the grief that flared within him, even after thirty years. "Yes, he's dead."

"I'm sorry. He was a Sentinel?"

"No, my mother was the Sentinel," he said brusquely. "She's dead, too."

"Oh. I am really sorry."

He shrugged. "It goes with the territory."

She was silent a few moments, then she asked, "So, is it common for Sentinels and conductors to marry each other?"

"It's fairly common for those Sentinels who want to have families. It would complicate matters for a Sentinel to be married to a non-conductor, and then engage in a conduction with another person."

"I never thought about that. Just as it never occurred to me that Richard might do a conduction with someone else, once we were together. Of course, he never did." She stared out the windshield, her expression distant.

"You know, I didn't totally believe Richard's wild story about being a Sentinel until that first conduction. Talk about a mind-blowing experience. Among . . . other things." A slight flush stained her porcelain skin.

"I'll bet."

A smile tugged her lips. "You're such a guy."

"So you noticed."

She turned and punched him lightly in the arm. "You actually have a sense of humor. Hard to tell, though, with all that macho attitude and testosterone swirling around you."

She became pensive again. "Richard rarely laughed. He was so serious all the time. Alex is so much like him. I wish Richard had lived to see his son."

"Unfortunately, being a Sentinel is a very dangerous occupation. Which is why I don't get involved with anyone." Now why the hell had he said that?

"Sometimes it's worth the risk," she said quietly. "I wouldn't trade what I had with Richard for anything. I'd do it all over again, even those last moments—"

Hearing the catch in her voice, he glanced over at her, but she was staring out at the road again. "Must have been tough."

She blinked rapidly. "It was horrible. But now I have Alex. And I have some wonderful memories."

Sometimes the horrors overrode the good memories, he thought.

They made the rest of the drive back to Zorro with very little conversation. He dropped her off at her office, over her protest that she needed to get her truck. "I'll pick you up when you're ready," he told her. "Just call my cell phone."

"I can drive myself. Besides, people will start to talk if they see you chauffeuring me around."

"And they're not going to talk when they see my car parked at your house all night?"

"They most definitely will," she said. "We'll become the center of town gossip. With Alex safe now, there's no reason you can't return to the Magnolia Bed-and-Breakfast."

"That's not an option. I can't—and won't—take the chance that the Belian might have identified Alex. Not to mention that, as the town's resident stranger, I'm automatically suspect, and we've already been seen together. I'm not going to risk anything happening to you."

Her eyes narrowed. "Oh, that's right, then you wouldn't have a conductor."

He felt a flare of unidentifiable emotion from her, but before he could respond, she said, "I'm sorry. I'm tired, and I miss my son, and I'm more than a little scared. I shouldn't be taking it out on you."

"Like I said, it goes with the territory. Do you have your gun with you?"

"No. I don't have a permit to carry it yet."

"That's right. Damn. I'll get you some police-grade pepper spray. You can keep that in your lab coat pocket."

"That will barely slow down a Belian, as you keep pointing out."

"It will cause any human body to react and cough and gag. That will buy you some time to escape."

"All right." She jerked open the car door, obviously unsettled.

"Call me when you're ready to leave. I won't be far. And Kara, be very careful."

She turned to look at him. "The same goes for you Sentinel. Watch your back out there."

Her concern shouldn't have mattered to him . . . but it did.

THAT evening, Kara brought home a stack of lab test results she said she needed to read before they were filed. She also brought medical files on her patients with serious health problems, as Damien had requested. They sat at the dining room table and went over the files.

There was Belle Williams with her breast cancer; Sal with his heart condition; Katie Woodward, an ovarian cancer survivor; Mary Roberts, who was battling lung cancer; and Police Chief Tom Greer, who'd had prostate cancer. There were also fifteen other patients whose names Damien didn't know, but would be checking out. And there was one surprise: Luz, who had severe asthma, and had to carry an inhaler with her at all times.

He tapped Luz's file. "This is very interesting."

Kara's eyes were troubled. "I brought Luz's records because you requested all those with ongoing serious medical conditions. But she's not the Belian. I can't believe that."

"The Belian could be *anyone*," Damien said. "They're very adept at hiding their true natures."

"But surely Luz would have picked up on Alex before now. He's had to be broadcasting from time to time."

"Maybe. But the Belian might not pick up on it if it wasn't consciously tuning in."

"I don't even want to consider the possibility." Kara closed the file and tossed it onto the pile. "At least not tonight. I'm too tired to think straight. And I still have to read those lab reports. I've been leaving the office early, and going in late, and I'm getting behind."

"I want to look through these records again," Damien said, pulling the stack over. "We might have missed something."

He studied the files, while Kara perused lab reports and initialed them and made notes on a legal yellow pad about the patients she needed to call. After a while, his stomach started demanding food. "I think I'll putter around in the kitchen and see what there is to eat."

"Good luck finding anything," she said absently, her brow creasing as she studied a report. "That cholesterol level is way too high. I'll have to call Bill Donovan tomorrow."

Her concentration appeared formidable, and it was matched by an impressive intelligence. Damien left her to it and went to the kitchen. Mac, apparently having decided he was a friend rather than a foe, followed him and settled by the back door, watching expectantly.

Damien found a well-stocked pantry and fridge, probably thanks to Luz. He also found leftovers in the fridge—a chicken and tomato sauce dish that looked very similar to the chicken cacciatore his father used to make, and tossed green salad. In the pantry, he found rice and packaged dinner rolls. He got to work heating up the chicken and rolls and cooking rice.

It felt strange to be preparing a meal for more than one. He often stayed in hotel suites where he had a microwave and fridge, so he was used to putting together informal meals. But Kara's bright, homey kitchen carried him back to his parents' big blue-and-white kitchen in Syracuse, New York, and resurrected memories of helping his father prepare family meals—and with them, emotions best left buried.

He didn't know why the memories were so vivid, because they were from over thirty years ago, and because he'd managed to keep them obscured, for the most part, until now. Maybe it was the surprising punch of nostalgia, or the cozy kitchen, or the easy familiarity of Kara working in the other room—as if they were a family unit—but he felt more at home here than he'd felt anywhere since his parents' deaths.

After they'd died, the family duplex in Syracuse had been sold, and he'd been sent to live with his newly appointed Sentinel mentor. He'd gone from a warm and loving family environment to a sterile, utilitarian condominium and a man who had no experience with ten-year-old boys, especially one who was inconsolable with grief.

All of that was in the past, Damien told himself firmly, and every event had a reason, was a part of the Divine plan. He was right where he was supposed to be, and his focus needed to be solely on tracking and dispensing the Belian. Nothing more, and certainly no emotional involvement.

Resolute, he pulled the chicken and rolls from the oven and took the rice off the stove. He got out the salad and some salad dressings, put everything on the kitchen table that he had set with plates and silverware, and poured iced tea, which was served year-round in Texas.

"Kara," he called out, heading for the dining room. "Dinner's ready. Prepare to be impressed by my culinary abilities—" He stopped, seeing her slumped over the table, her pen still clutched in her hand.

A soft snore verified she was asleep. He gently shook her shoulder. "Kara, wake up. The food is ready."

She didn't move. He knew she was exhausted, and maybe rest was more important than food right now. Pulling her chair back, he lifted her up. She settled against him with an incoherent murmur. Her breath was warm on his chest, and her musky, feminine scent wafted upward, assailing his senses.

The peach silk blouse she wore gaped away from her chest, revealing the lacy low-cut bra she wore beneath it. A dainty gold locket on a delicate chain was nestled between her breasts, which swelled enticingly above the cups. He knew from last night that her smooth skin would be soft and warm beneath his fingers, her breasts exquisitely sensitive.

Lowering his head, he inhaled deeply. Damn, she smelled good. His body hardened in reaction, causing him to suck in another breath. Even as he told himself he shouldn't let his libido get the better of him, he was remembering how Kara's lithe body had responded last night. *Cut it out,* he ordered himself.

As he turned to carry her to her bedroom, he was struck with the sudden image of his father carrying his mother. He'd only seen that once, when his parents thought he was asleep. He'd come quietly from his room, hoping to sneak a snack from the kitchen, and he'd seen his father carrying his mother to their bedroom. Even though he'd only been eight at the time, he'd noticed the incredible tenderness and caring between his parents, seen the way his father held his mother as if she were a precious treasure, and how her head rested against his shoulder.

His Sentinel mother had been far stronger than his human father, and could have carried *him* ten miles without breaking a sweat. Yet his father had always been protective toward her—even though it ultimately got him killed.

Just another reminder of a past that was long gone. Damien strode to Kara's bedroom, mentally opening the door. She murmured again when he placed her on the bed and slipped off her shoes. Her toenails were painted a glossy red, a feminine touch that sent another punch of desire through him. Damn, he definitely needed to get laid—but that required a willing party.

Determinedly he pulled the comforter and bedding from beneath her, and resettled it over her. She curled onto her side and sighed. Her auburn hair fanned over the pillow like flowing silk. She looked vulnerable and innocent—and sexy as hell. And very human, Damien reminded himself. Off-limits, except for conductions—and that was another murky issue.

He headed to the kitchen, where he and Mac would share dinner and celebrate their bachelorhood. Then, if the lust ravaging his body hadn't abated, he'd take another cold shower.

THE next morning, Kara stepped out of examining room three and walked into the nearby nurse's alcove to make a few notes on Betty Libby's chart. Mrs. Libby was the grandmother of one of Alex's soccer buddies, and was often at soccer games. Seeing the elderly lady had nudged Kara's thoughts of Alex into even higher gear. He'd only been gone one day, and she missed him terribly.

"Dr. Kara? Are you at the nurse's station?" came Bonnie's voice over the intercom. The receptionist had an amazing sixth sense when it came to knowing where Kara was at all times.

"You tracked me down, as usual."

"Chief Greer is on the phone. Line one."

Kara didn't think any phone call from Tom Greer could be good. She strode to her office, fingering the small metal cylinder in the pocket of her white coat. Pepper spray, courtesy of Damien. She'd gone outside early this morning and practiced the correct way to hold it, flip up the plastic shield, and discharge it. She just hoped an innocent patient didn't make a wrong move; her nerves were frayed to the point she felt like she might snap at the least little thing.

She picked up line one. "Hello, Chief."

"Kara. I have some news."

She took a deep breath. "What have you got?"

"The Travis County medical examiner's report on Doris Burgess came in this morning."

Kara fumbled for the chair behind her desk, slipped into it. "What did it say?"

"Miz Burgess died from an overdose of insulin. Seems she got confused. Maybe she forgot she'd already taken her shot."

"An overdose?" Kara shook her head. "That's not possible."

"Well, that's what happened."

"But Doris was very careful with her medicine."

"She was an old lady!" Tom snapped. "And old folks forget sometimes. Hell, I forget lots of things. It was an accidental overdose, doctor. So ruled by the chief medical examiner."

Kara wanted to argue, to insist Doris would never forget her medicine, to tell Tom she *knew* Doris had been murdered. But she held back, knowing he'd either never believe her, or he'd know exactly what she was talking about. For all she knew, he was the Belian. The thought chilled her to the core. "Has Doris's family been notified?" she asked.

"I reckon they have. The ME's office keeps up with that stuff." Tom's gruff voice softened. "I'm sorry, Dr. Kara. I know you really cared for Miz Burgess."

"Would you mind faxing me a copy of the coroner's report? For her file."

"I reckon. What's the number?"

Kara gave it to him, then hung up. She stared at the phone a long time, thinking she'd never feel safe again.

"DORIS would never mix up her insulin or give herself an overdose," Kara told Damien that night. "She was too sharp and too careful."

They were at the kitchen table, eating stew he'd started that morning in the Crock-Pot (which she hadn't even known she had). Tonight, he'd pulled more of the tossed salad out of the fridge, and heated store-bought biscuits. The stew was delicious. Kara decided he could take Luz's place in a pinch, although she hadn't observed his house-cleaning skills yet.

It felt very strange having him ensconced in her home, with his laptop and briefcase commandeering the dining room table, his suitcase in Alex's room, and his toiletries in the main bathroom. The house smelled of aftershave, sandalwood, and primal male. It had been so long since she lived with Richard, she'd forgotten the sensual perks of having a man around.

She didn't think she would be so intrigued with just any man, but then Damien was no ordinary male. She couldn't help but wonder what it would be like to have him sleeping in her bed, to be able to reach out, touch bare skin stretched over taut muscles.

She pulled back from her thoughts, shocked. Two people were dead and a Belian was stalking the citizens of Zorro, and here she was, daydreaming about sex. She looked over at Damien.

He was reading the coroner's report on Doris, his ebony brows drawn together and making his sculpted face look even fiercer. "This was no accident," he growled. "But then we already knew that." He put the report to the side, dug into the stew. "You're preaching to the choir here."

"I know." She set her fork down, no longer hungry. "So what do we do now?"

"*You* will eat. You haven't had a solid meal in the past two days." Damien sat back in his chair, his gaze steady on her. "As for the Belian, all we can do at this point is wait for it to make another move."

Kara had a bad feeling they wouldn't have to wait long.

The evening progressed quickly, with kitchen cleanup, a call to Alex and her parents, and reviewing another stack of lab reports. Even though she was exhausted when she finally fell into bed, she tossed and turned, haunted by dark, violent memories and a premonition something terrible was about to happen. She finally drifted into a fitful sleep . . .

A man was walking away from her. He was outside, and it was nighttime. The breeze ruffled his thick hair; with the moonlight reflecting off it, it appeared to be brown or dark blond. He wore a heavy suede jacket over Wrangler jeans. His shoulders were broad, and he moved with a slightly unsteady gait, like he was stiff or injured.

A sound rustled behind him, and he stopped, turned his head slightly to look over his shoulder. She could only see part of his face, and that was blurred in the darkness. But he was so familiar, she was certain she knew him.

"Oh, it's you," he said. "Whadda you want?" His voice, again familiar, was slurred.

He jerked impatiently and turned fully toward her, but the shadows obscured his face. She knew him, she was certain. But she couldn't figure out who he was.

"Look, I'm sorry about everything," he said. "But I already told you . . ." He paused, belched. He was drunk—that must be why his words were slurred.

"I've given you all I can." He raised his hands, staggered. "You'll have to settle for that. I'm sorry it's worked out this way. But that's it. It's over. No más.*"*

An arm came up, pointing toward him. The arm was encased in a bulky sleeve, and it took a moment for her to realize that whoever it was held a gun in his black-leather-gloved hand. Black malevolence radiated around the arm. No! Not this!

The first man's reaction was slow, probably blunted by alcohol. He squinted at the gun pointing toward him for a moment. "Whoa there!" He stumbled back a step. "What the hell are you doing?"

No answer, just the gun steadily pointing at him in silent menace. She already knew what was going to happen. Please, God, stop this. Stop this thing now.

"Hey!" the man said, alarm edging his voice. "You can't be serious. After all I've done for you?. We go way back . . . W-why are you doin' this?

The black-gloved thumb cocked the trigger. "Wait!" he shouted. "I'll do more. I'll—"

The blast hit him right between the eyes. Blood and brain matter flew toward her, splattering as if hitting a glass wall, obscuring her vision. All she could see was red, crawling downward in a sickening pattern.

She knew the man hadn't survived the shot between the eyes. And the blood, the blood . . .

She heard the screams without realizing they were hers. She felt hands on her shoulders, gripping them tightly. "Kara! Kara, wake up!"

"No!" she cried, trying to wrench away. She couldn't let it catch her, or it would kill her, too. "Let me go!"

"Kara, it's just a dream. Open your eyes."

She did, but everything was blurry. All she could see was a sinister dark shape bending over her. *It had found her.* Panic resurged, and she kicked wildly and rolled to the side.

"Kara!" Hands clamped onto her shoulders again, pinned her to the mattress. "It's me, Damien. You're in your house, in your bed. You're safe."

Lucid thought seeped slowly into her consciousness, and she sank down. Damien released her and stood back. Light streamed in from the hallway, illuminating the lower end of the bed. But her surroundings didn't seem real. She felt like she was still in that horrifying other world.

"Oh, God. Damien, I saw it."

He sat on the edge of the bed. "Saw what?"

"Another murder." She struggled to sit upright, and he angled the pillow behind her so she could lean back.

"Tell me everything." His low voice was utterly calm and devoid of emotion.

"I saw the back of a man. He was outside, wearing a suede coat. He was staggering a little, and his words were slurred. I think he'd been drinking. I felt certain I knew him, but I couldn't see his face."

She took a deep breath to calm her stomach, closed her eyes. The dream flashed back into her mind, the grotesque splatter of blood and matter sliding slowly down the invisible barrier. Gasping, she opened her eyes.

"What is it?"

"It's like I'm still linked somehow to the place." She raised a trembling hand to push her hair from her face. "Or . . . to the Belian." Her whole body began shaking then, as if she had a horrendous chill.

Damien's hand went to the crystal resting against his chest. She belatedly realized he wasn't wearing a shirt, just a pair of jeans that weren't snapped, but she was too shell-shocked to appreciate the impressive masculine view. Holding the crystal, he closed his eyes. Energy, fueled from unimaginable power, surged and circled around them.

Kara felt a faint tingling flow along her skin and knew she was enveloped in a protective Sentinel shield. She managed to draw in a breath, tried to relax. But the shaking didn't ease.

"You're safe. The Belian can't reach you through the ethereal now. And on the physical plane, it will have to go through me to get to you. Tell me the rest of the dream."

She did, and then he made her tell him everything again. "You can't think of any other details that might tell us who this man is or where this took place?"

She thought it through, shook her head. "No, I can't." She wrapped her arms around herself to still the shaking.

"You're fairly certain the dream was accurate?"

She nodded, feeling both miserable and frustrated. "I *know* it is. And it probably just happened. Shouldn't we call the police and tell them? Maybe the man is still alive." She thought of all the blood and brain matter she'd seen. "No, he's not."

"If you can't identify the man in your dream, or the place where it occurred, there's not much we can do. We can't just call the authorities and tell them we 'think' a murder has occurred, but we don't know where. We'll have to wait until it's reported."

He stood, leaving her feeling oddly vulnerable. "I have a police scanner set up in Alex's room. I'll keep listening through the night. Once the body is discovered, we can take action."

Kara looked at the clock by her bed, the red fluorescent numerals reminding her of the blood. Twelve forty-four in the morning. Funny, it seemed she'd been asleep longer than that. Another big chill rolled through her.

Damien tugged the comforter up around her. "You all right?"

She hated being needy. She and Alex had been completely on their own up until now, and had done just fine. But she still had that sick feeling and the violent shaking.

"I'm cold. And I'm scared." She hesitated, pride warring with fear, but she didn't want to be alone tonight. "Please stay with me a little longer."

"Let me get the scanner and set it up here."

She was inordinately relieved. Right now, she felt like an easily spooked child instead of the rational adult she prided herself on being. She'd feel foolish in the morning, but in the aftermath of the dream and in the dark bowels of the night, she was grateful for Damien's steady presence.

He returned a moment later with the scanner. It was smaller than the radio scanner Richard had used, but then technology was seven years more advanced. Damien set it up on the nightstand on the opposite side of the bed and turned it on. It emitted a burst of faint static.

He settled onto the bed, sitting against the headboard, his legs crossed at the ankles. He was still barefooted, but he had pulled on a black T-shirt that fit him like a second skin, stretching across an impressive display of muscles.

His beautiful physique wasn't enough to distract her from the nausea, cold, and uncontrollable shaking. It was all she could do to keep her teeth from chattering.

He finished setting the scanner, looked down at her. "Are you better?"

"A little." She clutched the comforter as another spasm of shivering racked her. "I j-just can't seem to stop shaking."

"Shock, probably." He watched her, a furrow between his brows.

"It was just a d-d-dream," she muttered, dismayed at her lack of control over her body.

"It was more than that. And you can have dream shock." He stood, slid beneath the covers. "Maybe I can get you warm."

She curled against him without hesitation, grateful for the heat emanating from his large body, even as she was aware of the erotic electricity that arched around them. She realized her hands were clenching his T-shirt, and released it.

He closed his arms around her, and she felt safe and secure. She hadn't been held like this in a long time. He felt so solid, and his warmth and scent wrapped around her like a soft blanket.

"I didn't react this way to the last dream," she said.

"The connection with the Belian is stronger now that we've linked twice with its energy."

His hand began moving up and down her back in slow, steady strokes. Some of his heat seeped into her chilled body. With a sigh, she relaxed a little. He kept stroking, and she felt oddly comforted.

"Thank you," she murmured.

His hand stilled. "For?"

"For staying with me. For giving me comfort."

His hand resumed it's stroking. "Don't expect that from me, Kara. I'm no good at emotional things. It's best if you remember what I am—an assassin. I serve The One, but that doesn't change what I do."

She didn't accept his declaration that he didn't care. He had also given of himself last night, touching her with surprising gentleness, even if it had been sexual. Or had it? His words flashed into her mind: *"Ah, hell, Kara. This was necessary for your well-being."*

She realized now he was trying to take care of her, as best he knew how. That understanding evaporated the anger she'd felt about last night. She knew from personal experience that caring and nurturing was a struggle for a loner Sentinel. Denying that they were emotionally involved was also a part of the persona. But they did feel—very deeply—for the humans in their charge. The God they served—The One—imbued them with light and compassion and a powerful sense of justice.

She snuggled closer to him, the shivering finally gone. "Thank you for caring."

"Maybe you should focus on getting some rest," he said gruffly, obviously deciding to ignore the issue.

She listened to the slow, steady cadence of his heart. "I can't stop thinking about that poor man in the dream."

"Relax, and go to sleep." His voice took on a hypnotic lull.

She felt her eyelids growing heavy, despite her conviction she could never sleep tonight. Already, she was drifting toward oblivion. She wondered if he was using a mental push, but was too drowsy to protest.

"You won't dream again tonight."

She knew then he was putting her under. That was her last thought, as a soft, welcome darkness enveloped her.

She was jarred from the void when someone called her name. *What—*

"Kara, wake up *now*."

The urgency in that voice cut through her sleep like a hot knife through soft butter. She snapped awake, saw Damien above her, his expression fierce. "What is it?" She pushed herself up.

"They've found a body at Jim's Tavern."

FIFTEEN

"THE tavern?" Still groggy, she shoved her hair from her face. Voices crackling from the other side of the bed drew her attention to the police scanner. She looked back at Damien, realized he had pulled on a sweater and had his boots in his hand.

"Police reports are coming in, officers and emergency vehicles are being dispatched. Someone saw a lone vehicle in the parking lot behind the tavern and went to investigate. That's when the body was discovered. We need to get over there."

The memory of her dream rushed back to her. "Do they know who it is?"

"No name was given. Come on."

She looked at the clock as she slid out of the bed: 6:02 A.M. Shivering again, she yanked down the long T-shirt she slept in and went to the dresser to get some jeans. "Give me a few minutes, and I'll be ready to go."

"Hurry. I'd like to get there before a lot of people arrive and energies get mixed."

Oh, gee, and she couldn't wait to see the carnage.

Damien got them there in record time without wrecking his car or running over anyone, for which Kara was grateful. Her nerves were tied in knots, but a part of her was glad he included her. It would have been far more stressful to wait at home, not knowing anything.

The police and emergency vehicles had drawn a small crowd, even at this ungodly hour. The flashing red and blue lights looked garish against the morning gloom. She saw there were two Blanco County sheriff cars, in addition to the two City of Zorro police cruisers, an ambulance, and several pickup trucks. Damien parked the car as close as they could get—about two blocks from Jim's Tavern. He got out without a word and moved toward the scene in a ground-eating stride, his duster flapping around his long legs. Kara had to jog to keep up.

A county sheriff was unrolling yellow police tape, barricading the sidewalk in front of Jim's. She caught glimpses of officers milling around in the back parking lot. Two Zorro officers stood in front of orange roadblocks that had been placed across the gravel drive leading to the parking lot. They were telling the bystanders to return to their homes and businesses—not that anyone was leaving.

Kara recognized most of the bystanders. They either lived close to the tavern or had businesses on the square. She saw Sal, looking old and tired, his complexion ruddy from excitement. "I can't go anywhere," he was saying. "'Cause I found him. Saw his truck from the road and thought I'd better check it out."

"Who?" she asked hoarsely, cleared her throat. "Who was it, Sal?"

Sal turned toward them. "It was Matt Brown."

"Matt. Oh no." She staggered back, felt Damien grasp her elbow.

"Tell us what you saw," he said.

"I was coming in early to do some extra cleaning in the store, and stock the stuff that arrived yesterday. Since I live on the southern end of town, by the river, I always come past Jim's—"

"What did you see?" Damien interrupted, command edging his voice.

"Well, I walked back there and thought the truck looked like the one belonging to Matt. I didn't see anything else at first, 'cause it was still dark and the truck was parked where I could only see the passenger side." Sal paused, looking around as if he wanted to make sure he had everyone's undivided attention—which he did. "When I walked around to the driver's side, I saw Matt lying there. He was staring straight up, and his eyes were open, and he had a hole in the middle of his forehead. And a lot of blood was everywhere."

Just like her dream. Kara willed herself not to fall apart. Matt Brown had been young and vital, and from all appearances, a decent person. She felt Damien squeeze her arm, and didn't know if he was warning her to be silent, or offering his strength.

"Hey! Don't you be talkin' to that reporter!" Tom Greer came around the barricades and strode toward them. "Don't be talkin' to anyone until we have all the information from you."

He stopped and glared at Damien. "What are you doing here? The bed-and-breakfast is clear on the other side of town. No reason for you to be here." His glare shifted to Kara. "Or you, either, doctor. There's *nothin'* you can do. Nothin' anyone can do for poor Matt."

His gaze returned to Damien, and his eyes narrowed. "You know what, Morgan? The more I think about it, the stranger it is that you showed up here right after Matt's body was discovered. You also showed up at Miz Burgess's house, right after we found her. Mighty suspicious, if you ask me."

"I'm not a reporter, I am a crime writer, which seems to be a difficult concept for you to grasp, Chief," Damien said. "Because I document crimes, I use a police scanner, which keeps me informed when something happens. I came when I heard the dispatchers and responding officers. Dr. Cantrell came because she's a doctor and thought she might be able to help."

"All I know, Morgan, is that you're a stranger in Zorro, with no apparent reason for being here. Do you have an alibi from about eleven last night until now?"

Tom's implied accusation sent a shock through Kara. "Now, see here, Chief—"

"Excuse me, doctor, but I'm the one talking here. You carry a gun, Morgan?"

Damien stared back at Tom steadily. "I do. And I have a permit to carry concealed."

"I'd like to see it."

Damien reached beneath his duster, pulled out his gun, and handed it to Tom. He also fished out his wallet and showed his permit.

"I'll need to have this gun tested," the chief said, after studying the permit carefully. He gestured one of the officers over. "Bradley, give this man a receipt for his gun. It's a"—he examined it—"Colt .45, semiautomatic . . ." He slid out the magazine. "Looks like a seven-round magazine, with seven cartridges in it—not that that means anything."

Kara felt a rapid rise of fury. "Chief Greer," she said, ignoring the pressure of Damien's hand on her arm. She was not about to let the chief accuse Damien when the real killer was out there somewhere. "I can vouch for Mr. Morgan's whereabouts since early last evening."

The chief raised a grizzly eyebrow. "Oh you can, can you?"

"Kara, don't—" Damien started, but she ignored him.

"Yes, I can. He was with me all evening—and all night." The murmur of voices reminded her she had an avid audience, and she looked around to see about ten Zorro citizens, most of them patients, staring at her as if she'd sprouted horns. *Damn.* That ought to make her the center of town gossip for awhile.

"Well, now, that's very interestin'," Tom said. "I understand you also have a gun, Dr. Cantrell. Heard you bought it last week. I'd like to see that weapon."

He was acting like a class-A bastard, but she had nothing to hide. "Of course, Chief. But the gun is at home, because

I don't have my permit yet. Wouldn't want to break the law, now, would we? I'll bring it by later." She forced herself to shut up then, before she said something she'd regret.

"You do that, doctor." Tom looked around at the gawkers, raised his voice. "None of you folks needs to be here. We've got a dead man, and crime scene people on the way, and all you're doin' is messing up possible evidence. Now get on home!" He turned back to Kara and Damien. "You two be sure to stay in town. I might want to question you later."

"I'm not going *anywhere*," Damien said, his eyes glittering. "But I suggest you start your questioning with Luz Pérez. I saw her arguing with a man she called Matt Sunday night, in the tavern parking lot. If it's the same Matt, she might know something."

Tom's return stare was just as cold. "I'll keep that in mind, Morgan."

"Come on Kara." Damien turned and walked away.

She followed, furious with both him and Tom Greer. *Men and their pissing contests.*

He turned to look at the scene one more time, spoke in a low voice. "Too many people and too much activity to read the energy now, especially since we're both under suspicion. I'll have to come back after dark."

She'd already figured that out, but it wasn't the main thing on her mind at the moment. "Why did you drag Luz into this?" she demanded when they were fully out of earshot. "She's going to be devastated when she finds out Matt is dead."

"Unless she's the Belian." Damien unlocked his car door, hit the master lock.

"You don't know that!" Kara slid into her seat, slammed the door. "Whatever happened to innocent until proven guilty?"

"Look, if she's innocent, the police won't find any evidence to link her to Brown's murder. But there are some things about Luz that I find very suspicious."

"Like what?"

Damien started the car, checked the mirror, and pulled

out. "She's got a chronic illness that weakens her physically, she drives a white Ford F-150—"

"Sal drives a white Ford F-150, so does Tom Greer," Kara said. "I know you're looking at them. Sal was the one who found the body. Don't murderers often return to the scene of the crime?"

"They do sometimes. I am looking closely at both Sal and the chief, but Luz stands out more strongly. We know she and Matt were dating, and your dream showed that Matt knew his killer. He also used a Spanish phrase, right? Sunday night, I saw Matt hit Luz, and I saw how angry she got. I sensed some sort of power from her."

"Matt hit her?" Kara felt sick and shaky all over again. "I can't believe that."

"He did, but he was drunk at the time. He might have treated her just fine when he was sober."

"It can't be Luz." Kara stared out the window, although she barely saw the scenery passing by. Her thoughts shifted to Matt, who'd come to her office a few times. He was a healthy young buck, and like most men, he didn't visit a doctor very often. But he'd needed the occasional stitches for minor wounds, and the required tetanus shot. He'd been handsome and charming, and her nurse and receptionist had been very attentive.

Now he was dead.

She hated herself at this moment. A young, vital life was snuffed out, and she could have done more to prevent it. "I'll bet you think I'm a selfish bitch," she said suddenly. *And maybe I am.*

Damien shot her a surprised glance. "Why would you say that?"

"Because if I'd had sex with you during the conductions, Matt Brown might still be alive. And there's no telling who else is going to die before we catch this monster."

He returned his attention to the road. "I know I've pushed you on the sex, and I won't deny that it might have given us a little more to work with. But it's no guarantee the Belian can be identified quickly, and it still usually takes several sessions to get a sure identification. This is a very powerful Belian. Second-guessing what may or may not have worked is useless." He looked at her again. "And, for the record, I don't think you're a bitch, or selfish."

She felt a flush of gratification that he wasn't judging or blaming her, but that didn't negate her feelings of guilt. Even the tiniest edge might bring them closer to the Belian's identity.

"Conduction sex might have helped." She stared down at her hands, and made the decision. With Alex safely out of the way, she was finally ready to fully engage in the battle. She would have to push away the painful memories of Richard. This was her town now, and she wasn't going to let a Belian destroy it.

She looked at Damien. "The next conduction will yield better results."

He turned sharply, met her gaze. "Meaning?"

Her heart started pounding in her constricted chest. *This is the right thing—the only thing—to do,* she told herself.

She forced a deep breath. "I'll have sex with you."

AH . . . the rush of a fresh kill, the power and glory of the blood. And all that wondrous energy from a young, vital life. The fear, the adrenaline—like the headiest of nectars. I should have drawn it out longer, made him beg for his life. The sniveling bastard. But it is enough. I can feel the strength of Belial coursing through my body, as pitiful a shell as it is. But I am becoming stronger, more powerful. Soon I will have a far better vehicle to represent the magnificence of Belial. I think I want an even younger, fresher life force for my next kill. Yes, younger . . .

Glory to Belial, to the blood, and to the undefeatable power of the darkness.

ALEX liked his grandparents. They were kind of old, but they didn't move slow like some old people did, and they exuded good energies. After they'd picked him up in Birmingham and driven back to Huntsville—*not* the place where the prison was—they'd taken him to dinner at a cool place called Ruby Tuesday.

Grandma and Grandpa talked about the things they were going to do with him—take him to the space museum, visit Guntersville Dam, look for arrowheads along the Tennessee River, and even a trip to Chattanooga to the aquarium. It all sounded iced.

He knew he would enjoy all that stuff, but he was kinda worried about his mom and the bad stuff going on in Zorro. He didn't like her staying back there with that Belian thing running around, although he wasn't exactly sure what a Belian was.

He was glad Mr. Morgan was with her, because Mr. Morgan had a lot of power. The power was something Alex didn't understand completely, but he knew it was like magic and he believed it could fight evil. Maybe even defeat Darth Vader.

He'd talked to his mom Tuesday and Wednesday, and she'd sounded okay. She just kept telling him to have fun. And he was, for the most part. He'd been okay until the ghost came to him Wednesday night. He was in bed, watching TV, when the strange stuff started happening.

Some books on the desk started moving around, and the pen on the little table by the bed lifted into the air, then fell to the floor. The light flickered, and he heard the same strange whispering he'd heard when the ghost came to his house last week. Then the TV started going on and off. It was freaky.

Mr. Morgan had told him the ghost wouldn't hurt him, and that he should listen to it, as long as he kept his shields up. But he was scared. He ran to his grandparents' bedroom and crawled into their bed. They thought he'd had a bad dream and they let him sleep with them, which was cool, because they had a *giant* bed, and because the ghost didn't come in there.

But the problem was he *knew* the ghost probably

wouldn't go away. And he knew he couldn't pretend to have a bad dream every night. He thought about it most of Thursday, and decided maybe he needed to talk to someone about the ghost. But he knew Grandma and Grandpa wouldn't understand. Mom had told him they didn't know about Sentinels or any of that stuff. There was one person he might be able to talk to, though.

Alex walked to the front door, which was open. There was a glass storm door that kept the heat in. He stared across the street, at a small house that Grandma said had been empty until yesterday. Then a man had rented it, which surprised Grandma, she said because it had been empty for months. She also said she'd never seen anyone move in with so little stuff—just some things in the back of a small truck. The man also had a motorcycle. A really cool, big motorcycle with a lot of chrome and black.

But the most interesting thing was that the man "felt" like Mr. Morgan did. He put off an energy that felt like the Sentinel power. Alex had watched him on Wednesday while he was moving in. Then he had carefully put out mental feelers, being sure his shields were up, and he hadn't sensed anything dark or bad—just the same energy he picked up when he was around Mr. Morgan. He was fairly certain the man was a Sentinel.

He knew he wasn't supposed to talk to strangers, and he knew he had to be extra careful talking about Sentinel stuff. But he was afraid the ghost would come back tonight, and he really wanted to tell someone about it.

Now it was getting late, and Grandma was fixing dinner—except she called it supper. Alex figured he needed to do something before it got dark. "Grandma," he called, "can I go outside for a little while?"

"Sure, sweetie," she called back, sounding a lot like Mom, only older. "Put on a jacket, and don't go far. Stay where I can see you. We'll be eating in about twenty minutes."

"Okay." He slipped on his jacket and pushed open the door and went down the steps. The man was in his driveway, drying off the motorcycle, which he'd just washed.

Alex walked slowly down his grandparents' driveway, studying the man, ready to bolt back to the house if he felt threatened. The man was big, like Mr. Morgan, but he had blond hair, which he tied back like Mr. Morgan, only it was longer, partway down his back. Alex took another step.

The man glanced at him when Alex reached the end of the driveway, but then he squatted and returned to the drying. This close to him, Alex could really feel the flare of power. He checked it carefully and still couldn't feel any darkness. He stood there a long time, debating whether or not to cross the street.

"Are you going to stare all day, or are you going to say what you want to say?" the man said suddenly.

Alex's heart jumped in his chest, and he almost turned and ran—almost. "Hi," he said uncertainly.

"Hi, Alex." The man sat back on his heels.

"You know my name." Alex wondered if this might be a trick.

"I know a lot about you."

Alex found himself taking a step into the road. "Who are you?"

"I'm Luke." The man stood and dusted off his jeans. "If you're coming over, I'd suggest you do it. I'm sure your mother has told you not to play in the street."

"I'm not supposed to talk to strangers, either."

"You're talking to me, aren't you?"

"Well . . . yeah."

The man—Luke, like Luke Skywalker!—smiled real big. He didn't seem as serious as Mr. Morgan. "So why are you making an exception and talking to me?"

"Because you don't seem like a stranger. You have the power," Alex blurted. Belatedly, it occurred to him that maybe he shouldn't be talking about the power to anyone.

Luke nodded. "Yeah, I do. You're pretty good, to pick that up. So what do you think that means?"

Alex considered, decided to take a chance. "I think you're a Sentinel."

"The same as you?"

He wasn't supposed to tell anyone, was he? "Uh, maybe," he hedged.

Luke laughed. "Good boy. You have to be very careful who you tell." He bent down and picked up a container and started spreading a white paste on the motorcycle. "What can I do for you?"

"I have this problem." Alex took another tentative step.

Luke gestured impatiently. "Look if you're coming over, do it all at once. You can stand on the other side of the bike if you're nervous about me. I promise I won't bite."

"Sentinels bite?" Alex asked in amazement.

Luke laughed again. "No. Well, at least not most of the time. That's just an expression."

"Oh." Alex decided to be brave—or at least pretend that he was. He walked across the street, stopping on the opposite side of the motorcycle from Luke.

Luke went back to waxing the motorcycle. "So what's going on?"

"There's this ghost . . ." Alex began.

SIXTEEN

KARA didn't tell Damien she was going to see Luz before she went to her office. It had been enough of a battle to get him to allow her to drive herself. She realized it was probably foolhardy for her to even consider visiting Luz alone, in view of Damien's suspicions and her own doubts—which she couldn't bring herself to acknowledge. She did pocket her pepper spray, but knew it would offer little, if any, protection against a Belian.

Most likely, she wouldn't be the one to break the news to Luz, but she needed to be there to offer support. Luz had been a good friend, and a surrogate mother to Alex. Kara wasn't sure how involved the relationship with Matt had been, but she knew Luz had been seeing him a long time, and would probably be grief stricken. Damien would not be a welcome presence.

Luz's house was a small cinder block structure similar to most of the old homes along River Road. Several gnarled live oak trees were situated around the house, which had the original tin roof and a small front porch with brick foundations for the wood support beams. The house and porch railings had been painted a sunny yellow, while the porch's cement floor, the steps, and the door were a forest green. Large clay pots and a wood-slatted, hanging bench seat with brightly colored patio cushions filled the small porch space; wind chimes and light catchers festooned the upper beams.

Two cars parked in the gravel driveway behind Luz's white Ford pickup indicated Luz had visitors and already knew about Matt. Kara parked partly in the yard and went up the green steps. A dog's distant barking and the melodic tones of the wind chimes drifted on the brisk breeze.

Luz's sister, Serafina, met Kara at the door. The smell of burning candles, incense, and fresh coffee drifted out around her. She looked tired and strained. "*Hola,*" she said softly.

"*Buenos días,*" Kara replied, knowing she preferred Spanish over English. "Is Luz here?"

Serafina stepped back, opened the door wider. "*Entrar.*"

Luz's living room was small, but the light coming through spotless windows made it look more open. Instead of curtains, Luz had put up natural-wood brackets and dowels, and draped them with white sheers that fluttered down each side. Tied bunches of drying herbs hung from the dowels.

Against the interior wall, there was a lace-covered table with a statue of the Madonna. White, blue, and green candle pillars surrounding the Holy Mother were lit. A heavyset, older Hispanic woman whom Kara did not know backed away from the table and crossed herself. She shot Kara a glance and disappeared into the kitchen.

Luz sat on a beige contemporary sofa flanked by sleek oak end tables. Her eyes were bloodshot in her color-leached face, and she was dressed in a gray sweat suit. Without her usual makeup and vivid clothing, she looked young and vulnerable.

Kara went to her and sank down beside her to give her a big hug. "Oh, Luz, I'm so sorry. So very sorry."

With a sob, Luz returned the hug. "I cannot believe it. *Mi novio es ido*. Who could have done such a thing?"

"I don't know." Kara sat back, well aware no words could ease Luz's pain. "Is there anything I can do for you?"

"No . . . there is nothing." Luz's voice broke. Serafina, who was hovering nearby, offered her a tissue. Luz blew her nose, then said, "Unless you want to call off that police chief, Greer. He's already been by to ask me where I was last night."

"Did he say anything else?" Kara asked, feeling guilty because she knew Damien had pointed Tom in that direction.

"Only that people had seen me fighting with Matthew, and that I should not leave town. As if I would run away." Luz sent Kara a startling, malevolent glare. "I know *that man* told him, that *Damien*. He hit Matt at the tavern on Sunday night. I told the chief he should be talking to him instead of me."

"Damien hit Matt?" Kara wondered why Damien had withheld this information. She couldn't see any point in asking Luz about Matt hitting her.

"*Sí*. And he threatened him. Now my Matthew is dead!" Luz's dark eyes glittered, and she started chanting in Spanish, her voice low and harsh. "I call *un maldición*—a curse—upon this Damien!"

"Luz! You don't mean that."

"Oh, *sí*, I do."

Serafina stepped beside the couch, her expression fierce. "I put my own *un maldición*. May this Damien die in *gran agonía* and rot with *el Diablo*."

Shocked by the venom in her voice, Kara stared at the young woman, who was usually quiet and soft-spoken. But her attention was drawn back to Luz, who wrapped her arms around herself and rocked back and forth, muttering in Spanish. "*¡Cabrón!*" she shrilled suddenly.

"Who, Damien?" Kara asked, totally nonplussed by her behavior.

"Matthew." Luz's expression grew hard, all traces of grief vanishing. "*¡Pinche pendejo!* How dare he go and get himself killed!"

"Luz," Kara said gently. "You don't mean that. You're not yourself right now."

Instantly, Luz's expression shifted back to one of sadness, and she sighed. "Forgive me, *camadre*. You are right, I am not myself."

"It's understandable." But Kara wasn't sure she believed that. "You're in shock, and you're grieving."

"You know me so well." Luz took Kara's hand and squeezed it. "I am glad you are here."

But the ugly head of suspicion reared inside Kara, and a disconcerting fear—of Luz—made her end the visit as quickly as she could.

"THAT was a great supper, Mrs. Cantrell. Spaghetti is one of my favorites, and yours was delicious." Alex's new friend picked up his empty plate and placed his silverware on it. "Let me help with the dishes."

"Thank you on the compliment, and please call me Jenny. I'd like to retain at least the illusion of middle age for awhile longer." Alex's grandmother smiled and started stacking dirty plates. She waved Luke back to his seat when he tried to help. "No, sit down. I'll do the dishes later. It's time for dessert. Homemade pecan pie and ice cream."

Luke's eyes lit up, just like Mr. Morgan's did when dessert was served. It was Alex's favorite part of the meal, too. It just was totally weird that Luke was here.

Over at Luke's earlier, Alex had told him about the ghost appearing in Zorro and then again at his grandparents' house. Luke asked him a bunch of questions, then put his motorcycle in the garage.

"Come on," he said. "Let's go meet your grandparents and see if we can sweet-talk them into letting me check out your room."

Alex didn't know what "sweet-talk" entailed, but he didn't think his grandmother would let a stranger—and a big, scary-looking dude at that—into the house. But Luke had smiled and introduced himself to both Grandma and Grandpa, and they'd let him in.

Alex thought he felt a flare of power during the introductions, and wondered if Luke was using something like "the force" to put his grandparents into some sort of trance. But they kept acting normal, except they invited Luke to stay for dinner.

The invitation to dinner convinced Alex that Luke had done *something* with his powers to assure Grandma and Grandpa that he was an okay guy, but it had been ultra fast, like a stealth bomber under the radar. *Sweet.* Alex hoped he could use his powers like that some day, without worrying about a Belian or other bad guy being able to figure it out.

Grandma brought the pie to the table, and Luke ate two big pieces with ice cream, along with a large glass of milk.

"Best pecan pie I ever had," he said finally, patting his belly. "You sure I can't help in here, Mrs.—I mean, Jenny?"

"I'm positive," she said firmly. "That's what the dishwasher is for."

"Great dinner and great pie, Jen." Grandpa rose and gave Grandma a quick kiss on the cheek. He looked at Luke. "NBA game just started—Dallas Mavericks versus the Miami Heat. Care to join me?"

"It's supposed to be a good game." Luke pushed back his chair and stood. "But I think Alex wants to show me his room." He smiled at Grandma, and Alex felt a brief flare of power. "If that's all right with you."

"Of course it is. I think it's wonderful that you're willing to spend time with him." Grandma stepped close and whispered, "He doesn't have a father. Some attention from a male adult would be good for him."

She thought Alex couldn't hear her, but he'd recently figured out he had much better hearing than other "regular" people did. He guessed it went with his special powers.

"Thank you for telling me that," Luke said. "I like kids, and I'll enjoy Alex's company during his visit here." He looked at Alex and gestured toward the hallway. "Come on, bro, let's check out your room."

They left Grandma in the kitchen, humming a tune. Alex had never heard her hum before. Grandpa was settling down in front of the big-screen TV, his attention focused on a bunch of women dressed in what looked like bathing suits and dancing all around.

Luke's attention also fixed on the TV. "Very nice."

Rolling his eyes, Alex tugged on his arm. "Come on. Let's go to my room." He led the way down the hall. "What does 'bro' mean?" he asked.

With another glance back at the TV, Luke followed. "It's short for brother. You're one of the brothers now, part of the White Brotherhood. Is this your room?"

"Yeah. What's the White Brotherhood?"

"It's what the priesthood on Atlantis was originally called." Luke looked around the room. "Sometimes it's still used when referring to Sentinels as a whole, although the term is misleading."

"Atlantis? What's that? Why is the White Brotherhood misleading?"

"Lot of questions there, bro." Luke sat on the edge of the bed. "Atlantis was a continent that existed many, *many* years ago, but it sank into the Atlantic Ocean. Most people believe it's just a myth, but that's actually where Sentinels originated."

Alex stared at him in amazement. "It sank, the whole country? The Sentinels didn't drown?"

Luke shook his head. "It's extremely complicated, and not my place to explain it to you. But when you're on the Internet, do a little research on Atlantis. I think you'll find some amazing stuff. Just remember a lot of it is wrong.

"As for the White Brotherhood, the term is misleading because it's not about ethnic race, like white or black or Asian. 'White' is referring to good, to the light of God. 'Brotherhood' is a loose translation from the ancient language, but it doesn't really fit since there are also female Sentinels."

"Girl Sentinels?" Alex didn't know what he thought about that.

Luke smiled. "Yeah. And some of them are pretty hot. Now, let's check out this ghost."

"I think it's the same ghost that came to my house in Zorro," Alex said. "But is that possible? Aren't ghosts trapped in one place?"

"No, that's a myth. Ghosts don't have physical bodies, so they're not tied to the physical realm like we are," Luke explained. "If this so-called ghost wants to talk to you, it can follow you anywhere. Give me a minute, okay?"

He glanced around the room again, closed his eyes. His hand went to his chest, rested there. Alex could really feel the power surge then. "Hey! Have you got a necklace like Mr. Morgan?"

Luke cracked one eye open. "If it's a quartz crystal framed in silver, then yeah, I do. I need you to be quiet now, and let me work."

"Cool," Alex said, already plotting to bug Mr. Morgan or Luke until he got his own necklace. But he remained quiet, watching Luke, who sat completely still, his eyes closed and his hand over his crystal.

Then the most amazing thing happened. Alex saw Luke start to glow, like he had a bright light outlining him. It was white right around his body, but it had other layers of color on the outer edges, dark blue and a kinda of purple. "Wow," Alex breathed.

"See something?" Luke asked without opening his eyes.

"You've got light and colors around you!"

"That's just my aura. Stay quiet a while longer, then I'll explain it to you."

This was so totally iced, Alex could hardly sit still. But he did, and while he waited, he concentrated on the energies Luke was using. They were becoming familiar to him now.

After a few minutes, Luke took a deep breath and opened his eyes. He smiled at Alex. "Okay, bro, this doesn't appear to be a bad ghost. It won't hurt you." He held out his hand. "Hold onto me and I'll show you what it looks like."

"You can see it?" Alex asked, not at all sure he wanted to go any further.

"The ghost isn't here now. I can see the energy it left behind. So can you, if you'll take my hand, and let me show you."

"Is it scary?"

"Nah. Nothing worse than Casper. Besides, you're a Sentinel, bro. You can handle it." Luke's hand remained outstretched, his gaze steady.

A Sentinel. The words whispered through Alex, beckoning him like a powerful lure, one even stronger than getting to watch *Star Wars* or *Star Trek,* or winning a soccer game. He finally belonged somewhere, with people who were like him.

Slowly, he stretched out his hand and placed it in Luke's.

IT was after dark when Damien returned to the house with a bag of hamburgers, cheese fries, and strawberry milkshakes from the Busy Bee. The aroma of fast food and ice cream wafted inside the house with him. The door closed behind him, and the bolt turned to the locked position, both without physical assistance.

Kara was curled up on the couch, trying to focus on the paperwork she had stacked next to her. She'd been pretty much unsuccessful, upset by her visit with Luz, as well as distracted by thoughts of the upcoming conduction. She watched Damien set the food on the dining room table. He pulled an indigo pillar candle from his duster pocket and also set it on the table. She knew it was for the conduction, and her heart skipped a beat.

"Any luck at the crime scene?" she asked.

"Yes." He took off the duster, walked over to hang it on the wall rack by the front door. "I picked up a strong energy trail. Should be able to get a good conduction."

He strolled to the overstuffed chair, sleek and graceful, reminding her of a very dangerous wild animal. He settled into the chair, looking deceptively relaxed. "Anything unusual at the office today?"

Kara didn't mention her solitary visit to Luz, although she'd been badly shaken by it. She didn't want to deal with Damien's certain reaction right now. She'd tell him later.

"Sharon Wills, Doris's oldest daughter, came by. She's staying in Zorro for the rest of the month, to close up Doris's house. The memorial service is tomorrow, at two o'clock." She tried to push away the overwhelming press of grief and sadness.

"I'll go with you." It was a command, not an option.

"That's fine."

He stared at her thoughtfully. "Anything else happen?"

"Nothing major." She sighed. "But four of my appointments cancelled. They told Bonnie they wouldn't associate with anyone who was living in sin. I guess they heard the latest rumors about you and me."

"You know Texas is part of the Bible Belt."

"Apparently a lot of those 'Bible Belters' are extremely interested in sin. Almost every adult patient I saw today asked about you. And Mike Johnson made a pass at me."

Damien's eyes narrowed. "Did he give you a hard time?"

"I can handle inappropriate remarks and occasional gropings."

"He groped you?" His voice chilled about a hundred degrees.

"I did *not* say that." Kara rolled her eyes. "Down, boy! You don't have to come to my rescue. You'd be surprised how many men lust after their female doctors, or fantasize about them. Some women do, too, but that's another can of worms."

"You don't have to come to my rescue, either," Damien said. "You shouldn't have told Greer we'd been together all night, especially in front of that crowd."

"He had no right to imply that you might be the murderer, and without any proof. Not only that, but I didn't want him focusing on you, when he needs to be looking for the real killer." She rolled her head, trying to ease the stiffness from her shoulders. "As you pointed out yesterday, your car parked in my driveway all night is pretty much the equivalent of waving a red flag and shouting *'Dr. Cantrell is having wild monkey sex with that stranger'.*"

His eyes took on a burning intensity. "They'll be right after tonight."

Desire flashed through her lower body, while her stomach felt like it was twisting itself into double knots. Her apprehension must have shown on her face—not that a mere human could hide anything from a Sentinel—because his expression softened. "Kara, you know I won't hurt you."

Not physically, but the emotional ramifications were another matter entirely. She managed a small nod. "I know."

He rose and crossed to the couch, taking her chin in his hand. He tipped her face up, forcing her to meet his mesmerizing gaze. "Do you trust me?"

"Yes, I do." She spoke the absolute truth. She'd trust this man with both her and Alex's lives. He was a warrior, sworn to protect the innocent.

"Good." He released her, stepped back. "Do you want to eat first?"

The double knots in her stomach twisted into triples. "I'm not hungry."

"I figured you wouldn't be able to eat now. I'll put the food away until afterward." He took the bags into the kitchen, and she heard the fridge open and shut. He returned to the living room as she stood and stacked the files. Her hands were shaking.

She straightened, smoothed her sweater. "I guess we'd better get to it."

He looked at her in that disconcerting way of his. "No sense putting it off." He went to the table, picked up the candle, and gestured toward the hallway. "After you."

She walked to her bedroom, the sound of his boots thudding on the wood floor behind her. She flicked on the light, moved over by the bed. He came in behind her and sat in her wingback chair to pull off his boots. She watched him, imagining how magnificent he would look naked.

In a few moments, she wouldn't have to imagine.

A sudden thought occurred to her. "What about protection?"

He set the second boot by the first. "Sentinels are not susceptible to sexually transmitted diseases, as you probably already know. And the only way you can get pregnant is if a Sentinel soul chooses you as a birth parent."

She pressed her palm against her belly. "Would birth control prevent such a pregnancy?"

"No." He stood and unbuckled his belt. "But a pregnancy won't occur unless The One and the Sentinel soul are convinced it's feasible for all involved parties." He slid the belt free, tossed it into the chair. "In other words, if it is God's will, then it will be. Some things are out of our control."

Another baby—one that would be a Sentinel? She didn't know how she felt about that. Part of her would love to have another baby, but to raise a child in the Sentinel world . . . "I don't know if I could handle having another child."

"If that's the case, then you won't get pregnant. You have to trust in the Universe, Kara."

She wasn't sure she was capable of trusting anymore. Yet she and Damien were the only things standing between the Belian and the town of Zorro. She could only hope she didn't get pregnant, although it seemed like Russian roulette to her.

Damien pulled off his sweater, shaking his gleaming hair free. He wore a white T-shirt underneath, which emphasized his dark skin and bulging biceps. Her mouth went dry. She didn't know if she could nonchalantly strip in front of this man and stretch out across the bed for his use in a conduction. Feeling the heat rise to her cheeks, she cursed herself for being such a prude. She was doctor, used to dealing with naked bodies.

Even so, she felt like that innocent schoolgirl again, about to experience her very first kiss. For a woman who'd dated very few men, and who had been celibate the past seven years, the thought of hot, uninhibited conduction sex with a man she hardly knew—and certainly wasn't in a relationship with—was daunting, to say the least. *Terrifying* would be more accurate, yet Kara hated to think of herself as a coward. Nor was she going back on her word.

"Well, then." Blowing out her breath, she started unbuttoning her sweater.

"Kara." He halted her with a hand on her arm. "Do you have a robe?"

"It's in the bathroom."

"Undress in there and put on the robe. I think that will be easier."

He was far too perceptive. She turned toward the bathroom, feeling like a fool. "I'm sorry to be so . . . silly about this."

"You're doing just fine."

Easy for him to say. He did this on a regular basis—which she found strangely unsettling. In the bathroom, she stripped with shaking hands and fumbled into the robe, tying it at the waist. The chill from the tiled floor wafted up her bare legs, and she shivered. Taking a deep breath, she stared at the closed door. *Now or never.* She opened the door, stepped into the room.

The lights were off, and the indigo candle had been placed on her nightstand and lit. Damien was on the far side of the bed, the covers just barely over his hips. He was impossibly large and imposing, dwarfing the queen-size bed. The candlelight flickered on his bare chest, over the sleek bulge of muscle, and the glint of his crystal. Glancing away, she saw his clothes draped neatly over the nearby armchair.

Aware of his gaze on her as she slid beneath the covers, she settled onto her back. She stared at the ceiling, tension invading her body. Some of it, of course, was the sexual energy he was radiating like a raging furnace.

"Turn on your side, facing me." His voice was like rough velvet.

She did, meeting his gaze. He shifted closer, lifted a hand to cup her cheek. She stared into the molten silver of his eyes, feeling heat and desire flaring from their two bodies, the sparks from his fingers tingling on her face. She felt a tug at her waist, realized he was untying her robe with his other hand, and pushing the fabric behind her.

He slid his hand lightly along her bare hip and midriff, his fingers leaving a scorching trail. Need rose like a brilliant sunrise, and in her mind, she saw two nude bodies entwined in raw hunger. *Dear God.* She was about to melt into an incoherent puddle, and they'd barely touched.

He settled his body mere inches from hers, although he didn't caress her again or kiss her, as Richard would have done. His hand remained against her face, and she resisted the inordinate urge to turn her lips into his palm.

"Don't be afraid," he said in that black-magic voice. "I'll be . . . careful with you."

She knew he couldn't honestly say "gentle," because there was nothing soft or easy about conductor sex. "I know," she whispered, shocked at the husky timbre of her voice.

"Tell me if you feel any discomfort at any time."

Of its own volition, her gaze shifted lower to the sizable, tented sheet above his groin. *Oh, my.* She managed to nod.

He took her hands in the ritual conduction clasp. "Don't let go, no matter how intense it gets."

It was already intense. The heat from his body had raised her temperature to a simmer; his touch elevated it to a full boil. The energy didn't initiate in a steady flow, but like a tsunami wave. The sexual surge exploded in her belly. A red haze filmed her vision. She felt like she'd been slammed against a wall. *Pop! Pop! Pop! Pop!* The four lower chakras blasted open almost simultaneously, and she jolted forward with a cry.

"Hold on," Damien's harsh voice came against her ear. "This is going to be wild."

He eased her onto her back, shifting his body over hers, setting every cell inside her on fire. She twisted, no longer concerned about propriety. She desperately wanted—needed—to touch him, to explore his body, but he had her hands entrapped in his.

The fifth and sixth chakras burst open, pouring vivid blues into her inner sight. "Damien," she gasped, unable to process anything but her body's erotic demands. She felt the aching wetness between her legs, needed him inside her *now*. Spreading her legs, she arched against him.

"Hang on." He settled between her thighs, and she felt his erection probing a burning trail right where she desperately needed it. She tilted her pelvis to give him better access.

"*Now!*" she cried fiercely.

He slid inside her as the seventh chakra opened and a violet mist enveloped them. He *was* big, and he filled her completely. But she was beyond ready; there was no discomfort, only perfection of fit and friction. She started climaxing with his first stroke. Rapid-fire images flashed through her mind, as waves of sensation erupted in her body. It went on and on, a mindless detonation of visions and pleasure. She lost all sense of time and reality. Yet she was acutely attuned to Damien, to him stroking hard and deep inside her, to his shuddering orgasm.

Gradually, she realized the energies were receding, while little aftershocks rocked her body. "Oh, God," she groaned.

Damien dropped his forehead to hers. "*Damn.*"

"Yes," she said weakly. "That, too."

He pulled out and rolled onto his back, his chest heaving. She had just enough strength to pull the covers over herself. At least there was no headache this time, no burning, unappeased need.

"You okay?" he asked.

"I'm fine." Although it might be hours, maybe days, before she could walk normally again. It had been seven years since she'd been with a man, so she'd probably be very sore for a few days. Willing her breathing to calm, she closed her eyes, setting off a series of startling visual flashes. Her eyes opened and she angled her head toward Damien. "I'm still seeing the images."

He turned on his side, the covers dipping low on his hips. "Take my hand. Let's see if you can link to my third eye, like you did with the ghost."

She reached out, and he grasped her hand firmly in his.

Electrical sensations coursed up her arm. "Concentrate on your other sight," he said. "My third eye should bring it into sharper focus for you. We'll both see the same thing."

She closed her eyes again, opening herself to him. The images clicked on, clear and vivid, as if she were watching a movie.

A pair of sleek, female legs, wearing stylish red pumps, walking languidly down a gravel driveway. They moved alongside a white vehicle; a momentary shift in the visual showed a dirty Ford F-150. The door opened, and the legs stepped up into the driver's side.

A feminine hand put the key in the ignition and started the engine. Then the truck was moving, with visual snippets out the window. It appeared to be on River Road; the sunlight reflected off the Blanco River as the truck drove. Another shift upward to the woman's head, but the face and hair were hazy.

Then everything went blurry and the vision did a Hollywood-style fade-out.

Damien pounded the mattress. "I just need to see the face. Just a glimpse. *Damn it!*" He sat up, thrusting his fingers through his hair. "This thing is way too powerful."

The state trooper/Belian stepped away from Richard's body, glowing with preternatural light. Richard's death seemed to have rejuvenated, empowered him. He moved toward Kara, grinning grotesquely, Satan incarnate . . .

Battling nausea, she clutched the sheet to her chest. "The longer it survives and the more it kills, the stronger it grows," she whispered.

"It doesn't have much longer." Damien's voice was colder than she'd ever heard it. "Its cursed soul will be burning on Saturn very soon. I want to see the medical files on your female patients again—all of those with ongoing health problems. I know there were five that caught my attention—Belle Williams, Luz, Mary . . . what was her last name?"

"Roberts." Kara pushed herself up, keeping a firm grip on the sheet. She'd already violated doctor–patient privilege, and she would do it again—anything to stop this monster. "There's also Katie Woodward and Beth Gonzales."

"That's right. I'm going to look at them very closely. Do you know if all of them drive white Ford trucks?"

"I know that Belle and Luz do, and so does Mary. I'm not sure about Katie and Beth."

"I'll find out." He tossed back the covers and slid from the bed, giving her a breathtaking view of one fine rear end, and a beautifully muscled torso and legs to go with it. He seemed comfortable in his oh-so-sexy skin, but then most guys were less self-conscious about their bodies than women were, Kara thought enviously. Moving to the chair with lethal grace, he stepped into his jeans, sans underwear, zipped them up, then pulled on his T-shirt and sweater.

"We can discuss this more over dinner." He picked up his boots and started toward the door, then glanced back at her. "You coming?"

That's one way of putting it, she thought inanely. She forced her thoughts away from sexual innuendo, nodded. "Yes. I'll be there in few minutes."

He stared at her as if trying to gauge her state of mind. "You know you did the right thing, Kara. We're very close now."

Close to what? she wondered. *Light or darkness? And which one would win?*

PRAISE be to Belial, my strength is growing, and my abilities are all powerful. How could the fools think I wouldn't sense such a strong sexual surge? Having a conduction to try and track me down, are they? My, my. And so early in the evening. Maybe they couldn't wait any longer, couldn't keep their supposedly pristine hands off each other, fucking like dogs in heat. Oh, my dear, was it as good for you as it was for me? *Ah, how I amuse myself.*

But I know, *even though they think I don't. Not that I care—I'm far too strong for them to find me. It has to be that nosy reporter, Morgan. Everyone else in this pitiful excuse of a town has been here forever; no one leaves for long. And if Morgan is the Sentinel—may he be cursed for eternity—then Dr. Kara must be the conductor. It is the only logical explanation, especially since she and Morgan have been shacking up together.*

Dear, sweet Kara. What a front you present to everyone. I, however, know you for the bitch you really are. I will enjoy your screams—and Morgan's, too—when I torture you both. I'll savor your pleas for mercy, and then I'll send your souls into the bowels of Hades, as my offering to Belial.

But first, I will increase my strength with another kill, which will offer me the boundless energy of a child. Not a challenge, true, but once I'm able to take over a better body, I'll be invincible. Too bad the kill can't be Kara's brat, but she's sent him away—for now. I'll deal with him when he returns for his mother's funeral.

And now, I'm going to drink to my perfect plan. Praised be Belial.

SEVENTEEN

KARA didn't feel the letdown until she was in the shower the next morning. After the conduction, the evening had been too busy for introspection. She and Damien had eaten, reviewed medical files, done some laundry, and she'd called Alex. Never once had they acted like a couple who had just had mind-blowing sex.

At bedtime, Damien had retrieved the police scanner and taken it to Alex's room, where he spent the night. Slipping into her bed alone, Kara felt a sense of desolation. She told herself it was simply fear of dreaming about another murder, but knew there was more, which she was unwilling to face right now.

She'd been so exhausted that she'd quickly fallen asleep, despite the lingering energies of the conduction. Thankfully, there had been no dreams.

When the shrilling alarm jolted her awake at seven A.M., she swatted it off and stumbled to the bathroom and into the shower. She stood beneath the warm spray until her mind began to function. Then, as she soaped herself, wincing when she reached the sore flesh between her legs—a part of her anatomy that had probably atrophied over the past seven years—she thought about last night's conduction.

Not about what had happened, but what *hadn't* happened. There'd been no tenderness, no affection, between her and Damien, although he had been considerate and respectful. No unnecessary touching, no tongue-tangling kisses; no kissing at all, for that matter. No true touching of souls, not in an emotional sense.

She'd had those things with Richard. She had finally accepted their loss, although she still grieved for the man and the love they'd shared. That didn't mean she wanted to live the rest of her life without finding them again. For the first time since Richard's death, she was coming alive, emotionally and physically, as a woman. Her needs were awakening, voicing their demands. But she wanted more than just sex.

She felt let down because she hadn't had that *more* with Damien. Which was ridiculous, she told herself; he had never represented the situation any other way. She had gone into last night's conduction knowing it was just that—a sexual tracking session. She needed to get her foolish longings under control before she set herself up for some serious heartache.

She dried off and dressed in a navy pantsuit and low matching pumps that would be appropriate both for seeing patients that morning and Doris's memorial service that afternoon. She added a gold silk scarf she found in her accessory drawer, although for the life of her, she couldn't remember where she'd gotten it. She brushed out her hair, added a touch of blush to her chalk-white cheeks, and applied mascara to her lashes—waterproof, so she wouldn't look like a raccoon if she cried during the memorial service.

Wondering if Damien was up yet, she walked quietly down the hallway. She saw him then, sitting in the lotus position in the middle of the living room floor, back erect, eyes closed, wearing nothing but his jeans and the crystal on its silver chain. He'd raised the blinds and situated himself in the center of the sunshine streaming in. The light blazed around him like an immense halo, and he appeared to be in a deep meditative state.

Her breath caught in her throat. She used to observe Richard meditate, sometimes had even joined him. The enlightenment of altered consciousness, the power of controlled chakra energies had been, in their way, more profound than a conduction. Joint meditation had always brought Richard and her closer together, and often ended in lovemaking.

Watching Damien now, she felt a rush of emotions. She wanted to go to him, to stroke her hands over his beautiful chest, to touch him everywhere, and have him touch her in return.

Not a good idea—not even an option, really.

She forced herself to turn away, quietly got her purse and coat, and let herself out the front door.

KARA spoke at the memorial service. Sharon had asked her to, and she felt honored to be able to share what a wonderful person Doris had been. "Doris had an amazing vitality and a zest for life," she told the group assembled at the Gateway Funeral Home. "She could do circles around people half her age, me included." A lot of people smiled and nodded.

"She had a huge heart and a loving spirit. She cared about those less fortunate, and was always helping with church and town fund-raisers. She was a wonderful baker and made the best cakes and cookies in Zorro. I owe at least five pounds to her." More wistful smiles and nodding.

"Doris did a lot of things to help others, quietly, without any fanfare. I've seen her—saw her—load her car with meals and blankets and clothing and take them into the poor neighborhoods around Zorro. She'd also take flowers from her garden—yes, she was an excellent gardener, too—and books and magazines to people who were sick.

"She loved children—everyone's kids—and was so darned proud of her own children and grandchildren. My son adored her." Kara paused, feeling tremendous regret that Alex couldn't be there to say good-bye, but he had written a letter right after Doris died, and she'd brought it today and propped it by the urn containing Doris's ashes.

Clearing her throat, Kara continued, "Doris was a modern woman, and kept up with the changing technology, despite her age. She surfed the Internet on her computer, sent and received e-mail, took yoga classes, and went on ocean cruises. She had a full and happy life, and I—" Her gaze skittered to the lovely portrait of Doris on its easel, and the golden urn beside it, and a sudden rush of tears filled her eyes. "We're all going to miss her terribly," she finished in a tear-choked whisper.

She stepped down from the podium, and Sharon, pale and wan with grief, flashed a thankful smile. Her heart heavy, Kara returned to her seat beside Damien. "Well spoken," he murmured.

The tears overflowed her eyes and she fumbled blindly in her jacket pocket for a tissue. A white handkerchief appeared out of nowhere. "Here."

"Thanks." She took it, blotted her eyes, feeling miserable. Losing Doris was painful enough. It was made worse by the fact that she'd been murdered, and by a Belian. Added to that was her guilt because Damien had warned her about the Belian, but she'd done her ostrich routine until it was too late.

"You are *not* responsible for Doris's passing," he said in a low voice, and she wondered if he were a mind reader.

Needing his strength and warmth, she leaned against him. She felt the slight hesitation before his arm came around her. Its reassuring weight was enough to get her through the rest of the service.

"WHAT a day," Kara said later, as they walked across the grass to her house.

The memorial service had been followed by a get-together at Doris's house. Neighbors and friends had brought enough food to feed the entire Texas National Guard. Damien made impressive inroads on the food, while managing to stay close to Kara. It was stressful being in the house where she'd found Doris, talking to the family and dealing with the curious stares and whispers aimed at her and Damien. She was glad when they were able to leave.

The sun was setting and the temperature dropping. The chill seeped through Kara's wool pantsuit. "Did you pick up anything?" she asked.

"Not even a glimmer. If the Belian was at the funeral home or the house, it was well shielded."

"Belle Williams didn't look very good," Kara commented. "She must have had a chemo treatment yesterday."

"Did you notice her legs? Very nice for a woman her age."

"She square-danced for years, until her husband died . . . the Belian has nice legs," Kara said slowly, remembering the vivid images from last night.

"That's exactly what I was thinking."

"Belle *is* on our short list of suspects." Kara turned to look back at Doris's house. Soon it would be sold, and her things would be distributed among her children. Kara couldn't shake the soul-deep sadness. And she missed Alex. Nothing was right in her world. "God, I need a drink." She felt, rather than saw, Damien's gaze swing to her.

"We can do that."

She knew his mega-rapid metabolism allowed him to drink large quantities of alcohol, while she could drink herself into oblivion—which sounded damn good right now. "I don't want to go to Jim's Tavern," she said with a shudder. "Let's just go to the Quik-Stop drive through and get something to bring back here."

"Fine." He had the measured tone of someone trying to soothe an upset or deranged person, but she simply didn't care.

She insisted on driving, so they took her truck and bought a twelve-pack of Shiner Bock, which she also insisted on paying for. She didn't bother to change her clothes when they returned, just grabbed two beers, popped the tops, and gave one to Damien.

She plopped onto the couch and kicked off her pumps. Damien was wearing that killer black suit, this time with a silver-and-black striped tie. He set his beer down to take off the coat and tie and drape them over a dining room chair, then retrieved the bottle and settled in the big chair.

She had a fourth of her beer downed before he took his first sip. His eyebrows lifted when she slugged another fourth in one long gulp. "You know, you didn't eat anything at the reception."

"Ask me if I care."

He didn't respond, but she thought she saw his lips twitch as he raised his beer to his mouth. He took a healthy swig, his powerful throat flexing as he swallowed. He'd released his hair from the tie, and it was loose around his shoulders, a stark contrast against the white dress shirt. With the sharp angles and lines of his face, tempered by the sensual fullness of his lips, he looked like a god. Watching him made her a little giddy.

"Besides, you ate enough for the two of us," she muttered in an attempt to divert her wayward thoughts.

"Yeah, there was some great food there."

She almost laughed at the reverence in his voice. He might be an all-powerful Sentinel, but he was such a *guy*. And what a guy—with all the right parts, slot A fitting perfectly into slot B. Damn, her thoughts were definitely unruly.

She drank more beer and pondered her reactions to Damien. Part of it was the sexual attraction that raged between them when they were in close physical proximity to each other, and that was nothing more than chemistry.

Yet even when there was distance between them, when she was away from the mind-clouding hormonal surge of the Sentinel–conductor link, she had lingering thoughts of Damien. His honor and integrity, his compassion and strength, his gentleness and easy affection with Alex—his basic *goodness*—all combined inside a gorgeous face and body to form one hell of a package.

One that was becoming harder to resist. *And maybe she shouldn't even try.* Gulping the rest of her beer, she rose from the couch. "You ready for another one?"

"Sure." He drained his bottle, handed it to her.

In the kitchen, she leaned against the sink, staring sightlessly out the window. She knew she was navigating treacherous waters, at a time when she was vulnerable. Her life was off course, everything she'd worked for threatened, and now she had inexplicable, *dangerous* feelings. They were probably just the result of the upheaval in her life. Yet, didn't she deserve some happiness, however fleeting? Deciding the answer was yes, she got two more beers.

She rejoined Damien in the living room, sipped the second beer more slowly. Her thoughts returned to last night's conduction, and to something that had nagged at her since then. "You didn't kiss me," she said.

"What?"

"Last night. You didn't kiss me during the conduction."

She'd caught him off guard, judging from his expression. "Kara—"

"Don't give me some bullshit answer! I asked a simple question. A straightforward reply would be nice, for a change."

His jaw tightened. "No, I don't kiss my conductors. It makes things too personal, raises . . . expectations."

Ah, emotion, commitment. She understood Sentinels couldn't get involved with every one of their conductors. But many took mates and had families—to propagate the species, if nothing else, as she had just learned. Yet she sensed there was something else underlying Damien's isolation.

"Does this have anything to do with what happened to your parents?"

The pain flashed across his face before he could hide it.

Then he schooled his features into an unreadable expression. "That has nothing to do with any of this."

But she knew it did. He had done the same thing she had, she realized. His pain from his personal loss had been so great, he'd shut down emotionally. In that regard, they were kindred souls. Both wounded spirits.

She was so damned tired of being wounded.

She was on her feet without a conscious decision, her legs carrying her to Damien of their own volition. His eyes flared, but before he could react, she leaned down, trapped his face between her hands, and kissed him.

He jerked back as if he'd been burned. "What the—"

She pressed her fingers against his mouth. "Shut up. This isn't a conduction, Damien, where you can keep your distance by claiming it's for a higher cause. There's no Sentinel and conductor business tonight. Right now, we're just two people who need each other."

He grabbed her wrist, pulled her hand from his mouth. "That's the alcohol talking. You don't know what you're doing."

It wasn't the beer—she could drink at least three before she got tipsy. She felt as if she'd made a monumental decision, had already taken the leap off the cliff. She couldn't go back now, didn't want to go back.

So she reached for her wings and took control of the fall. "The hell I don't! You keep telling me that life goes on, that we do have free will in some things. Well, I'm choosing to *live*. I guess you're going to hide behind your Sentinel heritage, instead of facing life head-on. You're a coward, Morgan."

Anger sparked in his eyes. "You know that's not true."

"Really? You're letting the past dictate your life, and you're refusing to let yourself feel. I'd call that cowardice."

Maybe her words were the pot calling the kettle black, since she'd done exactly what she accused him of, but at least she had finally been willing to take the leap. And her wings seemed to be working just fine.

"You don't know anything about my life," he said, and started to move her back so he could stand.

She shoved him hard, catching him off balance, and he fell back into the chair. "I know you're a man, with feelings and needs, just like any other human male. And I'm assuming you want me. *So kiss me, damn it!*"

Not giving him another opportunity to protest, she grabbed his head and kissed him again. She felt his resistance, his hands coming up to her shoulders to push her away. She angled her head, teased her tongue between his lips. *Please,* she thought, *please, please don't reject me.* She needed this right now, needed to feel alive and maybe cared for, even if only for one night.

As if again reading her mind, his hands cupped her shoulders, and she sensed him wavering. With a groan, he took command of the kiss, began ravishing her mouth with devastating finesse. Dear God, he kissed every bit as good as she had fantasized, and then some. With a little hum, she crawled on his lap, straddled him. Felt him leap to life between her legs, the immense hardness of him pulsing against her.

Her own body's response was immediate, her breasts swelling, wet heat flooding her lower extremities. Damien knew—his senses were too keen to miss her reactions. Still kissing her, he let his fingers tease against her crotch for a brief moment, then swept his hand up to cup her breast. She reciprocated by cupping him back, only much lower, and it was like throwing gasoline on a fire. Need and heat exploded between them, and things got a little crazy.

She jerked his shirt open; he unbuttoned her jacket and unsnapped her bra. They couldn't get enough of each other, kissing and touching, the fire now a roaring inferno. She got his belt unbuckled and his pants unzipped. He groaned as she freed him and wrapped her hand around his hard length.

Wildness flared through her, along with an intense craving for physical and emotional intimacy. She slipped down to kneel before the chair. Damien had given her back her humanity, and she wanted to revel in it. She wanted to take him to the depths of an intimacy he'd been avoiding. To let him know what she had just learned herself.

That it was good to feel again.

As Kara knelt between his splayed legs, Damien knew what she was going to do. He was too far gone to resist, could only watch as she looked at him with those luminous gray eyes, as she lowered her head and took him into her mouth.

Then sensation decimated all rational thought—not that there had been much during the past moments of sensual frenzy. Moist warm heat stroked him, as silky auburn hair tantalized the inside of his thighs. All he could do was lay his head back and take the exquisite torment.

Until it was almost too much, and he was on the edge of exploding. He wanted Kara along for the ride, so he stopped her, pulling her up with him as he stood. She tried to protest, but he swung her into his arms and carried her to the bedroom, then stripped off the rest of their clothing. Bits of mental clarity returned, but he ignored the clamoring warnings.

He shouldn't be indulging in this, couldn't be what Kara deserved and needed. Yet he'd been alone and isolated for so long, he couldn't step back from this. It was like letting the wind loose and then trying to corral it, or attempting to stop a tidal wave. He knew on some level that giving in to his feelings would damn him, but he was determined to taste paradise before he burned in Hades.

He needed this too desperately to take his time with Kara. Placing her on the bed, he feasted on her like a starving man, his mouth flowing over satiny skin. She didn't seem to mind, arching against him, trying to touch him in return. There was no talk, just her sweet moans, and the pounding of his heart.

Her breasts were as sensitive as he remembered, only

this time he got to taste them, to swirl his tongue over turgid nipples, and hear her breath catch. With hands and mouth, he got to map the curve of her body, the texture of her skin, as he moved down her.

He discovered she had a tiny gold ring in her navel—which was sexy as hell—and that she was a true redhead. Her natural feminine scent beckoned, and he lowered his head to kiss her intimately. He focused on giving her pleasure, vaguely aware of her fingers tangled in his hair, of the breathy sounds she made. He hurled her over the edge, savoring the way she cried out his name. He slid back up, his own need now taking center stage.

"Damien," she whispered. She pulled his head down and kissed him fervently. Settling between her legs, he took her wrists and pressed them against the pillow, and began sliding inside her.

"No." She wiggled free and pushed against his shoulders. "Lady's choice, Morgan."

With a groan, he allowed her to shove him onto his back and straddle him. "Kara, you're going to"—he groaned again as she lowered herself over him, sheathing him to the hilt—"kill me."

She smiled wickedly, began to move, way too slowly. "Oh, I think you'll survive."

She was right, although at one point, he felt certain he'd died and been shot like a rocket into the heavens. But then, as he gradually returned to terra firma, he knew he'd survived very nicely.

SARA Thornton checked her appearance in the corroded wall mirror in the small space that served as a foyer. She wasn't sure tonight was a good idea, but she hadn't had much of a life since David—she blocked the thought before it could complete itself. Had it only been eight weeks? Sometimes it seemed like it had happened an eternity ago, while at others, it felt like only yesterday that he'd gone off to fish in the Blanco River, and never returned.

She pushed the thoughts away. She needed to get out—had to get out, before the four walls of the tiny house closed in on her. She couldn't believe her babysitter hadn't cancelled, after Wednesday night . . . Zorro had seen more unusual happenings in the past two months than it had all of Sara's adult life.

A knock came on the front door, and she thought it might have been nice if David had gotten around to putting in the peephole he'd been promising for years. But who would have known there was a murderer living in Zorro? She cracked the door to find Luz standing on the narrow cement steps. Opened the door to let her in.

"Thank you for coming. I thought maybe with what happened with Matt and all, you'd—"

"I need to stay busy," Luz interjected. "I need to just keep going, as if . . ." She shook her head.

"I know." Sara closed the door. "I was sorry to hear about Matt."

Luz glanced around, her face unusually pale and devoid of emotion. "Where are the children?"

"Michael's in his room, and Julie is at the Millers, two houses north of here. She's supposed to be home by eight. There's leftover macaroni and cheese in the fridge, peanut butter and jelly on the counter." Sara hesitated. "You sure you want to do this?"

Luz's expression became determined. "*Sí*. I *want* to do this."

Sara felt a rush of relief. "Okay . . . good. Well, then, I'll get going."

"Where will you be?"

"Beth Gonzales and Mary Roberts and me are going down to Gruene for dinner."

"To the Gristmill and maybe the Dance Hall?" Luz asked discerningly.

The lure of a drink called to Sara; she could almost taste the whisky going down. But she didn't like the knowing smirk on Luz's face. "Maybe. But I deserve a good time. I've been workin' my fingers to the bone, taking care of these kids and trying to hold things together ever since David went off and drowned."

"Of course you do. Go on, and do not worry about *los niños*. They will be fine."

Sara did, grabbing her purse and coat, and feeling a heady rush of freedom as she left her responsibilities behind her.

OH . . . *God* . . . Kara dug her fingers into Damien's slick shoulders. Her back was pressed against the wet shower tiles, her legs wrapped around his waist, with him deep inside her. She needed just a little more . . . just a little harder.

He gave it to her, stroking in a powerful rhythm as the water pounded around them. Her spine felt fused to the tiles, but she didn't care. She came apart, detonating like an atom bomb. Wrapping her arms around his neck, she held on for dear life as she dissolved into fine particles that felt like they were flying at light speed into outer space.

Much later, she stumbled into her bedroom, her towel flapping around her, and collapsed on the bed. She'd forgotten about the phenomenal Sentinel endurance, and that it was enhanced by water, but it was coming back to her now. She lay there and drifted for a few moments, listening to the faint sounds of Damien moving around the bathroom across the hall, then the blow-dryer going on.

Their relationship didn't appear altered by non-conduction sex, maybe because they simply weren't talking about it. Last night, she'd felt Damien draw away from her as soon as they left the bedroom. Although they'd slept together later, she'd been the one to curl against him.

She'd also been the one to instigate lovemaking this morning, but he hadn't refused; he'd even taken the lead once things heated up, giving her two shattering orgasms before he found his own release. Once they got out of bed, however, it had been all business.

They'd visited the three known murder scenes—those of

David, Doris, and Matt—and this afternoon, attempted another conduction. Despite the powerful sexual crescendo, they hadn't been able to garner any more information on the Belian.

After dinner tonight, when Damien went to shower, she had joined him. One thing led to another, and the shower ended with a very satisfactory outcome. She knew her actions were wanton, but she also knew her moments with him were fleeting.

The three times they'd been in the throes of non-conduction sex, he had been a passionate, intoxicating lover. But after each time, he withdrew emotionally.

Kara got up, retrieved her robe from the bathroom, and put it on. Then she sat on the bed and toweled her wet hair. Despite the myriad concerns nagging at her, she couldn't stop thinking about Damien. That's when the realization hit her, with the impact of a physical blow.

She was falling in love with him.

Stunned, she dropped the towel. What was the matter with her? Why couldn't she go for the *normal* men? Because . . . maybe she wasn't supposed to. She'd been born to be a natural conductor for certain Sentinels; her son was a Sentinel. If there really was a divine plan, as Damien insisted, then maybe this was part of that plan.

She drew her knees up and rested her chin on them. *Damn.* She had no idea if Damien returned that love, but if he did, she might never know it. Oh, she knew he cared. She knew it on a primal level, as evidenced by his protective attitude, how he looked at her when he didn't think she was aware of it. And by the way he touched her during lovemaking, with the same reverence Richard had shown her.

Damien might never admit to his feelings, even to himself; he would probably never be willing to commit to a relationship. Maybe she should feel hurt, but this wasn't a high school crush, and she fully understood. She knew Sentinels had to be careful that their conductors didn't fall in love with them. They carried tremendous responsibilities, and faced very dangerous—and often fatal—situations. All too often, they lost loved ones, as Damien had. She didn't know if he could ever get beyond the emotional baggage from his past.

She would have to live with that. Life would go on, and so would she. One day at a time, just as she had done after Richard died. She had Alex to think about, and taking care of him was a full-time job—in addition to her medical career.

Yet the irony of the situation wasn't lost on her.

She was finally ready to love again—with a man who might not be capable of returning that love.

IT was late Saturday night. His grandparents had gone to bed, and Alex was in his room, looking at the day's treasures. They'd gone to the Tennessee Aquarium in Chattanooga, which had been totally iced, and he'd gotten some great souvenirs. He really liked the "Shark Dudes" T-shirt and the ceramic otter mug (he planned to drink hot chocolate in it tomorrow) that Grandpa had bought him. With his own money, he'd gotten a cool plush Day-Glo stingray for his mom.

Still too hyped to sleep, he put the items on the dresser, got into his pajamas, and turned on the TV. To his delight, *Farscape* was on the Sci-Fi channel, and he settled in bed to watch it. Sleepy now, he was nodding off when the blinds at his window started rattling. Startled, he sat up and looked at the window. The blinds banged back and forth like there was a strong breeze coming in. Only the window was closed.

His senses tingled, and he felt the crawl of a foreign energy along his skin. His heart started racing. It took a moment for him to remember to raise his shields. A wall photo of him and Mom tilted sideways, static blared from the TV, and items skittered along the dresser. The handle of the door to the hallway began turning back and forth. Afraid to try to make it through the door, Alex huddled under the covers. He knew on a logical level that it was probably just the ghost trying to talk to him; on a gut level, he was scared stiff.

"W-w-what do you want?" he whispered, scrunching his eyes closed. He knew from what Luke had showed him that the ghost was leaving wavering energy trails, which experienced Sentinels would be able to see in their minds. But he couldn't see anything. He pushed his shields up further, tried to listen, like Luke had told him to.

He heard a high-pitched whisper, barely audible over the TV static. *"Help . . . my . . . say . . . Say . . . no. Help . . . my . . . My!"*

"Help you what?" Alex asked, afraid to look.

"Stop! My! Say . . . no . . . No!"

He tried to make out more words, but he couldn't figure out the strange hissing sounds. The energies around him escalated. There was a crash, and his eyes flew open. His new otter mug was on the floor in a bunch of pieces. The picture of him and Mom rocketed to the floor. The blinds were pounding against the window now. All kinds of stuff went flying through the air, and the hissing became more of a wail, like wind in a storm. Only it was inside the room. *"My . . . myyyyyy!"*

He knew Grandma and Grandpa wouldn't come to his rescue. They couldn't hear anything because Grandma slept with some sort of sleep machine and a mask over her face, and Grandpa snored real loud.

The pillow next to Alex levitated and rotated, spinning faster and faster. Utterly terrified, he leaped out of bed and lunged to the door, flinging it open. He ran down the hall, stopped outside his grandparents' closed bedroom door.

A noise had him looking back toward his bedroom. He could almost see the flow of energy coming down the hallway; he heard popping sounds as pictures on the walls began spinning. Then the hissing. *"Myyyyyyy!!!"*

It was coming straight at him. He turned and ran. He fumbled with the front door bolt, his heart pounding furiously. At any second, he expected to feel fiery claws grabbing him. Then he was out, racing across the cold grass, gasping for breath. He looked behind him, fearful that something might be after him. But he saw only the dim glow from the lamp Grandma kept on in the family room, illuminating the open doorway.

He leaped onto Luke's porch, pounded on the door. He hit the doorbell three or four times for good measure, heard it chiming inside the house. "Luke!" he yelled. "Luke, it's me, Alex!"

Dancing back and forth on his icy feet, he looked back at his grandparents' house. So far, so good, but he sure didn't feel safe. It seemed like an eternity before the porch light went on and the door swung open. Luke stood there in nothing but a pair of jeans. His long hair was messed up and he looked kinda sleepy.

"Alex! What the hell's going on?"

"The ghost! It's back and it's *really* upset!"

IT took Sara Thornton four tries to get her key into the lock. Of course, it didn't help that the porch light was broken—another one of David's uncompleted projects—and that the door seemed to be moving. On the road, Beth and Mary leaned out the car windows and hollered comments.

"Hey, Sara, locked out of your own house?"

"Shut up!" she yelled back. "I just can't find the keyhole."

"It's supposed to be the man who keeps missing the hole." Both of them dissolved into laughter over Beth's remark.

"Go get screwed," Sara said, but she was feeling too good to really care about their comments. She finally shoved the key home, fumbled the lock and door open, and swept grandly into the house. Beth honked the horn twice behind her, then the car screeched away.

Sara stumbled and almost fell, cursing. Who had left the rug edge flipped up again? And who was that asleep on the couch? Oh, yeah. It was Luz. Couldn't stay awake, the stupid woman. And it was only . . . Sara squinted at her inexpensive gold-toned Timex—a gift from cheapskate David—but her vision blurred. Well, it was after midnight—she knew that much.

"Sara? Are you all right?" Luz sat up and swung her legs off the couch.

"You fell asleep," Sara said accusingly. "You're supposed to be watching my kids."

Luz's dark eyes narrowed. "I did watch them. And I fixed them their dinner, made sure they got their baths, and put them to bed—after I washed their sheets. I even cleaned your bathroom and scrubbed your kitchen floor. They were both filthy." She stood and began folding the blanket she'd been using.

"I guess I should be grateful." But all Sara felt was angry, her alcohol-induced euphoria starting to fade. How dare Luz insinuate she wasn't a good housekeeper?

Unable to concentrate on much of anything, she decided to let the insult pass. "How were the kids?" There. She sounded perfectly normal.

"They were fine." Luz stared at her. "They are good children."

When they weren't driving Sara crazy. Swaying, she pressed a hand against the front door.

Luz tossed the folded blanket on the couch. "You are drunk. Again."

Another insult. "I deserve a drink now and then." Sara sauntered over to the slat-back rocking chair and tossed her purse at it. She missed, and the purse slid to the floor.

"I knew you would come home in this condition. Like old times, eh?"

The bitch. But Sara forced herself to smile. She needed Luz, who was one of the few people willing to come to the poorest part of Zorro and to put up with Sara's kids. Without Luz, Sara would never be able to escape her miserable life.

"Oh, yeah, like always," she muttered, staggering over to pick up her purse. She got so dizzy, she almost fell, but she used the arm of the rocker to heave herself back up. She dug around in her purse, pulled out two crumpled twenties—which her mother had sent her to buy clothes for the kids—and held them out to Luz. "Here."

"One is enough." Luz shoved the other twenty back into Sara's shaking hand. "Use the rest to buy *los niños* something more to eat than peanut butter and macaroni."

One of these days, Sara wouldn't need Luz. Then she could blow off the bitch. "Sure," she muttered. "Thank you, and all that stuff. Good-bye."

Luz's eyes glittered for a minute, and then she smiled. That smile chilled Sara to the bone. "*Buenas noches,* Sara." She picked up her coat and purse from the end of the couch and sauntered to the door. She looked back over her shoulder, her eyes still gleaming. "May your dreams be . . . sweet."

"Good riddance," Sara muttered as the door closed behind her. She started for her bedroom, but the floor was uneven, and she couldn't seem to keep her balance. Besides, the couch was so much closer than her bed. It had a pillow and a blanket, except Luz had folded the blanket. Now why the hell had she done that?

Sara made it to the couch, sank down with a groan. She dropped her purse again, kicked off her shoes, giggling as they hurtled off into the darkness edging the dimly lit room, and fell back on the couch. She managed to get her head on the pillow, grabbed the square of blanket, and plopped it, still folded, over her middle.

And passed out cold, oblivious to the edge of darkness creeping over her.

EIGHTEEN

ON Sunday morning, Kara and Damien sat at the breakfast table, lingering over a second cup of coffee while he worked on his laptop. She was reading the semiweekly Zorro paper, and she couldn't help herself—she turned to Matt's obituary.

"He was so young," she murmured as she read it, her heart going out to Matt's father, Glen.

Damien looked up. "Who are you talking about?"

"Matt Brown." Kara folded the paper. "Do you think there will be another murder soon?"

"Absolutely." His eyes turned arctic. "The Belian is definitely escalating, and enjoying the kills way too much. We won't have to wait long. We'll take the scanner with us today."

Nowhere to run from the darkness, she thought, carrying her mug to the sink and dumping her unfinished coffee. "I'm ready when you are."

They began driving by the homes of the women on their list of suspects. They parked a discreet distance away and walked back, getting as close as they could without drawing attention. Damien did psychic readings around each residence. He asked Kara to link with his third eye to enhance the energies, just as they had with the ghost.

"I didn't know a Sentinel could use a conductor like this," she commented as they walked through the wooded area behind Katie Woodward's house. Richard had certainly never done it, but then he'd also never taken her to a Belian crime scene.

"Not many do. They either haven't realized it can be done, or they want to spare their conductors the physical and mental drain, to reserve their energies for actual conductions." Damien shot Kara an apologetic look. "I'm sorry to use you like this, because I know it's draining. You'll be tired later."

She already was, but how could she complain, when three people had already lost their lives? "I'll be fine. Are you picking up anything?"

"Nothing of note. Who's next on the list?"

"Mary Roberts," she said as they walked back to the car. She looked up at the overcast sky. It was a dreary day, cool and damp and gray. An ominous presence seemed to drift in the chilled air, or maybe it was just a reflection of her macabre mood. If the grim set of his face was any indication, Damien felt the same.

They got in the car and he started it. Instantly, the police scanner, which was plugged into the car power outlet, hissed to life with static and voices. He turned up the volume and they heard the dispatcher say: "Adam Six, code three."

"Adam Six, code three, go ahead."

"We have a DB at 1021 River Road, juvenile, possible homicide."

"Copy. I'm headed that way."

"What exactly did they just say?" Kara asked, although she'd picked up the alarming words *juvenile* and *homicide*.

"They have a body, and it might be a minor. Do you recognize the address?" Grimly, Damien swung the car around with a screech and floored it toward River Road.

"Not off the top of my head. Oh, not a child." Sickness and the presence of evil seeped through Kara.

Damien let the scanner run through the channels, and they heard more jargon: Blanco County Sheriffs also being dispatched, along with an ambulance and other emergency vehicles. It was like a replay of Matt Brown's murder. The actual scene was similar, too, with two police cruisers, Chief Greer's white pickup truck, and a jumble of onlookers filling the road.

When Kara saw which house it was, she didn't wait for Damien. She leaped out and raced toward the people, her heart hammering. She heard the screaming before she saw the woman.

"He's dead! Oh God, he's dead! My baby's dead!"

Kara knew that voice. She shoved through the onlookers and saw Sara Thornton crumpled on the ground. Officer Allen Spears was on one side and Nancy Miller on the other. Nancy had her arms around Sara, but Sara shoved her away and screamed, "My Michael is dead!"

Michael Thornton? *Mikey was dead?* Kara's legs went weak. She stumbled back, felt Damien's hands close over her upper arms. "Steady now," he murmured.

"Ma'am, I know you're upset, but if you could just come sit in the cruiser." Officer Spears tried to take Sara's thin arm, but she wrenched away.

"He was fine last night, before I left." Tears streaked down her ravaged face. "He was fine, I tell you! Luz Pérez stayed here with them last night. She killed my boy!"

Another shock wave for Kara to absorb, and she felt the cold sliding through her. Tightening his hold, Damien started pulling her back from the crowd.

"Ma'am," Spears, a young man fresh out of the police academy, pleaded, "if you could please calm down and wait, we'll take your statement after Chief Greer finishes inside—"

But Sara was like a wild woman, and she spun away from the officer's outstretched hand. "My baby's inside! I should be with him. I have to go to him." She scrambled toward the house, but Spears, his face turning red, grabbed her arm again. Another officer came to his assistance, and with one on each side of her, they towed her toward one of the squad cars.

"She killed him!" Sara wailed. "Luz killed my baby! He was fine when I left him last night! When I went in to wake him this morning, he didn't . . . he—" She collapsed, sobbing brokenly as the men placed her in the front seat of the car.

Kara stood there, too shocked to fully process the situation. Damien leaned down and said in a low voice, "I'm going around the house to see if I can pick up anything before the police get more organized."

"Wait!" She spun around. "I'm going with you." She followed him to the far side of the house. Most of the people were clustered on the south side and in the front, and the area hadn't been cordoned off yet, nor had the ambulance arrived. Distant sirens indicated more emergency vehicles would be arriving soon.

They went around the corner and Damien said, "Wait here. I've only got a few minutes to work."

Michael Thornton was dead. She was still trying to take it in, even as sharp-edged grief slashed through her. "Let me help. If you can use my energy, you might pick up more. I'm not letting this thing get away. He was just a little boy." Her voice caught, but she forced it under control.

Damien's steel gaze bored into her eyes. "All right." He took her hand, tugged her further along the side of the house. Touching his necklace through his shirt, he inhaled deeply.

She mentally reached for him, and opened herself to the despised abilities lurking deep within her. A scene unfolded in her mind.

A distorted image of a person stepped into what was obviously a child's bedroom. The moonlight drifting through the window illuminated soccer and baseball posters on the walls and a soccer ball on a dresser. But the figure moving toward the bed was murky, blurred by powerful supernatural abilities.

Michael was sleeping peacefully on his back, sweet and innocent. A pillow covered his face, was yanked down so hard, Kara felt her body jerk.

"Stay with me," Damien ordered. "Don't break the link."

She dug deep, sheer determination keeping her in the vision.

Two feminine hands gripped the ends of the pillow, pushing down. The only color in the nightmare scene was the glaring white pillow case and the bloodred fingernails on the killing hands. Michael, obviously a deep sleeper like most children, didn't move, didn't know he was being suffocated. With a sigh, the life left his small body. Then the killer looked right at Kara, as if posing for a picture. The face was shadowed, but white teeth flashed in a taunting smile. The face began to come into focus—

"What are you doing there?"

Kara jolted back to reality, met the glare of a man in a county sheriff uniform. "I don't know what the hell you're doing," he growled, "but I can arrest you for tampering with a crime scene."

"I'm sorry," she said lamely, still stunned from the vision. "I heard the news and I-I—"

"She's a friend of the family," Damien interjected. "She was so upset when she heard about the boy that I brought her around here to give her some privacy. I'm sorry, officer. I didn't realize that would be a problem."

The sheriff studied Kara. She must have looked like death warmed over, because he nodded. "Get back around the house, and go on home. There's nothing you folks can do for the boy now."

The truth of his words struck like a hammer on an anvil. Little Michael Thornton was dead, brutally murdered by a monster. She was barely aware of Damien leading her around the carnage of people and vehicles and back to the car. She gave a brief nod when he asked her if she was all right—a colossal lie—and tried not to think or feel during the silent drive home.

He pulled the car into the driveway, his face rigid. "Damn! I needed just one more minute!" He acted like he wanted to hit something, thought better of it, rested his clenched fist on the steering wheel. "I'll have to go back later."

Kara had been barely holding it together; now she began crumbling inside. She wrenched open the door and ran for the house, digging her keys from her purse. She reached her bedroom, slammed and locked the door, and collapsed on the bed.

Pain rolled through her in great waves. She curled into a miserable ball and sobbed. So much death, so much suffering. A lively old lady killed as casually as one would swat a fly, and now the life of a child taken. Memories of Richard's death took their place in the gruesome queue, another layer of grief.

She didn't know how long she lay there; she only knew that it seemed as if her life force drained out of her with the tears. Now she was empty inside, except for the pain. She felt a familiar touch of energy, followed by soothing warmth.

"I locked that door for a reason," she muttered.

"You've grieved enough." Damien's voice washed over her with another wave of warmth. "I can feel your exhaustion. Rest now."

"You can't keep doing this," she protested, feeling the pull toward nothingness. She rolled over and glared up at him. "What about free will?"

"Mine is stronger than yours."

Arrogant male, she thought, battling the pull. She was going to have to . . . to . . . sleep . . .

She awoke with a start, completely disoriented. It took her a moment to realize she was in her bedroom, and that it was late afternoon, judging from the dim light coming through the partially open blinds. The quilt from the foot of the bed was thrown over her.

It took another moment to remember that Michael Thornton had been murdered. A fresh wave of pain swept through her, and more tears threatened. She sat up, blinking them back. She was through crying. It was time to go after Mikey's murderer.

She went into her bathroom, splashed some cool water on her face, but there was no help for her red, puffy eyes. She rinsed her mouth, ran a brush through her hair, and changed into a pair of sweats. Then she went to find Damien.

He was the only light in the darkness.

DAMIEN sat in the large chair in the living room. The blinds were closed, but the dim room was bright in comparison to his dark mood. After he'd sent Kara to sleep, knowing it was the best thing, considering her fatigue and distraught state, he'd spent an hour in meditation. He hoped that would help firm up a psychic imprint from what he'd gathered at today's BCS. But it wasn't enough, damn it to Belial and back. He'd need more before attempting a conduction.

He'd listened to the police scanner as he fixed and ate two sandwiches, but hadn't garnered any helpful information. He typed a report of the latest murder and e-mailed it to Sanctioned headquarters, then sat down to center himself and think through every event of the past two weeks. There might be something, even the tiniest clue, he had overlooked. But nothing jumped out at him. He thought of Michael Thornton—just a *child*, about the same age as Alex—and a mixture of rage and pity roared through him. He had to stop this thing *now*.

A whisper of sound snagged his attention, and he looked up to see Kara standing just inside the room. Her hair fell loose and simple around her pale face. She'd changed into a slate blue sweat suit. With no makeup on, and her slender figure, she looked incredibly young. But he knew from firsthand experience she was all woman beneath that bulky fabric.

Her gaze locked with his. She looked sad and . . . alone. Just as alone as he felt. He should be used to loneliness by now. He'd been isolated, either self-imposed or by circumstances, for over thirty years. But sometimes the emptiness closed in on him, although he'd always had another hunt to keep him going. And sometimes . . . sometimes he wished for companionship, for a kindred spirit to ease the barrenness of his existence.

Motivated by emotions he didn't dare examine too closely, he held out his hand to Kara. Wordlessly, she came to him, folding that lithe body into his lap, tucking herself against him. He wrapped an arm around her and rested his cheek against her head. She smelled like lavender—from her shampoo, he knew—and the classic Chanel perfume she favored. She felt soft and warm and . . . wonderful. A dangerous exercise in futility, he told himself.

Yet the door had been opened when he'd let her get too close, when he'd taken her—and allowed himself to be taken—in non-conduction intimacy. But he wasn't quite ready to close that door. Not yet. It was hard to return to the loneliness.

He felt her shiver, realized the room was cold. With a flick of his hand, he ignited the gas logs. Another gesture and the afghan over the back of the couch floated to them.

He tucked the cover around her. "Are you feeling better?"

"I'm not as tired as I was." She placed her palm on his chest. He wondered if she could feel his heart speed up. "We're going to have to talk about your overbearing and macho attitude, Sentinel. You do *not* decide when I go to sleep."

As long as there was danger, and innocents were involved, he *would* have the final say in everything. But he merely said, "Let's get through this, then we'll discuss your sleeping habits."

She sniffed, but didn't argue. "What now?" she asked. "Shouldn't we do a conduction?"

"Not yet. I need that last bit of the psychic signature. We can't do much until the activity at the Thorntons' calms down and I can go back over there."

"I was afraid that sheriff's interruption messed up the

reading." She was silent a minute. "If Michael was mur—" She shuddered. "If it happened last night, why didn't I dream it?"

Feeling the tension invading her body, Damien splayed his hand over her back, rubbed in slow, calming circles. "I don't know. But you're not going to dream about everything the Belian does. Or you might have dreamed about the boy, but your subconscious buried it. Even if you had dreamed on a conscious level, you couldn't have stopped it."

"I know." She shifted to look up at him. "Have you been listening to the scanner?"

"Some, but there's really nothing new—except they picked up Luz for questioning. It wouldn't surprise me if they officially charge her for murder."

"Oh no." Her hand clenched against his chest. "I shouldn't be so shocked but . . . her nails were red when I saw her."

"What?"

Kara sighed. "I didn't tell you about this, but I went to see Luz Thursday morning, after Matt was murdered. She acted very odd, which might have been because of the grief. But her nails looked freshly painted—in bright red."

He should read her the riot act for going to see a Belian suspect on her own, but she was so upset right now, he'd save the lecture for later. "Another clue," he murmured.

"I don't want it to be Luz. She's been a good friend since I moved here. I hate to think of her being in jail."

"If she is the Belian, everyone is safer with her behind bars. If she's innocent, then she's better off in jail—safe from the Belian and from those who believe she's a murderer."

"I guess you're right." She settled closer to him, and they sat quietly for several moments before her whisper broke the silence. "How do you stand it? How can you watch innocent people get murdered, day after day?"

He slid his hand up beneath her hair, kneaded the tension in her neck. "Knowing I'm going to stop the things responsible for those acts, knowing I'm fighting evil—and maybe even winning the war—makes it bearable." *Just barely.*

She looked up at him. "Mikey was a child, hardly older than Alex. How am I going to tell him his best friend is dead?" Tears filled her eyes and she swiped at them. "Damn it. I'm not going to cry anymore."

"Sometimes all you can do is to mourn for those departed. We're not always the ones in control."

"I hate that!"

"I'm not wild about it, either, even though I have faith in The One."

She stared at him solemnly. "You do, don't you? That's something I admired about Richard—his total and absolute faith in a supreme being. I wish I could have such conviction." She lifted her hand to his cheek. "But I have total faith in you. I know you won't stop until this evil is destroyed."

No one had ever looked at him with such complete trust. He felt a wrench inside, prayed he could keep her and Alex safe. She slid her hand behind his head, tugged him down. He needed no further invitation to lower his mouth to hers, to take what she offered so freely. Trust. Faith—*in him.* Compassion. Light, in an existence dominated by darkness.

Exploring her mouth, he savored the sensuality of kissing, something in which he rarely indulged. He slipped one hand beneath her sweatshirt, stroked the smooth skin of her back. No bra, which made it all too tempting to slide his hand around and cup one perfect breast. With a little moan, she shifted to her knees, straddling him and working his sweater up. She ended the kiss, moved her lips along his neck.

"Damien . . ." Her husky voice heated his blood. "Make love with me."

He had every intention of doing just that, even if he'd be damned for his actions. He cradled her against him and stood, carrying her to the bedroom in a few rapid strides. Placing her on the bed, he swept off her sweatpants and panties. Then he ran his hands along her legs, parting them so he could look at her.

"Hey," she protested. "I want you naked, too."

"Soon." He stroked her, watched her shudder. Slipping a finger inside her, he found her hot and wet. God, she turned him on. He settled beside her and pushed up her shirt, teased a nipple with his tongue.

"Damien!" She twisted toward him, tried to touch him.

He ruthlessly used his strength to keep her where he wanted her, to slow down the pace. Their first three times had been wild and urgent. This time, he wanted to show her what he would never be able to tell her. That he respected her, admired her, found her worthy. *That he cared.* He told her with his lovemaking, using his hands and mouth to give her the first orgasm.

Then he stood, stripped, and returned to her arms. He started again, still controlling the pace as he built desire back to a fever pitch. When he finally entered her with a slow, drawn-out stoke, he entwined his fingers with hers, pressing their hands against the mattress. Exerting extra effort to keep the chakras closed to conduction energy, he stroked slow and deep.

Her gaze locked with his, her feelings reflected in her radiant eyes. He committed this moment to memory, for those future times he'd again embrace the darkness. *Alone.*

Then he took them both over the edge.

THE breeze stirred Damien's hair. It was a clear day, and the bright sunshine warmed the air, making the temperature almost balmy. Last night, he and Kara had driven out here to the Thornton house, but there had still been too much activity for them to attempt a reading.

Today, however, the area was deserted. Except for the yellow crime-scene tape flapping in the breeze, the small, unpainted cinder block home looked nondescript. There were no vehicles in the driveway or on the street, so Damien figured no one was there. Not surprising. The remaining Thorntons were probably staying with family or friends.

He strode around to the back of the house, where he wouldn't be visible from the road. There wasn't much grass here, just barren, rocky earth. A rusted swing set, minus the swings, and a large, torn trampoline took up much of the yard. Someone had started a garden, with an area of ground dug up. A shovel and a rake were leaning against the house.

Walking to the edge of the lot, he stared out across the Blanco River, which flowed in a narrow, sparkling ribbon about twenty yards away. It was a beautiful day, and yet he sensed the evil, felt the dark psychic energy drifting around the house.

Closing his eyes, he pressed his hand over the crystal beneath his shirt, shielded, and then opened himself to the energies, which were enhanced by the nearby water. Darkness raced toward him, reaching out insidious tendrils—

"What are you doing?"

The soft female voice jolted him from the beginnings of a trance. He reoriented himself, looked around at the slight figure standing behind him. Her hands jammed into a threadbare cardigan sweater over a knit crewneck top and worn jeans, Sara Thornton appeared fragile and vulnerable.

"Mrs. Thornton." He walked toward her, sending out calming energy so she wouldn't feel threatened. "I didn't realize you were here."

Her pale skin made her eyes seem even darker. Her face had that pinched look of someone who was suffering, and her dark brown hair was tangled. She took a distrustful step back. "Who are you?"

He stopped. "I'm Damien Morgan. And I'm very sorry for your losses."

Her lips trembled, but she kept her composure. Her gaze was wary. "You're that reporter."

"I'm not really a reporter. I'm a writer for *Society Magazine*."

She took another step back, staggered slightly. "What are you doing here?"

Her voice slurred a little, and he wondered if she had been drinking. "I write about crimes, and since there have been several unexplained deaths in Zorro, I've been investigating them."

"I don't want you here!" Her voice rose to a hysterical pitch. "This is a private matter. I've lost my husband and my s-son, and—" Her composure crumpled, and she turned away, sobbing.

"I'm very sorry, Mrs. Thornton." Damien knew she wouldn't appreciate his touch, so he sent her reassuring energy instead. "I didn't mean to intrude. I'll get off your property now."

He turned to leave, but something caught his eye. A scruffy live oak tree. It was on the southern boundary of the lot, which was probably why he hadn't seen it yesterday. A big branch had been severed, leaving a jagged edge. Down the front of the tree, the bark had been sheared off, as though it had been struck by lightning. It was the same tree he had seen in the first conduction with Kara.

His internal alarms went on full alert. Reaching for the gun tucked in his waistband, he spun around. Just as he saw a flash of silver coming toward him. Then darkness.

KARA'S patient load was light this morning, which was a good thing, since she was exhausted and distracted, and she had a grueling conduction to look forward to later. Maybe she could sneak a nap in her office at lunchtime. She was headed toward exam room two when Bonnie intercepted her.

"Dr. Kara, you have a phone call. It's Sara Thornton, and she sounds upset."

Dread snaked through Kara. What could she say to Sara, after a loss of such magnitude? No parent should have to bury a child. It was unimaginable. Yet, if Sara needed her, she'd do her best. Taking a deep breath, she picked up the phone and engaged the line. "Hello, Sara."

"Dr. Kara. I'm so glad you're there!"

"How are you doing? I'm so sorry about Michael. I-I don't even know what to say."

There was a moment of silence, then a little sob. "I can't believe he's gone."

Kara's heart ached for her. "What can I do for you?"

Sara sniffed loudly. "I'm not calling about me. I'm calling about Julie. She's sick."

"What's wrong with her?"

"She has a fever over a hundred and three, and she's shaking and says her throat's hurtin' real bad. Will you take a look at her?"

"Of course. Bring her by, and I'll see her right away."

"I don't have my truck. We stayed with Beth Gonzales last night, and she dropped us off at our house so we could . . . so—" A soft sob. "I'm sorry. Anyways, Beth's off to work, and I didn't realize how sick Julie was until I just took her temperature."

"The poor baby. I'll come by your house, then. Give me thirty minutes. I have one more patient to see before lunch."

"Bless you, Dr. Kara. I knew you'd come."

"See you soon." Kara hung up, and hustled off to see little Joy Mason. She quickly diagnosed an ear infection and took care of that.

Then she told Bonnie where she was going, and that she planned to be back in time for the afternoon appointments. She packed some medical supplies, including antibiotic samples, in her briefcase, and got her purse and jacket.

As she drove, she wondered if Damien was still there, if he'd seen Sara and Julie—or they'd seen him. He'd been planning on heading there around ten, after people got to work. She glanced at her watch—almost noon. He should be long gone.

But as she headed north on River Road, she saw Damien's gray sedan parked on a dirt turnaround three houses south of the Thornton home. That was odd, unless he was staying with Sara and Julie until she got there. He had a deep well of compassion, and it would be like him to use his powers to make Julie feel better.

Her thoughts flashed to yesterday, to images of Damien lacing his fingers with hers as he moved inside her, of the emotion she'd seen in his eyes. He hadn't tried to hide his feelings for her, even though he hadn't expressed them verbally.

She hadn't hidden her feelings, either, but she refused to burden him with words that would only cause him more pain. She knew he'd leave as soon as the Belian was identified and dealt with, just as she understood he was too emotionally damaged to commit to a relationship.

But man, oh man, she had it bad for the guy. And it was going to hurt big-time when he left. Bittersweet emotions swept through her as she pulled into Sara's driveway. As she got out of the car, she noticed a white Ford F-150 truck parked farther up on the road, just clear of the Thornton lot. Whose vehicle was that, if Sara's truck was at Beth Gonzales's house?

She shrugged it off. Lots of people owned those trucks. She got her briefcase from the backseat and walked up the cracked cement steps. The front door was slightly ajar, so she knocked lightly, pushed it open. "Sara? Julie? It's Dr. Kara."

Nothing but silence answered her. She walked farther inside. "Hello! Anybody here?" Still only silence, and a familiar oppressive feeling that she'd felt . . . *at Doris's house, the day she'd found her body.* A chill swept through Kara. She put her free hand in her jacket pocket, fingered the pepper spray there.

"Sara? Julie? Where are you?" She looked around as she walked toward the kitchen at the back of the house, but there was no sound or movement, no indication of anyone around. Where was Damien? Maybe they were all in the backyard. It was a beautiful day, and it would be nice by the river.

Kara walked toward the back door. It felt even more oppressive in the kitchen. She wondered if it was residual energy from Michael's murder. Thinking about that chilled her more. She found the back door unlocked and stepped outside.

At first she saw nothing, but when she looked to the right, she saw a form on the ground. *What—?* Shock roared through her when she realized it was Damien, lying on his side, blood on his face.

"Damien!" Dropping the briefcase, she leaped off the stoop and ran toward him.

As she got closer, she realized his hands were secured behind his back. He was conscious, and he glared a warning at her. *"Go!"* he shouted. "Get out of here! *Now!*"

Shock made her sluggish, but she understood the urgency in his voice. Just as she understood, with abject horror, the Belian must be nearby. But she wouldn't leave him here, defenseless like this. Her gun was in a case in her trunk, for target practice tonight. If she could just get to her car—

"Hold it right there!" came a female voice from behind her. "Turn around, slowly, dear Kara. No tricks now, you hear? I've got a gun on you. And I know how to use it."

A voice Kara knew. Another shock wave went through her.

"Turn around. *Now.* Or I'll shoot the spawn of The One."

Kara turned and faced the Belian.

NINETEEN

ALTHOUGH Luke assured him he could handle the ghost if it came back, Alex avoided his room on Sunday, and sneaked into his grandparents' bed after they were asleep that night. It hadn't returned, though, and he felt better on Monday. It seemed safer in the daytime, especially since he was outside in the backyard, playing with a neighbor's cat. Grandma was inside, fixing their lunch, and after that, they were going to go play miniature golf.

It happened so suddenly, Alex didn't sense it coming. One minute, Princess, a gray tabby, was chasing the string he was dangling. The next moment, she hissed and arched her back, her fur standing out like porcupine quills. The low, eerie growl coming from her throat had Alex's own hair standing on end.

He felt it then, the energy tingling along his skin. Heard the insidious whispering. Her tail puffed as big around as her body, Princess hightailed it out of there. A breeze whirled around Alex, jerking the string he held. A *Star Wars* action figure lifted from the ground and hovered there. Yep, it was the ghost, all right. His heart pounded like a Death Star explosion.

He looked toward the back door. Maybe he could make it past the ghost and get inside, and maybe it wouldn't come after him, especially with Grandma in there. And maybe—

Maybe he needed to act like a Sentinel.

Alex remembered what Luke had told him Saturday night: *"You can't understand the ghost because you're listening with your physical self, instead of your spiritual self. You have to use your third eye."*

Luke had explained a lot of stuff about colors and chakras—a word that sounded like chalk the teacher used. Then he'd shown Alex how to go inside himself and hook up to his sixth chakra and his third eye—an invisible eye everyone had! Only you could hear with it as well as see with it.

The wind picked up, and the whispering became louder. *"Aaaalex . . . Heeeeelp . . ."*

Shaking like a wobbly wheel on a Rollerblade, Alex shored up his shields. He was going to do it—try to listen to this ghost, like Mr. Morgan or Luke would. Taking a deep breath, he turned inward, as Luke had showed him. He "looked" for the purple/blue color of the sixth chakra. He was terrified, but he reached for it, felt like his head was getting bigger. The muttered sounds became clear words. He could hear the ghost!

"Aleeex . . . help."

"Help who? Who is this?"

"Tho-rn . . . Tho-rn-ton."

"Thornton?" Confused and disoriented, Alex tried to think. "Mr. Thornton? Is this Mr. Thornton, Mikey's dad?"

"Yesssss."

Somehow, knowing the ghost was even more frightening. His heart doing somersaults in his chest, Alex tried to stand. He wanted to get inside to Grandma.

"Heeeelp your mommm."

Did the ghost say *mom*? "What?"

"She's after your m-mom."

My mom? Is my mom in danger?

"Yessss. And Mooorrgan. St-stop h-her."

Freaked, Alex rocked back and forth. "Stop who?" His voice squeaked.

"Ssssaaaarrr."

"Who?"

"Saaaraaaa."

"Sara?" Wasn't that Mrs. Thornton's first name? Alex made it to his feet. He didn't know what to do. "Where's my mom? Where's Mr. Morgan?"

"M-my hoooooouse."

"Mom and Mr. Morgan are at your house? Mikey's house?"

"Yessss."

"And they're in danger?"

"Yessss. Got M-Miiikey. Stop her!"

Alex didn't understand the reference to Mikey, but he understood his mother was threatened. Fear raced through him, and he couldn't hold the link. The ghost wailed as the connection slipped, but Alex had heard enough. He had to help his mom!

Instinctively, he knew Grandma wasn't the person he needed. He raced around to the front of the house, down the driveway, and across the street. "Luke! Luke!"

Luke was just coming out of the garage as Alex hurtled up his driveway. "My mom's in trouble!"

"Whoa, slow down!" Luke squatted, laid a reassuring hand on Alex's shoulder. "Take a deep breath, bro, and tell me what's going on."

He listened intently as Alex gasped out what had happened, and what the ghost had said. His eyes glowing with approval, he squeezed Alex's shoulder. "Good job, young man. You handled that like a true Sentinel."

Pride swelled inside Alex. He had done it! He had talked to a ghost! But worry quickly took the upper hand. "We gotta help my mom. What do we do?"

"No tough decision there." Luke stood, pulled his cell phone from his belt clip, and flipped it open. "We call in the troops."

"PÉREZ." Kara stared at the Belian. "I can't believe it."

"You would never have figured it out. You're too stupid." Serafina Pérez jerked the gun toward Damien. "Just like him. Idiots, both of you. I'm going to enjoy watching you suffer."

Kara saw Damien was sitting up. Blood oozed from a nasty cut on his right temple. Even though his ankles were bound together with a length of chain, he managed to shift to his knees. His shoulders and arms strained against the handcuffs pinning his hands behind him.

"Give it up, Sentinel. Even you're not strong enough to break those handcuffs. They're police issue, made of the finest carbon steel." Serafina's smile was like an evil caricature. "I took them from Allen Spears's house, after I fucked his brains out. Men are so easy to fool. Easy to kill, too."

Memories of Richard's death flashed through Kara's mind. *No.* If only she had her gun. She reached into her jacket pocket, found the pepper spray. She wrapped her fingers around it, thumbed off the cap. She'd have to wait for just the right moment to use it. Having a plan calmed her a little, and she suddenly remembered Sara Thornton. "Where's Sara?"

Serafina gestured toward a crumpled form on the other side of the yard. "Such a weak being," she sneered. "Drank so much, she ruined her liver, and what few brain cells she had."

She looked back at Kara, still holding the gun steady. "It was easy to control her mind, to get her to call you, and plant exactly what I wanted her to say to lure you here. Easy to make her sound convincing. And you fell for it. Then I brought her outside and . . ."

She mimed shooting the gun, looked over at Damien with another sneer. "Nothing you could do about it, could you, Morgan? I know how you light-seeking Sentinels claim you can't stand to watch innocents die. Hey, at least she didn't suffer—not like you're going to."

Kara battled rising nausea. She had to stay calm. Had to find some way out of this. She eased the pepper spray higher in her pocket, adjusted her grip.

Serafina stroked the gun tucked into the waistband of her jeans. "Nice of you to carry two guns, Sentinel, even if the smaller one is only a .38. Gives me plenty of bullets to use on you." She glanced back at Kara. "But I'm not going to kill you, bitch. I was planning to at first, but you have a young, healthy body that I can use. And you're a respectable citizen in Zorro, a doctor, no less. No one will suspect you of the kills to come. And there will be many more, praise be Belial."

"What's wrong with the body you've got?" Damien asked, shifting subtly.

"Serafina was another stupid being."

"Was?" Kara asked, wondering what had happened to the soul, the essence of Luz's sister.

The Belian gave that chilling smile again. The person/thing standing there looked like Serafina, with the same long, wavy midnight hair and dark eyes, the general build, and resemblance to Luz. Even the nails on the hand holding the gun were a glossy red. But it wasn't Serafina facing Kara. It wasn't even human. There was no spark of humanity in those cold, dead eyes.

"That pitiful excuse of a spirit is long gone from this Earth plane, an offering to Belial," the Belian said. "It was easy to force it from its weakened body. That slut fucked any man who paid the slightest attention to her or offered her cheap trinkets. She didn't care who they were.

"Screwed David Thornton, right under that tree over there—the one you found so interesting, Sentinel. Even went behind her stupid sister's back and fucked Matt Brown. Managed to get infected with HIV. Her weakened body provided my entry into this plane, but its usefulness is at an end. For that matter, so is yours, Sentinel." It cocked the gun, swung it toward Damien.

Kara lunged forward, bringing the pepper spray out and up. The Belian whirled with superhuman speed, grabbing and twisting Kara's wrist. It was strong; Kara felt her wrist snap, as intense pain shot up her arm. She dropped the spray.

"Bitch!" It backhanded her, sending her to her knees.

Whirling, it raised the gun toward Damien, who was on his feet, jumping toward them. The explosion of a gunshot ripped through Kara. *Damien!* She clambered to her feet, her wrist throbbing.

"Stay right there! Or I'll shoot him again," the Belian said.

Feeling utterly helpless, Kara studied Damien anxiously. He was faceup on the ground, his chest heaving. Red bloomed just below his left shoulder. He shook his head at her in warning.

"See?" it jeered. "It's a nonfatal wound, and I used the .38, so he won't bleed as much. Killing him too quickly would take the fun out of it."

But he could easily bleed to death from that shoulder wound. Kara watched the blood spread down his sweater. He had to be in pain, but he didn't show it. Instead, his focus was on the Belian, his expression feral.

Turning the gun on Kara, the Belian reached down and picked up the canister. "And what is this? Pepper spray? How quaint. As if that could stop me. But it might stop you. Let's see, shall we?" It shoved it toward Kara's face, pressed the discharge.

Kara tried to turn away, but the wind blew the spray on her. Fire raced over her skin and into her lungs. It seared her eyes. She'd never felt such agony. She staggered back, gasping and coughing, tears streaming from her burning eyes. She couldn't catch her breath. Felt like she was suffocating, as her chest heaved in a desperate attempt to draw in oxygen. Her efforts left her throat raw and feeling on fire. She couldn't see, either, her vision distorted and blurred through the tearing.

"Oh, I like this," the Belian crooned. "Here, Sentinel. You try it."

Kara heard Damien gasping and coughing, and cursed

herself for her clumsy attempt to spray the Belian. She should have known better. Still in pain, panic rising faster than she could control it, she squinted at the Belian, saw its attention was on Damien. *Nothing to lose,* she thought, whirling and running for the road. Maybe she'd draw it away from Damien. She'd always heard it was difficult to shoot a moving target with a pistol.

The excruciating pain shooting through her leg proved that theory wrong. She went down in the dirt, rolling and grabbing her left thigh. Felt the slick flow of blood covering her hands. Her right wrist screamed at the contact.

"Kara!" Damien yelled.

She felt like a turtle on its back, helpless and terrified, as she stared up at the Belian.

"If you move even one inch in this direction, Sentinel," it hissed, pointing the gun at Kara's head, "or if you try to use energy to jerk my arm again, like you just did, I'll kill her. I can always find another body."

"Kara, are you okay?" Damien asked.

"Yes. It's just a flesh wound." Even so, her thigh was bleeding heavily and hurt like hell. Her eyes were still burning, but her vision had cleared enough that she could see him. He was sitting up again. His face and watering eyes were red. Blood flowed from the shoulder wound.

"What a perfect scene." The Belian smiled again. "The two of you on the ground, injured, bleeding. Beautiful, beautiful blood. All for Belial. But it's time to get on with it." It stepped back, shifted the gun toward Damien. "Guess what, Dr. Bitch? You get to see your Sentinel lover die, just like before."

Like before? How could it know? "What are you talking about?"

"Oh, I checked you out. Once I realized you must be the conductor, I researched you. The Internet is an amazing resource, don't you think? I know all about your precious Richard Wayman. I know you watched him die."

Kara closed her eyes to block out the monster's sneering

face. *Richard. His body jerking as the knife sank into him.* Tremors surged through her body.

"You remember. That's good. The shock of seeing Morgan killed will be a nice addition to your memories. He won't try to stop me, or I'll kill you, too. Your foolish guilt and grief will make it child's play to cast your puny soul from your body."

This was too close to the nightmare in Birmingham. Kara felt herself going numb with horror, with hopelessness. She looked at Damien. He was much paler, his face sweating, but he was still straining against the cuffs. And he was inching closer. He met her gaze, his eyes like silver flares. She wished she'd had a chance to tell him she loved him.

"How about a matching wound on the other side, Sentinel?" The Belian aimed the gun toward him.

"Police! Drop your weapon!"

Tom Greer stepped around the south side of the house with Steven Smith behind him. Both men had guns trained on the Belian.

"Drop the gun," Greer said quietly. "You don't want to shoot him."

"All right. I'll drop it." The Belian acted like it was lowering the gun. A sudden energy surge sent both officers' arms jerking upward. It shot Steven, spun toward Tom.

But Kara had already hurled herself forward, using her good leg to kick the Belian's legs from beneath it. The second shot going wild, it went down with a roar of rage, becoming entangled with Kara. Its arm holding the gun was rigid, as if being held in place by an invisible force. Probably Damien's doing. Screeching again, it struck Kara in the face with its free hand.

But Kara was beyond pain. Fury and grief drove her; adrenaline gave her super strength. Like a wild woman, she clawed at the Belian. She felt the smooth butt of the pistol tucked inside its jeans, closed her fingers over it like a lifeline. Yanked it free.

It was hard to hold it steady with just her left hand, but

she dug deep. Angled it toward the Belian and pulled the trigger. Pulled it again. And again.

The Belian's eyes opened wide in shock. "I'll kill you," it hissed. It tried to say more, but a gurgling sound came from its throat; blood oozed from its mouth. The body went into spasms.

Blood was everywhere.

Just like Birmingham.

The Belian stepped over Richard's body, his malevolent gaze on Kara. "And the woman becomes mine." He stalked toward her, the crystal pendant dangling from his fist, reflecting the flashing lights and the blood. The knife that had claimed Richard's life was in his other hand. "Come here, sweet thing. Treat me real nice, and I might let you live."

She'd gotten the Belian's gun after Richard sent it spinning from his reach. But by then, he and the Belian had been locked together and rolling on the ground. She'd been unable to shoot, afraid she'd hit Richard. Now it was too late.

The Belian was almost to her. Somehow, she retained enough presence of mind to realize the element of surprise was her only chance. She didn't pull the gun from behind her back until the last moment. Then she emptied the magazine into it . . .

"Kara! I need you."

Damien. She shoved Serafina's body away. He was pushing himself toward her, bending his bound legs at the knees and digging into the ground with his feet, and with his hands behind him. She tried to scrabble to him, difficult with a bad leg and wrist, and the slick blood that was everywhere. He looked pasty white, and the shoulder wound was still bleeding.

"Lie down," she ordered, trying to yank her shirt open with one hand. She needed something to press against his wound, and fast. She was weak and dizzy from her own blood loss, didn't know how much longer she'd be functional.

Looking over, she saw Greer working on Steven. He

was talking on his hand radio, so she knew help was coming. He glanced her way, and she called, "I'll take care of Damien." He nodded and leaned back over Steven.

"Stop," Damien rasped. "Reach behind me and take my hand."

"What?"

He jerked his head toward Serafina's body. "The body is still dying. The Belian hasn't left yet. I'm too injured to dispatch it without your help."

It took her a moment to realize what he wanted. "Forget it. It will weaken you too much. Lie down and let me stop the bleeding."

"Not until I send the cursed thing to Saturn."

"It's not worth it. Nothing is worth your life. I need to stop your bleeding, now." She managed to slide the shirt off, balled it up.

"Kara, this *is* my life. It's what I am, what I do."

She stared into his eyes, saw his resolve. "I don't want to lose you," she whispered. "I . . . I love you."

His gaze softened. "Then let me do what I have to."

She stretched up, pressed her lips to his for a brief, sweet moment. She heaved out a sigh. "All right. But if you die on me, I'll never forgive you."

"I'm not going anywhere. Take my hand."

"In a minute." She lifted his sweater, pushed her shirt up inside, and pressed it to his shoulder. He winced. Leaning against him to maintain the pressure, she reached behind him, took his right hand in her left. Closing her eyes, she slipped into that other consciousness inside her. The link with Damien's third eye clicked into place.

She heard his deep voice, intoning in a beautiful, ancient language. She knew he was psychically restraining the Belian, while at the same time summoning the High Sanctioned, basically the high priests of the Sanctioned. They would exorcise the Belian from the Earth plane, exiling it to Saturn for spiritual rehabilitation—not a pleasant process.

She felt the tremendous drain on Damien, felt his body

shaking from the effort. She sent him as much of her rapidly dwindling energy as she could, praying it would be enough.

A growling moan rose from Serafina's body as a near-blinding light encircled it. Four brilliant starbursts erupted into the light circle. The Belian screamed its defiance. It burst from the body, a black, shapeless form that slithered and twisted to evade the High Sanctioned, its shrieks growing more frantic. But it was no match for the four luminous beings that surrounded and pinned it, as Damien continued the chant.

Richard had told her the basic translation of the final incantation: *Be thou removed from this plane of existence. Be thou restricted to Saturn, to be purified by the flame of the Karmic Initiator. Be thou to remain there until thou recognizes The Light, The Truth, The One. Then shalt thou return to do penance.*

As if suddenly sucked into a vacuum, the black form disappeared with a howl, and the light beings along with it. Then there was nothing left but poor Serafina's shell.

Kara had been present one time when Richard performed a BE, the Sentinel term for a Belian expulsion, but she hadn't been a participant like this. Her third-eye link with Damien allowed her to see what was actually happening; Tom Greer wouldn't have seen anything but their strange behavior.

She felt utterly drained, yet a dark residual energy lingered within her, the destructive aftereffects of the Belian. Then she felt Damien's touch inside her, clean and bright. He disintegrated all remaining traces of the Belian, replacing it with warmth and light.

That done, he leaned his forehead against hers, heaving an exhausted sigh. She released his hand, placed her palm against his clammy face. He eased back to meet her gaze, his eyes glazed with pain. He tried to say something, but his eyes rolled back in his head. He passed out in her arms.

TWENTY

THEY were flown to Brackenridge Hospital in Austin. Sheer will keeping her conscious, Kara managed to slip Damien's crystal into her pocket before he was loaded into the helicopter. No way would she risk a Belian seeing that necklace while he was weak and helpless. Then it was her turn to collapse onto a stretcher, and she finally surrendered to the exhaustion and pain, barely aware of the flight to Austin.

At the Brackenridge level II trauma facility, Damien was whisked off to surgery. Kara's thigh was stitched up and her right arm set and encased in a temporary cast. She spent the night in the hospital and was released the next morning.

Steven Smith, Sara Thornton, and Serafina Pérez had all been pronounced dead at the scene. Tom Greer had escaped injury, while Julie Thornton and Luz each received another knockout punch of losing yet another loved one.

But the Belian—at least this one—was gone, bringing Damien's assignment in Zorro to a close. Kara tried not to think about that, tried not to have any hopes or expectations.

What Damien might feel for her and what he could commit to were not necessarily in sync.

She stood outside his hospital room. This was his third day here, and he'd be released tomorrow. He'd healed faster than a normal human with the same injuries would have. The doctors and nurses had been amazed by his progress. Even so, he'd had a rough time of it. His fast metabolism broke down pain medications too quickly to offer relief. He'd had to rely on drawing in energy to heal and control the pain, difficult to do in his weakened state.

Even so, the side effects from the concussion he'd suffered when the Belian hit him with the shovel were gone by the first day. And today, the last of the tubes and drains were supposed to be removed. Kara opened the door and stepped inside, limping slightly. Damien was resting against the elevated head of the bed. His eyes were closed; sunshine from the nearby window streamed over him. He'd kicked the covers back and wore only long cotton pajama bottoms, a concession to modesty, as he preferred to sleep in boxer shorts or nude. None of the nurses had complained about his bare chest. Imagine that.

That magnificent chest was marked with white bandages covering his left shoulder and an arm sling to keep that side immobile. The bruises on his face were fading. His hair was loose and his features relaxed. A few days' beard growth made him look dark, dangerous, sexy. He looked good enough to eat—a sure sign of her own recovery. He opened his silvery, mesmerizing eyes.

"Hey," he said.

"Hey, yourself. I see you lost the rest of your accessories."

"Damn tubes," he muttered. "Especially that catheter. Belial had to have invented that article of torture. They'd never have done that to me if I had been conscious."

"They took it out after the first day."

"One day too many," he growled.

She repressed a laugh. "Hopefully the equipment hasn't been damaged."

His eyes took on a heated gleam. "I would think not."

Desire snaked through her body, but she ignored it. Since the Belian had been exiled, they'd danced around their private issues, acting like impersonal friends rather than lovers.

"Where's Alex?" he asked.

"He having lunch with Luz, then she'll bring him here. She met me at the airport, and we both picked him up. She really missed him. I thought it would be good for them to have some time together." Feeling the press of guilt, she turned and walked to the window. Outside, Austin traffic inched along 15th Street. "I think Luz needed to get away from all the relatives coming into Zorro for the funeral. I hope she never learns I'm the one who shot her sister."

"You're not the one who killed Serafina. She was long gone before we got to the Belian. And I don't think Chief Greer will tell Luz exactly how things went down at the Thornton house." He paused. "That's the second physical incarnation you've ended."

Maybe her shock should have been greater, but she was worn down from the guilt and the memories. She turned to face him. "You know about Birmingham?"

"I checked it out as soon as you told me about Richard Wayman." There was no judgment in his eyes, only understanding. "Kara, you had to shoot that trooper. It was no longer human, and it would have killed you."

"I'm a doctor. I'm supposed to help people. Not shoot them and watch the blood spurt out." She'd been grappling with a lot of things the past few days. Still, she'd kill again, if necessary to protect her loved ones or herself. Her fingers tightened on the bag she was holding.

"I almost forgot. I brought you some food." She placed the bag containing fruit, peanut butter, crackers, and cookies on the table by his bed. The hospital fare wasn't enough to satiate his enormous appetite, even though the nurses took turns bringing him ice cream and leftover desserts from the cafeteria.

"Thanks. Any Oreos in there?"

"Yes, two packages."

His smug satisfaction had her smiling and dissipated some of her dark mood. He was such a guy. She eased herself into the visitor chair to take the weight off her throbbing leg. Absently, she rubbed the cast on her arm. After Damien was discharged from the hospital tomorrow, he'd probably leave the area entirely. Luz and Alex would be up to the room soon, and she had some things she wanted to say only to him.

They needed to address their relationship—or, more likely—its closure. It was frightening—terrifying, actually—to even consider they had a relationship; or to try to salvage one that maybe had never existed in the first place. Disconcerting to throw pride to the wind, to bare her soul to a man who might toss her feelings back in her face. But she'd opened the door, and she'd told him how she felt when she whispered *I love you*. She didn't want to close it back.

"What is it?" Damien asked.

As usual, he was too perceptive. "I've been thinking about some things you've said to me over the past few weeks."

"My words coming back to haunt me?"

"Something like that." She met his gaze. "You shared some very wise insights. One is that there are no guarantees in life. We can't always play it safe. Sometimes we have to take chances. You also said a Sentinel soul chooses its destiny. I'm assuming other souls also do that."

He nodded slowly. "They do."

"So probably I—or my soul—chose a life as a conductor."

"That's very likely."

She drew a deep breath. "Then maybe I'm supposed to use those abilities. Maybe I need to be conducting on a regular basis."

His brows drew together. "Kara—"

She rushed on before he could finish. "And you told me that sometimes we have to trust in the Universe."

He didn't respond, just watched her. Not encouraging, but she plunged on. "I'm ready to take a leap of faith. To take a chance. That includes being willing to love again. I think you should do the same."

He sighed. "I almost lost you on Monday. Almost got you killed because I didn't identify the Belian soon enough." His face took on an expression of abject pain. "I couldn't bear losing someone else I cared about."

Her heart felt like it was sinking. Now she knew. He couldn't get past the pain of his past—not a surprise. He didn't want to risk experiencing such grief again. She'd taken her best shot. He knew how she felt. But he wasn't responsible for her feelings. She wouldn't beg or make him feel guilty.

"So I guess that's it, then." Barely holding onto her composure, she opened her purse and pulled out his crystal. "Let me give this back to you."

She rose and placed the necklace on the bedside table. Then she turned to go. She knew she'd see him again, that they'd have to make some decisions about Alex. But right now, she needed distance, needed time to pull herself together. "I'd better go find Alex."

"Kara." His fingers closed around her good wrist, pulled her back. "Come here."

She turned, vision blurring, as she fiercely told herself she would not cry. "There's nothing more to say."

He tugged hard, making her lose her balance and stumble forward. She couldn't use her broken arm to brace herself, so she ended up sprawled across him. "What—"

His big hand grasped her chin as his lips commandeered hers. Stunned, she started to protest—which may or may not have been a mistake, depending. It gave him full access to her mouth, and he took it. God, the man could kiss.

"Ummm," she managed. Then her mind stopped functioning, overruled by hormones going on full alert. Somehow, she ended up in the bed with him. And somehow her leg got slung across his, while his hand slid beneath her sweater. How did he always manage to do that to her—

"*Mom!* What are you doing?"

Alex's voice was like a wave of ice water. She jerked

back and scrambled off the bed. "Alex! I was—We—I—" She yanked down her sweater, which had ridden halfway up her midriff, and felt a flush heating her face.

Alex was grinning from ear to ear. "You were kissing Mr. Morgan."

"Just telling him good-bye," she muttered, deciding a change of topic might be her best defense, while she studiously avoided looking at Luz. "It might be nice if you remembered your manners and greeted Mr. Morgan."

"Hey, Mr. Morgan." Alex waved at the bed. "Luke said hi." He raised his backpack, which he'd refused to let Kara put in the trunk with his suitcase. "I've got the . . . you know."

"Who's Luke? And what have you got?" Kara asked. Damien and Alex just looked at each other.

Luz touched her good arm. "I need to get back to my mother's *casa*."

Kara finally looked at her and was disconcerted by the knowing expression on her exotic face. "I'm glad you came. I know Alex was delighted to see you."

"I missed my *chico*." Luz smiled at Alex. "It was like part of my heart was gone." Pain flashed into her eyes as she turned her attention to Damien. "I am sorry my sister shot you, and you, too, Kara. I do not know why she did such a thing." Her face crumpled, and a sob escaped her lips.

"Your sister wasn't herself," Damien said quietly. "I have no hard feelings."

Luz's shoulders shook from her sobs. Kara enveloped her in a comforting hug. After a moment, Luz pulled back, dabbing at her eyes with a tissue. "I am sorry." She took a deep breath. "Some of the responsibility for what happened is mine, *Señor* Morgan. I always knew something was wrong with Serafina. She was a lost soul. She went from man to man, was never satisfied. But I should have suspected something when she started acting strangely."

"When was that?" Damien asked.

"About two months ago. My sister became angry and withdrawn. I sensed a new darkness inside her, but I thought it was just a temporary depression. I should have done more to help her."

Damien exchanged a glance with Kara. "Sometimes there's nothing we can do to change fate. Your sister's problems, and her actions, were not your fault."

Luz shrugged, radiating sadness. "Perhaps you are right." She looked at Kara. "I will be back to work next week, if you still want me."

Kara hugged her again. "Of course, we want you. You're part of our family."

"Gracias."

"We'll see you on Saturday, at the funeral," Kara added. "But if there's anything you need, anything I can do, call me."

"Si." Luz leaned down to hug Alex. "Take care of yourself, *hijo. Te quiero*."

"I love you, too, Luz." Alex waited until she was gone, then he whirled toward Damien. "Now?"

"Now is good."

"Now what?" Kara asked, looking from one to the other. Damien was as impassive as ever, but Alex was squirming with excitement.

"I got you something really neat from the Tennessee Aquarium." He opened the backpack and lifted out a sizeable object crudely wrapped in glitter tissue paper, held on with about twenty pieces of tape. He offered it, glowing with pride. "I wrapped it myself."

"So I see." She took the gift, her heart lightening. "How sweet of you to bring me something."

"Open it now, Mom." Another glance at Damien. "I think you'll really like it."

"All right." She settled back in the chair and carefully undid the crumpled paper. She held up a plush stingray that was over a foot long, and was light purple with dark purple dots. "It's adorable."

"Purple is one of your favorite colors," Alex said proudly.

"Yes, it is." She swept her hand over the plush surface. "I love it. Thank you, sweetie. Come give me a hug."

"But there's something else. Look at the tail, Mom."

"Where . . . is this it?" She saw a silver band toward the base of the tail, held with tape. She peeled the tape away, slid it off. It was a ring, with a large, oval-cut pink diamond—at least she thought it was a diamond—and three smaller pink stones framing each side.

"It's a ring, Mom!" Alex's voice pitched up with excitement. "It's from—" He glanced at Damien. "You tell her."

She forced her gaze from the gorgeous ring to Damien. His eyes were like molten silver, his expression as warm and open as she'd ever seen it. "It's from Alex and me," he said. "We want the three of us to be a family."

"W-what?" She could only stare at him, her mind too shocked to function clearly. "What are you talking about?"

"He wants to marry us!" Alex crowed.

"I—" She looked at the ring, then back at Damien. "Why didn't you discuss this with me first?"

"I already had a pretty good idea how you felt. But Alex needed to agree to the idea as well."

"I voted yes!" Alex was practically glowing. "And I helped Luke pick out the ring, although Damien gave us a lot of instructions. We used one of your old rings to get the size."

"Who the hell is Luke? Will someone explain what's going on?"

"You're not supposed to use words like *hell*," Alex said. "Luke is this really cool Sentinel who moved in across the street from Grandma. He was keeping an eye on me, and he showed me lots of neat Sentinel stuff. He helped me talk to the ghost. And he called Chief Greer when I told him what the ghost said."

Her eyes narrowed. "The ghost? Sentinel stuff? Damien, you promised—"

"Mom, pay attention! I'm trying to 'splain. Mr. Morgan and I wanted to surprise you with the ring. But he was in the hospital, so me and Luke went to get it. It was way cool. I got to ride on his motorcycle—a *Harley*—to the jewelry store and—"

"You rode a motorcycle?" She was getting sensory

overload from so much information crowding her mind. "Your grandmother let you do that?"

"Actually, it was Grandpa, and he thought Luke's bike was iced, so he said yes."

"Men and their toys," Kara muttered. She stared at the ring. "I don't know what to think."

Damien sat up, swung his legs over the edge of the bed. "Come here."

"Oh, no. I'm not doing that again. There's a child in the room, Morgan."

"Then I'll come to you." He stood, steadied himself. He'd been taking regular walks through the hallways, and his strength was returning. He moved around Alex and took the two steps to her. Grasping her left arm, he pulled her to her feet. She stared up at him as he unfolded her clenched fingers and took the ring.

"I love you, Katherine Jennifer Cantrell," he said in a husky voice. "And I think that boy of yours is pretty special, too." One-handed, he slipped the ring on her finger, fumbling a little. "I want to be part of your lives."

"I still don't understand," she said, wondering if maybe she'd taken too many pain pills and was dreaming all this.

"I've had a lot of time to think," he said. "Especially that first day, when I was drifting in and out of consciousness."

"You made this decision based on drug- and pain-induced hallucinations?"

"Kara." His voice was a caress, melting her insides. "Of course not. My weakened state merely allowed me to drop the barriers created by fear and the past. I had nothing to do but think, especially about some things that *you* said."

He slid his free hand against her face, his molten gaze stealing her breath. "You were right. I was a coward, and I was denying my feelings. Love is the truest and purest expression of The One. It's our divine birthright, and it's supposed to guide our actions. I was terrified when I thought the Belian was going to kill you. I realized how much you mean to me, and I'm not letting another chance to be with you slip away."

The reality began to sink in, and she began to believe. Part of her was elated, while another part remembered her earlier mortification. "Damien Morgan! You sat in that bed and let me bare my soul—and you didn't say anything. You let me think you didn't want to be involved with me. You—"

He was getting pretty good at cutting her off with that sensual mouth of his. And she couldn't seem to resist kissing him back.

"Wow," Alex said. "I've never seen anything like that, not even on TV."

She broke off the kiss, tried to pull away, but Damien tightened his arm around her. "Come over here, Alex, and join in this hug," he said.

Still grinning, her son stepped forward and tried valiantly to put his skinny arms around both of them. They were wrapped in a group hug, in a wonderful cocoon of love and warmth.

"Well?" Damien demanded, those silver eyes mesmerizing her again.

"Well?" Alex echoed.

Her heart was singing, but she still felt the need to regain some dignity. "I think we'll have to come to some understandings about equal rights in our relationship."

"Ah, negotiations." Damien gave her a suggestive smile. "One of my specialties."

"I'll just bet." She angled her chin, sent him an unspoken challenge. "Better get used to me winning, Sentinel."

"Sweetheart, with you and Alex, I can't lose." He kissed her again, and this time, she didn't even care that her son was watching.

Life was good.

No, life was *wonderful*.

Author's Note

I've been fascinated with Atlantis most of my life, and I'm certainly not alone. Atlantis has long been a topic of intense interest and speculation, going all the way back to Plato, who discussed it in his works *Timaeus* and *Critias*, which was around 350 B.C.E. Since then, much more has been written about this mysterious place.

Despite the numerous books on Atlantis, no one really knows if it actually existed, or if any of the speculation is remotely accurate. So anything goes when writing about Atlantis in fiction. The author can make up any details that fit with his/her story vision, and many have done just that.

What I wanted to do with the premise of this Sentinel series was to incorporate my fascination with Atlantis and my lifelong interest in the psychic Edgar Cayce. Many of my details about Atlantis were inspired by the Cayce readings—and there were over seven hundred on the topic. There are a number of books discussing Cayce's Atlantis readings. The two that I find the most fascinating are *Edgar Cayce on Atlantis* by Edgar Evans Cayce, and *Edgar Cayce's Story of the Origin and Destiny of Man* by Lytle Robinson.

If you'd like to learn more about Edgar Cayce, you can visit www.edgarcayce.org/. You can also visit my website at www.catherinespangler.com for a complete list of my Atlantis reference books. Also posted on my website is a talk I presented on Atlantis some years ago.

Thank you for sharing this mystical, magical, and emotional journey with me.

~ Catherine